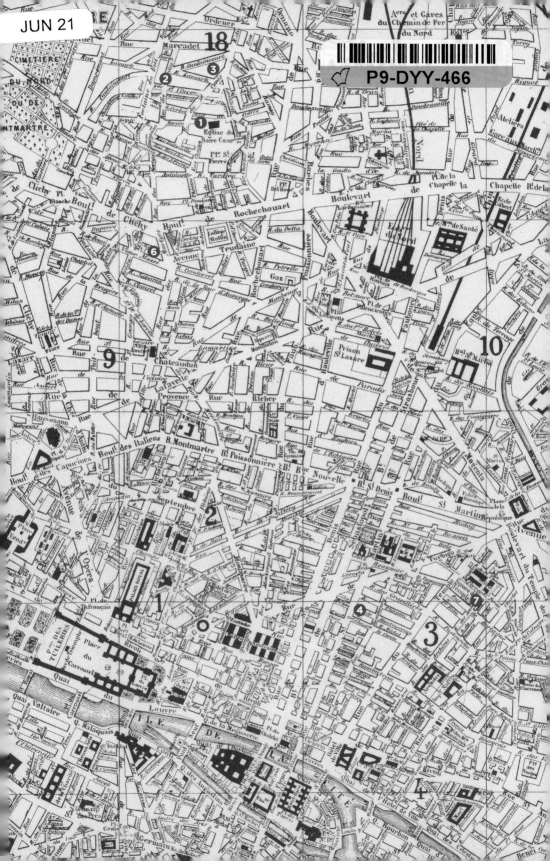

THE PARIS LABYRINTH

By the same author

L'Exil des anges, Fleuve Éditions, 2009; Pocket, 2010
Nous étions les hommes, Fleuve Éditions, 2011; Pocket, 2014
Demain j'arrête !, Fleuve Éditions, 2011; Pocket, 2012
Complètement cramé !, Fleuve Éditions, 2012; Pocket, 2014
Et soudain tout change, Fleuve Éditions, 2013; Pocket, 2014
Ça peut pas rater !, Fleuve Éditions, 2014; Pocket, 2016
Quelqu'un pour qui trembler, Fleuve Éditions, 2015; Pocket, 2017
Le premier miracle, Flammarion, 2016; J'ai lu, 2017
Une fois dans ma vie, Flammarion, 2017; J'ai lu, 2018
Vaut-il mieux être toute petite ou abandonné à la naissance ?, with Mimie Mathy,
    Belfond 2017; Le Livre de Poche, 2018
Comme une ombre, with Pascale Legardinier, J'ai lu, 2018
J'ai encore menti !, Flammarion, 2018
Les phrases interdites si vous voulez rester en couple, with Pascale Legardinier,
    J'ai lu, 2019

The Paris Labyrinth is the author's first work to be translated into English.

GILLES LEGARDINIER

THE PARIS
LABYRINTH

A NOVEL

RESEARCH AND DOCUMENTATION
Chloé Legardinier

TRANSLATED FROM FRENCH BY
Kate Robinson

Flammarion

To those who feel like strangers in this world;
to those who doubt their ability to protect their loved ones
from what the future holds, who wonder where to look for hope,
I say this: do not dread the days ahead,
but accept nothing without discernment.
Follow your heart, be prepared to serve or to resist
with all of your might, or to wage battle, even.
Do not be afraid to call upon your imagination.
No path is forbidden.
The best paths are still secret, and at the heart of our best self
is the only key that will unleash the possibilities.

1

It was dark, with a chill in the air. In the tree-filled gardens of a mansion in a wealthy Parisian neighborhood, five men stood guard on the immense lawn sprawling behind the building. The glow of lanterns projected their long shadows onto the surrounding plants. The men were armed with revolvers, loaded and ready to fire. Alert, they scanned the area, listening carefully.

In the center of the perimeter that they had formed stood a man who was beginning to lose his patience. Dressed in a luxurious fur-collared coat and a meticulously polished top hat, he glanced periodically at his pocket watch. He'd waited months for this meeting. If, in one minute, the person he was expecting did not appear, the delay would not go unpunished.

The clatter of iron-rimmed wheels on cobblestones in a nearby street caught his attention. He knew, however, that the strange individual with whom he had an appointment would not arrive by carriage. Vincent always appeared as if by magic. He was surprising in every sense of the word. It was difficult to say how old he was; impossible to know where he lived; even his surname was a mystery. And yet he was well known by the powerful and wealthy, for whom he worked with the greatest discretion.

The clop of horseshoes rang out as the carriage continued on without stopping.

Suddenly, a silhouette emerged from a grove of trees, right under the nose of a guard holding a lantern, who grunted, taken by surprise in spite of his watchful vigilance. His companions took aim, then relaxed as the man in the coat spoke a few words in a foreign language.

"You know how to make an entrance, Vincent," he greeted his visitor in a Russian accent. "You almost frightened me."

"Please forgive me, Your Highness. It's a risk that comes with the profession."

Athletic in build, Vincent made his way across the grass with a light step. Unlike his illustrious client, he was not dressed in the latest fashion. Nor did he wear a hat or cap, which was unthinkable for anyone else, except perhaps a young child. His dark, close-fitting clothes gave no indication of profession or social status. The fabric was of good quality, but the style might befit a laborer. Was he a craftsman of some unidentified trade? A circus tightrope walker? A thief? No doubt a bit of all three.

The man in the coat avoided his handshake and barked, "I hope you're not going to inform me of a delay."

"Have I ever kept you waiting?"

"No, I must admit, you have not. Everything is ready then? After entrusting my home to you all winter, can I move in safely now—at last?"

"I think so, Your Highness."

"You think so? Must I be satisfied with what you *think*? Are you aware of the danger for an exiled prince here in your capital, with everyone flocking in for this preposterous World's Fair?"

"A crowd is a much better guarantee of secrecy and safety than any secluded retreat, Your Highness."

"I am not counting on a crowd in order to escape an attempt on my life; I am counting on your plan."

"You may indeed."

"How can I be certain? You are costing me a fortune, my dear Vincent, and though you have a reputation for being the best at your craft, I do not want to be the victim of your first mistake."

Vincent took a step forward, calmly breaching the distance that propriety imposed between a modest service provider and his prestigious client. He lowered his voice.

"Your Highness, I would like to offer you a deal that will give you complete peace of mind."

Disconcerted by the sudden proximity, the man in the coat stiffened, but steeled himself from backing away.

"You'll get neither more time, nor more gold than we agreed upon."

"I ask for neither."

Vincent paused to take a deep breath before adding, "When you asked me to create an entirely undetectable shelter, you trusted me with your life."

"That's right."

"Would you be reassured if I did the same?"

"What do you mean?"

Vincent didn't respond. He glanced around, savoring the moment. Each time he delivered a secret passage or a hidden room, he particularly enjoyed presenting it to the client, even when fewer risks were required than this evening. It represented the result of several months of hard work for him and his team. In that moment, his clients, as important as they might be, were obliged to listen to him with the greatest respect and to treat him as an equal. Nothing less than their safety or their most secret desire was at stake. Rank, title, and fortune dissolved, leaving just two men, face to face. He felt that only under these conditions did civilization reveal its true nature. The rest was a charade.

Certain that he now had his listener's full attention, Vincent murmured, "If you gave them the order, Your Highness, your bodyguards would not hesitate to kill me. Isn't that right?"

The prince seemed embarrassed at having to answer, but Vincent's steady gaze left him no choice.

"Of course, but why would I do that?"

"To prove that my work can save your life, let me risk my own." Vincent drew closer and whispered, "I'm going to make a run for it and hide in your mansion."

"But…"

"Order your escort to follow me and kill me. Without warning or mercy."

"Have you lost your mind?"

"If I survive, you will be reassured, because you will have personally witnessed the system's effectiveness."

"And if they kill you?"

"Then you shall keep your gold, and I beg you to accept my corpse as respectful evidence of my shame for having failed."

The man in the coat hesitated. He looked back and forth from Vincent to his men.

"I am warning you, Vincent," he said finally. "They are loyal assassins. They will not fake it."

"Your Highness, no one survives by faking it."

2

Vincent set off in the moonlight. No sooner had he left the lawn than the prince barked his order in his incomprehensible language, in a tone that brooked no discussion. His men raced after Vincent like a pack of wolves on the hunt, silent and determined.

Vincent was not afraid. Ironically, he was happy. He ran at a steady pace. A form of elation arose in him. Without slowing, he leaped over flowerbeds and sidestepped obstacles on his way towards the mansion. The prince's bodyguards were in hot pursuit. Vincent knew that to avoid alerting the policemen on patrol in the wealthy neighborhood, they would rather stab him than shoot him. They could not kill him from a distance, which would give him a few extra yards of safety.

He bounded up the back terrace steps, entered the sitting room that looked out over the gardens, and stole a glance behind him. In the darkness, he could not tell how much distance separated him from his pursuers. Oh, well. In any case, it would be a close match.

Without a moment's hesitation, he stepped into the hallway leading to the front of the building. Vincent could hear his pursuers' voices, but he was too concentrated to entertain worry. In fact, he saw this test as just a game, really. He was risking his life, but that didn't matter much to him. He was no longer aware of the fragility of existence. He knew how useless it was, in the rush of the moment, to think of the future. What mattered was to be present, to give in to the moment entirely without thinking of anything else, and to count on there being an afterwards. Living is an act of picking oneself up from the minutes preceding the present moment. He'd certainly had the opportunity to learn how.

What was now taking place was nothing more than an ordinary game of hide-and-seek, like the ones he enjoyed so much back when his life was uncomplicated. This evening, however, he was treated to a much more sophisticated hiding place and far less friendly opponents. If he were so unfortunate as to lose, he would not be able to laugh and pick himself up again.

He stopped running halfway down the hallway when he found himself between two alcoves where imposing Greek statues stood facing each other. A goddess and a god: Aphrodite and Ares, love and war. Vincent slipped behind the goddess. He would need her benevolent protection, for his pursuers had already swarmed the living areas.

He wrapped his arms around the goddess, respectfully embracing the folds of her stone robe. With his foot, he triggered the secret mechanism located behind the pedestal, immediately setting the entire alcove into motion. Like an elevator, it descended towards the basement, taking Vincent, still clinging to the life-saving statue, with it. With a swift vertical movement, the alcove was replaced by an exact reproduction lowered from above. It was a perfect replica.

Supported by a complex set of pulleys and counterweights, Vincent's alcove landed softly in a secret room constructed in the bowels of the building's foundation. If necessary, a person could stay in this buried hideaway for three days, equipped with enough supplies and in sufficient comfort. The system, impossible to breach, became the obvious solution when the prince refused an escape tunnel, which he deemed too expensive and too time-consuming.

Still clinging to his plaster savior, Vincent listened carefully. The muffled sounds of pounding feet drifted down from the floor above. The assassins continued down the hallway, without a thought for war or love. He smiled.

He murmured thanks to the goddess and released his hold. Curious to see what would happen next, he walked over to a panel lined with openings. Connected to a network of tubes, they enabled him to hear everything that went on in the residence. The sound of voices slipped from the tube labeled "main hall," to one labeled "office," then "master bedroom": the prince's men were moving on to the upper floors. They searched every room. Doors were opened unceremoniously, even the closets. Some of the assassins were already back in the garden, no doubt convinced their target had fled.

Savoring the fact that he was still alive, Vincent slipped delightedly into an elegant velvet armchair in the middle of an oriental rug. That night, it was his. That night, he was in complete control. The work he had accomplished with his team had saved his life. He exhaled. His breath and his heartbeat gradually slowed. He thought of his brother, Pierre, and of his friends, the ones who helped him build these unique mechanisms, these little masterpieces of engineering.

Hiding places and secret passages, as varied and imaginative as they were, served to accomplish a single goal: to guarantee the safety of that which mattered most to the client. A person, a treasure, a secret. These illusions—a combination of trompe-l'œil and virtuoso mechanisms—existed for that purpose alone.

The intelligence of design and the excellence with which it was implemented were secondary to function. That was a golden rule of his profession—which, strictly speaking, wasn't one.

Vincent heard raised voices coming from the spy tube in the hall. He recognized the prince's phrasing. He may not have understood his words, but he sensed his anger. Why was His Highness so angry with his men? Had he really hoped that they would kill him? Didn't he realize that his troop's inability to force Vincent from his hiding place was the best guarantee of his own protection?

Vincent didn't care what the prince thought, as long as he paid up. The work was complete, the mission accomplished. As happened at the end of every project, other much more important questions arose. Fears, above all.

A particularly intense one surfaced: what would happen to his team if he died? Although they only worked together, they were all he had to call family. Vincent felt responsible for them.

The adrenaline dissipated. He was sorry to feel it fade, for when he was running, when he put his remarkable sleight of hand into action, everything moved so fast that suddenly there was no room for existential questions. Urgency smothered all doubts and banished any concessions. There was no time to drift along in fog and shadow. When the race began, only his deepest self emerged; his most private nature guided each of his actions. He was suddenly untouched by time, escaping for a brief interlude everything he knew and everything he feared.

Vincent felt the weight of the world fade. Just for an instant, like a glimpse of eternity.

3

The first rays of dawn stained the few clouds in the sky a deep pink, signaling the arrival of a beautiful clear spring morning, the kind that retains a bit of the invigorating chill of a recently departed winter.

The path up to Montmartre had always felt to Vincent like a shortcut to another world, the border between two universes. As he wound his way back to his neighborhood, he left the capital behind. Although Paris had annexed Montmartre almost three decades ago, the area still remained apart; another spirit reigned here.

As a child, Vincent dreamed of one thing: to race down the very same slope and discover the city and the wonders it promised. Wearing an oversized cap that his father had given him, he would spend hours at night on the summit gazing out at the city's multitude of captivating lights. He could follow the lamplighters as they progressed from point to point, street to street, spreading their glow like a swarm of fireflies.

Standing on his hill, overlooking the city and its countless streets, he imagined women in beautiful dresses and well-attired men living lives so different from his own. Unidentified sounds sometimes drifted up to him on the wind, and he amused himself trying to guess what made them.

Oddly, now that he was a grown man, he was never happier than when he was on his way "back up" to his home. A weight lifted when he turned towards his village. The climb was liberating. Up there, he no longer needed to stay in character. He was no longer obligated to take extra care with his words. There was no need for comparison or self-justification. Up there, he could just be himself.

With measured steps, Vincent finished his climb through what remained of the thickets. He had barely reached the summit when he had to sidestep the workers who milled about on the immense worksite of the future Basilica of Sacré-Cœur. As it had every day for years, an unending procession of carts fed the monstrous structure with blocks of a rare, hard stone that had the distinctive character-istic of turning white in the rain. They were brought from south of Nemours. It was hardly surprising that construction had been hard to finance, despite the successful underwriting. The ogre had not finished expanding its grip, rising little by little, hungry for every-thing the people's devotion could offer.

Although far from complete, the structure already promised to be imposing. The foundations alone had made all the headlines: the first set was accidentally swallowed up by the left-over galleries of the old gypsum quarries that honeycombed the hill.

The monument was already visible from all over Paris, and many had forgotten about the neighboring Saint-Pierre de Montmartre church, the oldest place of worship in the capital. The venerable church had been abandoned after falling into ruin during the Revolution and subsequent wars. Shameful. The bell no longer tolled. The oldest building in Montmartre—and the most sacred still in existence—had been reduced to silence. The local inhabitants were not pleased that their neighborhood had been muted. They refused to make do with the bells of the churches down below to mark the rhythm of their day.

Vincent wove in and out of the construction site. Early in the morning, an army of carvers was already busy at work on the immaculate stones before they were hoisted by laborers up to masons perched on the enormous scaffolding. Each piece of the puzzle found a place in the walls that grew higher and higher. Colossal wooden supports prevented a clear view of the entire building, even though the entrance with its three Byzantine arches was complete. If it hadn't been dedicated to Christ, the building would have been cursed, given how much its appearance and very existence were being criticized. No one knew when the baffling nave would cease to rise.

Below, pavers and convicts reshaped the hillside. It was said that a spectacular staircase would soon descend the hill replacing the fields and winding paths.

Once, the only things visible from this precise spot had been the sky and the blades of windmills rotating in the breeze. Where there had once been fourteen, only two remained, one of which survived only after being converted into a rock crusher.

He paused for a moment on the site of the future parvis. He was beginning to feel the effects of his sleepless night in the prince's mansion. Indifferent to the flurry of activity around him, he gazed at the horizon and at the capital spread out below.

Take a step back, see the big picture—he knew how important that was. This very spot was where he had learned the value of rising above it all—in every sense of the term. The city holds a thousand curiosities for those who venture into it. On the bustling streets, everything can delight, entice, and spark longing or desire. But while that may aid the passage of time or serve as a distraction, it rarely helps anyone determine where they really need to go. The uncertain quickly lose their way.

Gustave Eiffel's 984-foot metal tower rose—despite public pro-testations—above the freshly paved avenues and after a mere two years and two months of construction. Everything was happening so fast these days. Now the tallest structure built by human hands anywhere in the world, its slender red silhouette slashed the horizon and challenged the brilliant azure sky. At night it became a beacon casting its blinding light over the capital. Just weeks before, on March 31, the tower began welcoming visitors from all over the world, but its elevators would only begin running in early May, for the inauguration of the World's Fair that sprawled at its feet.

Paris was changing. Everything taking place pointed to a new world. The future basilica had already claimed its place in this emerg-ing world of inventions and progress that was upsetting the course of things in many ways.

Most of Vincent's beloved landmarks had disappeared, one after another. But the corner of Rue des Saules and Rue Saint-Vincent was still home to the Lapin Agile, a cabaret where laughter and singing drifted out onto the street at all hours of the day and night. Back when it was still called the Rendez-vous des Voleurs, his father would go there almost every evening to banter and to secure work for the following day. Despite Vincent's attachment to the emblems of his childhood, he would have preferred to see this particular establishment obliterated without a trace.

He was startled by an order shouted at a laborer dallying nearby: "Get back to work!"

This roused Vincent from his daydream; his conscience might very well have bellowed the same thing. He was expected somewhere.

4

As day dawned, the neighborhoods sprung to life. The rag-and-bone men were already going about their business, cursing the Poubelle bins that were stealing their livelihood. The street sweepers finished clearing debris, and stalls were set up. Water carriers, knife grinders, glaziers, caners, and other craftsmen began their rounds, offering their services at the top of their lungs.

Vincent headed for Montmartre's north slope, sheltered from the tumult of the capital. As he descended Rue de l'Abreuvoir, the din of construction gave way to birdsong.

He walked down the middle of the cobblestone path unconcerned about traffic; carriages never came this way, for the slope was too steep, and those who lived here couldn't afford to have anything delivered anyway. A few months earlier an automobile had tried, on a dare, but it stopped a quarter of the way up Rue Mont-Cenis. None of the residents had ever seen such a machine, and the ungodly noise of the combustion engine had terrified several of the locals.

Without slowing, Vincent had already entered another world. In the shadow of the ruins of the Château des Brouillards, coal men and scrap-metal merchants crowded together in a tangle of shanties and hovels belching smoke. This anarchical maze overrun with vegetation was known as "the maquis." No one ventured in unless they lived here, and it was a refuge for many outcasts. It wasn't a place for wandering; here people just did their best to scrape by, hoping for brighter days. There were no roads lined with wide sidewalks, no lights illuminating the twilight, and no water flowing in the houses; here the paths became torrents of mud after each rainstorm. Penniless artists flocked here in ever greater numbers, conversing and debating in the midst of the less fortunate. They had a wealth of dreams and found sustenance in their ambitions, although none of that was worth a decent hot meal.

The cries of children mingled with the scents of reheated soup and laundry. Even after washing, the linens hung out to dry were far from pristine. Sometimes a street singer could be heard warming up and practicing popular songs from inside his shanty before heading out to perform on more respectable thoroughfares. People with twisted—or broken—fates lived together, united for better or for worse by a life that spared no one. Even so, Vincent felt more at ease here than in Paris's smarter neighborhoods.

He became more alert as soon as he entered the maquis. He checked periodically to be sure he hadn't been followed. His hideout wasn't far, and he was keen to keep its location as secret as the passages he designed.

Skirting a fence covered in posters that touted the area's new dance halls, Vincent suddenly slipped between two boards, supple as a cat. He crossed an abandoned grain and flour depot to enter, unnoticed, the backdoor of a house on Rue Caulaincourt. Although he was the official tenant, he never used the front door. The deserted business located just behind the residence provided a much safer means of access, hidden from curious eyes. By cutting through the former repository, now reduced to a few empty storage spaces covered with a thin layer of dusty old flour, he came out into a small wild garden at the foot of the service door to his own house. It took more than a key to open it: he had been careful to protect the entrance with an array of traps and alarms.

After wiping his fingers clean to avoid leaving any trace, he turned one of the iron moldings on the doorframe, which disarmed the load that was trained to fire on unwelcome visitors, and simultaneously rang the bell that alerted his friends of his approach. Then he entered the large empty house.

What had once been a guesthouse was dark and dirty, nothing like the lavish places where Vincent most often operated. But that didn't matter; aside from sleeping in one of the upstairs bedrooms—constantly changing place as a precaution—he and his companions passed the majority of their time elsewhere. The heart of their hideout was located below.

Vincent approached the fireplace in the abandoned kitchen. He slipped his hand into a hole on the side left by a missing brick. With his fingertips, he pushed the trigger that activated the opening mechanism. With a click, the back wall of the hearth shifted to reveal a small stairway that led beneath the building.

When Vincent and his younger brother, Pierre, had looked for a larger location to develop their unique business, they hadn't been attracted so much by the size of the house as by the large vaulted cellars, the remains of a monastic annex belonging to the royal abbey; only the section above ground had been altered. They decided to set up their workshop here, shortly before Konrad, the German carpenter, and Eustasio, the Italian artist, joined them, completing the team. Their craft required no storefront—quite the contrary.

Vincent raced down the steps.

5

The secret entrance locked shut behind Vincent. He felt reassured as he inhaled the familiar musk of the cellar and felt the solidity of the steps and the massive walls of the ancient stairwell. The warm light of oil lamps greeted him at the bottom, setting him immediately at ease. He had returned home, to safety.

Since the day he and his younger brother had been driven from their childhood home, he had never felt safe or in his rightful place anywhere but in this underground space. It had once served as a wine cellar for the Benedictine nuns of the Montmartre abbey, back when vineyards covered acres of what at the time was still countryside. Now all that remained was an immense vaulted chamber supported by columns. Barrels and casks had given way to the tools of other trades. The space now accommodated the team's various activities: an abundance of gear and equipment piled between the work stations gave an impression of general disorder. The sheer quantity of tools and materials needed to carry out their projects generated a bizarre accumulation that could rival the set department of an opera house.

On the left, Konrad's carpentry and cabinetry workshop housed a lathe and a bandsaw; the scent of turpentine often dominated the mingled fragrances of the wood varieties he employed. Above the vise hung an assortment of chisels, planes, files, gouges, and cans of wax and wood stain.

Across the room, Eustasio had strewn out pots of paint, pigments, brushes, and cloths that he used to create his remarkable optical illusions. He mastered all manner of camouflage and subterfuge: in his hands, steel could be mistaken for a cloud, and cloth for granite. He could make something new look old, or something hollow appear solid. Equally skilled with plaster, fabric, leather, and glass, he was also tasked with creating scale models of future projects—they never failed to persuade clients.

In the center of the space, between the various trial maquettes used to test Vincent's inventions, stood a long table piled with blueprints and sketches in a deceptively untidy jumble.

The basement workshop was completed by a forge equipped with a smoke evacuation system and a large counter for metal work. That was Pierre's domain; like his older brother, he specialized in mechanisms of every kind.

He was waiting for Vincent, leaning against a pillar where he had been standing since hearing the alarm bell ring.

"Took you a while," he called out in greeting.

"Long enough to perform for the prince and come back."

"Everything went okay?"

"I wouldn't be here if it hadn't. I risked my neck, but everything turned out all right in the end. He yelped out in terror at the sound of my voice coming through the spy tube in the hall."

Vincent's younger brother frowned. "You shouldn't take it so lightly. I worry every time. Not all of our clients are honest. I don't like you going by yourself, it's dangerous."

"Everything is dangerous in our business, little brother. So what good would it do to put you at risk as well?"

"Still, waiting for you is torture. It's actually getting worse. With every hour that passes, I worry I won't ever see you again."

Vincent placed his hand on his brother's shoulder. "I know how it feels. But don't worry, I always come back."

A tall man with a thick beard appeared from behind a pillar to join them.

"Greetings, Vincent."

"Well, hello there, Konrad."

"What kind of welcome did the prince have in store for you?" Konrad's German accent was strong, but his speech was impeccable.

"He forced me to run very fast and he tried to have my throat slit. Otherwise it was rather gentlemanly. The usual. If Aphrodite had refused to drop, I would be dead and good riddance!"

The two men laughed.

"His Highness is very happy with his hideout," added Vincent. "He sends his congratulations."

Pierre shrugged his shoulders. "Your prince doesn't even know who we are."

"That's one of the company rules. It's for your own protection."

"Did he pay us?" fretted Konrad.

"The gold was delivered on schedule. Henri confirmed as much."

The German clapped his hands with delight. "Then project forty-eight is officially complete, and we are a little richer!"

Vincent looked around their hideout and said, surprised, "Where is Eustasio?"

"He's in Passy, with the Comtesse de Vignole," explained Pierre. "Project forty-two. The hidden door to her secret boudoir needed another touch up."

Vincent burst out laughing. "This is at least the fifth time the door to her boudoir has needed a paint job!"

"Every week," said Pierre with a knowing smile.

"Let's hope she doesn't send our handsome Italian home too exhausted. Did he take his tools with him for show? Or just his strapping good looks?"

Konrad pointed to the toolbox at the foot of Eustasio's work-bench. The three men chuckled at their friend.

Pierre was the first to grow serious and change the subject. "I hope you didn't forget about the meeting with Alfred Minguier later this afternoon."

"The industrialist? What exactly does he want?"

"He didn't say. He wants to explain in person."

"Who recommended us?"

"Françoise de Fremensac. Her daughter is engaged to Mr. Minguier's only son and heir to his fortune."

"Nobility bows to industry. That's a sign of the times. Power is changing hands."

"The powerful used to wave a sacred sword, now it's a donkey wrench!" quipped Konrad.

"It's 'monkey,' Konrad, a monkey wrench. But you're right."

A brief scraping sound from the back of the workshop caught Vincent's attention.

"Did you hear that?"

Pierre and Konrad shook their heads in perfect unison. Vincent squinted to get a better view of where the sound seemed to emanate. But there was no light in that part of the cellar where the men tossed unused scrap materials.

"It's probably a rat," said Vincent's brother in what he hoped was a reassuring voice.

Vincent raised his eyebrows. "A rat?"

"I'll take care of it while you're at Minguier's."

Something about Pierre's behavior was off, piquing Vincent's attention. He was too quick to respond, and his tone of voice too unsteady for such a simple matter. Vincent peered again into the far corner.

"A rat?" he repeated, increasingly intrigued by his younger brother's strange manner.

He turned to Konrad, but the carpenter raised his hands, feigning incomprehension. For the first time, Vincent had the feeling that his colleague, reputed for his candor, was uncomfortable. Determined to find out what was going on, he grabbed a lantern and headed to the back of the chamber.

He walked straight towards the dark area where no one ever went.

This time, Pierre caught up with him, ran ahead, and tried to block his path. He raised his voice: "Why don't you ever listen? You only do as you please!"

His brother did not slow down.

"Even mother complained about it! No wonder she didn't last long!"

Vincent froze. Suppressing a flash of pain and anger, he turned to face his brother who had never spoken to him that way before. "Why did you say that, Pierre? What are you accusing me of?"

The young man knew he had gone too far.

"I'm not accusing you of anything," he said, trying to smooth things over. "I'm just saying... you should let me try to get rid of the rats. You have more important things to do."

In the lamp light, Vincent could see that Pierre had gone pale and avoided his gaze. He was now convinced there was more than a rodent to be found in the cluttered mess. He stepped forward and began his inspection. He shone his light onto the heaps of boards, piles of unused scenery, various scraps, and stacks of models, project after project. His brother tried to resume the conversation.

"Come on, let's head back to the table. We're arguing over nothing."

"Be quiet," ordered his older brother.

Vincent listened hard in the silence. Finally, he detected the sound of breathing—quiet, but fast—that confirmed his suspicions. He took a wary step forward. With a fluid motion, he pulled an ebony-handled folding knife from his belt where it always hung and opened the blade.

"Please," begged Pierre. "Don't go any further..."

Vincent wasn't listening. He had just caught sight of a glistening eye between two wooden friezes. It stared at him unblinking. Whether it was predator or prey was impossible to say. Warily, his knife raised, Vincent called out in a calm voice, "Whoever you are, come out immediately."

"You're going to hurt me!" said a fearful voice. A woman's voice.

Vincent insisted, "I'll only hurt you if you don't come out."

Nothing happened at first, but the boards eventually began to move and shift apart. In the hiding place under the scrap pile, Vincent discovered a young woman crouched in a torn bodice, with disheveled hair and filthy skin but an incredibly beautiful face.

6

Furious, Vincent grabbed his brother by the jacket and shoved him against the wall.

"Do you realize the danger you've put us in by bringing that girl here? What were you thinking?"

Pierre was terrified. It wasn't the first time he'd seen his older brother lose his temper, and he knew what he was capable of. But until now, Vincent's anger had never been directed at him.

"You reckless idiot! Have you lost your mind? She saw our faces. She knows where we live. She knows about our inventions! She could give away our secrets to anyone!"

"I didn't let her in," said Pierre defensively.

"Excuse me? You mean to tell me she got in by herself? She dodged all of our traps?"

"Last week she fell in through the delivery hatch. I swear I'm telling the truth."

"The delivery hatch? The one we sealed closed together?"

"Go see for yourself. Everything we put in rotted through. I was at my workbench when I heard a cry. I rushed over and found her on the ground, half unconscious. She was being chased down the street by a group of thugs and ducked into the first spot she could find. They wanted to sell her to the brothel on Rue Letort."

Unsettled by what he had heard, Vincent loosened his grip slightly, torn by conflicting feelings.

His brother continued. "I considered sending her back out the way she came, I really did, but I couldn't find the heart to do it.

Throwing her back out there would have been the end of her."

Vincent listened. With slightly more calm he asked, "Why didn't you tell me?"

"I was waiting for the right moment, between two emergencies. In the meantime, I took it upon myself to hide her. I told her to stay away from the table and the blueprints."

"How long has she been here?"

"Three days."

Vincent's anger flared again. "She's heard everything we've said for the last three days? And you have the gall to tell me that you're worried because I don't get home fast enough?"

"She doesn't know what we're talking about."

Vincent spun around, looking for the carpenter, who had slipped away.

"Konrad!"

"Over here!"

"Did you know about this?" Vincent curtly asked the approaching German.

"I heard her cry out when she fell…"

"So you knew. And it didn't occur to you to inform me, knowing how hard I work to keep us safe?"

"I respect you, Vincent, you're an honest man. We get along well and I would never betray you, but I couldn't denounce your own brother. You're close, inseparable even. It's not my place to tell you what your brother won't. That's your business. However, please, I would like you to let go of him; it pains me to see you fight like this."

Vincent took a deep breath and complied.

Konrad went on, "I must admit, I would have done the same thing if I were him. And I bet you would have too."

Vincent straightened his jacket. "First I would have asked myself if she was a spy!"

"Sent by whom, *mein Freund*? If you had seen her eating, shaking, and crying in Pierre's arms, you would have known she was just a lost, starving young woman."

Vincent looked directly at Pierre, who no longer averted his gaze.

"Now that you've decided to save her, what do you intend to do with her?"

"We could let her stay here for a while."

"A girl, here? When we don't know anything about her?"

"I trust her more than many of our clients," retorted Pierre.

"You know, Vincent, we can adapt," said Konrad reassuringly. "It would only be for a little while. Plus, she knows how to cook, and well."

Vincent gasped.

"She cooked for you?"

"She made last night's stew."

Vincent didn't know what to say. True, the stew had been excellent, but that's not what was on his mind. He looked towards the back of the room. She watched them, a frail silhouette barely visible against the darkness.

The young woman stood waiting for them to decide her fate. Her scrawny arms dangled by her sides, but she held herself upright. Her shoulders drooped, but she stood firm, her chin raised, attentive. Even when a person has been stripped of everything, their true nature remains.

Vincent wanted to remain impassive; his responsibilities demanded it. Forever condemned to make the right decision, he had to resist all sentiment to carry out his duties. Pity was not an option, and anyway, she would probably refuse it. He already had enough to manage without adding a young woman who had stumbled onto them by accident. If only she had holed up in some other corner, anywhere but here. But fate had decided otherwise, and Vincent could no longer pretend that nothing had happened, especially since he knew exactly what she was going through. He felt it. He remembered. He had been in the same situation, that hellish moment when one's fate lies in someone else's hands. Truly nothing would be simple in this life, thought Vincent.

He turned to the woman. "What's your name?"

"Gabrielle."

7

"Who shall I say is calling?"

"Tell Mr. Minguier that Vincent has arrived. He'll understand."

The butler frowned doubtfully. "Please wait here." He pronounced the request with effort. The manservant turned on his heels, discreetly motioning to a maid to remain near the entrance. He wasn't about to let someone who presented himself by first name only out of sight. These days, delinquents would try anything.

Vincent studied his new environment, as he always did. He had had occasion to notice that a housekeeper at the entrance to a mansion indicates great wealth; a butler at the door suggests even more.

Vincent scrutinized the entrance hall, which conveyed the image of power its owner sought to project. First to catch his eye was an enormous chandelier made entirely of steel chains. Elsewhere their girth would have served to hoist heavy loads or secure a boat, but here they were mere decoration. And yet the chandelier's imposing size created a curious impression of balance, and the disparity between its classical form and the material was enchanting. Where others displayed crystal, the industry baron had decided to showcase what he manufactured.

The walls were hung with dramatic paintings of battles, including one lost by the French—which supporters of the Republic might find to be in poor taste. Between two paintings hung the blazon of a noble line the industrialist did not belong to, and below that, more surprisingly, two large photographs of factories. Vincent stepped closer. On the front window, he could make out the words

"Minguier & Bellair, manufacturers of the best welded link chains." Vincent had seen very few photographs in his life, and never any this large; it was rare to see them displayed like this. He was still studying the images when the butler reappeared, visibly unnerved.

"Please follow me. Mr. Minguier will see you now." He seemed surprised to be pronouncing the invitation. Out of habit, he motioned the maid to gather the visitor's things, but checked himself. No coat, no hat: there was definitely something odd about the fellow.

A short man with a round, red face appeared in the hallway and walked towards them with his hand outstretched. "Mr. Vincent! I'm so delighted to meet you at last."

"My respects to you, Mr. Minguier."

The handshake might have felt sincere if it hadn't been so overly emphatic. It revealed more about the man's technique than his character—a real businessman's handshake.

The industrialist teased him good-naturedly. "It's more difficult to get a meeting with you than with the commissioner of the World's Fair!"

"I beg your pardon."

Vincent's formality and restraint contrasted with the man's gregarious spontaneity; he invited Vincent into his office. "Please, come in."

He pointed to an armchair and turned to his manservant. "Joseph, see that I am not disturbed. And try not to eavesdrop for once."

Joseph was outraged, but his master couldn't have cared less. The butler disappeared. As soon as the door closed, the two men settled in across the desk from each other.

"Cigar?" offered Minguier.

"No, thank you. I don't smoke."

"Neither do I, except when other people do. Cigars are all the rage in manufacturing—the bosses seem to want to produce as much smoke as their factories!" He laughed at his own joke.

"What can I do for you, Mr. Minguier?"

"You're quite right, let's get down to business." The man straightened in his seat, then leaned towards his visitor. He lowered his voice and said gravely, "Let's be clear: everything we talk about here is absolutely confidential."

"Of course. You have my word. And it will stay that way, should we work together or not."

Alfred Minguier nodded his head appreciatively and began. "I'm preoccupied with one affair in particular, and when I learned of your existence, I immediately pegged you as the man for the job. Let me explain: I inherited an old house that holds a great deal of sentimental value for me. Several months ago, by sheer accident, I discovered that it contains a secret passage. But I was given no information about how to open it. So here I am, knowing that it exists, but completely unable to access it. You see the problem."

"Is the mechanism blocked? Would you like to have it changed?"

"Before we resort to that, I'd like you to try to make it work."

"You know nothing about how it operates?"

"Absolutely nothing."

"Do you have any idea what purpose it serves?"

"Given the building's history, I imagine the passage leads to a secret hideout, but I'm not even certain about that."

"When was the passage last used?"

"No idea. Given the condition of the furniture near the entrance, it's probably been closed for over a century."

"A century! Good gracious! What made you suspect the existence of a hidden room?"

The question seemed to surprise Minguier. He hesitated before answering.

"I found allusions to it in correspondence between the former owners."

Vincent noticed the man carefully weigh each word of his brief response. So it was a sensitive topic. "Did they mention anything about how to enter the room?"

"Not a word. I find myself—literally—faced with a wall I can't get past."

"Have you tried to force it open? After all, it's your house, and you must have the mechanical means at your disposal in your factories."

Minguier shook his head.

"I fear the entrance may be booby-trapped. If we resort to violence, the contents might be destroyed by who knows what kind of curse—fire, flood, or collapse, I really can't say. I can't take that risk."

"I understand. You would like me to bypass the locking systems and regain access to the room."

"Exactly."

"If I may, do you have any idea about what you will find behind the door, Mr. Minguier?"

The man was taken aback.

"Am I obliged to answer?"

"Certainly not, but I think it would be preferable. There is often a connection between the value of the contents and the complexity of the methods used to protect it. Being able to evaluate this factor with a maximum of information will help me to advise you and prepare my research without incurring unnecessary costs. Rest assured, I know how to keep a secret."

The industrialist was clearly displeased at the idea of revealing the hideout's contents.

"I'm not sure what I'm going to find," he said reluctantly. "Let's just say that it could be vital for me. I will tell you what I know when the time comes. First I want to know if this mission falls within your expertise. That's the first step."

"I've devoted myself to studying secret passages and their mechanisms since I was in my teens. I've analyzed masterpieces by the craft's best minds, and I work hard to carry on their talent. Normally I'm hired to build mysteries, not to uncover those created by others. I must admit, I've never been presented with a challenge like this, but I'm keen to try. I can hardly sing my own praises, but at least I'm certain no one else has as deep an interest in the subject as I do."

"So my sources tell me, and full of praise. I understand you work with a team."

"Indeed."

"Are they trustworthy?"

"I answer for my men as well as myself. But they specialize in construction."

"Then you won't need them."

"In theory, no."

"Perfect."

"If you are interested in my services, I will need to visit the site with you to begin my investigation—and to determine the fee for the operation."

"Money won't be a problem. Once the passage is open, you'll be paid whatever you like."

"Pardon me for broaching the subject, but we're accustomed to receiving payment in gold, if you don't mind. No paper notes, no shares."

Minguier waved his hand.

"Satisfy my request, and you'll have all the gold you want."

Vincent was surprised by this reaction. Businessmen are not in the habit of handing out their profits with such generosity, unless doing so could generate even more. He had noticed the contrast in the quiet way Alfred Minguier expressed himself and the intensity of his sharp gaze, which missed nothing. He considered the discrepancy between the man's enthusiastic cordiality and his reluctance to respond to perfectly reasonable questions: he had a gray area; there was something ambiguous about him.

"When would you like us to go there, Mr. Minguier?"

"We can only do it at night. I'm too busy during the day. My presence is required in the Galerie des Machines to prepare for the imminent opening of the World's Fair. My associate and I will be presenting a new machine capable of producing ten yards of chain an hour."

Instinctively, Vincent knew that this reason, though entirely valid, was not, in fact, the truth.

8

Laughter thundered and insults flew in the din at the Brasserie des Martyrs. The place had quite a reputation around Pigalle. Foremen from the many surrounding construction sites gathered there at the end of the work day, before the artists and poets who arrived and lingered much later than the laborers, who had to be up at dawn.

The pediment of the narrow hallway leading to the bathroom was inscribed with a maxim: "The worker washes his hands before pissing, the intellectual washes them after."

The large first-floor dining room was occupied by those there to be seen, while conversation flowed easily on the more informal second floor.

In a back corner, glasses were filled to celebrate the completion of project forty-eight. Vincent raised his.

"Let's make a toast, my friends. To all of you! Let us never forget: nothing would be possible without each other."

The whole team had gathered. Even young Henri was there, although, unlike the others, he neither developed nor created passages. His role was to manage food supplies—including fetching water from the well in the courtyard—and, most importantly, acting as messenger. He collected letters but also delivered them, which he did with unrivaled speed thanks to his talent for latching undetected onto horse-drawn carriages and other vehicles. In this way, he could cross Paris in less than an hour with the involuntary assistance of successive coach drivers, who always grumbled when they spotted him. Henri—nicknamed the Nail for his leanness—also carried out other, more confidential tasks for Vincent. When their companions asked for specifics, the boy replied that he ran security, and Vincent eluded the question with a wisecrack.

That evening Henri discovered that, for the first time, his fingers were finally long enough to completely encircle his glass of wine when he held it in one hand. He could now cup it in his palm, his thumb and index finger touching. He wasn't going to say anything for fear that his older companions would tease him yet again and call him, as they often did, "kid." He had been waiting for this moment for years, as project after project came to an end. He had been drinking wine like a man for three years, and from now on he could hold his glass like an adult. He kept his pride to himself, happy that someone else, for the moment, was on the receiving end of the teasing. The Italian was the target this time.

"So, Eustasio, tell us about this 'touch-up' at the countess's house."

"And don't forget the technical details!" ribbed Konrad.

"Knock it off, the countess is a respectable *signora*..."

"And to stay that way, she receives her lovers in her secret boudoir!" teased Pierre.

The table burst into laughter, Eustasio included.

"It's true, she is passionate," he confided. "She says I have an ardor that aristocrats are incapable of. She thinks they're boring and keeps saying they're only interested in themselves. So it's only inevitable..."

"...the countess is consorting with a commoner!" said Vincent. "I hope she's generous with you."

"She doesn't pay me or give me anything! I'm not that kind of man," Eustasio countered. "She's gentle, and it's true, we have a good time together. You can laugh all you want, but in the wee hours of the morning, we forget about everything that separates us and just enjoy what we share. I'm not ashamed."

"I'm sorry, Eustasio, I didn't mean to offend you. What matters is that you're happy with the relationship—or rather, with the repairs!"

The five companions burst out laughing again. Konrad took a swig of coarse wine and changed the subject.

"With the payment from the last project, our little treasure has grown substantially. I don't know about you, but I find myself wondering more and more often what I'm going to do with my gold."

Pierre motioned for him to lower his voice.

"Soon, we'll be living like princes, isn't that right?" continued Konrad more quietly. "Don't you ever think about it?"

He turned to his Italian friend.

"Eustasio, are you planning to stay in Paris or go back to Italy?"

"Who knows where my destiny lies? I'd like to bring my parents here. My mother is French, after all. Maybe buy them an acre of land and a little house."

With a faraway look in his eyes, he added, "And why not buy a studio for painting or sculpture?"

"Specializing in nudes!" quipped Konrad. "You already have a model!"

"What about you?" chuckled the artist. "Will you go home?"

"Home... I don't really know where home is. I have no ties, no family to help or to find. I would like to travel a little, and lend my furniture-making services to churches or cathedrals in Europe. I learned to speak several languages during my time on the road, and clergy are often in need of good craftsmen. They pay well. I also thought about investing in an apartment, or in those new shares that the rich are snatching up, in a far-off mine that promises incredible profits."

Each man weighed in, saying how audacious the idea was; just look at the run of bad luck that had befallen the underwriters who invested their savings in the Panama Canal. Investing money in a business managed by an obscure board of directors? Vincent didn't set much store by it and Eustasio didn't understand it.

Pierre said he had other plans. As the others turned to look at him, he calmly explained his idea, which suggested he had probably thought more seriously than any of them about his future.

"There's no way I'm leaving Paris. I'd like to stay in Montmartre and rent lodgings with a view, despite Sacré-Cœur. As far as my work is concerned, Mr. Eiffel and his metal tower have demonstrated what steel makes possible. Even though the attraction will be taken down when the World's Fair is over, it has ushered in the real steel age. I bet that metal will define the next century, and I'm certain there will be plenty of exciting opportunities for a guy like me."

Henri piped up, "I'd like to become a doctor."

The boy ignored his companions' mockery. "For sure I could! With my share of the gold, I'll be able to pay for medical school. I can do it. I learned to read in less than a year!"

Vincent was the only one who didn't tease him.

"You're right, Henri. Don't be discouraged by what others say. Ever. If you're determined and if you work hard, it's possible. Read, learn, study. Don't forget arithmetic. In a few years, these unbelievers will be more than happy to have you minister to their sorry bones!"

"True enough!" exclaimed Konrad. "Hurry up and become a doctor, because my vision is going and I'm short-winded."

Pierre winked. "Eustasio's conquests will eventually earn him a shameful disease!"

The Italian laughed cheerfully, but once the hooting had settled, he turned to Vincent.

"And what do you plan to do with your little fortune?"

Vincent paused a moment before answering, then looked at each of them in turn.

"What matters most to me is not what I do with it, but with whom I do it. Our business is exhausting and dangerous. Our clients are complicated and sometimes perverse. Each project is a puzzle, a tightrope act without a safety harness, but I enjoy what we do. I especially love doing it with you. It's funny, but even though I'm in charge of our team, you will ultimately decide what happens to me."

"I want to stay with you!" Henri gushed.

With these words, the boy suddenly seemed younger than he usually tried to appear.

The five friends spent a while considering how their money might be used. Eustasio even compared their ramblings to the adventures of Perrette and her pot of milk in Jean de La Fontaine's fable. Like the milkmaid, they imagined so many possibilities—some quite ridiculous—of what they might get for their treasure.

Although no one could hear their words over the noise of the dining room, one man was watching them intently. Peering out from under the visor of his cap, he observed them with an unbroken gaze, all the while playing with a leather shoelace that he wrapped with mechanical dexterity around his long, thin fingers. He had gotten lucky that night. All he needed to do was follow one of them to identify the whole group. He hadn't expected it to be so easy. He now knew the faces of those who so carefully protected the secrets of the powerful.

The rest would be neither long nor complicated.

9

The night was well underway—too late for the foremen, but still too early for the artists. Vincent checked to be sure the street was deserted, then disappeared himself, the last to slip between the fence boards. Keeping equal distances apart, the five companions crossed the old abandoned mill without making the slightest sound. They met outside the backdoor of their hideout. Still immersed in their pleasant time at the brasserie, they continued their banter, but in hushed voices.

Konrad activated the molding in the doorframe, then methodically unlocked the door. The panel was half-open when he froze: a glimpse of light from the kitchen had caught his eye. Gabrielle had been allowed to stay in the house, with access to everywhere except the cellar, and on condition that she didn't draw attention. For a moment, the carpenter entertained the thought that she had betrayed them. The vixen might have taken advantage of a rare occasion when the place was empty to loot it with her accomplices. If that turned out to be so, he would be disappointed.

Konrad quickly motioned for Vincent to join him. As soon as their leader noticed the suspicious light, he whipped out his knife and stepped through the door.

The hallway had been swept. Even more surprisingly, a pleasant fragrance hung in the air, quite different from the usual musty odor. Vincent tiptoed forward, with Konrad close behind him. Pierre and Eustasio waited at the entrance, flanking Henri in case of an ambush.

Vincent carefully peeked around the kitchen door. He was immediately relieved to see the wall to the cellar still closed and intact.

Leaning further forward for a better view, he caught a glimpse of a corner of the table—draped with a tablecloth. Places were set. He stretched a little further and spotted Gabrielle with her back to him, busy drying the dishes in front of the stone sink. His eyes widened in surprise as he entered the room.

"What have you done?" he demanded.

The young woman started and nearly dropped the bowl she was holding before regaining her composure. "You scared the living daylights out of me!"

"So did you."

The others joined them in the kitchen. The five men looked around, astonished. They had never seen the place in such a state. Usually it was a drab antechamber they merely crossed on their way to their subterranean hideout, but this evening, they discovered a real kitchen.

Henri sniffed the air like an animal picking up a trail.

"You made a cake?" he exclaimed.

"A pie. I found some apples in the pantry of a room on the first floor."

Eustasio blanched. "My apples! You went into my room?"

Gabrielle didn't seem to hear him and continued. "I thought you might be hungry after your night out. I grew up with uncles who drank. They were always starving when they got back from the tavern."

"We're not drunks!" grumbled Konrad. "None of us is inebriated."

"I helped myself to the butter and flour. I found the reserves."

"She found the reserves," moaned Henri.

Pierre stepped towards her. "Thank you for the pie. You didn't have to..."

"I was here, going round in circles. May as well be useful. After all, everyone does their part for a place here. Why shouldn't I do the same?"

Vincent's mind raced, as usual. "Did you visit the entire house?"

"I swear, I didn't take anything," cried Gabrielle. "I'm not a thief!"

"My main concern is whether the neighbors might have seen you from the street. They're very curious and we wouldn't care to..."

"I understand that you don't want to attract attention. I was careful not to turn on any lights in the front of the house.

That's fine with me, especially since those pimps are probably still prowling around out there. They're not likely to give up. If they catch me, I'm done for, and if they know you're helping me, they'll give you trouble. I don't want that."

Gabrielle grabbed the dish sitting on the cast iron stove and removed the cloth that covered it, revealing her pie. She set it on the table.

"I didn't know what time you'd be back, so I kept it as warm as I could. I hope it's not too dry."

She motioned to the men to take their seats at the table and began to cut the pie.

"Don't you want any?" she said, pointing to the pastry.

Five plates rose at once. Gabrielle served the pie, starting with Vincent, then with her foot pushed a stool between Henri and Pierre and sat down.

This late and very unexpected snack in Gabrielle's presence had a decidedly different ambiance than the tavern.

For Konrad, the delicious pastry, warm light, and silverware on the tablecloth conjured memories of when he still lived with his parents, in the Ruhr district. As for Henri, the moment held everything he had always imagined but never experienced: a home. Vincent and Pierre exchanged looks. The scene stirred in them an ease forgotten since the day their childhood was cut short. Magic is fleeting, but profound.

It was some time before they finished, as if they were doing all they could to make the moment last.

A little later, while Konrad and Henri clamored to help clean up, but without knowing where to start, the two brothers snuffed out the candles one after another. Then everyone went upstairs to sleep.

Before closing his door, Pierre leaned towards Vincent. "I'd like to use my money to buy her some decent clothes. Is that all right with you?"

"Why would I object? You're free to do as you like."

Pierre smiled. He was worried his brother would try to talk him out of it. But Vincent knew that there are some forces that shouldn't be opposed.

10

A blinding explosion set the Parisian sky ablaze over the imposing rotunda of the Palais du Trocadéro. The colossal circular concert hall flanked by two square towers appeared to have caught fire, but it was in no danger. The light was so intense that Gustave Eiffel's scarlet tower, standing across the water on the south bank of the Seine River, was illuminated. The rooftops were also bathed in light, as if it were suddenly high noon. Darkness eventually reclaimed the night, but not for long.

The aerial explosions were followed by giant streaming candles; a spray of sparks erupted into the starry sky. It was an extravagant show.

Vincent didn't miss a bit of the action; he was far better off on his hillside than packed into a gawking crowd. From his comfortable seat, he had an unobstructed view, probably the best in the city. As far away as he was, the colorful flashes reached him before the sound of the explosions. For a moment, he thought he heard the applause of captivated onlookers, but it was probably just his imagination playing tricks on him. A different celebration was held practically every night in a run-up to the grandiose official inauguration. No one could remember exactly what was being celebrated in a preview of events to come, but the fireworks were a daily occurrence.

The workers deserted the Sacré-Cœur worksite at nightfall. All was calm; darkness had overcome the frenzy of activity. Scaffolding, chains, ropes, and hoists were all still. Nothing moved. The blocks of stone, abandoned where they sat, awaited the return of forces that would raise them into place. Only the wind whistled now and then through the timbers of the scaffolding.

The echo of racing footsteps suddenly erupted from the unfinished walls of Sacré-Cœur. Vincent turned around and caught sight of Henri running towards him, out of breath.

"Hey, why are you running? Trouble?"

"No! I heard the explosions! I want to see the fireworks."

"They're finished for tonight, but I'm sure there will be more tomorrow."

Disappointed, the boy sat down next to Vincent with a loud sigh.

"Did you have supper?" Vincent asked.

"Gabrielle made broth. I had two big bowls. And Pierre gave me bread and cut some ham. He told me I'd find you here."

The boy pulled a sealed letter from his knapsack.

"I found this at the cemetery."

"Did you see who left it?"

"No. I stopped by at sunset, and I didn't hang around. I don't like being there when it gets dark. But I did fix up the flowers that the wind had blown around."

"Thank you. Did anyone see you pick up the envelope?"

"No chance. Goddamn, if there's one thing I'm good at, that's it!"

"Don't swear. Ever. I keep telling you: language and diction are to your mind what clothes are to your body. Sully neither your words nor your appearance..."

" '... or risk being passed over before being given a chance.' I know."

Vincent opened the envelope. He skimmed the lines and made a face when he reached the end.

"Bad news?" asked Henri.

"I can't say for sure. It's strange. The sender wants to meet me for a future project."

"That's promising."

"Except he doesn't mention his references."

"Maybe he forgot? Someone must have told him about us, otherwise he wouldn't have known where to leave the message."

"He's also proposing a very odd meeting place."

"Are you going to go?" asked the boy with sudden interest.

"I have to."

The Nail pointed at the Eiffel Tower.

"If it's down there, can I come with you? Please, Vincent? You'll see what they're preparing for the Fair. It's huge! This morning, I saw the elephants arrive; it was amazing!"

The boy stopped suddenly, aware that he had said too much. Vincent grumbled.

"I don't like you hanging around down there."

"It's not dangerous. The only ones around are laborers finishing-up the pavilions before opening day."

"You can be sure that criminals will be the first visitors, even before the crowd arrives."

"I'm not a kid anymore."

"Perhaps. But that doesn't mean you're capable of handling everything you might encounter."

"I know how to defend myself! Konrad taught me."

"Oh, really?"

"Hey, will you take me to the Fair? Please?"

"That's not where the meeting's been set."

For the second time that evening, Henri was disappointed.

"But I'll go eventually," Vincent reassured him. "To see what the future holds for us. They say there will be automobiles and new machines capable of playing classical music without an orchestra. They can record everything they hear on rolls of wax."

The Nail shifted from dejection to enthusiasm in an instant, like only the young can. "We'll go see them together!"

"We'll see."

Over time, the boy had found a way to make himself useful. He collected the mail clients left behind a burial vault in the Saint-Vincent Cemetery. But later Henri had been given another, more important mission: he guarded the team's fortune. He kept watch over the hiding place where they stored the gold that accumulated with each new project. For his own security, he didn't know how to get in; Vincent and his partners had outdone themselves to protect the fruit of their labor.

Neither spoke for a moment as they sat side by side, taking in the view. At last Vincent broke the silence.

"Did you finish the book I bought you?"

"I read it three times already."

"Why don't you read me a few pages, for practice?"

He didn't need to ask twice. From his knapsack, Henri pulled Jules Verne's popular novel *The Mysterious Island*, carefully wrapped in a square of fabric with frayed edges, and quickly leafed through it.

"I love the part where Cyrus Smith realizes that he and his friends are being watched by Captain Nemo."

"I can't wait to hear it—even if you just spoiled the plot."

"You didn't know that? I thought you had read it."

"I never got the chance."

The Nail hesitated, afraid to offend his mentor, but dared all the same to ask timidly, "Can you read at least?"

"Not as well as you can," admitted Vincent, ruffling the boy's hair. "I'm better with blueprints than with words."

"I could teach you, if you like!"

"Why not? As you grow up, you'll probably teach me many things."

"What would you like me to teach you?"

Vincent knew his answer, but he couldn't say it for fear that it would never come to be. That's how real wishes worked. He would have liked Henri to teach him that no one's fate is predetermined, and that even a street kid can make it out.

The boy's voice drifted into the night sky.

"Cyrus Smith ordered Nab to fetch wood for the fire. The night promised to be a dangerous one."

11

Vincent turned off Rue du Temple and headed down Rue de Montmorency. Although the street was not long, he had to walk the length of it to reach the largest of the gabled houses at the far end, at the intersection with Rue Saint-Martin.

When he reached the building, Vincent was surprised to find it dark. Unlike its neighbors, the imposing house appeared deserted. But he was certain this was where Alfred Minguier had suggested they meet that evening.

The columns on the front of the house were embellished with symbols faded with time. A fine inscription ran along the width of the pediment, but the half-eroded letters were impossible to make out in the darkness.

Vincent knocked on the door, hoping he hadn't crossed half of Paris in vain. To his great surprise, it opened immediately. It wasn't a butler standing before him, but the industrialist himself.

"Good evening, sir, I hope…"

Minguier interrupted him.

"Hurry up and come in."

The little man grabbed Vincent's arm and literally pulled him inside. As soon as the door swung closed, he quickly secured it with two metal bars.

"Forgive the conspiratorial welcome, but I must avoid drawing attention. Follow me. I'll explain everything downstairs where we'll have some quiet."

Carrying only a small lantern, Minguier guided his visitor through the rooms of the empty house. It looked like the old boardinghouse Vincent rented and gave off the same odor of dust and damp.

"Are we alone?" asked Vincent.

"We have to be. I want to keep our meeting secret. It's essential."

The man led Vincent to a storage room that opened onto a stone staircase leading underground.

"Watch your head."

The unadorned architecture and worn stair treads suggested the building was very old, probably dating to the Middle Ages. A curt echo reverberated from the walls, mingling with Minguier's labored breathing.

"Is everything all right, sir? There's no rush, I have plenty of time for you this evening."

"Thank you, my good fellow, but unfortunately I can't say the same for myself. I have high hopes for our visit, and time is a cruel mistress whose embrace I cannot escape."

The two men came out into a room with vaulted ceilings and dirt floors, which the industrialist crossed without pause. Vincent couldn't make out much in the weak lantern light, except for the shadow of a few piled crates and a splintered barrel. Two more low-ceilinged rooms led to a fourth, where the entrance was blocked by a wrought-iron grate that would have been at home in the dankest dungeon. Minguier stopped in front of the thick, intertwined bars.

"Here we are."

He took a large key from his pocket, unbolted the imposing lock, and pushed open the rasping grate. Then he set about lighting a half-dozen kerosene lamps. As the light increased, Vincent began to make out more of the room.

It was longer than the previous rooms, but the ceiling was lower. He could almost touch the highest part of the arch without standing on tiptoe. The curved ceiling was supported by columns partially incorporated into the walls. A jumble of dismantled furniture, rusted scrap iron, and buckled shelving lined the walls.

Only the back wall had been cleared. The porous floor showed traces of repeated trampling. Minguier stepped forward and spread his hands respectfully on the blocks of stone that formed the wall. His manner was surprising: he appeared reflective.

"This is where the passage lies." He lowered his head.

Observing him from behind, Vincent first thought he might be tired, but his posture appeared to be one of veneration.

The man turned around and spoke gravely, "I would like you to help me open it."

Vincent stepped closer and began to inspect the wall. Several things surprised him, but first he needed to examine certain details. He ran a finger along the angle formed by the top of the wall and the vaulted ceiling.

"May I borrow a lamp?"

"Of course, of course. You didn't bring any tools?"

Vincent smiled.

"When faced with a riddle, the mind is the only worthy tool. Using anything else at this stage would be an admission of failure."

He examined the masonry assembly in minute detail.

"The surfaces show no trace of friction or rubbing that would suggest having been opened."

He blew on the stones and their mortar joints, then ran the tip of his finger along them to glean a fine dust, which he tasted.

"The material is old," he declared, "perhaps as old as the building. The sharpness of the cut edges and the precise positioning tell us unequivocally that the blocks were new and not salvaged."

He knelt down and studied the floor, scratching at it. He shook his head in silence: the base of the wall seemed in keeping with the rest of the construction.

He stood up and brushed the dust from his knees. He grasped his knife and, without opening the blade, pressed his ear to the stone and tested the wall by tapping it with the handle. He did this several times at different heights, under his client's watchful eye.

"Do you know what the area behind a secret passage is called?" asked Vincent.

"I have no idea."

"The 'great beyond,' Mr. Minguier. It's what we're all striving for, because a better life might be waiting for us there."

The man didn't even crack a smile. Vincent continued his examination.

"Are you certain there's a passage hidden here?"

"Entirely."

"Please forgive me for insisting, but are the indications that suggest it so credible?"

"Without a doubt. In fact, they corroborate each other."

"You mentioned documents left by the former owners. Is that what you're referring to?"

Minguier vaguely moved his head in confirmation. He seemed reluctant to provide more information.

"Have there been other occupants in the house between those who wrote about the passage and yourself?"

Minguier thought for a moment.

"Two, three at the most."

"Might one of them have done some work to permanently wall off the passage?"

"Impossible. If by some chance they knew about it—which is highly unlikely—they might have tried to open it, but they would never have sealed it off. As I said before, there is a way to open it. That's for certain."

Vincent put away his knife and stepped back to take in the entire wall.

"Would you happen to have a candle, please?"

Minguier didn't understand at first.

"The lamps are not enough?"

"I need the live light of a candle."

The industrialist grumbled but complied.

"I should have some upstairs."

He hurried away with short, rapid steps, leaving Vincent alone. He reappeared shortly holding a candlestick.

"Here," he panted. "What are you going to do with it?"

"You're about to find out."

Vincent removed the glass from one of the kerosene lamps to light the candle wick, then turned back to the mystery. He ran the candle along the contours of the stones.

"What are you looking for?" asked Minguier in surprise.

"A draft. The slightest breeze that would cause the flame to waver and reveal the smallest crack between the stones."

The industrialist kept his eyes on the candle, but the flame remained hopelessly straight. After examining the full width of the stonework, Vincent turned to his client.

"I'm going to be honest, Mr. Minguier: I see only two solutions to your riddle. With all due respect, either you're mistaken and there's nothing hidden behind this wall—"

"I can assure you, the secret entrance is there."

"Or this is one the most sophisticated passages I've ever encountered and, believe me, I've seen my share."

"I'm not surprised that it's remarkable. But I guarantee you that it does indeed exist, here, right in front of us." The industrialist pointed confidently at the wall. Vincent remained puzzled.

"I'm going to need several nights to work it out."

"We don't have that much time. You must act fast."

"I'll need something else."

"I told you, you'll have all gold you want, Mr. Vincent."

"That's not what I was going to say, although what I'm about to ask for may cost you as much."

"You're scaring me."

"Please forgive me, but in your best interest, I must insist. You have to tell me everything you know about this passage, and most importantly of all, in all secrecy, you must tell me what it protects. That's the only way we can hope to understand the people who designed it and have any chance of figuring out how they proceeded."

Minguier clenched his teeth. He would much rather it did not come to that.

12

Whenever Vincent was in doubt, he mentally revisited the moment when everything began. Eyes closed; reliving the spark. He was young when he first discovered the power of illusions and the ingenuity they require. In one instant his fate changed, as if he had been born at that precise moment. The shock was so great that he immediately forgot everything miserable about his life. A blinding flash in the night: his first glimpse of eternity. He had been returning to draw strength from the memory ever since.

There he was, as if it were only yesterday. He had just finished his delivery route. The bags of coal leaking black dust weighed more than he did. As he did every Thursday, he saved the watchmaker's for last, hoping he could linger there a while. He felt at ease in his store, but even more so in his workshop.

That particular night, the kind man had a little more time for the curious boy, whose face was as dirty as his hands. He pointed to a bucket of cold water where the boy could wash himself and said, "Come, I'm going to show you something you'll like."

Vincent followed him. The man pulled back the curtain on a miniature theater, revealing a building the size of a dollhouse. The watchmaker cranked a handle and set the mechanism in motion. Tiny sheet metal figures began to move in the windows: A woman hung up her laundry and a man put on his hat. On the roof, a tabby cat paced back and forth between two chimneys. They repeated their cyclical movements over and over again. Suddenly, tiny cut-out flames appeared in the windows. They were painted red and orange and danced to a regular beat. The building was on fire! The man, the woman, and the cat froze. Their cries for help were almost audible.

A fire-carriage appeared on stage, moving forward on a track to stop in front of the building. As if by magic, the ladder pivoted and unfolded, sending a firefighter towards the blaze. The flames disappeared. The man, the woman, and the cat resumed their activities, and then the mechanism stopped.

The boy was left speechless and amazed. It was like a waking dream, except it was all real. He had seen it with his own eyes.

Vincent would never forget how he felt upon discovering the automaton. At first, he thought it was a toy intended for the child of a millionaire. But when his mentor showed him the mechanism hidden in the back and told him about the brilliant magician who had invented it, he was overcome with wonder; he was no longer standing before an opulent plaything, but on the threshold of a fabulous world into which he stepped and never left.

Vincent realized all that could be created, and chose his path then and there. Nothing could be more enthralling than devoting his life to this art. The boy later learned that even the most amusing trick is the result of immeasurable knowledge and perfect execution. It took him several more months to realize that the simpler the effect appeared, the more complex it actually was.

Years went by and Vincent never tired of the small mechanical theater. In fact it was the only physical keepsake he ever received from his mentor. He repaired the worn-out parts, meticulously maintained the paint work, and, now and then, allowed himself to operate it. But only very rarely, fearing that the feeling it provoked would fade with repetition. Sometimes he waited months for the right moment; to serve as a reward or to fulfill a vital need.

This marvelous automaton was a remarkable concentration of most of the principles of the craft. Vincent found in it both an inexhaustible well of inspiration and a constant reminder to remain humble.

Pierre interrupted his daydream: "What are you waiting for? Try it."

Vincent returned to the present. It was time to test the device he had designed for a new kind of secret compartment, under real-life conditions in the workshop.

While Konrad, Eustasio, and Pierre kept their eyes trained on the mechanism, Vincent moved a fragment of magnetic pyrite towards the fine wood partition. When the ore was near enough, the magnetic pull attracted the metal plate inside, which shifted at once and freed the spring it was holding in place. It opened with a click.

"Your idea works!" rejoiced the German.

Eustasio rubbed his hands together. "*Fantastico!* It's the right solution!"

Smiling broadly, Vincent put down the pyrite. "An invisible key. No hole, no mechanism. You just have to know where to hold the magnet to unlock the panel."

He returned to the table and finished sketching the mechanism.

"The wood component shouldn't be too thick, or it will create interference."

He corrected the measurements and adjusted the position of the spring.

"*Wunderbar!* Our clients will think it's magic," exclaimed Konrad.

"Good!" remarked Pierre.

Vincent nodded in approval.

"We should only use this device with those capable of fully appreciating it."

Gabrielle's voice travelled down the spy tube from the kitchen and rang out in the cellar.

"Gentlemen, dinner is ready!"

All four men started. Although the young woman had been living in the house for over a week, her presence still surprised them. Yet she had managed to fit in, and they all viewed her arrival as a piece of good fortune. She understood that she shouldn't venture into the underground workshop, so she kept to the ground floor and upper levels of the house. She spent her days there, busying herself from morning to evening, never going outside—she hadn't left once since her theatrical arrival.

Inside that closed world with its reassuring boundaries, she regained her confidence and a taste for life. The occupants were kind to her, even though they remained wary. Sometimes she wondered if it really was a lack of trust, or if they just weren't used to being around women.

Gabrielle was determined to do what she could to convince them to let her stay, so she tried to add a little extra comfort to their days. Besides preparing meals for the whole team, she also attended to the house with unusual care. The rooms were aired and the beds made; disorder and dust diminished.

As she began to reiterate her invitation, Pierre called back, "Coming!"

"Go on, I'll be up in a minute," said Vincent. "I have to record a few details while they're still clear in my mind."

The other three men didn't wait for him. Once they had disappeared up the staircase, Vincent pulled a small notebook from his pocket. He opened it and wrote down his thoughts. He didn't know why or how, but he had been convinced for some time now that it would be crucial for the future.

13

Vincent had barely set foot in the dance hall when he was jostled by a pair of dancers. They didn't even notice him, carried away as they were by their own momentum, glued together, too busy consuming each other with eyes and hands.

Every Wednesday night, hundreds of people came to enjoy themselves in the Waux Hall on Rue de la Douane, in the Jardins de Tivoli, one of the most popular dance halls in Paris.

Petticoat dresses swirled and mustaches gleamed. Strong, seductive arms supported supple, confident hips. Plunging necklines lent to the giddiness of a party only Paris could offer.

On the stage, thirty musicians played loudly, but not loud enough to drown out the men's laughter and the women's cries of delight. The house orchestra featured a virtuoso on the newly fashionable saxophone. In a capital city with a growing nightlife, hundreds of couples, often illicit, formed to frenzied rhythms in dance after dance: wild square-dances and covers of light comic operas alternated with pieces from far-flung places like New Orleans in America. No one cared where the song came from, as long as it had a swinging beat. Over the music, an announcer in a tired suit could already be heard calling out the next act by the famous contortionist Valentin the Deboned.

Vincent fought his way through the festive crowd. He had never been to one of these events. He would probably have enjoyed yielding to the merry, superficial ambiance, but the reality was, he didn't have that luxury. Necessity had taught him to favor the virtues of dawn over the charms of the night.

He was not there to be entertained, seduced, or intoxicated. As strange as it might seem, work had brought him to this temple of dance and libertinism. That was a first. He'd never paid a single franc to attend a meeting, and yet that's what it had cost him to get in. What kind of man, who had no references for that matter, would organize a serious interview in this kind of place?

Vincent wandered randomly, wondering if he would recognize the person waiting for him. Indifferent to the bodies brushing past him, male and female alike, he peered up at the walkway that skirted the room. Logically, the person who wanted to meet him should be up there. He saw many couples and groups of friends seated at tables. Suddenly, he caught the gaze of a man sitting alone. He held himself erect; graying temples framed a thin, angular face. The man emanated undeniable nobility. He gestured subtly to Vincent.

Upstairs the ambiance was just as frivolous, but fortunately showed more restraint. Vincent paid no heed to the persistent looks he received from women. He walked straight toward the man, who stood to greet him. Vincent noticed the stranger's well-groomed hands: so he was not lower class. The handshake was cold and just firm enough to be reassuring. He also noticed a bowler on the table next to the man, a more ambiguous symbol of social status than a cap or a top hat.

"Thank you for accepting my invitation. Have a seat, please."

Vincent slid into a chair. They had a fine view of the dance hall.

"Don't watch them dance for too long," joked the man. "You'll get seasick."

Making no effort to avert his gaze, the stranger looked with easy frankness at Vincent, who was almost intimidated.

Downstairs, the orchestra began playing a gavotte. In response the crowd rearranged itself in an orgy of noisy gesticulating.

The man seated before Vincent remained strangely silent.

"To be honest, sir," began Vincent, "I hesitated to come."

"I can imagine. Rest assured, I did not choose this place because I like it, but because it serves my purpose. A crowd provides a remarkable guarantee of secrecy."

The comment caught Vincent's attention. He thought he was alone in thinking as much.

"May I ask who recommended our services?"

"No one. Your creations led me to you. Finding you was not easy."

"How did you discover us?"

"Let's just say that circumstances led some people who know you to tell me of your wonders. But to be honest, I had no idea what you looked like."

"Yet you recognized me as soon as I entered the hall."

"Recognized, no. Identified, yes. No man comes here alone, Vincent. We are exceptions, and I can only imagine what certain people make of that."

The idea seemed to amuse him. Vincent felt uneasy.

"You signed your message 'Mr. Charles,'" he said, steering them back to their conversation. "Is that your real name?"

"A wise question. Charles is my first name. Like you, I don't share my last name, Mr. Vincent."

A voluptuous woman in gaudy attire approached and wrapped her arms around them unceremoniously.

"What's your pleasure, gentlemen? Wine, love?"

Charles responded without losing his composure.

"Bring us wine! *That* you can sell honestly."

"Yes, sir."

The woman walked away.

"What do you want from me?" asked Vincent.

"A skill, most likely. Perhaps even support."

"Explain yourself."

Below, the army of twirling couples began an Austrian waltz played to an operetta tempo. The two men took no notice.

"What do you believe in, Vincent?"

"Excuse me?"

The man looked him straight in the eyes.

"Where does your life force come from? What or whom do you fight for?"

Vincent raised an eyebrow. There was something inappropriate about asking so personal a question in so artificial a setting.

"Excuse my candor, sir, but those are personal subjects I don't discuss with strangers in places that hardly seem appropriate."

"If we don't talk about them, Vincent, then we shall indeed remain strangers. As for the location, the very principle of integrity implies enduring in a world that constantly threatens it."

The words echoed inside Vincent with strange intensity.

"I'm asking you what keeps you going because I need to know who I'm dealing with—without wasting time. I haven't come to negotiate a contract. I respect your refusal, but I hope that you at least know the answers for yourself. For the man who doesn't, doesn't know himself."

"Of course."

The woman brought the wine, which Charles paid for generously without hesitating. He raised his glass.

"To our odd encounter, Vincent. I hope it is the first of many."

Then he turned towards the dance hall.

"To the people down there enjoying themselves, unaware that they should be thinking of what's to come."

Vincent raised his own glass.

"To you, sir, whoever you are."

The two men took a sip. They both made a grimace that suggested they at least felt the same way about the drink. Vincent began to relax, but he needed reassurance.

"Don't take my reaction as a sign of disrespect. I'm a simple craftsman, and I make it a point of honor to satisfy my clients. Yet I'm afraid we've gotten off on the wrong foot. Put yourself in my place, sir: you have no references, you arranged a meeting at a dance hall, you've bought me a drink, and yet I still don't know anything about the work you would like me to do."

"Your suspicion is warranted. Usually you design secret passages for people who want them. This time, if you accept, that won't be the case. I don't need your services for myself, but the cause I represent depends on them."

"A cause? Are you an anarchist or in one of those pseudo-parties that wants to revolutionize the world? If so, our conversation ends here. I have little regard for people who preach about liberty only to turn around and kill those with different opinions."

"No, Vincent, I'm not driven by violence. I'm sorry I can't tell you more for the moment, but before I reveal anything to you, I must get to know you. I need to know I can trust you."

"And I as well."

"What would you like to know about me?"

Vincent hesitated. He decided to be honest.

"Who are you, really?"

Charles turned to look at the dance hall.

"Let's just say that I've experienced enough to know that what we do for ourselves is never what matters. I'm old enough to have learned that this life can take from you everything it has given. I've come far enough to know that the real battles are silent and that sometimes they demand we make sacrifices."

His words deeply affected Vincent.

"What do you want from me?"

"I want you to think, Vincent. About what you've experienced this evening, about the questions I have the presumption to ask. About the impression I first made on you—I'm sure you've learned to pay attention to that. You will take your first step towards me. You won't be asked to work for nothing, but you must commit yourself. It is not just another contract, and telling you otherwise would be a lie. Take your time. In a few days, I'll suggest another meeting. Perhaps you will decide not to come. Then you will never hear from me again. However, if you accept for us to become more than strangers, then we'll have a lot to do together."

"That's all you'll tell me tonight?"

The man leaned forward and locked eyes with Vincent.

"I have not come to you to conceal a secret. I need your help to protect a truth that has changed the lives of everyone who has encountered it."

14

Unable to sleep after his puzzling interview, Vincent agreed to accompany Konrad on a walk to clear his mind. They had just visited a residential area being built on Rue Le Peletier; the German was considering investing in an apartment there. He liked the neighborhood. In addition to the colossal Printemps department store erected nearby, more businesses were expected to be built, along with a greater concentration of shops, offering a selection unlike any in the capital.

The weather was beautiful. Women had abandoned their shawls at home to drink in the sun's intense heat, while carefully protecting their pale skin with umbrellas and large-brimmed hats. Curious passersby slowed to peer into shop windows brimming with novelties. They were constantly approached by men selling padlocks who advised them to lock up their belongings to avoid being robbed. Everything on these thoroughfares was made to tempt those with the means to buy it and to capitalize on their gullibility one way or another.

For the second time, the two companions noticed a man sporting strange-looking glasses with dark-tinted lenses that protected his eyes from the blinding sunlight. This touch of eccentricity, most likely brought over from the Americas, could very well become a fashion. It was a time for eccentricity; the many visitors rushing to the city for the Fair, which would finally open the next day, brought with them their share of absurd inventions and strange customs from around the world.

At an intersection, a young street singer performed the timeless song "Temps des Cerises" in a high-pitched voice. Further on, a newspaper vendor shouted the headlines, announcing that anarchists had threatened the Fair's official inauguration and were considering turning against President Carnot. These dire announcements did nothing to dampen the general feeling of good cheer. Over time, the press's continued focus on the sensational had eroded its credibility.

On that beautiful spring afternoon, Konrad was not thrilled at the idea of returning to their underground workshop. He had an idea.

"Since we're in the neighborhood, let me show you an unusual place. Then you'll see how I manage to earn a little extra money."

Without waiting for his friend to respond, Konrad strode off across the street. Vincent had no choice but to follow him.

The two men wove in and out among the different modes of transportation bearing down on them from all directions. Seated on the upper levels of large three-horse omnibuses, men held their hats in place while ladies sheltered in the lower cabins. Carts and wagons pulled by tired old nags dragging their hooves along the sidewalk were pelted with insults by fiacre drivers with much faster teams champing at the bit. This two-way ballet was growing denser, and Paris would soon be paralyzed by its traffic and interminable construction.

Konrad headed up Rue de Châteaudun and turned onto a cross street. In the span of several steps, the world around him changed. There were no horse-drawn carriages here, no displays or enticing shops, no perfectly aligned buildings. Well-dressed women and their handsome beaux did not stray into this area—they stayed in the light.

The buildings in the narrow street, out of the sun's reach, had not been remodeled by developers. Handymen offered their services. These secondary streets were home to many modest lives, and only the most necessary trades. The buildings here were nothing more than a jumble of houses that had been tacked together over time, giving an overall impression of chaos, far different from the orderly lots being built on the new roads.

Konrad strode confidently towards a shop. Standing between a mattress stuffer and a shoe repairman who worked in the street, the establishment was striking both for its dilapidated appearance and its activity. The sign hanging on a post out front read "Quasimodo," written just above a horrible-looking head—the pitiful paint job no doubt added to the ugliness of the model.

Konrad stopped at the entrance and turned to his companion.

"Whenever I have the time, I give it a try," he explained, "and it always works. You're lucky, there aren't many people at this hour. At the end of the day, the line often stretches outside."

The poster plastered to the door proclaimed: "Meet the ugliest Monster in Paris! If you can bear the sight, win up to twenty sous!" Another smaller sign stated that children, women, and clergy were forbidden from entering.

Pulling Vincent along with him, Konrad strode confidently in. A dark corridor led to a single ticket window. When they reached it, a man with a mustache and a cap launched into a rote explanation.

"The encounter costs twenty sous. If you don't show any sign of fear, you leave with your money, plus a bonus of twenty sous. But if you show the slightest hint of terror, if you cry out, if you fall off your seat, or if you run away, you win nothing. The boss will be watching you, and he's the one who decides what your courage is worth. Should you disagree, the monster himself will settle the score. Is that clear?"

Konrad nodded his head and placed two coins on the counter. "I'm paying for my friend."

The man whisked the coins away. "Fine. But you'll go in separately. Wait here."

There were already two people standing in line. Vincent wondered what he was doing there. Suddenly a howl rang out. A man burst from the booth at the end of the corridor and ran straight for the exit without stopping. The next person in line was already moving to take his place.

Vincent chuckled. "Looks like the poor guy just saw the devil."

"If only it were the devil," replied Konrad. He was eager to see how his friend would react to the sight he himself had been able to overcome.

He lowered his voice. "Behind the curtain, there's a little stool that you sit on. When you're in position, the curtain will part, and you'll see a shapeless monster staring at you with bestial eyes. He's no more than arm's length from you. He's so close that once I even felt the warmth of his breath. The thing is, the stool is tiny and bolted to the floor. If you recoil in the slightest, you'll fall off, and then you've lost the game. The first few times, I fell for it, but I knew I could bear it. So I came back."

"That's the game? Not to be frightened by a carnival freak?"

"Laugh all you like, but it's not that easy! To do it, I concentrate, and I freeze. I imagine my feet are screwed to the floorboards, and I keep my hands plastered to my thighs. I hold my breath. When he appears, I pretend to be a statue just long enough for the boss to think I'm not afraid."

The person ahead of them also ran away wailing. One more and it would be Konrad's turn. It was over quickly, and the candidate reappeared white as a ghost. Though he didn't holler like the other, he staggered out as if he'd been stunned.

Konrad disappeared behind the curtain, leaving Vincent alone. He heard movements, the rustle of cloth, and a groan. After a few excruciating seconds, a muffled voice called out, "Congratulations, you braved the monster. Achille, give the big bearded guy forty sous."

Konrad came out. His proud demeanor could not hide his panic-stricken gaze. He collected his coins and pushed his friend into the booth.

"Be strong."

Vincent went behind the thick curtain. The space was dark, tight, like a secret cupboard hung with tapestries. His eyes had difficulty adjusting to the dimness. He sat on the stool and looked straight ahead, placing his hands flat on his thighs as Konrad had advised him. He was ready, although what for he didn't know.

Just then the curtains parted before him to reveal an inhuman face perched above a torso draped in coarse cloth. The low lighting accentuated the lumps that deformed the forehead and sketched the contours of a horrifying face. The eyelids looked like waves of flesh that had crashed onto the vile protuberance that must have been the nose. Deformed lips framed a twisted mouth from which a horrifying wheeze escaped.

Vincent didn't move; he remained stone-faced. However, the immobility of his body contrasted sharply with the inner storm that racked him. An intense emotion had overcome him the instant he laid eyes on the creature.

It was not the abnormal face that he noticed first; it was the eyes, filled with infinite pain in a silent cry for help. He forgot the rest. He was incapable of looking away, his mind raging with thoughts. How could he sit there without flinching, while everyone else fled at the sight? Was he so incapable of experiencing the slightest feeling? Unless this appalling face had opened in him a chasm, an abyss, and at the bottom he had somehow managed to glimpse something utterly human.

Vincent was suddenly overcome by a feeling he'd never experienced before: in that hopeless gaze, he felt as though he were seeing for the first time what he felt. A troubling window onto his own existence: he had just put an image to the solitude that overwhelmed him at times.

Vincent could have spent hours contemplating the sight that had stirred him so, but the boss was already making his announcement.

"Congratulations, you braved the monster! Achille, give forty sous to the handsome dark-haired man who lost his cap. Next!"

15

Vincent leaned against the wall near the dormer in the room he occupied these days and peered discreetly down at the street below. Always take the higher ground to study and soak in life's parade. The light permitting, he scribbled now and then in his notebook. He looked at nothing particular, but let himself enjoy the movements of the many-faceted ballet that took place each day. Shopkeepers served their last clients. A few rascals chased each other between passing carts, which dwindled in number as evening fell.

Vincent could not forget the eyes of the unfortunate creature that had won him twenty sous. Absorbed in his thoughts, he didn't hear Gabrielle sweeping the hallway.

Lost in her own thoughts, she hadn't noticed Vincent standing there motionless. She went through the open door to continue cleaning and prepared to make the bed.

As she began to fluff the pillow, Vincent jumped in surprise, frightening Gabrielle, who stifled a cry and put her hand to her heart.

"You scared me!" she cried.

"So it seems each time we meet. Back in the kitchen..."

"I thought the room was empty."

"And I didn't think anyone was up here."

Standing there facing each other, they were both embarrassed. Vincent noticed the young woman's new clothes. It wasn't so much what she wore that caught his attention, but the way she wore it.

The last time Vincent had seen a woman of such beauty, she had been made of plaster and saved his life.

"Are you sleeping in here?" asked Gabrielle.

"For now, yes."

"I thought Eustasio was."

Vincent didn't respond. The young woman put the pillow back on the bed. She spoke suddenly, not daring to look at him. "You don't like me, is that it?"

"What makes you think that?"

"You don't trust me."

"I have to be cautious. You have to admit that you arrived under rather peculiar circumstances."

"I didn't choose them," retorted Gabrielle.

"I believe that now. I don't blame you for anything."

The young woman's shoulders relaxed.

"I didn't get a chance to tell you earlier, but thank you for allowing me to stay."

"That was Pierre's decision."

"You would have kicked me out?"

"Who knows? My friends don't think so. But since there are no dress rehearsals in life, we'll never know what role I might have played if I had been the one to find you."

"If you had given the order to throw me out, no one would have dared oppose you. I owe you my protection here."

"It's not that simple, Gabrielle. If I'm not mistaken, you haven't gone out since you landed in our home."

"I feel safe here, which doesn't happen to me often. I know what awaits me in the street. This world is cruel, especially to women."

"Do you plan to go out again one day?"

Her clear gaze met his. "Go out or leave?"

"Go out."

"Maybe, at least to the market with Henri."

"Who taught you to cook?"

"My mother. She always said, 'for those who aren't lucky enough to receive an education, knowing how to feed one's own is a saving grace.'"

Vincent smiled.

"Are you amused?"

"I'm impressed. People who suffer in this life have a wisdom that those who have everything could never afford."

Vincent continued, "My father claimed that a woman's fidelity could be ensured by clothing and housing her as lavishly as possible. He never forgot to point out that the same result could be reached by truly loving her."

Gabrielle smiled broadly.

"Are you amused by my father's words?"

"I'm moved. People who are capable of love have a power envied by everyone."

"Your family must be worried about you. If you like, Henri could take a message to them."

"I don't have anyone, except for a sister I lost track of."

Gabrielle turned away and repositioned the bedspread. "You were working. I'll leave you alone. Sorry for bothering you."

"You didn't disturb me. Thank you for everything you do for our little troupe. Everyone appreciates it."

"But not you?" There was a trace of worry in her voice.

"I do, but as Pierre says, I'm overly aware of the threats to our safety, so I tend not to know how to enjoy myself in the moment."

The young woman turned to go, but suddenly spun around in the doorway. "Can I ask you a personal question?"

"You can try."

"How did you come to create secret passages?"

He laughed. "Well, Pierre was wrong. You understand what you hear perfectly well."

"You thought I didn't?"

"Not for a second."

"Does my question upset you? Do you still think I'm a spy?"

"No. And my story holds no interest for anyone interested in competing with us. But to be honest, no one has ever asked me."

His gaze drifted towards the window. Night was falling. The memories slowly surfaced and Vincent began to tell his story.

"Pierre and I lost our father when we were very young. I was actually younger than Henri. I had to find work to help my mother. One day I delivered coal to a watchmaker, and his workshop fascinated me. All the tools, the mysterious, perfectly formed pieces. Few discoveries have captivated me as much as that collection of cogs, those ingenious mechanisms that we can rely on, that make us believe we master time and that all is right in the world. I immediately developed an admiration for the man; his work was all the more precious because no one was aware of it. I went back to see him more and more often, even when I had nothing to deliver. Day after day, I would stop in front of his window to watch him. He warmed to me and entrusted me with an errand, then two, then odd jobs. I expected nothing more than this; then one evening he offered to make me his apprentice. That was probably one of the most wonderful moments of my life. For the first time, I had been chosen by someone who had seen in me something other than a dirty, lost boy."

He lowered his eyes.

"He taught me mechanics, every kind of metal work, both for watches and pendulums, the kind that adorn monuments. He was demanding and he could be harsh, but he was never mean. I never mistook him for my father, but he was my benefactor. He gave me an education and a skill, and instilled in me a sense of curiosity.

"Several years later, he confided that he sometimes created mechanisms for secret passages and rooms. One day when he fell ill, I went to a meeting in his place. That's how I met the man who trained me—a true genius. It was eye-opening for me, as if I had discovered what I was made to do. It's strange to be talking about the man who reached out to me, especially now. The only good years I've had since childhood were in the service of that honorable man."

"He must be proud of your success."

"He never knew about it. He died before I set up my business."

"Pierre joined you then?"

"I made him my associate, but he would have found his way without me. He has talent and he's not afraid of hard work."

"I think he likes me."

"That's true. If he didn't, he would have asked me what to do when you fell in through the hatch. But he made his own decision, without any second thoughts."

"And that isn't like him?"

"Saving you was the first decision he's ever made on his own."

16

Konrad put down his wood plane and freed the piece of mahogany from the jaws of the vise. With a gentleness that belied his stature, he caressed the rounded edge to be sure he had achieved an uninterrupted curve. This component would complete the decoration on a bookshelf rigged with a secret compartment he and the rest of the team were preparing for a politician who collected forbidden books. The bookshelf was one of their classic models and probably the project for which they received the most orders. So many, in fact, that when Konrad, Eustasio, Pierre, or Vincent spotted one in a home, they immediately suspected that it might hide a secret passage or room.

Seated nearby at the large table, Vincent thought while he drew, making short, precise motions and distinct lines. Sketching always helped him work through his ideas. This time, he was drawing Alfred Minguier's vaulted cellar. He had taken a new approach to solving the riddle of the passage that was supposedly hidden there: he was trying to imagine how he would have installed one himself, if he had been the creator. By putting himself in the shoes of the designers, he hoped to arrive at the same solution they had.

The layout consisted of three elements: the wall, the vaulted ceiling, and the pillars. An equation with three unknowns. There were no fixtures or furniture to hide the entrance, and no false partitions. No matter how he approached the problem, he arrived at the same basic question: how could the wall shift, rise, or pivot? The second issue: where the devil could the trigger be hidden?

Vincent deepened his investigation by coming up with more hypotheses and diagrams. Pierre had noticed his brother racking his brain over a blueprint, but he hadn't dared to ask him what it was.

But Henri did. The Nail circled the table for a long time, watching out of the corner of his eye for the right moment to arise. The second Vincent laid down his pencil, he was at his side.

"A new project?"

"You could call it that. But it's an odd one."

Seeing that he had not been turned away for his curiosity, the boy stepped closer.

"What did you draw?"

"The floorplan of an underground room. This is a top view and this is a cross-section."

"What are those arrows? And there, are those pulleys and levers?"

"I'm trying to understand how to move this wall. For once, we're not being asked to make a passage, but to open an existing one. The owner doesn't know how it works and asked for my help."

"Sort of like an honest break-in."

The analogy was unexpected, but it pleased Vincent.

"You could call it that."

"Will you figure it out?"

"I hope so. For the moment, I'm just like anyone else—I don't know the secret. However, I suspect that the people who created it must have applied the same principles that govern any hidden passage."

"There are rules?"

"Like in any science."

"Will you teach them to me? Please?"

Vincent turned to the boy and looked him straight in the eyes.

"You think I'm going to entrust you with such precious information? Just like that, chatting about it because we're friends?"

"I'd like that."

"My masters waited years to share some of them with me, and since then I've gone out of my way to add to, assemble, and formalize them. They are the keys to our profession, the sum of an experience acquired over centuries that also applies to the art of magic and illusion. Like all rare knowledge, they cannot be passed on carelessly. They're not for entertainment."

"I don't want to play around with them. I want to think, like you."

"Are you capable of keeping them to yourself?"

"Promise, I won't say anything, to anyone."

Vincent motioned him closer and whispered, "All right, I'll give you one today: every good secret passage respects five key principles. The first is discretion."

"Discretion," repeated Henri, concentrating hard.

"Exactly. The best passage is one nobody suspects exists. No one bothers with what they can't see."

Henri's eyes were shining, but his mind quickly set to work again.

"The one in the underground room: you've gotten past that. You know it exists."

"Indeed. And yet the creators so successfully applied the first rule that I still doubt its existence. Amazing, isn't it?"

"Teach me more!"

"Just one for today. We'll see about the others later, if you really want to learn, and if you remember what I just shared with you."

"I really want to!" cried the boy fervently.

Gabrielle's voice ringing out in the cellar interrupted them, "Time to eat!"

The Nail made a face that amused Vincent.

"What a face!"

"I'm starving, but I also want to keep learning!"

"The person who taught me my profession said, 'Only a satisfied body can be receptive to that which is not a vital need.' Let's go have lunch."

17

That evening, Vincent had a date with a dead man, in the Saint-Vincent Cemetery, on the corner of Rue Saint-Vincent, across from the famous tavern that was once called the Cabaret des Assassins. Certain coincidences could only lead him to question the true nature of chance; the people who had made him a man coalesced at this intersection that bore his own name—here, where the worst rubbed elbows with the best, his father met his tragic fate and the man who had taken him under his wing was laid to rest. Sometimes fate unleashes so much power that you can't flee, bringing you back again and again to the place that shaped you.

Vincent had reached the rowdy cabaret. The young never suspect that the tragedies endured by their predecessors could have happened in the very place where they think they've found happiness.

Each time he passed it, his heart tightened, flooding his veins with a painful poison. Images and sounds came back to him; violence, too. Although he had no desire to linger, his steps grew heavy and his shoulders sagged under the burden. He lowered his head. He squeezed his fists until the knuckles turned white. A full-bodied anger snarled within him. But he couldn't give in to it; he had to keep walking. Some obstacles can't be destroyed; so they must be circumnavigated in order to keep moving forward.

He crossed the street without looking back and continued along the back wall of the small cemetery. Vincent preferred to wait for nightfall to jump it. He had nothing to be ashamed of, but he would be more at ease. The realm of the dead didn't frighten him; he knew many of its residents.

He glanced around to be sure the street was empty, then easily climbed the outer wall, holding on to his knapsack that tinkled as he did so. He was there to celebrate an anniversary he wouldn't have missed for anything. The fifth of May was a sacred date.

He landed on his feet, slipped between the tombs, and took the stairs down from the upper terrace. Vincent would have liked to offer his father his own grave, where he would have buried his mother when she passed. But at the time, he and his brother didn't even have enough to eat. Vincent had resorted to stealing to feed his younger brother, and pretended to gorge himself so that Pierre wouldn't feel guilty gulping down what little they could glean. They had no parents to protect them. They didn't go to their father's funeral because their mother didn't have the money to pay for one, or their mother's because they hadn't even been informed. Vincent believed their remains were buried in a potter's field in the large new cemetery below. When he thought about his parents, he wanted to believe there was a paradise after death, because that gave him hope that they were finally sharing a happiness that this life had refused them. When he tried to remember his father's face, its features grew less and less clear. Only his words, his gaze, and his rare gestures of tenderness remained etched in Vincent's mind.

He slipped between the headstones. Even in the moonless night, he knew where he was going. His reference points were the imposing mausoleums lining the main path. Like the entrance hall in a mansion, each of the funeral monuments conveyed the image that the deceased or the family wanted to project—pride resists death for as long as buildings remain standing.

The wind had picked up, and the cemetery was dark and deserted. At that very same moment, on the other side of the hill, the official inauguration of the World's Fair was in full swing. Vincent couldn't hear any of the festivities, or glimpse even the faintest glow of fireworks in the sky.

He had come alone to be among the graves in the name of the past, while the world's celebrities were gleefully reveling in the future.

He soon spotted a burial vault as tall as it was wide; it belonged to the powerful Picard family. The dead man he had come to visit that evening was buried just to the left, under a much more modest slab. Vincent bowed before the grave.

"Étienne Begel 1830–1880." The line underneath it read: "Genius watchmaker." Even though this mention had cost Vincent a handsome sum, he was determined to see it etched on his mentor's gravestone. This evening marked the anniversary of the day Mr. Begel hired him as an apprentice. Though he never talked about it, Vincent thought about that moment every time he received a new order. He did not forget those rare individuals who opened their doors to him. Strangely, he never mentioned his former employer to his companions, or even to Pierre. He didn't like to share his feelings. It had taken a near stranger's personal question for him to open up, and that was just yesterday. Another coincidence. Mr. Begel often joked, claiming that coincidences were the ties bound to us by the Great Watchmaker to remind us of our own history.

A sharp crack caught Vincent's attention. He turned around and peered into the dark, discerning only the silhouettes of headstones. Everything was still. Just as he had convinced himself it was nothing, he heard another sound.

"Henri, is that you? Come here, don't be afraid. It's me. Did you come to check the mail?"

No answer. He waited a moment, then turned back to the grave. It was probably just one of the many cats that prowled the area at night. From his knapsack he pulled two glasses and a bottle of red wine. He crouched down before the tombstone and filled each glass, then raised his.

"I wish you a happy anniversary, Mister Begel. Blessed be the day I met you. Thank you for giving me a chance. I am reminded every day of what you did for me."

He clinked his glass lightly against the etched name and took a swallow.

"A lot has happened since my last visit. Business is going well, although we do have to be careful. Five of us are able to live off the work."

He spoke as naturally as if the man had been standing in front of him.

"The clients are getting stranger all the time. Rich men, politicians—there is less and less to protect and more and more to hide. The times are taking a funny turn. Even though I miss you, sometimes I'm glad you aren't here to see how things are being done today. There's less honor, more self-interest. Maybe I'm just getting old. Other than that, Pierre is doing well, and so is Henri. Soon the Nail will be as tall as me. I would have liked for you to know him. He would probably remind you of me as a young man! Konrad and Eustasio do excellent work. Tonight, our Italian is out, in the arms of his countess. He's celebrating the inauguration of the World's Fair. Henri was dying to go, but I asked him to stay with Gabrielle, at our place. Oh, yes! Gabrielle... I have to tell you, the house is no longer inhabited only by men. We are housing a young woman—very beautiful by the way—who's in serious trouble with a gang of misfits. I think Pierre has a soft spot for her."

He was interrupted by another suspicious sound. This time he didn't believe it was a cat, or even a rat. He tiptoed onto the path. All five of his senses were alert. He unfolded his knife, ready for anything.

He spent a good long while inspecting the neighboring graves, in vain. Had he scared away a prowler?

When he returned to the grave, Étienne Begel's glass had not moved. But a sealed letter had been placed beside it. A shiver ran down his spine. He looked around, but still saw nothing.

He opened the letter with trembling hands. It was too dark to make out the message's few lines.

Whoever dropped it off still had to be in the area. Maybe he was even watching Vincent. Maybe he had heard everything he had told his master. He bent down on one knee. Laying his hand respectfully on the tombstone, he bowed and murmured farewell to the man he had come to see that evening.

"I'm sorry, Mister Begel, but I have to go."

Vincent was right, he was being watched. And while it wasn't the man with the leather lace who had left the message, he was there, very close by.

18

Vincent was growing obsessed with the riddle of Alfred Minguier's secret passage. He couldn't stop thinking about it. When the industrialist suggested several possible dates to continue his research onsite, he jumped at the first one. He was eager to return and tackle the mystery, not to try to outdo the minds of the inventors, but to learn from their expertise.

Vincent no longer doubted that a secret opening existed; he had seen with his own eyes the notes left by the former owners clearly indicating its presence. However, Minguier had been careful not to let Vincent read too much, and he had learned nothing about what might lay "beyond." The businessman once again remained evasive, politely arguing that none of that concerned him.

That evening, Vincent had decided to rely on method to increase his understanding. While Minguier lit the lamps around the wall, Vincent turned back towards the rooms they had quickly walked through—perhaps too quickly.

"What are you doing? Are you leaving already?"

"No, don't worry. I'm just starting at the beginning. May I borrow a lantern?"

Minguier watched him, doubtful. His specialist turned and positioned himself at the bottom of the staircase they had taken to the basement. He examined every last detail, down to the steps and partitions. Vincent made a systematic study of all that surrounded him. Minguier grabbed another lantern and joined him.

"Let me give you some light."

"Thank you. More light is always welcome in a case like this."

He slipped behind the crates, leapt up onto the empty barrels to get a view of the room from above, then moved them aside. He examined every crack and fissure in the stone walls, peering more closely at each block that might seem suspect. The little man followed his every movement. Vincent began to rummage around in the pile of odds and ends in the second room.

"I understand that you do not wish to tell me what might lie behind your wall—"

"Simply because I have no idea!"

"—but do you at least have more information about the people who installed the passage? If I knew who they were, it might help me work out their thought process."

"Their thought process?"

"Over the centuries, all across Paris, many people have imagined ways of hiding their goods or their intentions. But they don't all do so in the same way. Criminals, clergy, mystics, and simple merchants each take a different approach rooted in their mentality and their environment.

"In your experience, who might have had reason to install one here?"

"We would need to examine the history of the house, beginning with its construction. I don't think criminals built it. If they committed their crimes in the city center, they would have preferred to establish their hideout further afield. To my knowledge, neither clergy nor knights ever owned this neighborhood. Perhaps mystics..."

Vincent raised great clouds of dust and frightened spiders away as he picked his way through the jumble of items abandoned in the cellars. Then, behind a pile of old cracked wicker baskets, he spied a ring sealed in the wall.

"Now here's something interesting."

"What did you find?" asked Minguier with interest.

Unconcerned with dirtying his fine clothes, the industrialist joined Vincent in the clutter. Vincent studied the rusted ring with caution. He didn't touch it at first; he smelled the metal. Then, from his pocket, he pulled a white cotton glove and slipped it on before gripping the ring tightly.

"You think it might be poisoned?" asked Minguier over his shoulder.

"I've heard some surprising stories."

Vincent tried pulling on it at first, but nothing happened. Then he tried turning it like a key. Still nothing. He combined different movements, then got up to see if anything had changed in the adjoining room. Nothing had moved.

"What do you think it is?" asked Minguier excitedly.

"Just a ring, sir, nothing more. We must continue our search."

19

Although the countess was a curious woman, she hadn't dared sit next to the window; she let Eustasio sit there. They had waited a long time to board the strange little car, and every seat was occupied. The passengers lucky enough to have made it aboard were already talking about what they were going to experience. They were as excited for what was about to come as they were about the prospect of being able to say they had been there.

Since the inauguration, Madame de Vignole and Eustasio had been spending their free time visiting the Fair's pavilions. But until today, they hadn't ascended the soaring 984-foot metal tower.

The event made for many chance encounters. When the countess bumped into someone she knew, she presented Eustasio as a young Italian noble on a trip to discover Paris. All the women smiled at the handsome stranger with the attractive physique and charming accent. They eyed him while admiring his command of the language. The men immediately tried to determine how much he was worth, the only area in which they had a chance of outdoing him. How many shares in the Brazilian Mines Company did it take to overshadow such an attractive pair of shoulders?

The countess had carefully explained to her protégé how to behave in front of these people. Instead of telling him what he should say, she advised him to keep quiet. In high society, every snippet of information became a weapon, and every disclosure was a stepping stone to power. This mawkish jousting required a faintly distant attitude, vague responses, and easy compliments, all delivered with an unfaltering smile. Eustasio's was perfect, bright and virile, but he wasn't in the habit of giving it on command. When he complained about having to force a smile, the countess suggested he imagine it was for her. His devastating grin had worked wonders ever since. He called her "madame the countess" in public, and he was the "Duke of Perenote." When they were out of range of eavesdroppers, they were simply Hortense and Eustasio.

Eustasio enjoyed most of all those moments when the two of them were just a couple like so many others lost in the crowd of curious sightseers. He liked that no one could tell them apart from the rest; they were anonymous in broad daylight, free to enjoy their unique relationship without having to play a part. He'd had difficulty accepting the beautiful clothes his lover had given him. He promised to reimburse her, down to the cufflinks and tiepin.

The car was about to depart. An operator closed the doors after wishing them all "a pleasant ascension courtesy of Mr. Gustave Eiffel." Word had it that the great man himself often came to welcome his visitors. The operator motioned to the driver seated in a cabin on the car's exterior and the trip began.

The revolving cables produced a continuous muffled rumbling as the car climbed the east pillar. The futuristic vessel travelled smoothly within a lacework of riveted girders that in no way spoiled the surrounding view.

The Fair was the most talked about place in the world since opening to the public. Crowds flocked to the Eiffel Tower, which had already proven to be the main attraction. Thanks to the tower and its lights, Paris shone—in every sense of the term. People hurried to see it from across Europe and even the Americas, traveling by boat, train, and horse.

The car had risen past the treetops and now seemed to be flying over the rooftops of the highest buildings. The feeling of height was striking. Apparently after the first floor, the incline at which the device travelled imperceptibly compensated for the curve of the monument's leg—yet another technical feat among many that defined the extraordinary construction.

Awestruck, Hortense inhaled deeply. With a subtle movement she pressed herself closer to her admirer, who took notice.

Although the view was fascinating, her sudden closeness distracted him from the spectacle.

The car slowed to a stop. The doors opened, and the passengers spilled out onto the immense terrace. There was a theater, several restaurants, and bars—all of them the highest of their kind in the world—but everyone hurried first to the guardrails to admire the view. In her long afternoon gown, the countess appeared to glide along the floorboards.

The spectacular sight elicited gasps of wonder. The stunning view was only accessible to the birds and those adventurous enough to clamber aboard a hot air balloon. Madame de Vignole's heart was pounding wildly. The expression "to have Paris at your feet" took on its full meaning here, and there was no need to be a star, a king, or a president to make it one's own.

They had a view of the entire Fair—a city within the city, or more accurately, an entire universe within the world's most spectacular capital. To think that it would exist for no more than a few months only added to the dizzying impression.

The jewels of industry were on display, but the past and history had not been forgotten. Entire neighborhoods of far-off cities had been recreated at the foot of the tower. Visible from above was a street from the Orient and others from the East, the Great North, and Africa. All the world's nations, and economic and political powers, were represented by pavilions, each more grandiose than the last, presenting each in their best light.

At the far end of the Champ de Mars, just past the central hall and the Galerie des Manufactures, towered the enormous Galerie des Machines, the largest building ever constructed in the history of humanity. Its high angled chimney stacks spewed a dense, white smoke symbolizing the power of progress. Seen from such heights, the crowd below resembled a colony of ants.

As the two lovers were taking it all in, a man approached them and bowed respectfully to the countess.

"My respects, madame."

To the woman's puzzlement he replied, "We met last fall at Mr. Fauvel's. He supplied most of the windows for the tower's amenities. I am Bertrand de Montereuil, and I recently became his associate."

Hortense proffered her gloved hand, which he honored with a perfect display of etiquette.

"This new flat glass, so resistant that a stone couldn't shatter it, has contributed much to the building's success," he continued. "If madame the countess is not interested, perhaps the gentleman would like to invest?"

Eustasio didn't know what to say. The worst of the lowest rank of noble dandies expressed themselves better than he did. Encumbered with a hat he didn't know how to hold and shoes that hurt, he simply didn't measure up. Hortense would have been just as comfortable on the arm of this Bertrand. She would have been as elegant, and he wouldn't end up speechless and at risk of putting her at a disadvantage.

Sensing his embarrassment, the countess interrupted.

"Thank you, my dear Bertrand, I wish you every success in this new endeavor. My friend is an Italian duke and his business is in neither glass nor steel."

The man bowed respectfully and withdrew without insisting.

"You saved me once again," Eustasio said thankfully. "I'm not worthy of you."

"Please, don't misplace pride where you just need a bit more practice."

"It infuriates me that I'm not of your standing. Everything would be so much simpler."

"Rank does not make the man, Eustasio, otherwise these little princes wouldn't have to resort to using their wallets to seduce women. Incidentally, that one now works for a commoner. Come, let us leave this place."

20

The Fair took on another atmosphere after dark, probably because the visitors who came primarily to be seen left as soon as the day's society events ended. But it was also because the artificial lighting gave the site an altogether novel texture. Science had overpowered the night. Only the truly curious had stayed to enjoy the show—the countess and Eustasio among them.

Under the cloak of growing darkness, when she was sure there would be no more awkward encounters, Hortense finally allowed herself to walk closely with Eustasio. This change in manner reassured him more than any declaration of love could have.

Together they discovered the extraordinary Electricity pavilion, a building large enough to contain a mansion and lit by a multitude of blinding lightbulbs, far brighter than any kerosene lamp. Incandescent bulbs had been arranged to form giant flowers and geometric figures; the couple had to crane their necks to see the embellishments on the ceiling that flooded the space with light. The generators that kept them burning were so powerful that it was impossible to hold a conversation in their vicinity. To prove the point, a sign invited visitors to try.

As they were leaving, an astonished Hortense dragged her lover towards the Fair garden to see the luminous fountain created by the sculptor Coutan. An army of criers had just announced the start of the last spectacle before the Fair closed for the night.

The crowd had gathered around a pool. At the far end, a military orchestra sounded the opening notes of a march. The first jets of water soared in front of the monumental sculpture: a tangle of silhouettes topped by the goddess of Progress. All at once they were illuminated from within, and in different colors. The audience was enthralled. The jets of water radiated upward to form shapes that resembled giant precious gemstones: a ruby pillar, an emerald waterfall. Aquatic columns rose from the fountain and took on supernatural hues. Thousands of diamond-like droplets glided through the darkness before tumbling into the watery reflections below. There were more than three hundred water jets lit with gold and oscillating tones. The crowd grew more excited. The light followed the rhythm of the music. The show united strength and poetry in an original alliance.

Hortense was content; the day ended like a magnificent dream. After the Eiffel Tower, diamonds in the South Africa pavilion, and the admirable Arabic mosaics, she was bound to have trouble falling asleep. As the fountain unveiled new shapes, she tucked her arm into Eustasio's. It was the first time the countess had allowed herself this degree of intimacy in public. She had always shown her companion tenderness, but had never before dared to do so outside the secrecy of her boudoir, where he was now her sole visitor. He was startled but tried not to show it, overwhelmed as he was. Her gesture moved him more than all the magic of human accomplishment laid out before him.

"Do you like it?" he whispered in her ear.

"I love it," she replied, holding him closer.

He wished he had the courage to ask her if she liked *him*. He dreamed of hearing her say she adored him, but was careful to focus his question on the show. One letter or a word added or taken away can change everything.

The Italian had never been confident. He knew perfectly well that if he hadn't been so handsome, his life would have turned out differently. He had been obliged to develop his craft far beyond what others did so that he would finally be noticed for his accomplishments rather than his appearance. As the music soared and the aquatic spectacle culminated above the fountain, Eustasio realized just how lucky he was to have built, with his companions, a life that had enabled him to meet the one he so boldly thought of as his beloved.

When the music ended, after an enchanting finale, the jets subsided and the fountain went still. The orchestra had finished playing. The crowd applauded and dispersed. The water that had been so alive and bright a moment before was now a dark, barely rippling mass. The spectators set off for home on paths that corresponded to their rank and means. Some would walk for miles on feet already sore from long hours wandering through the fair. Others would pay for the luxury of riding in a fiacre, a sort of horse-drawn hackney coach. The wealthiest were awaited by their own horse and carriage. To avoid the crowd, Eustasio had instructed Madame de Vignole's carriage to meet them behind the Middle East neighborhood.

"Let's go, Hortense. It's getting chilly and I don't want you to catch cold."

While fairgoers headed out the main entrance, the couple took a different route and disappeared between the Egyptian buildings. They passed beneath the finely wrought arch that marked the entrance to the fair's exotic street. The atmosphere there was suddenly different. The path was now deserted and the lighting sporadic. Numerous balconies and hanging tapestries created a play of moving shapes and shadows, but the foreign exhibitors had disappeared.

Hortense was still caught up in the exhilaration of her day. "What an astonishing show, don't you think?"

"*È magnifico!*"

"Next time we come, I would like to visit the Galerie des Machines. A friend described it as appallingly loud and of the utmost mechanical violence, but I think that woman is too fragile to have grasped the point."

"We'll go wherever you like."

"Tomorrow?"

"I have to work, but I will have time on Friday."

"I'll wait for you then, and if you take too long, I'll demand that you come for another touch-up in my secret room!"

She laughed and kissed him. The street grew darker and darker, and the crowd had dwindled to a distant murmur. They were alone.

Suddenly, a silhouette loomed before them. It was joined by a second, then a third. Thinking they were guards, Eustasio began to explain: "Good evening, gentlemen. Don't worry, we're just heading to madame the countess's carriage that awaits us up ahead."

None of the strangers moved. The first simply said, "We're not worried. But you should be."

His tone was icy and the threat palpable. Eustasio moved quickly to shield Hortense.

"We don't have any money with us," he said, "and I suggest you leave the *signora* alone. I'm warning you."

Two of the strangers broke into a wicked laugh. The one who had spoken first didn't react; his behavior was by far the most troubling. The Italian began to think that he wouldn't get away without a fight. Whatever happened, he would deal with it. He was in good shape, and the thought of someone harming Hortense magnified his fighter instinct.

Eustasio kept Hortense behind him to protect her from their assailants. After confirming that retreat was still possible, he whispered, "Run, *bellissima*, run to the central walkway and seek shelter there. I'll protect you."

She clung to him. The man who appeared to be the leader suddenly flashed a knife.

"She doesn't need protection. We don't care about your old mule."

Eustasio bristled. "How dare you talk about Madame…"

The man charged him. Eustasio narrowly avoided the blade and landed a punch in passing. Combat was not his specialty, but his speed gave him a bit of an advantage. Hortense let out a cry and retreated, surprised by the aggressiveness of the attack. The other two men charged at her beloved Eustasio. He fended them off somehow, and delivered as many blows as he could. Despite his clumsiness, some of them landed.

Now there were three knives pointed at him.

"Leave him alone!" shouted the countess. "Take my necklace and leave!"

She loosened the jewelry and threw it at the men, but they paid no mind, instead doubling down on their prey. Eustasio was already cut on the arm and the side. He contorted his body as best he could to escape their thrusts. Even though he had no chance of regaining the upper hand, he refused to flee.

"Scoundrels!" cried Hortense. "Help! You animals! Leave him alone!"

She berated them, ready to jump into the melee, but she didn't have time. Eustasio had just received a more serious blow. He staggered, clutching at his chest before collapsing to the ground.

Hortense shouted at the top of her lungs and, without thinking, ran to him. There was blood on his shirt. The horrible stain was spreading quickly. The young woman tried to sit him up and hold him in her arms.

The three attackers considered the result of their work without remorse. One of them muttered, "I think he's done for."

They didn't have time for a closer look. A whistle shrieked in the night. Two gendarmes came running from the main entrance.

"What's going on here?"

"Help!" moaned Hortense hoarsely.

The three attackers fled.

"Stop where you are!" cried a gendarme.

But such men don't heed an officer's orders. They were already gone.

21

Vincent and Pierre were out of breath by the time they finally reached the home of Madame de Vignole. The maid hurried them in.

Alerted by the noise, Hortense appeared at the top of the staircase overlooking the entrance. Her hair was down and she was dressed in a simple housecoat.

Vincent bowed. "Good evening, Madame Countess, please excuse us for calling so late—"

"I would have informed you sooner, but I didn't know where to find you."

"We found your message this evening. We came immediately."

"Come upstairs. He's resting in my room."

The two brothers bounded up the stairs. The countess met them on the landing.

"How is he doing?" asked Pierre with alarm.

"I called for my doctor. He says Eustasio will survive, but he truly had a brush with death. Half an inch more and it would have been over. When I think back... He lost a lot of blood."

"How did it happen? In your message you mentioned an assault."

"We were attacked as we were leaving the Fair."

"And you?" asked Vincent. "Were you harmed?"

"Eustasio protected me. I was nothing but a helpless witness to this horror."

The countess searched the faces of the wounded man's friends. "Weren't you concerned about his absence?"

Vincent lowered his eyes, "Pardon, madame, but we imagined he was lost in love."

"In love, that I can believe, but not lost. That's not like him."

Pierre explained, "When he talks to us about you, it is with the utmost praise and respect. We know how much you mean to our friend."

The countess led them to the door to her room, then opened it. "Enter. He asked for you. He will be happy to see you."

Vincent and Pierre found Eustasio dozing, lying in a sculpted bed made up with flowered sheets in sumptuous fabric. It was strange to see their friend in such lavish surroundings, as though he were suddenly no longer himself. His chest was bandaged tightly. Usually so dignified and careful about his appearance, Eustasio now seemed fragile. Pierre approached, visibly shaken. The injured man's eyelids fluttered and Pierre took his hand gently.

"Eustasio, we're here." He encouraged poor Eustasio to open his eyes, but the light blinded him.

Eustacio muttered a few words in Italian and finally opened his eyes a crack. He didn't recognize his friends at first, but a feeble smile eventually brightened his face.

"You came."

"As soon as we heard," said Vincent, kneeling at his bedside. "How do you feel?"

"Tired, very tired. But that's not the worst of it."

Hortense was standing at the foot of the bed. Vincent looked up at her and said, "Don't worry, the doctor said you're going to recover. Madame the Countess is here to make sure of it."

"I thought my time had come. *Che Dio mi protegga...*"

"We're going to take care of you. Soon this will be nothing more than a bad memory."

"My health doesn't matter. Those criminals could have attacked Hortense."

"Thank God, they didn't."

Eustasio grabbed Vincent's hand. "Listen to me. They weren't thieves. They weren't there to rob us. They were there for something else."

"What do you mean?"

"Those *bastardi* were there for me. They wanted to kill me, I'm sure of it."

Pierre frowned. "Ordered by someone jealous of your relationship with Madame?"

"No one knows about our relationship," interrupted Hortense. "And despite what you might think, I don't have that many suitors."

"So who then?" asked Vincent. "Do you know who would have reason to kill you?"

"No. I have no debts, nor enemies."

"A family affair? Revenge?"

"Our *famiglia* is peaceful and no one bothers with them. In fact, few of them even know that I'm in Paris."

"Damn it, we have to find an explanation!"

"Maybe they got you confused with someone else?" suggested Pierre.

"That's what I thought at first, but after thinking about it, I realized that can't be it. *Dannazione!* They did their research. They must have been following us for several days to have known our routine. They knew that we were going to take a shortcut to meet up with Madame de Vignole's carriage, the only one parked on that side. There was no mistake. Madame the Countess was not their target; they said as much before attacking. It had to be me."

He moaned. Hortense came around to his bedside and sponged his forehead.

"The doctor ordered rest. Don't work yourself up. You're safe here."

"I can't stop thinking about it," Eustasio insisted, "but I still don't understand. There were three of them, but only one spoke to me. He knew who I was. He was very calm, as if he were used to that kind of ambush. He was there to eliminate me, plain and simple. He had no problem with killing me."

"Would you be able to recognize the scoundrel?"

"It was too dark to see his face. But I did notice one detail."

"What?"

"When he stepped in front of us, before he lunged at me with his knife, he kept playing with a thin leather lace, wrapping it around his index finger."

"We're not likely to find him with such a meager clue," lamented Pierre.

Eustasio winced in pain and tried to sit up a little more.

"The more I think about it, the more I'm convinced they weren't really there to attack me."

"You just said they knew exactly who you were."

"Yes, and that's true, but I don't think these knife wounds were meant for me alone."

"For whom then?"

"For us, Vincent—our team."

22

An emergency meeting was held in the cellar. The situation was serious. Gabrielle had not been invited, or even informed about what had happened. Vincent sat with his elbows planted on the drawing table. Konrad had just learned of Eustasio's attack. He was having a hard time reining in his anger and paced the room like a caged lion. Pierre tried to reason with Henri, who was not taking the news well either.

Vincent spoke with unusual gravity.

"Until we get the whole story, we have to be very careful. Henri, starting now, you're no longer in charge of picking up mail at the cemetery. I'll do it. Focus on watching our cache of gold, and be more vigilant than ever. Move only in daylight and take streets where you know you won't be alone."

"Got it."

"Do you think our fortune is in danger?" asked Konrad.

"I have no idea, but now is not the time to leave it unguarded."

"When can we bring Eustasio home? He would be safer here."

"As soon as he can be moved, but I'm afraid that won't be for another few days. Don't worry, in the meantime, he's well protected in the countess's home."

The German punched a pillar in anger.

"Why would they want to attack us?" he thundered.

"For plenty of reasons," replied Pierre. "Forty-eight and counting—as many passages created as secrets hidden. I keep telling you, not all of our clients are reputable. We know a lot about them, about what they're hiding, and what they own. And we're well positioned to access it."

"Are you thinking of the art dealer and his investment certificates?" asked Konrad. "He never looks people in the eye. Or that dirty traitorous general who sells information to other countries?"

"You can add the chairman of the board who collects compromising dossiers on his colleagues so he can blackmail them. The list of potential suspects is long. Many of them might be tempted to eliminate witnesses to their darker side."

"Like the pharaohs who silenced the laborers who built their tombs," added the carpenter.

Vincent interrupted them. "I don't think the clients you've mentioned are scheming to get rid of us. They may have the motivation, but they don't have the means. That takes unscrupulous men and contacts in criminal networks."

Konrad suddenly stopped his pacing. "*Warten Sie, meine Freunde!* I didn't pay it any mind at the time, but something strange happened to me two days ago. And in light of what happened to Eustasio..."

"Tell us!" cried Henri.

"I went to visit a new residential development in the center. Several times, I had the impression that a carriage was following me. To my surprise, it kept pace with me, staying always a little behind and taking the same streets. I thought I was imagining things, and I didn't give it any more thought. But when I crossed the street further along, a carriage charged straight at me, knocking over everyone in its path. If I hadn't thrown myself to the side, it would have run me over."

"Did you see the coach driver?" asked Vincent. "Did he have a passenger?"

The carpenter shook his head.

"It all happened too fast. In the time it took me to turn around, he'd disappeared. At first I figured the horse got excited, but it really seemed to be the carriage that had accompanied me earlier on the way."

Pierre spoke up, "None of us should leave the house alone anymore. Maybe we should also increase the number of alarm systems around the house and warn Gabrielle."

"You're right," agreed Vincent. "I'll let you take care of it. I'll be back to help you, but first I have to get to a meeting that might shed some light on things."

23

After a closing prayer, the service ended. Bending a knee as they crossed themselves in the direction of the choir, the faithful trickled out of the church of Saint-Leu-Saint-Gilles. The pews emptied as they did so. The priest tidied the altar, then disappeared into the sacristy, and the nave was soon deserted. Only Vincent remained seated, as he had been told.

The door closed behind the last parishioner, echoing throughout the church. The calm that immediately settled over the pews was not unpleasant; in fact, it felt to Vincent like the eye of the storm that was ripping through him. He felt peaceful there. But he had never been a churchgoer. His mother had taught him several prayers, but he hadn't had many occasions to recite them, and even less to believe in them. However, he would have had many things to ask of God. Not for himself, but for the people dear to him, whom the Almighty had often mistreated.

A man sat down next to him. Vincent hadn't heard him enter, but he wasn't afraid. He was used to making such appearances himself. He didn't even try to see who it was. His gaze remained concentrated on the crucifix that reigned above the choir, although he perceived smooth, calm movements beside him.

Charles crossed himself, joined his hands, and said in a low voice, "I'm pleased you came. May I conclude that you thought things over?"

"That's all I've been doing."

"Do you prefer this meeting place to the dance hall?"

"I'm surprised by the address—Rue de la Grande-Truanderie, in one of the most dangerous neighborhoods in the city. I'm almost tempted to take it as a sign. At least it's quieter, but I'm still no closer to knowing why I'm here."

"So why did you accept my invitation?"

"Because I need answers, and I'm betting that you have a few."

For the first time, Vincent turned toward the other man. They were close, much closer than they had been at their first meeting. There was no table between them. Charles's face appeared just as noble, but Vincent was less intimidated this time.

The man smiled and murmured, "I sense anger in you."

"And for good reason."

"Am I the cause?"

"I don't know yet, but I intend to find out."

"Explain, Vincent."

"You delivered your letter to the graveyard while I was there."

"I didn't do it myself, but indeed, I was informed of your presence."

"One of your men?"

"I have no men. Just someone I trust."

"Why didn't he make himself known?"

"It was not his intention to meet you. It was pure coincidence that you were there at the same time."

"Coincidence. Of course. Was he alone?"

"He was. Why these questions?"

"Because I had the clear impression that two people were watching me that night."

"My messenger was not there to spy on you, and I know that he was unaccompanied. He did not mention the presence of anyone besides you."

Vincent noticed that, despite his inquisitive tone and the directness of his questions, Charles remained calm.

"What's going on, Vincent? Why are you in this state?"

Receiving no response, he insisted, "What do you suspect me of?"

Vincent slowly turned toward him.

"Did you order the murder of one of my companions? Perhaps even attempt to have another run over?"

For the first time, Charles allowed himself a reaction that escaped his control.

"One of your companions was killed?"

The man seemed sincerely concerned. Realizing that Charles assumed the attempt on Eustasio's life had been successful, Vincent chose not to say otherwise.

"Are you the one attacking my team?"

"I came to you for help. Why would I want to weaken you?"

"To isolate me, for example. To alienate me and make me easier to manipulate."

"Remember: one of the first questions I asked you was for whom or for what you fight."

"I remember very well—and that's exactly what's being attacked."

"Are you sure these murderers are targeting your team?"

"Everything would suggest so."

Charles sighed. His hands parted.

"You know something!" said Vincent.

"I fear I do."

"You have to tell me."

"Vincent, we're going to have to speak openly. This may be very confusing for you, but I no longer have a choice. We have even less time than I feared. Follow me."

24

The underground room below the church did not resemble a crypt so much as it did a place of worship. There were no burial vaults, just a modest altar tucked into a chapel crowned with a simple rusty iron cross. The walls of stone enveloped each sound with a distinctive muted echo that did not reverberate. Charles seemed familiar with the place.

"We'll be safe here," he said.

His voice was different, more chiseled. Nothing interfered with it in the sepulchral silence.

"Vincent, what I'm about to tell you is going to seem outrageous. You are not obligated to believe it, but I must warn you that you will never be able to forget it. You will no longer be able to envision our world as you do now, at this very moment. Do not think I am exaggerating; I am choosing my words carefully—I experienced it myself. However, you can make the decision to escape it before I begin. If you ask me to be silent, I will obey. Your life will continue as it was, but that won't protect you from those who know of your existence."

"For God's sake, who are you?"

"My name is Charles Adinson. I've been officially dead for nine years now. I was buried in a small cemetery on a bluff in Normandy overlooking the sea. No one visits my grave, not even me. I'm dead because I had no family, dead because I believe in a better world. I died so I could be free. Now I am nothing more than a first name—like you, Vincent—because unlike many, our lives are not defined by the surname we carry, but by the things we accomplish. Of my own volition, I formed an alliance with certain people who share the same hopes as I do. I joined forces with them. Like them, each working in their respective field, I devoted my energy and my resources to serving what I believe in. I obey no one blindly. I am simply supporting what I think is right. I am not always the one to make the decisions, but I devote myself without reservation when I am convinced. I know enough about you to believe that these words may find an echo deep within your soul."

"You know nothing about who I really am."

"Are you sure?"

"Surprise me."

Charles peered at Vincent as if he were deciphering a riddle.

"Are you challenging me? Do you want proof? Beginners often need it. But are you ready to receive it?"

"Let's just say, I'm old enough to have learned that this life can take from you everything it has given. I have nothing to lose."

Adinson smiled. "So be it. You've made your choice."

He paused before continuing.

"Your name is Vincent Cavel. You and your brother Pierre lost your parents when you were very young. Your father was killed one evening, before your eyes, by a laborer, jealous of a job your father had secured instead of him at the cabaret across from the cemetery where you went the other night."

Vincent tensed and his gaze hardened.

"How could you know that?"

"From a reliable source."

"Only my brother knows about that. I never told anyone else. Did you know my family? My father?"

"No. Contrary to your assertions, you did confide in someone else. I am certain that you remember."

Vincent was reeling. That a stranger he was wary of could reveal his deepest secrets made him nauseous. He staggered. The words reverberated in his increasingly agitated mind.

"After your mother died, you and your brother were thrown onto the street by your landlords, despite your offer to work for them. You decided to hide to avoid being placed in an orphanage."

Vincent was stunned. He raised his hand, a pitiful shield against what he was hearing.

Without wavering, Charles continued. "You met Étienne Begel, watchmaker, locksmith, and a grand specialist in mechanical systems who, in addition to his official activities, also worked on more confidential, even secret, projects. He took you under his wing and trained you."

Vincent wheezed in pain. In his shock, he was physically forced to step back and lean against the wall to keep from collapsing. He brought his hands to his temples; he thought he was losing his mind.

"He helped you develop your skills. He taught you the history and techniques of secret passages."

Vincent had heard enough. Each word Charles uttered chipped away at the armor he had so carefully built up over the years. Suddenly, his muscles tensed, shaken by a fit of rage. Defensively, he leapt up and lunged at Charles, grabbing him by the collar and shouting, "How can you know all of this?"

Adinson did not seem startled. He didn't even fight back. He acquiesced and continued, speaking deliberately. "You knew that Étienne Begel often worked for a famous magician—a visionary illusionist, automaton enthusiast, and exceptional inventor."

Vincent no longer knew if he had a hold on Adinson or if he was clinging to him to keep himself from falling. His strength evaporated; he collapsed against the other man. Breathless, as though trying to convince himself, he murmured, "No one knows, it's impossible."

"That's how you met Jean-Eugène Robert-Houdin, founder of the renowned Theater of Magic, uncontested expert at sleight of hand, and creator of the greatest conjuring acts. But you knew only too well that he also had other interests: spiritism, occult science, and secret passages. You worked directly with him when Étienne Begel fell ill."

"You're the devil. No one else could have known," Vincent cried.

"I'm not the devil, Vincent. Jean-Eugène was my friend. He told me about you. He told me everything. He also introduced me to the people who are now my fellow researchers. He was one of them."

"Did he belong to a secret society? Do you?"

"Not the kind you're thinking of. Those aren't secret. They do nothing but draw attention to themselves with thinly veiled rumors, so that everyone hears about them. Nothing more than amateurish clubs plundering the past so their members can claim loyalty to a spirit that fascinates them, even as they subvert its very essence. No. Forget about such false secrets. Like Robert-Houdin and Begel, I belong to a brotherhood that shares more than a name—we share an ideal. We act according to our deepest-held convictions in the only domain with real power: the shadows."

Vincent trembled to his very core.

"Mr. Robert-Houdin and Mr. Begel never mentioned anything about it."

"You were too young. They probably would have eventually."

Adinson helped him up.

Vincent straightened and hesitantly asked, "Is Robert-Houdin really dead, or did he disappear, like you?" His question betrayed how much he longed to see his mentor again. His absence had left a gaping void.

"I'm sorry, Vincent. Jean-Eugène is no more. Fate didn't give him time to die any other way. The only disappearing act the master bungled was his own."

Vincent lowered his head, exhausted. "Please, sir, I don't want to hear any more."

"Pull yourself together, Mr. Cavel. We're not done yet."

25

Pierre was now certain of it: something bad had happened. First he thought his brother was still sleeping—that would be possible, but surprising, especially since he had never seen his older brother rise after him. He was always the first up and often the last to go to bed. So he waited impatiently, but Vincent didn't appear.

No longer able to bear it, Pierre searched every room in the house, in vain. He hadn't alerted Konrad yet, but the young man had been worried sick since dawn. Gabrielle noticed, but Pierre remained silent, more to shield her from worry than out of caution.

The attack on Eustasio, committed with a knife no less, had brought back awful memories for both brothers. Then there was that mysterious meeting Vincent hadn't want to tell him about. No one had seen him since.

Pierre paced the house wondering what he should do. Vincent would have told him to consider everything. The smallest lead, even the most improbable, should never be overlooked.

While checking the house for a second time, he noticed that the door to the tiny room at the back of the attic was closed. He didn't remember that being the case previously. He listened carefully. His soft knocking was met with a groan. Carefully, he entered. Daylight filtered down through the roof tiles. There, at the foot of a dusty old trunk, lay a shapeless mass covered with a blanket.

"Vincent?"

Another groan; Pierre sighed with relief.

"Thank God, you're here."

Vincent grumbled.

"You can't blame me for being on the alert, with everything that's happened!" Pierre retorted.

Curled up under a tattered bedspread wheezing feathers, Vincent responded, "But don't worry, little brother, I always come back." His voice was thick, and his words uncertain.

Pierre frowned. "Why did you hide away in this hole up here, like an animal? You're not injured, are you?"

Vincent mumbled something, but his words were inaudible. Pierre knelt down and placed a hand on his brother, insisting, "Answer me. I need to know. We agreed not to go anywhere alone, and yet you went to that meeting without anyone by your side."

His older brother stretched, and his head surfaced above the torn bedspread.

"Believe me, it was better for everyone."

Inwardly, Vincent wondered if instead of facing Charles's revelations, he wouldn't have preferred being stabbed. Adinson was right. The world hadn't looked the same since their meeting. Everything that had once seemed self-evident to him no longer did. Begel and Robert-Houdin were two of his mainstays, and he wasn't certain anymore if he knew who they had really been. The few certainties in his life had dissolved. Yet his admiration for the men had not diminished; he was even beginning to understand them better.

Unaware of his brother's inner turmoil, Pierre sat on the floor beside him.

"What's going on, Vincent? Talk to me. You can't bear everything alone forever. I know that you do that to protect us, especially me. But I'm no longer a child who needs constant supervision."

"You're not the only one to tell me that these days."

"You didn't want to tell me anything about Minguier's request. But I heard you talk about it with Henri."

"The Nail asked me questions, and I responded."

"And these meetings we're told nothing about. The other night at the dance hall and last night I don't know where."

"That's something else entirely."

"If I ask you questions, will you give me answers too, like you did Henri?"

Vincent straightened and leaned against the trunk. Dust motes danced in the sunlight.

"I have nothing to hide from you, Pierre. Everything I do, I do it for you. You are the only family I have left. I have no one else. If something ever happened to you…"

"The same is true for me. That's why I hate the fact that you take so many risks. It seems like you've always got something on your mind. Your nighttime rendezvous with the industrialist; sketches I don't understand that you leave lying around with the blueprints; clients I suspect aren't honest. I feel threats lurking everywhere."

"I do too."

"That was already the case before the attempt on Eustasio's life, but it's only gotten worse since then."

"You have to trust me, Pierre."

"Trust you? You're asking me to trust you? That's all I've ever done! As soon I could walk, I followed you. Always. And I've never regretted it. When we played hide-and-seek with Clément, you were the one who told me where to sneak off to for the best hiding spots; he and the Villars brothers could never find me. You even let yourself be found so they wouldn't capture me. I'm aware of everything you've done and everything you do for me. It's not a question of trust, Vincent. It's a question of safety. I don't want anything bad to befall you either. With everything that's happening, we would certainly be stronger together. You think you're sparing me, but you're pushing me away and depriving yourself of your best ally."

Vincent didn't respond. But Pierre wanted an answer. He pressed his brother, "What do you have to say to that?"

In response, Vincent grabbed his younger brother behind the neck and pulled him close in an animal gesture, a pack reflex. They stayed close like that for a long time, just like when they were children. Their shared reality overpowered Vincent's current state of mind. They might both have been men, but childhood was never far off, and in it they found a saving grace. They were safe there, far from the stormy swells of their life, on an island that belonged to them alone, and to which only they knew the way.

Vincent broke the silence at last. "You're right. I'm going to tell you everything and you're going to help me."

Pierre was pleased. Even if things were bad, he preferred to be close to his brother. Vincent ruffled his hair affectionately. The chestnut-brown cowlick that he tried so hard to tame always sprang up again, making Vincent smile.

"But first," he said, "I have a question for you."

"Go on."

"What do you want most of all in this world?"

26

Listening to Charles speak in the echo of the underground chapel, Vincent couldn't help but feel uneasy. Although the circumstances were different, the place reminded him of the first time Adinson had revealed what had been haunting Vincent ever since.

This time the content of their exchange was quite different, and Charles tried to explain the research he participated in, without revealing too much.

"Just think, Paris is an ancient city! Life has been taking its course here for millennia. From the earliest days of Antiquity to the Gauls to the Franks, then from the Romans to the Merovingians, the different peoples who have inhabited the city have left evidence of their expertise and their ambitions. They have, each in their turn, contributed to the edifice that we have inherited today. As different as their origins and their beliefs were, their cultures and their rituals, they always left the most impressive trace of their skills in their places of worship." Vincent watched him as he paced the room.

"These sanctuaries concentrate expertise and symbolize ideals. They also house certain treasures, some displayed for all to see as relics or masterpieces, and others still more precious hidden within their walls. Documents, sacred objects—the quintessence of what our civilizations have produced. All of that is under threat now. Our century is intent on remodeling Paris. Neighborhoods are being carved up, and places are being rearranged. New roads are constantly being built. For the first time since Lutetia appeared, it is no longer enough to build outwards; now everything that once existed is being obliterated to make way for the new. Those who have been here for generations are being chased out to make room for others, more fortunate. Thousands of homes are being torn down and hills flattened; there is drilling, ripping, and restructuring to build new residences, restaurants, shops, and places of entertainment. The city is devouring its outlying lands to build factories capable of producing everything the new people are so hungry for. Practical trades are disappearing in favor of new professions that satisfy no need, only desires. Geography is evolving to reflect the mentality."

"I understand perfectly, but I'm not sure I see what that has to do with us."

"You'll understand shortly where I'm going with this. These construction projects batter the city. They threaten sanctuaries—some of which are a thousand years old—and the treasures they hold along with them. Those that were already known to us can be moved, but some are not so easy to work with. Especially since moving them would reveal their existence, which is not necessarily desirable."

"Explain."

"The church under which we currently find ourselves is a perfect example. The Saint-Leu-Saint-Gilles parish resembles dozens of others like it in Paris. Yet, its history tells of much more than the faithful can discern. This church is the only surviving religious structure of those that lined Rue Saint-Denis. The subterranean chapel in which we stand was dug in the year of our Lord 1780, exclusively for use by the knights of Saint-Sépulcre, who were going to lose their chapel, located not far from here. Not so long ago, the surface building itself lost the extensions off its apse when Boulevard Sébastopol was opened. As you can see, the city's redevelopment poses a constant threat to sites with immeasurable value, not always recognized by the engineers."

"What can we do about it? No one can oppose the forward march of progress."

"That's not what we want either. We are simply trying to save what is hidden in this city, and what the era is destroying without even realizing it. It is a race against time. There's already talk of digging tunnels for underground trains, like those in London. The World's Fair is exacerbating appetites for major construction works.

Business has little use for faith; it's clear that this city is going to succumb to the mirage of material possessions. We are on the threshold of a future ruled by the science of men."

Everything in Charles's delivery reflected his conviction.

"Faced with the massive industrialization of souls," he went on, "it is up to us to preserve what has been passed down to us from time immemorial. We cannot sacrifice centuries of knowledge, spirituality, and power that are beyond our perceptions simply because other ways of thinking are in favor at the moment. Humanity was not built on the quest to satisfy incessant desires, but on ideals that give meaning to that which is essential. The highest building in a city has long been its cathedral. Today it is an extraordinary metal perch that, for a few francs, transports individuals to dizzying heights. The body is easy to elevate; not so with the spirit."

"Even if I agreed with you, what would I do?"

"My companions and I are archeologists of the sacred, Vincent. We unearth treasures and buried secrets to save them from destruction or discovery by non-believers who would only see in them another source of profit. These wonders do not belong to us. We are only removing them from the damage inflicted by modernity's madness. Contrary to other secret societies, we do not claim to have any divine mandate. Our mission is not to have at our disposal knowledge or powers that are beyond our mastery, but to protect them."

Vincent shook his head. "I admire you, Charles. Not only for everything you seem to know. You fascinate me because you believe. I envy your hope, your faith in a better world. I would very much like to share that with you. Perhaps you appeared too late in my life. I've witnessed so much injustice that sometimes, I admit, I find myself doubting the existence of God."

"I pity you. You are depriving yourself of great strength."

"And yet I'm not unhappy. I've learned to do without Him."

"Are you sure of that?"

"Charles, you are a man of great experience. Do you really believe that one day wisdom and knowledge will guide the world? Are you really so blind to human nature?"

"Life has not spared me any more than it has you. But I choose to preserve the knowledge, wealth, and messages from the depths of time so they may serve our descendants. Perhaps they will be better than us? I dare to hope so. I pray that they will be stronger than us. Perhaps they won't need God to guide them anymore because they will have acquired the capacity to act with righteousness and humanity."

"I'm afraid by the time that happens, I'll be dead and you'll have died a second time."

"That is probable indeed, but even if I never live to see it, I still believe this must be seen through to the end—Vincent, do you understand the deeper meaning of what I'm saying? Because therein lies the key to our actions. Men will die from acting only for their own interests. Should we sow only that which we are certain to reap? And if not, the only valid question is: are we ready to be nothing more than the seeds of a fruit that others might pick? Are we capable of acting without glory or benefit, so that one day those who follow will have a chance to do better than us?"

Vincent had no response. These questions went far beyond any that he had faced beforehand.

"There are powers much greater than the inventions with which people distract themselves. Voltaire said it more than once: the universe is too beautiful a clock to exist without a clockmaker. Do you not find the image of the clockmaker relevant? The astronomer Nicolas Copernicus was in the profession, as was Galileo, Huygens, and of course Mr. Begel and Mr. Robert-Houdin, my old friend. We are all cogs in a world that transcends us, Vincent. How do we want to see it turn?"

The reference awoke new possibilities in Vincent.

"Beyond new industrial technology," continued Adinson, "beyond the misguided actions of clergy who at times altered the message of their fathers, everything that sets us apart from animals must be preserved. Each manifestation of that which surpasses us must be saved. We are entertained, we marvel at the tricks our science performs, but it is not by exhilarating ourselves to the point of believing we are the creators of everything that our species will earn its salvation. Our century is coming to an end; the twentieth is on our doorstep. The future has arrived. It will likely hold many discoveries, but what will we do with them? Soon the time will come when humanity must decide between behaving like an irresponsible child grasping for toys or a being capable of choosing and taking charge of its own destiny. This crucial moment will come, Vincent, I promise you. It approaches with every revolution of the dial."

Long accustomed to day-to-day survival, Vincent had never permitted himself to reflect upon the world from such lofty heights. Yet the idea of considering things from a distance was familiar to him.

"Who am I to involve myself with such grand plans?"

"The most modest among us is always a precious ally when he acts out of good will. Accomplish the small things before attempting the larger ones. Robert-Houdin considered you to be the most promising apprentice he had ever met. Before it is too late, we need your help to find—and hide—priceless treasures."

"When the occasion arises, I'll see what I can do."

"The occasion has arisen, Vincent, sooner than you and I would have hoped. Tonight, in a place you know well."

27

In the dead of night, the lights of Paris were extinguished, and the Eiffel Tower was barely visible in the mantle of darkness that covered the capital. Surrounded by scaffolding, the unfinished church of Sacré-Cœur resembled a slumbering monster that would burst through its stony carapace upon waking. Cats kept watch on the parvis, seated loftily on the waiting limestone blocks, like sphinxes.

Compared to that massive heap, Montmartre's historic church was but a shadow of its former self. The recently erected calvary cross seemed powerless to protect it. From their stone perch, Christ and his two companions in crucifixion, frozen in their torment, rose like frail sentinels before the burgeoning basilica.

Saint-Pierre de Montmartre church bore the scars of all the offenses it had endured. The last vestige of the former royal abbey that once occupied the entire hillside, it was pillaged and profaned during the Revolution, converted into a temple of reason, then used as a base for the telegraph before being occupied by Russian troops in 1814, then finally turned into a storage depot and barracks before being abandoned. Although Mass was held there from time to time, rain fell on its sagging roof, and its fissured walls, overrun by vegetation, remained standing only with the help of buttressing struts. Its demolition now seemed inevitable.

Climbing the slope behind the building where excavations had been carried out, Vincent wove his way through the small cemetery bordering the church's north wall.

As he rounded a burial vault, a shape appeared before him. The man, wearing a fedora and a long leather coachman's coat, asked in a low voice, "Password?"

"I have a meeting with Charles."

"Password?" he repeated tersely, pulling a blade from inside his mantle.

Vincent stepped back. "Easy friend, he's expecting me. He gave me his damned password, true, but now..."

He concentrated as hard as he could. The man was already moving toward him. At the very last moment, Vincent blurted out, "August 15. The password is August 15."

The man sheathed his weapon and motioned for Vincent to follow him.

Vincent made out several other guards standing watch around the building. They all wore coachman's attire, which was a surprising choice for the circumstances. Vincent's escort invited him to enter the church through the partially collapsed wall of the sacristy.

Inside, several lamps illuminated three men whose elongated shadows stretched over the pitiful walls. They were busy dismantling a bit of masonry in the back of the choir. Vincent recognized Charles's figure standing near them. Stepping over debris that had long since fallen from the ceiling, he walked straight toward the man.

"What are these men doing, Charles? They are desecrating this place. Is that how you protect the past?"

"There can be no sentiments in action, Vincent. Sometimes we must cut away the skin to save the heart that beats beneath. We are obligated to take urgent action; the quarrymen have already begun pillaging the earth below."

He indicated an area of the nave that had been trampled as though a cavalry had stampeded through it.

"They're stealing the flagstones?"

"With a preference for funeral tablets, and without bothering to see if they mark a burial site, or if they were simply used as material."

He pointed to a tombstone set tightly in the choir floor.

"As a precaution, we're going to move the tombstone belonging to the founder of the former abbey, Adelaide of Maurienne. These thieves would not even respect a queen of France."

Vincent was outraged. "We have to tell the authorities!"

"The authorities couldn't care less about a crumbling old church and a forgotten queen. However, we can count on these criminals coming back to help themselves. They'll sell their loot to superstitious fools who will use them to decorate their sinister curiosity cabinets of the occult. It matters little to them whether the demolition notice is signed or not."

"Did you ask me to come for this tomb?"

"No, even though it would merit as much. Something even more important awaits. Somewhere around us is buried a coffer that must in no event fall into the hands of these pillagers."

Vincent looked at the devastation around him. The last time he was here, he had still been a child, accompanied by his mother, for a mass paid in his father's honor. Few people had attended.

Charles motioned him closer. "This has been a sacred site since Antiquity. This is where the cult of Saint Denis was formed, the saint to which the church was originally dedicated and the first bishop of Paris. Recent excavations revealed the existence of a vast Merovingian necropolis dating most likely from the sixth century. The church has been cited as such since 1096, almost eight hundred years ago. Few are aware of it, but it was here in this church—when it was still the sanctuary of the royal abbey—that on August 15, 1534, Ignatius of Loyola, Francis Xavier, and Peter Faber, and six of their companions, laid the foundation for the Society of Jesus."

"The Jesuit Order?"

"The very same. This is where the vow came into being and the founding act was accomplished. Almost a century later, in July 1611, workers—while drilling in the foundations behind the radiating chapel—unearthed a buried crypt that had been carved into the raw gypsum. They discovered a rudimentary altar, decorated with an engraved Latin cross. The walls bore traces of inscriptions but the fragile material had not been protected from humidity. With none of it decipherable, the site was soon considered to be the refuge of the first Christians, when Paris was still Lutetia, and it became a pilgrimage site."

Inviting Vincent to follow him, Charles crossed the passage that the workers had finally succeeded in opening and descended to the site of the former crypt.

"In one of his messages written during his distant wanderings, Ignatius of Loyola mentions a coffer 'of the utmost importance' that he intends to send to one of his brothers from the Holy Land. He asks him to hide it in the symbolic birthplace of their order. No information on its contents is provided. However, he recommends burying it in the 'hidden crypt.' We concluded that this small room, unearthed quite accidentally long after, was already known to him and his companions. We managed to trace the response he received several months later, confirming that his request had been fulfilled. That's how we know that whatever Loyola sent is hidden here somewhere."

Vincent examined the floor of the crypt. It was made of large flagstones of varying dimensions. Some, taken from graves, bore carved inscriptions.

Charles placed an encouraging hand on his shoulder. "Here we are, my friend. This is where I need your talent."

"Do you have any idea how big the coffer is?"

"None.

"Since you are also unaware of its contents, why the hurry to unearth it?"

"The identity of the sender alone is more than enough to urge us to bring it to safety. At the time it was buried, the Jesuits would have believed that the hiding place was secure, being situated as it was in a sacred space considered eternal. However, today even the sacred is being challenged and the site is dangerously compromised."

Vincent examined the area.

"Can your men probe the soil?"

"Of course, but that takes more time than we have. The sun will rise in a few hours and no one can know about our search. Only your experience will enable us to find what is hidden before it is too late."

"Bring me more light and move back."

28

Vincent had been pacing the small crypt for over an hour. Holding a lantern in one hand and his knife in the other, he walked across it, then crisscrossed the floor in every direction, muttering to himself. He even scoured it on all fours, closely examining every stone in the floor. He squatted in the back to give himself time to reflect and continued making observations. He asked himself what Begel and Robert-Houdin would have done.

Overcome by excitement, he had asked Charles's men to move one of the slabs and dig underneath, but nothing came of it. Charles and his workers had been sitting at the edge of the entrance, watching him, ever since. He paced back and forth, stopped, turned around, and came up against the altar as well as the rough walls.

"Far be it from me to send you into a panic, Vincent," said Adinson gently, "but the day will soon be upon us."

"Your 'coachmen' are protecting us, aren't they?"

"From potential attacks, of course, but not from the curiosity of residents and the publicity they could bring us."

Vincent nodded without losing his focus and retraced his steps once more, thinking out loud. "So many possibilities in such a small space. Let's be pragmatic: the stone concealing the coffer is sure to have characteristics that assure its identification. That would be essential in order for the Jesuits to be able to find it again."

Charles acquiesced silently to avoid disrupting Vincent's thought process.

"Each of the slabs—there are 278—can be distinguished according to four parameters: shape, the quality of the stone, position in the paving arrangement, and what may be carved on it," Vincent continued.

He spun around and added, "After meticulous examination, I chose to rule out differentiation by shape and stone quality; too many of the slabs look alike, and those criteria are not selective enough. That leaves position and the inscriptions."

Vincent stood in a corner of the crypt and spread his arms wide. "To efficiently define a position, one must be able to rely on an indisputable reference point. A corner of the altar, a direction indicated by the cross or intangible architectural elements that would allow for a combination of stable coordinates such as abscissa and ordinate."

"The walls are irregular, the altar itself doesn't seem level. I don't really see any reliable reference points," remarked Charles.

"I came to the same conclusion," Vincent assented.

Just then one of the coachmen entered the crypt and walked toward Charles. He murmured something in the man's ear. Charles gave a brief reply and the man hurried out.

"Is there a problem?" asked Vincent.

"Nothing more than what we already know. Time is running out. Stay focused. You were saying that the position of the stones was probably not the best solution."

"Exactly. That leaves the carvings, probably our most promising hypothesis. They are all different and scattered across the floor. But that still presents more than a hundred possibilities."

Vincent took a deep breath. "Moving all of them to search below would be a gargantuan task that time does not permit us."

He took a few steps and bent to look at one of the stones. "Most of the stones with legible inscriptions are from tombs dating between the late fourteenth and early sixteenth centuries, entirely in keeping with the assumed date of burial."

"Indeed."

"The oldest are no longer legible because of wear, imprecisely carved characters. To save time, I chose to ignore them to concentrate on the most probable. But the probable is not the possible. Now that I have finished analyzing those that I could read, and none seem to contain any coded sign or reference, I wonder if perhaps I missed something."

Still caught up in his thoughts, he pointed to the white marble stone that he had asked the men to move earlier. "This one caught my attention because the name of the deceased is illegible while, paradoxically, both the inscription above it and the date are legible."

"Yet there was nothing under it."

"Much to my regret."

He continued his thorough examination of the carvings. "I imagine the clue indicating the correct location will be relatively obvious, supposing we know what we're looking for."

"What makes you believe that?"

"The room itself was secret. One would have to find the crypt before reaching the stone. Therefore, there was no reason to further complicate its concealment to the same extent necessary if it were in a public space."

Vincent suddenly stopped on a very worn stone, among the oldest, carved with a single roman numeral. He knelt down and brushed the tip of his finger over it.

"This inscription appears to be much older than most of the others, enough to be out of the running, but..." An idea had just crossed Vincent's mind: the Jesuits could very well have called on the services of someone like Eustasio, capable of aging material well enough to deceive any observer.

He ran his finger along the depressions to feel what was engraved there: "S J M D X X X I V."

He stood up.

"If we look at the last seven letters, they could correspond to a date."

"And the first two?"

"A code. SJ. Perhaps Societas Jesu, the original name of the Society of Jesus."

"Why not?"

"Followed by the year 1534. Wasn't that the year Loyola and his companions decided to create the order?"

Charles confirmed. "August 15."

Outside, a mighty horn sounded. Charles and his men sprung to attention.

"Don't worry," Vincent reassured them. "That's the signal to announce the start of the work day at Sacré-Cœur."

He pointed to the stone on which he knelt. "Please, gentlemen, help me lift this slab. If my reasoning is sound, this will be the last one we move."

Armed with a crowbar, and not without difficulty, the three men removed the stone and probed the dry earth with fine metal rods. Charles rolled up his sleeves and helped them clear away the soil as they went along. Their work paled in comparison to what was taking place just a few dozen yards away, but it quickly bore results.

"I've hit something," said one of the workers as he removed his probe.

They all set to work clearing away the dusty soil. Finally Vincent freed a rectangular form the size of a letter box that was enveloped in several layers of thick fabric. The first few layers, dried brittle by time, fell away in shreds, but the remaining fabric was intact. From it Vincent pulled a dark wooden case, which he handled with extreme care. He blew on it to remove the last remaining fibers.

The cover bore three letters, "IHS," under a curved line and above a stylized fleur-de-lis; the image was encircled by a sun—the first symbol of the Society of Jesus.

Released from its shroud, the centuries-old wood still gave off a scent that Vincent recognized immediately. "Juniper," he declared, breathing it in.

Charles watched him. Vincent looked up and caught his gaze. With an easy gesture, he handed Charles their discovery. "Here."

"Wouldn't you like to know what it contains?"

"That's not my mission. 'Accomplish the small things before attempting the larger ones.'"

Charles smiled. The first rays of dawn began to illuminate the nave through the gaping roof.

29

Breathless from climbing the stairs with his friend in his arms, Konrad laid Eustasio on the bed that had been prepared for him. Freshly washed sheets and newly stuffed pillows greeted the Italian, who groaned in pain as his friend released him. Gabrielle helped him get settled. The window had been shaded to avoid tiring his eyes. Each detail had been carefully thought out for his comfort.

"You have the best room in the house," whispered Pierre. "It's not as lavish as your countess's rooms, but we're all at your service. All you have to do is ask and we'll serve you!"

Eustasio didn't have the strength to smile. The return journey had tired him more than he had imagined it would. The team stood around his bed. He tried to utter a few words. "Thank you, my friends, I'm happy to see you again. I feel like I've come home after years of being away."

He drew his hand to his side. His wound had reopened, probably from being jostled by so much movement. Blood seeped through the white bandages, staining them red. Gabrielle shivered at the sight.

"Don't worry, Eustasio," said Konrad reassuringly. "I wrapped so many bandages when I was an apprentice in the sawmills that I can handle yours—no problem."

He made sure that Eustasio was comfortably settled and began to uncover the cut. His movements were as precise and gentle as if he were working with a particularly fragile piece of wood. Vincent handed him the gauze. In the silent room, everyone observed as Konrad went to work and the wounded man gritted his teeth.

Henri, usually so curious about his elders' activities, seemed uneasy and hung back. Vincent thought he seemed tense; he couldn't catch his eye. When the wound was uncovered, the boy turned away.

"I'm going to get hot water from the kitchen," murmured Gabrielle as she left the room.

Pierre nodded his approval and placed eau de vie, camphor vinegar, and cotton on the nightstand. Konrad removed the last layer of bandage. Of the many wounds covering Eustasio's naked chest, one in particular was worrying.

"That's some gash!" said Pierre with a whistle.

"Those *Mistkerlen* really wanted to do you in," seethed Konrad between his teeth. "They cut you up all over."

With a change of tone he winked at the wounded man and added, "Look on the bright side: they say women love scars."

"I could have done without," groaned the Italian. "The wounds, not women!"

The German smiled. He poured a bit of eau de vie on a piece of gauze and set about disinfecting the open wound. Henri looked away again. Vincent noticed and murmured to him, "If you want to become a doctor, you'll have to toughen up. Watch Konrad and learn. You can help him."

The Nail didn't answer. He remained unusually silent and distant. Vincent chalked it up to the sight of blood, but maybe there was something else. However, he didn't have time to dwell on it; the alcohol Konrad patted on the wound made Eustasio groan, and Vincent returned his attention to his suffering companion.

Gabrielle's hurried steps in the hall signaled her return. She entered, wringing out the cloth soaking in her basin of hot water and sat down on the edge of the bed.

Trying not to press too hard, she cleaned away the bloodstains on the injured man's chest. Her fingertips brushed Eustasio's skin several times. She tried to avoid meeting his gaze so he wouldn't notice her embarrassment at being in the presence of a half-naked man.

The Italian let her continue and spoke to his companions. "Do you have any information about my attackers?"

"Not yet," said Vincent.

"Has anything been attempted against any of you?"

Henri surprised everyone by responding first. "Suspicious stuff, but nothing for certain."

"Now we avoid going out alone," explained Pierre.

Henri remarked in a strange voice, "Some of us take the risk anyway." The Nail stared strangely at Vincent, who chose not to engage.

"Work is calm at the moment," he said. "That's a bit of luck."

Eustasio reached out a hand for the glass of water on his bedside table. Gabrielle moved to help him.

"Thank you," he sighed after taking several sips. "I'm thirsty all the time. I could eat a little something, too. As generous as the countess is, I missed your cooking."

The young woman lowered her eyes.

"I'll go down and get you something to eat," said Henri, scrambling to the hallway, where Vincent caught him.

"Is there a problem, Henri? Is something bothering you?"

"Nothing at all," he growled stubbornly.

The boy's reaction seemed overblown, but considering the circumstances, Vincent had to be content with this response. "You would tell me if something was wrong, wouldn't you?"

"Of course."

No doubt it was his youth that prevented Henri from being a good liar. This time Vincent was certain: something odd was going on.

Cutting their conversation short, the boy bounded down the stairs and disappeared.

30

Every time Konrad placed an order with Marcel Flaneul, the man was happy to celebrate the sale by offering him a drink at the bistro adjoining his business. Few of his clients purchased such rare and expensive wood varieties, and paid cash for them, too. These days, Flaneul and Fils sold mostly shoring and timber for scaffolding. Construction projects were booming. Concrete was in fashion with dozens of tons being poured each day, so wood casings were also an excellent prospect. The buildings popping up like mushrooms were a boon for sales of ordinary wood, but the cabinetry market was growing increasingly marginal. The taste for beauty was being replaced by a race for volume at a reasonable price. True specialists were harder to come by, but Konrad was definitely one of them. That was clear by the way he evaluated the lots he was presented.

Inviting him to enter the crowded café, Flaneul said, "Although I've sold you quite a lot of precious wood, I've never seen a single one of the pieces you've made."

"You know how it is: as soon as they're finished, off they go."

"If photographs weren't so expensive and hard to make, you could keep images of them. One of my customers is a decorator and he does just that. He earns his living well enough to have pictures taken of all his creations. That way he can demonstrate his skills without bothering his former clients."

"That's not a bad idea."

The room was steeped in the atmosphere of Paris's outlying neighborhoods. People spoke loudly and drank hard. There were no bowlers here and even fewer top hats; instead there was a swarm of caps and scarves wrapped around necks. It wasn't hard to guess the occupations of the men raising their glasses. Each trade was easily recognized by the clothes they wore: masons in plastering jackets, and laborers in singlets and thick gloves. The plumbers who worked above ground were the cleanest. They could almost have passed for shopworkers, if their tools hadn't been hanging like garlands from their belts. However, the underground plumbers and cesspit drainers never came in because they smelled so bad. They drank separately, together, often outside and in any weather.

Konrad and Flaneul made their way to the bar. The wood dealer called out, "Maurice, two *vin cuits*!"

Neither man noticed the stranger who entered immediately after them, and who had been following Konrad since he left the center of Paris. The individual greeted the room like anyone else and headed to the bar as well. Two roofers entered behind him, followed by a coachman.

Maurice poured two glasses and plunked them roughly on the zinc counter. Flaneul and the German were entirely absorbed in their conversation. They agreed on the fact that no one worked like they used to and that it was probably the end of an era.

Taking advantage of their inattention, the man trailing Konrad discreetly added several drops of a transparent liquid to the German's glass. Having accomplished his mission in the blink of an eye, the stranger backed away and left several seconds later without attracting any notice.

Flaneul continued his train of thought. "You have to constantly adapt. My son wants me to venture into machine sales. He says that in addition to providing wood, we could equip our clients with tools."

"The idea is bold, but it merits thought. In the meantime: to business!"

The instant the carpenter raised his glass to his lips, he received a rough push. The impact was so strong he spilled his wine.

He groaned: his shirt was stained. He turned around and found himself face to face with the coachman who had collided with him.

"Excuse me, friend! I tripped. I'm so sorry. Let me buy you another. Boss, the same thing for the gentleman. It's on me!"

Konrad peered at the man who had run into him. He wore a long dark leather jacket with gilded buttons that covered him from neck to feet. A small gray feather was tucked into the braid of his hat. The carpenter was surprised: given the man's small stature, he must have completely lost his balance to jostle Konrad to that point.

The German noticed another detail that Vincent had told him never to ignore: his hands. They always have more to say than any title or suit: they bear the unmistakable trace of their owner's occupation. The coachman's were well cared for. The skin was clean, with neither callous nor crack. Those were not hands that tugged on leather reins in summer and winter.

But the carpenter didn't have time to linger, for Flaneul invited him to raise his glass anew. Konrad did so willingly. The wine was excellent. He was in great form and had already forgotten the incident.

Things had come very close to ending differently.

31

Once he finally stepped outside, Vincent inhaled deeply, filling his lungs with fresh air. He wanted to dispel the oppressive weight he was feeling. After hours spent in lamplight, he squinted in the bright morning sun. It was later than he thought.

An ice block delivery driver grazed him with his cart. On the corner, a flower seller was offering bouquets of violets to passersby. She alternated between just two sales pitches: to men she swore that her bouquets would please their beloved; women, she assured the flowers would showcase their dazzling beauty. Vincent felt separate from the bustle around him.

The night he had just spent trying to solve the secret of Alfred Minguier's hidden passage had left him exhausted, especially since, once again, he'd discovered nothing, not the slightest clue. The mystery of the wall remained intact, to the great displeasure of the industrialist, who was losing his patience. As the hours passed, and after enduring several increasingly discourteous remarks, Vincent had been obligated to remind Minguier that his investigations weren't costing anything; he could, if he was not satisfied, ask Vincent to abandon his search. The man had relented. It wasn't so much Minguier's attitude that troubled Vincent as the fact that he still hadn't figured anything out, which he had expected of himself.

He strolled randomly in the direction of Rue Saint-Martin. He avoided those who were carving their path with determination. Usually he counted himself among them, but not this morning. Vincent didn't want to go home; the few projects underway were not urgent, and he was reluctant to confront the questions that Pierre was sure to ask him after another night spent away from the house.

A strange idea suddenly occurred to him, the only one that seemed clear enough to constitute a goal: he would return to see the monster. The detour wouldn't take him long. Vincent set out for his destination with renewed motivation.

On the way, he took careful note of what was going on around him; postures, exchanges, gestures. He was attentive to the interactions between people and curious about their relationships. It was his nature to constantly draw information from everything around him: each action, each movement—from the most innocuous to the most spectacular—bore the trace of what had motivated it. A merchant and his client, a mother and her child, a police officer and a beggar, a pair of laborers, a couple of lovers: Vincent tried to decipher them all, like secret passages that lead to the truth of human beings. There are those who act out of duty, kindness, profit, desire. The women and men who populated these streets were all driven by one of those compulsions. They might appear to be impelled by several, but in reality, only one motivation dominated their actions. From his observations, Vincent sketched a very personal cartography of what life might be like among others.

His analysis of human relations had only deepened since he began taking an interest in it; but while feelings seemed unchanging and universal, the context in which they arose and the way in which the present enabled them to be expressed were changing—from where people lived or worked to what businesses were selling or which means of transportation were available. The details he gleaned in passing confirmed this. Evolving customs revealed what was changing at the core. Vincent was not very old, but he still remembered a time when Paris was different. He didn't go into shops, he never went dancing, and he still hadn't visited the World's Fair. He was not attracted to these new entertainments, as if none of the novelty this world had to offer concerned him.

As he turned the corner, he could see from a distance that a line had already formed beneath the placard announcing Quasimodo. Surprised to see such a turnout, Vincent joined the waiting crowd. As he listened to the conversations around him, he noticed that many people were there for the first time, determined to make a little money fast and easily—hoping to profit.

The intent gaze of the man behind the counter where Vincent laid down his twenty sous told him that he had been recognized. He then waited patiently in the corridor and showed no reaction, even when the other contenders left, beside themselves with fright. He had worked out the ruse. First, you were ushered into an increasingly dark space that made you uneasy. Then the corridor grew narrower to exacerbate the feeling of confinement. The ambiance became more stifling, fed by the terror of those fleeing the site as quickly as possible. By the time it was your turn, your imagination was white hot. The sudden discovery of the "monster" crystallized everything that the mind might have produced and left even the braggarts unnerved.

Vincent had overcome all that. He was not interested in the approach. As usual, he wanted to get to the heart of things.

When he finally entered the vestibule, he had just one thing in mind. He sat on the stool and, without even realizing it, rubbed his hands together. The curtain parted. There was the face. In the chaos of flesh, Vincent noticed the ugly trace of a blow on what appeared to be the cheek.

Vincent looked straight into the eyes of the poor devil, who growled weakly. He whispered, "I have to talk to you, I want—"

A large thug immediately appeared between two curtains. "Never speak to the monster!"

He brandished a menacing fist. "You've already been and you've already won. Good for you. Now get out of here, and I suggest you never come back."

"I just wanted—"

The man didn't let him finish his sentence. He grabbed him by the collar and shook him, causing Vincent to fall off the stool.

"Do you understand what I just said?" he repeated. "Get out of here, and I better never see you again—or else!"

As he got to his feet, Vincent caught a final glimpse of the monster's eyes. He thought he discerned a tear.

32

"It's just a text? Some report notes?" Vincent was perplexed.

"Five sheets," said Adinson. "Written by Ignatius of Loyola himself."

"What does it say?"

"He records a testimony received in confession while he was staying near Jerusalem. The coffer also contained a key, a strange one, and your expertise will no doubt be useful in determining what it might open."

"I thought confessions were confidential."

"The remarks were too strange even for a man of his stature to bear alone. So he chose to write them down on paper and entrust them to the secret of his order, knowing that his message would not be read during his lifetime."

"If you hadn't looked for the coffer, his missive might have remained buried until the end of time."

"Fate decided otherwise, Vincent. Or the Clockmaker. The fact remains that his letter has particular resonance today. He alludes to 'troubled days when those who claim to lead the world will be convinced they master its mysteries.' He speaks of humanity's new powers. Don't you find that strangely relevant?"

"It is surprising. Is the key connected to his letter?"

"I believe so. But a more precise study of the text is necessary to be certain, for several passages—including references to locations that no longer exist—are proving problematic."

"Will you keep me informed?"

"You, like me, are tied to this discovery, and I'm counting on your help to reach a complete resolution. I trust in you, Vincent."

"Is it proper that I be made aware of a confidential confession?"

"It's more than three centuries old. We can let bygones be bygones, even if the information passed on by the dying knight still retains its importance."

"A knight?"

"A descendant of the Knights Templar. As he himself was childless, the secret passed on by his ancestors would have died with him, but he couldn't let that happen at any price. What he knew must not fall into oblivion. That's why, before he departed, he confided in Loyola, a man he must have deemed worthy of receiving it. The knight mentions a sanctuary, formerly located right here, in the capital, to house relics brought back from crusades and various expeditions."

"Does he indicate a specific place? A church?"

"No. It's much stranger than that. He mentions an underground temple, a secret site buried in the depths of the city."

"Places of worship do exist underground; some have been found in the catacombs."

"None are as sacred as the one he describes. They're often relatively recent, and nothing has been discovered there that could have been brought back from the Holy Land or elsewhere."

"Does he explain what he means by 'relics'?"

"Not really."

"Does he give any indication as to the location of this sanctuary?"

"He only briefly describes a mysterious 'labyrinth' that allows access."

"Do you think such a place could exist? Could it not be the ramblings of a dying man lost in the tales of his ancestors that Loyola transcribed in good faith?"

"I wondered that myself. But there's a remarkable coherence to the whole story."

Vincent thought for a moment. "Why didn't Ignatius of Loyola search for the site?"

"He didn't have time to. He never came back, and he was the only one to know what the confession contained."

"Until we found it."

"If such a sanctuary had been found, we would know about it. If you agree, I would like to involve you in the search for it."

"With pleasure."

Charles suddenly seemed embarrassed. "Before we go any further, Vincent, I must inform you of an essential fact."

"Are you going to shatter my convictions again? Try to go easy on me, now—I'm still trying to get my bearings."

Charles smiled briefly but remained serious. "Pardon me, Vincent, but my goal is not to sow confusion in your mind. Like you, I am forced to bend to the urgency that requires me to share this information with you."

"What is it this time?"

"One of your friends—he escaped an attack far more insidious than a stabbing."

Vincent's heart began to race. "Tell me!"

"Someone tried to poison your carpenter while he was having a drink with one of your suppliers. He owes his life only to the intervention of one of my coachmen who was following him."

Vincent was stunned. Questions raced through his mind. "Why didn't he tell me? And why was your coachman following him?"

"Your friend was unaware that anything was amiss. Feigning a stumble, the coachman knocked over his glass before he could ingest the poison. He was following him to protect him. This is how our deal works: you assist me in my research and, in return, I do everything in my power to protect your loved ones. That's what we agreed to. You began fulfilling your part of the contract by discovering the coffer, and I am fulfilling mine."

A flash of pain seared through Vincent's head again. His jaw tightened; he growled between clenched teeth, "After Eustasio, they tried to kill Konrad."

"Even though we were unable to analyze the poison, we are certain of it."

"Good Lord."

"I understand that you are shocked, but I warned you: you've been identified, as well as your companions. We know neither by whom nor to what end, but there can no longer be any doubt.

The party that has entered the game wields powers that are not to be taken lightly. I know not what lies behind these attacks, but I have a suspicion that they are closely tied to the sacred subjects that led me to contact you. Perhaps they too are tracking down spiritual treasures, but one thing is for certain: they are doing it neither with the same intentions, nor with the same methods. They have invited themselves to our quest but respect no rule. They do not share our spirit. You must be wary of everyone."

"I'm accustomed to that." Vincent thought quickly, then announced, "Since we're sharing secrets, I have to tell you something: Eustasio isn't dead."

"What are you saying?"

"That he was only wounded."

Adinson pondered his words gloomily. Then he said, "You lied to me."

"No. I let you believe it. There's a difference. You're not the only one who needed to know if trust was possible. You just advised me yourself to be wary of everyone."

Charles took a moment to absorb these words. "I understand," he said at last. "How is he?"

"Better. His life is no longer in danger."

"So you are mourning no one."

"Not recently, in any case," said Vincent ironically. He contemplated the situation and sighed. "If you hadn't assigned one of your guardians to Konrad, and if Eustasio hadn't been lucky, I would have already lost my team without even knowing whom I'm supposed to be fighting against."

"I'm afraid it's only the beginning."

Vincent looked at him, chagrined. "I don't know what to do, Charles. I'm losing control of my life. I feel like I'm drowning. I'm afraid of dragging my loved ones down with me. Everything I thought I'd built is collapsing. What I thought I knew no longer does me any good. I am completely lost."

"I've been in your shoes, Vincent. Everyone confronts this uncertainty one day. It is a contemptible phase that puts us to the test—just before we decide what we really want to do with our lives."

33

Excited and bursting with curiosity, the visitors hurried from one pavilion to the next, tracing disorderly trajectories that formed a milling chaos. It was an assorted multitude in which social classes, languages, and ages mingled in a shared thirst for discovery. The sun had ushered out the parasols and ensured good fortune for the refreshment stalls. Lemonade and the licorice-flavored "coco" water flowed freely, but a new aniseed beverage was all the rage. To avoid fatigue, society ladies went about in wheeled chairs pushed by porters in livery. The music of fanfares and exotic orchestras drifted upwards to mingle in a fantastic cacophony.

Henri had been walking backward from the luminous fountain, incapable of tearing his eyes from the Eiffel Tower. "Henri, watch out. You're going to run into someone!" Pierre admonished him.

"Look at it, it's so beautiful! I really want to go up there."

"There are too many people for the moment. We'll go later. Be patient. And watch where you're going."

The boy did an about-face and discovered the central pavilion. It was the official site for ceremonies, where fiery speeches celebrating national pride and success were held. The majestic open-air hall was embellished with symbols of the French Republic, down to the smallest details of an excessively gilded decor.

Henri nevertheless found it less interesting than the splendid Galerie des Trente Mètres, a spectacular one-hundred-foot-wide structure looming behind it. Although it wasn't his ultimate destination, the Nail was impressed by its proportions and its central aisle, which led to specialized sections on both sides.

The best of what the factories had to offer was assembled here, in a series of wings overflowing with all manner of treasures. Goldsmithery, tableware, weaving, and furniture was on display. For the occasion, each trade had designed a monumental door presenting its talents in specially crafted masterpieces. Gabrielle stood astounded before the entrance to the crystal glassworks area: a theater curtain made entirely of precious stones. Pierre stopped short in front of the clockmakers' area: an immense dial the public could walk across, as if they had been reduced to the size of insects visiting a pendulum with oversized mechanisms. To see them so astonished, with Henri twirling around them, one might think they were a family.

As they visited demonstration after demonstration, none of them realized how far they had walked. Except for Henri, who was waiting for just one thing, the grandest, the most astonishing, the one the illustrated pamphlets in the press showered with superlatives: the Galerie des Machines!

When he had reached the end of the factory area, and the gallery's facade appeared before him, the boy froze and slowly raised his head in an attempt to take it all in at once. But that was impossible; it was so immense. The building could have contained an entire neighborhood, and it was tall enough to accommodate five-story houses. It was the largest covered structure ever built. The chimney stacks rising in the back gave it the appearance of a divine forge.

Eager to explore it, the boy began to run, to the amusement of Gabrielle and Pierre, who followed him at a more moderate pace, walking side by side.

As she explored the Fair, Gabrielle often had the impression she was walking in a setting out of a dream. She was living a fairy tale. There she was, propelled into a world where everything was novelty and abundance. It was also the first time the young woman had left the house since finding refuge there. The fresh air, the sun, people. She wasn't used to it anymore. Everything she experienced set off a whirlwind of emotions that left her breathless at times. Her last excursion had been a desperate attempt at escape. She had been hunted, threatened, and intended for a miserable fate. Today she was strolling along, accompanied by a handsome young man who took care of her, and wearing the most beautiful dress she had ever worn. Even though he didn't dare offer her his arm, Pierre gazed fondly at her.

No sooner had they passed through the monumental entrance to the gallery than the deafening roar of machines, amplified and augmented by the echo of the immense glass roof overhead, enveloped them. Pierre leaned toward the young woman and raised his voice to be heard.

"Is the noise too much for you?"

"I don't care! It's the most wonderful day of my life."

Henri ran left and right, reciting commentary from reviews about the Fair that he'd been wearing his eyes out reading for weeks.

"Look at these electric motors! They can lift a load greater than what a hundred Percheron horses could. Their strength is even referred to as horsepower."

He was already off somewhere else. "A steam-powered electric turbine! I read that with just one of these, they'll soon be able to light an entire city. Light in every house at the turn of a button!"

He pointed to a railcar displayed for the curiosity of visitors. "Can we see the car? Pierre, please, it's free! We're allowed to go in even without a ticket! Come on, I've never taken the train."

The first-class railcar was presented by the Compagnie des Chemins de Fer de l'Ouest. It intended to offer voyagers as much comfort "as aristocrats in their sitting room."

Fortunately, the line leading to the footboard was not very long, and Henri was soon exploring the richly furnished compartments, equipped with padded velvet seats and with walls decorated in marquetry. He even visited a four-bed suite with a private "water-closet." What an extravagant luxury! Pierre had a hard time keeping an eye on the boy, since he was also paying rapt attention to Gabrielle.

As they exited the car, Henri didn't know which way to turn. He quickly spotted the stairs leading up to the giant moving footbridges overlooking the gallery and decided to head in that direction. The immense steel balconies moved sideways above the central section, offering a unique panorama of the machines they hovered over.

This time, Henri didn't give the couple a choice. He slipped between them, grabbed their hands and pulled them along. Gabrielle and Pierre followed him, laughing. Pierre thought to himself that perhaps one day soon he would have the courage to take the hand of the woman he found himself increasingly enamored with. Gabrielle seemed even more beautiful outside the humdrum context of the old boardinghouse.

As the trio climbed the steps, the gigantic scale of the gallery became fully apparent. Pierre looked for Minguier's chain-making machines, but they must have been further on.

With each back-and-forth motion of the moving bridge, passengers descended at one end while new visitors boarded at the other. Henri counted: they would likely have to wait two rotations before taking their turn. But for once, the wait didn't bother the Nail. There was so much to observe that he had enough to keep himself occupied. As far as the eye could see, machines whirred, manufactured, rose, and produced before an audience stunned as much by the noise as by the technological feats before them. He even spotted the stand presenting automobiles, vehicles without horses capable of traveling up to ten miles in a single hour! An example was on display: it had two rear wheels and a single front wheel, and was designed by a German by the name of Benz. A large crowd had gathered around the high-priced marvels, and Henri was eager to go admire them.

The trio finally was allowed to board the moving footbridge. Henri rushed to the metal guardrail to claim the best lookout spot. The couple joined him in the space he had claimed by elbowing his way in.

Once the bridge was full and the guardrails closed, a man announced through a megaphone, "Stand clear for departure!"

The enormous structure began to move on its rails. They could feel the hefty steel mass moving under their feet. With a slowness that rendered the phenomenon even more impressive, the bridge began its aerial journey across the gallery.

Henri looked above and below. He was captivated by everything around him, both the building and everything it contained. He flew over machines as large as omnibuses; he could see their innards. He tried to show Pierre what interested him the most, but his interests kept changing, and he didn't even have time to finish his sentences. Other wonders were already parading before his eyes—printing presses, mechanical cyclones intended to grind ore, machines to cut or shape sheet metal, electric elevators. Each one triggered new excitement. Pierre spent more time watching Henri—who leaned much too far over the security rails—than enjoying the journey.

Gabrielle was also watching in wonder. Luckily she wasn't afraid of heights. However, she was wary of the creaks and vibrations of the metal floor, which worried her a little.

Suddenly Pierre felt himself literally being lifted. Was this a new sensation brought on by the revolutionary machine? Drunk on the new visions he had accumulated over the day, he didn't immediately realize what was happening to him.

Someone had grabbed hold of him. In an instant, he found himself above the metal handrail. He heard cries all around him. He struggled violently and tried to turn around. His body acted reflexively.

Pierre suddenly understood his situation: someone was throwing him over the edge, onto the furious machines below that would crush him to death.

34

The atmosphere in the kitchen was as heavy as the silence. Eustasio had resumed his place at the table. It was the first time he had come down from his room. He couldn't stay in bed after what had happened. He who drank so little had not refused the glass of plum spirits the team was sharing. There was nothing to celebrate, quite the contrary; but they all hoped for a little comfort.

Vincent was leaning against the closed chimney. Everyone turned their attention to Pierre, who was having his head tended to by Konrad.

"The gash is not deep," the carpenter reassured them. "Stitches aren't required; a bandage will suffice."

Gabrielle sighed in relief and laid her hand on Pierre's shoulder. She hadn't said a word since he had nearly lost his life. Tears rose from time to time, and she was powerless to stop them, so she turned away to dry them discreetly. Henri was seated closest to the survivor, as if he didn't want to let him out of his sight.

Konrad grabbed some gauze and a bandage.

"We'll have to buy more," he said. "At the rate we're going through them, soon there won't be any left."

Pierre said nothing. He remained prostrate, reliving the attack. He could not shake that feeling of flight, blurred by the movement of the bridge. As soon as he closed his eyes, he saw the gaping emptiness open before him, growing to swallow him up. He would never forget the moment when his disbelief brutally turned to panic before the thought of his impending death. It was a very close call;

a few instinctive movements and Henri's life-saving reaction. If Pierre hadn't managed to grab hold of the handrail, and if the Nail hadn't caught him, his poor body would have been torn to shreds by the enormous can-forming machine. He was obsessed with the sight of that specter, ready to devour him in the din of an inhuman clinking.

Eustasio tried to break his silence with a question. "Nobody managed to get anything out of your attacker before he died?"

Henri responded, "He wasn't in a state to say anything. Everything happened so quickly. The man was cornered. Sure to be captured, he preferred to throw himself over the edge."

"It wasn't panic that drove him to jump," interjected Gabrielle. "I was right next to him, I saw his eyes. He knew what he was doing. The arms outstretched to capture him prevented escape. When he turned toward the edge, he was strangely calm. He willingly chose to end his life. He fell right where he intended to drop." Her sentence went unfinished as she turned to the stove.

The German tried to lighten the mood. "What matters is that our Pierre is still alive and well. Here we are with two wounded men. This is no longer a boardinghouse, it's a hospice!"

Pierre turned to Henri. "If you hadn't grabbed my wrist as fast as you did, I would have died like the attacker. Thanks, kid. I didn't realize you were that strong."

Henri was filled with pride, but not enough to unravel the knot of tension tight in his chest since the attempted murder.

Eustasio shook his head. "Two deadly attacks in a matter of days."

Vincent turned around. "Probably three. Konrad, is it true that when you went to buy your wood in Montreuil, a man bumped into you, spilling the glass you were about to drink?"

"That's true," said the German in surprise. "In fact he bought me a new one right away." The carpenter frowned suddenly. "How could you know about that?"

"The man was dressed as a coach driver."

"Exactly. A long coat with gold buttons and a top hat. But how in the devil..."

"He saved your life," Vincent interjected. "The glass you were about to drink had just been poisoned. Three of you have now escaped death. To stabbing and a fall we can add poison. "

They all turned to look at their leader.

"Vincent, what's going on?" asked Eustasio.

"I would pay handsomely to know."

"You know things that we don't, so tell us!" insisted Konrad.

Vincent stepped closer to his companions and took a swig of alcohol to steel himself.

"A man warned me that we are at risk of becoming targets," he revealed.

Pierre replied at once. "Is it the man you meet without telling us about it?"

Vincent nodded his head and met his brother's gaze. "An older man, about whom I know almost nothing. But I believe he means well."

"Why would he warn us?"

"Because he needs us alive."

Pierre thought for a moment. "Did he explain why we're being targeted?"

"He thinks it has something to do with our profession and the secrets that we know."

"Why didn't you inform us?" replied his brother, annoyed.

"I found out about the danger after the attack on Eustasio, and I asked you to no longer travel alone. But I clearly underestimated the threat. I did not for a moment suspect that they would try to attack you in public, and in the middle of the day."

"Does this man know who the assassins are?" asked Henri.

"No. It's quite probable that he's also on the killers' list."

Silence settled over the room as they all pondered their own speculations.

A moment later, Gabrielle spoke up. "Do you think this house is still safe? They'll end up discovering the address, if they haven't already. Then they'll come..." She shivered. Pierre took her hand.

Vincent sighed and sat down with his friends. "Our safety is no longer guaranteed anywhere. I've been thinking about it constantly. We urgently need to increase the number of traps protecting the entrances. We might be forced to shelter in the workshop downstairs. It's the safest part of the house, and it will resist entry."

Konrad and Eustasio nodded in approval.

"If necessary, we can take turns keeping watch," suggested Henri.

Vincent acquiesced and added, "Limit your movements to strict necessity. When you're outside, consider yourselves in enemy territory. You'd best not consume food or drink anywhere where we usually do. Be unpredictable. Don't go where they could be waiting for us. Let's shuffle the cards. Change supply locations, hours of movement, and the routes you take. Never be alone and stay on your guard at all times."

The team approved of these recommendations.

"It would also be prudent to repatriate our nest egg. Because it's so far away, Henri has to take risks to keep watch over it. I don't want that anymore."

"Where will we put it?" asked the boy.

"I don't know yet. Your suggestions are welcome."

Vincent looked at Pierre. "I know you're in shock, but we also have to think about better protecting our project archives. Maybe we should distribute them across several hiding places. The strong cabinet is no longer sufficient. It's possible that the people targeting us are trying to get their hands on what we know."

His younger brother replied, "There's even a chance that the killers have orders from one of our former clients."

"Even so, out of loyalty to our clients who are not malignant, we have an even greater responsibly to protect their interests."

"So it's decided," said Henri. "From now on, no one goes out alone."

The Nail insisted on the words "no one," and fixed their leader with a look. Vincent could not contradict him, because he was right. But he already knew that was a rule he couldn't respect.

35

"Charles, do you realize they went after my own brother?"

The words thundered in the muted echo of the underground chapel. Adinson nodded in sympathy.

"I foresaw as much; they are capable of anything. However, I'm not certain they are aware of your family connection. To them, Pierre is just another member of the team. However, the brutality of the attack and the fact that it was carried out in public reveal just how urgently they want to strike. It is a safe bet they will not give up. Ironically, you have an advantage over them."

"By all the saints in heaven, what advantage? We know nothing about them. They attack whenever they want, however they want."

"Exactly! For this reason, they probably believe they successfully eliminated your Italian friend and the carpenter. Therein lies your opportunity. If your friends remain in hiding without being detected, they will no longer be targeted. They could then reappear at a convenient time."

Vincent imagined this possibility like a lifeboat for his sinking ship. "You're right!"

He began to think aloud. "Eustasio was left for dead, and he was brought home in secrecy. I don't think Konrad has left the house since his business in Montreuil. Indeed, there's a good chance they've both been taken for dead."

He frowned and reined in his enthusiasm. "Pierre's case is different. Hundreds of people were witness to his rescue and the violent demise of his attacker. The press is hungry for stories like that and probably reported on it."

"Let us appreciate what is working in our favor for a start. You have two men more than they believe, and as many aces in your sleeve."

"Why didn't those cowards come after me?"

"I don't know, but it troubles me."

"And yet," argued Vincent, "I often go out alone. I would be an easy target."

"I'm certain they've accounted for this parameter. Perhaps they've even discovered our acquaintance."

"So they suspect we're working together?"

"Whatever they think, they have no way of knowing who I really am."

Vincent grumbled, "If we only knew why they're attacking us. And in the middle of the Fair, no less! And here I thought a crowd guaranteed safety."

"So did I. But we're living in a time when limits are being obliterated. The worst among us no longer have any principle to hold them back. The only boundary is whatever is possible. From now on, let it be known: if something can be done, it will be done."

"Why didn't one of your coachmen protect my brother?"

"Because the one assigned to him lost him in the crowd. And your brother, the young lady, and the boy constantly changed direction. Their guardian angel had just entered the Galerie des Machines, hoping to catch up with them, when he was alerted by cries from the moving footbridge. At first he thought he had arrived too late, until he saw your brother hanging over the edge, clinging to your young protégé."

"Henri thinks the attacker jumped to his death to avoid capture."

"Quite likely," Adinson acquiesced.

"What kind of low-life is capable of killing himself to keep quiet? Who gives his life to protect something he knows?"

"I don't think an ordinary low-life would be capable of such a sacrifice. He likely wanted to protect much more than just information. His cause or the people for whom he gave his life are worth more in his eyes than his own existence. At least that gives us one thing in common."

"You would be willing to give your life?"

"I've already done so, Vincent. Since my burial, I no longer exist for myself."

Vincent remained thoughtful. "I'm impressed. I still haven't found an ideal I would sacrifice myself for without a second thought. I could only do so for a handful of people."

Charles's gaze drifted. "Long ago, I too once thought as much. I was like you. Then life tore from me those I cared for. One day, I found myself alone." He paused before continuing in a low voice. "With no one left to protect, I decided to make sure the unhappiness I had experienced would not befall others. I stepped into the darkness, so that the innocent may enjoy the light."

Vincent asked timidly, "Did you have a family?"

"A wife and a daughter; Éléonore and Sarah."

It was the first time that Vincent detected fragility in Adinson. The man seemed lost in memories so painful that Vincent avoided questioning him further.

Guessing his thoughts, Adinson raised his eyes toward Vincent. "You dare not ask what happened to them?"

"You don't have to talk about it, Charles."

"They both succumbed to illness, while I was traveling. Sadly commonplace. Poorly cared for, cheated by charlatans, no doubt. When I left, they were alive and affectionate; when I returned, they had departed this life. I have never forgiven myself for not being there to protect them. Deep down, a voice keeps telling me that they would probably still be alive if I had stayed with them."

"It does no good to torture yourself with guilt."

"I have overcome that feeling. Wherever they are now, they urge me to do everything I can in the name of what they, too, believed in—even for those I do not know."

Vincent suddenly saw in Charles a projection of himself in a future he feared. Would he also lose those he loved one day? Crushed by the same regrets, he would probably utter the same words. But would he still have the strength to remain standing? His mind raced, and some of his ideas frightened him.

Adinson pulled himself together; the fragility disappeared behind his mask of noble service. He regained his calm, at least in appearance, and said, "I'm going to assign more men to protect your loved ones."

"Thank you."

Adinson pulled a small velvet pouch from his jacket.

"Although the circumstances are not ideal, Vincent, I need your opinion now."

"About what?"

"Yet another mystery."

36

Charles opened the pouch and carefully removed a key as long as his index finger.

"This is the key that was in the coffer we unearthed," he explained. "The account recorded by Ignatius of Loyola mentions the existence of a secret underground site, and several times for that matter. The access is protected by a kind of maze that he calls 'the labyrinth'; it is impossible to escape it alive without knowing its secrets."

He handed the object to Vincent, who accepted it carefully.

"Does this key open the labyrinth?"

"Loyola mentions nothing about it," clarified Charles. "Although that would seem logical."

Vincent held the object at eye level and studied it carefully.

"It's a beautiful piece," he said, praising the key. "Remarkable workmanship."

At the tip of the shaft, the ring intended to be grasped to turn the key was shaped into a small solid disk the size of a thumb and finely engraved. The junction with the shaft was pierced through with a minuscule hole, and the key blade meant to activate the lock mechanism was split to resemble a cross pattée.

Vincent hefted it in his hand and said in surprise, "It's dense. It shines as though it was made of silver, but it isn't. It's probably solid, polished iron. Astonishing!" He tested the metal by scratching a nail against it.

"Despite the sophisticated craftsmanship, there is no precious ornamentation."

Charles acquiesced. "Those were my thoughts exactly when I discovered it. The humblest of metals, worked as carefully as possible. Usually pieces of this quality are gilded or decorated with jewels."

"Don't you find it odd that after centuries spent in a box, underground, it shows no sign of rust?" asked Vincent. "And yet it has no finishing coat."

"Perhaps it is protected in a way unknown to us."

"An unknown alloy? In any case, the smith concentrated his talents on engraving these interlaced symbols."

Vincent drew near a candelabrum and held the little key up to the light. "They're interwoven with extreme precision. The harmony of the ensemble in no way detracts from the individuality of each element. It is without doubt the work of a true artist."

He squinted to better discern the characters. "I can make out several different alphabets among the ornamentation."

"I noticed that as well."

"It appears the characters are from different languages: Latin, Hebrew, Arabic… even runes, what looks like a hieroglyph, and others that I've never seen. The engravings are so fine, I'd need a magnifying glass to make them out."

"Did you notice anything else?"

Vincent turned the key to look at it from all angles. A silvery flash of polished metal glinted. "What am I supposed to see?"

"Nothing, actually," responded Charles. "I was surprised to see that the key bears not the slightest scratch. It is perfectly smooth, down to the key blade, which is intended to carry out a mechanical action. It is as if it had never been used."

Vincent ran his finger along the edge and examined it closely.

"Exactly. Intriguing, indeed."

"You of all people know that any craftsman, especially one capable of this quality of work, would be sure to test it at least once in the lock it is intended to open."

"Correct. But as you say, the surface has in no way been altered."

"The account given by the descendant of the Templars mentions four entrances to the labyrinth. He likens them to the four elements of Creation."

"Fire, earth, air, and water?"

"Supposedly these access points are hidden somewhere in Paris."

"The association of mystical elements evokes the fundaments of ancient magic." He turned the key over again in the light of this new information, but its secrets remained intact.

"If the dangers of the labyrinth prove to be as formidable as the confession claims," murmured Adinson, "then we can't afford to make any mistakes."

37

Quite unexpectedly, the night turned out to be calm. Konrad's muffled snores resonated throughout the house. Vincent was methodically deactivating the traps on his way out the back door when a voice caught him by surprise.

"You're going out again?" Pierre emerged from the shadows.

"I have to meet Mr. Minguier."

"Alone? Despite the people out there who want to do us harm?"

"Don't worry, this will probably be the last time."

"Did you figure out how his wall works?"

"No."

Vincent hesitated before admitting, "I don't think I can. I'm going to tell him that I'm giving up. Besides, I don't like the way his behavior has changed. I'm growing increasingly wary of him. I can feel he isn't being honest with me."

Pierre looked relieved.

"You'd be better off heading upstairs to rest," Vincent advised him as he deactivated the final trap. "Have your headaches stopped at least?"

"It depends on the time of day. The worst is at night; I get migraines. I hear the constant clicking of that machine I almost fell into. It vibrates in me like the clacking mandibles of a giant insect waiting to devour me. It wakes me up at night."

"It will take time, but I'm sure it will pass. What about Gabrielle? She doesn't say much anymore."

"The poor thing. What happened troubles her even more than it does me."

"She was frightened for you. She saw what nearly happened, and the thought of losing you probably terrified her."

"It's not just that. For her, the day was the first day of a new life, a happy one. And that's what I wanted to give her. The attack was a reminder of the worst sort of violence, the kind she experienced before coming here."

"Take care of her; she's a good woman."

"I'm doing my best, even if it's not easy at the moment."

Vincent turned his collar up and prepared to leave. "You aren't going to tell me where you were this afternoon?" said Pierre.

"I can't. Forgive me."

"You met with that man who saved Konrad from being poisoned."

"Yes. It's in our best interest."

"Is he going to join our team?"

Vincent smiled. He had not considered things from that perspective. He nearly blurted out that he was more likely to be joining Charles's brotherhood, but it was too early to bring that up. "No, he won't be joining us."

"I feel like you trust him more than you do me. He seems to know everything."

"Don't be mistaken, Pierre. I am not and never will be closer to anyone than I am to you."

"I'm afraid, Vincent. When I thought I was done for, hanging over that machine about to grind me to bits, I thought of only one thing: I remembered the night you came home without our father."

He paused. "You were crying. You were choking. You couldn't even speak. That was the only time I've ever seen you cry. I understood immediately that something had just shattered, that our lives would never be the same. I don't know if you remember this, but I didn't run to our mother's arms. No. I clung to you like a lifeboat, like the handrail of that moving bridge. To survive. That night, I learned what it means to lose someone. You haven't stopped carrying me since, as if I were still clinging to you. I'm only now beginning to understand the effort that must have cost you all these years. Believe it or not, these attacks aren't what frighten me the most, nor is it the idea of being killed. I'm terrified because I see you changing and, for the first time, I don't understand you."

He was quiet a moment before blurting out, "I don't want to lose you."

Vincent pulled Pierre close and embraced him. "I'm afraid too," he murmured. "I'm as shaken as you are. But I'm not changing. An insidious war is playing out. I don't understand the rules or what's at stake, but we're involved, whether we like it or not. We have everything to lose. I cannot run away. I can see no way out, so I'm trying to stay the course in a raging storm. I swear, I'm doing everything I can so that nothing changes."

Pierre freed himself and took his brother's face in his hands. His eyes glistened with tears. "Promise you won't ever leave?"

"I will always be with you."

38

Vincent knocked at the door of Minguier's house. A gust of unseasonably cool wind blew down the deserted street, chilling his face and hands. He shivered, suddenly gripped by doubt. Without going so far as to call it a premonition, he felt vaguely apprehensive.

He cast a glance around, but nothing disturbed the calm night. He heard the sound of a lock opening. The industrialist opened the door and ushered him in with his usual haste.

"Good evening, Vincent. Thank you for being on time."

"Good evening, sir."

Without further discussion, the two men crossed the darkened house to the cellar stairs. Vincent followed Minguier, whose round silhouette stood out against the light of his lantern. He was already anticipating the right moment to announce his decision.

Once in the basement, Vincent noticed that the oil lamps were already set up and lit.

"Have you been able to consider other leads?" asked Minguier.

"Several, sir. But I don't wish to arouse false hope: none of them seems promising."

The man was annoyed. "That is vexing."

Vincent wondered whether to announce then and there his intention to withdraw his services but ultimately he deemed it more appropriate to perform a final investigation first.

"Where would you like to look today?" continued the industrialist.

"As close as possible to the passage."

The two men reached the last room, where the thick-barred grate was open and the lighting in place. Minguier stopped on the threshold and let his visitor enter alone. "We have reached a dead end, my friend," he said.

"We've been looking at one since the beginning, sir. In fact, you recruited me to get past it."

"Indeed. However, the results are lacking."

Vincent rummaged around in the jumble as a matter of principle, but without any real hope. He put up a front by continuing to busy himself and avoid having to face his client—for the first time in so many years of doing this job, he was about to give up on a mission.

"You're right, Mr. Minguier. I've made no progress whatsoever. I'm not pleased to admit it, but I'm probably not up to the task."

His client didn't respond or move in the slightest. Vincent was relieved. Perhaps that meant he understood his reasoning and would accept his resignation.

He heard a creak and, for a moment, Vincent thought he had activated some mechanism, but it was coming from somewhere else. As he stood up, he saw Minguier closing the grate: he was going to lock Vincent in.

Vincent sprang over the planks of wood and rushed to the grate. "What are you doing?"

The clanging of the lock rang out. It was too late. The grate was locked.

Minguier removed the key and backed away slightly. "Neither the promise of a generous reward, nor the time that you have been given were motivation enough for you."

"I considered everything, explored every possibility! None of them work. Neither money nor time will change that! For the love of God, open the door!"

"There must be a solution, because this secret opening exists. Since the easy way yielded nothing, I am offering you the best reason to succeed: you have no other choice. You will not leave here alive until you open that door."

With a hoarse cry, Vincent threw himself against the bars and tried to reach Minguier by thrusting his arm through them, but his fingers only grazed his frock coat. Vincent crushed himself against the iron bars, huffing and puffing, hoping to elongate himself by an inch to grab the man, but it was no use. Minguier simply took a step back without taking his eyes off Vincent, regarding him with a certain detachment even.

Vincent had to give up. "What are you looking for, really?" he shouted, enraged.

"Never mind that. You could have been one of us, Vincent. Your knowledge would have guaranteed your fortune in our group. I might give you the opportunity to join us if you succeed in the time you have left. Since we are laying all of our cards on the table, I can give you one bit of information that might help you succeed, and thus survive."

Vincent was all ears. It was his only hope. Minguier went on.

"This house was built by the illustrious alchemist Nicolas Flamel nearly five centuries ago. He never lived in it, but he did business and housed workers and the needy here. Flamel is remembered as the man capable of transforming lead into gold, which supposedly explains his infinite fortune. However, we have reason to believe he did not know how to make gold, but that he did know where to find it. We are convinced that he hid a treasure under this ancestral residence, behind the passage, whose secret I am asking you for the last time to unlock."

He paused before continuing. "You see? I answered your questions in the end. I told you I would give you the information when the time was right. Now you know what lies hidden behind this wall. Now you know as much as we do."

The disclosure gave Vincent pause; his mind began to race. "Nicolas Flamel's treasure..." he murmured to himself.

He let go of the grate and turned toward the back of the cellar. Ideas began to take shape and come to life, but the reality of his situation soon overshadowed them.

"Release me and I will keep searching for you," he said, spinning around to face Minguier.

"We're past that point, my friend. But you are indeed going to search for me, and this time, I strongly advise you to find something."

Vincent suddenly stiffened. Far behind Minguier, in the first room, he glimpsed a silhouette appear out of nowhere, its face hidden by a leather mask. The apparition approached in absolute silence, appearing to glide along the floor.

The individual was now behind the industrialist, who felt his presence and addressed him without turning around.

"I demanded not to be disturbed. What do you want?"

The silhouette leaned toward him and murmured in his ear. Minguier's face broadened into a smile. With a wave of his hand, he dismissed his visitor, never once taking his eyes from Vincent. With an air of satisfaction he declared, "We're in luck. I'm going to give you another reason to succeed."

39

When Vincent heard the voice shouting in the stairwell, his blood froze. Two masked men appeared at the bottom of the steps, clutching Henri firmly in their grasp; the boy struggled like a wild animal between them. He fought with all his might and lashed out randomly with his fists, but his captors were far too strong for him. They dragged more than carried the frail boy, grabbing him now by an arm, now by his disheveled clothes, or even by a leg. Their prey was a bundle of nerves.

Vincent pointed a finger at Minguier. "Let him go! He's just a kid, he doesn't know anything."

Receiving no response, he pressed his face between his hands where they clutched the bars and said through clenched teeth, "You won't force me to do anything under duress. I'd rather die."

"Die if you like, but so will the kid. And it will be your fault."

"Violence won't get you anywhere, Minguier!"

"Think again, my friend. Contrary to what popular wisdom peddles, violence is often the best of methods. Nothing important was ever accomplished without it."

After much kicking and twisting, Henri managed to free himself, leaving his jacket hanging between the two men, but his escape was short-lived. One of them gave him a swift kick that sent him flying against a barrel. The Nail collapsed to the ground.

Vincent closed his eyes in pain and rage. Being reduced to helplessness before this revolting scene was more than he could bear.

Henri, stunned, was unable to stand up. He didn't even struggle when the men gathered him up like an empty flour sack.

Vincent grew livid. Suddenly everything became clear. "You're the one who's been attacking my people!"

The industrialist made no attempt at denial. "We want you, and you alone. The others are of no use to us. Why let them interfere or even exist? We eliminate those who stand in our way. Your talents must serve no other interests than our own."

Vincent was disgusted.

"Times are changing, Vincent. Real power will not remain in the shadows for much longer. A new era is on the horizon, a pristine, blazing dawn. We will use every means at our disposal to see our ideals prevail. The old world is dying. You should realize that. But can you? In spending time with you, I've come to know you. Your mind functions like your brilliant mechanisms: precise, reliable, but with a rigor that prevents you from accessing what you don't know, and what you can't even imagine."

"What the devil are you talking about?"

"The occult, magic, and ancestral knowledge that—despite what political mouthpieces claim—alone governs the progress of the world. We can conjure up kingdoms, empires, or republics, and create more distractions to occupy the people, but the real rules will not change. At best, they will be skillfully concealed. The powerful know as much and adapt to it. The cleverest use it to their advantage. They are aware that forces beyond themselves are writing history. Contrary to what you seem to believe, not all enchantments are the fruit of astutely orchestrated illusions. Some wonders owe their reality to things entirely beyond the rational."

In response, Vincent howled in rage and shook the grate with all his strength, shouting, "You want to kill my friends and you expect me to help you?"

Minguier didn't respond.

Vincent tried to negotiate. "Let me go, leave us in peace, and I agree to keep quiet about your activities. You'll have nothing to fear from me."

The industrialist began to laugh, but his shortness of breath distorted the sound into a shrill mousy squeak. "You're in no position to 'agree' to anything. I'm making you a final proposition: open the passage and the boy will be safe."

"And if I don't succeed?"

"Then you'll both discover a 'beyond' that isn't hidden behind those stones. You have twelve hours. That's all I can give you. When I come back, you'll have a solution—or a serious problem."

One of the men drew a revolver and curtly ordered Vincent to step back. Minguier unlocked the grate and they tossed the boy into the cell like a sack of rags. He rolled in the dust, curled up in a ball.

Minguier closed the grate and motioned his accomplices to go upstairs. He followed them without haste, taking care to snuff out the lamps in the first rooms, where darkness gradually settled.

Before ascending the stairs, he turned around one last time. "I would sincerely have preferred things to unfold differently. I will be back later. Don't waste any time."

Minguier disappeared. Vincent remained immobile behind the bars, distraught; Henri lay prostrate at his feet, racked with sobs.

40

A deathly silence settled over the cellar. Vincent took a deep breath. Despite the storm raging through him, he tried to calm down. He had to, for Henri's sake.

He gently grasped his young friend, who was clinging tightly to his legs, and tried to prop him up. The Nail finally released his grip and sat on the floor. His face was smeared with dust and tears. He sniffled.

Vincent crouched down in front of him. "They didn't rough you up too much? Are you hurt?"

The boy shook his head.

"How did they capture you?"

"I followed you."

Vincent frowned. "What were you thinking, following me?"

The Nail defended himself between sobs. "The first time, I didn't want you to go alone. I wanted to help you. I followed you to Saint-Pierre de Montmartre church the other night. It seemed strange to me. I couldn't get near enough to see what you were doing because of those coachmen standing around. They frightened me. You stayed until dawn, and when I saw you come out again, you snuck away like a thief in the night. I started having doubts and imagining things. I didn't know if you were still who I thought you were. So I decided to keep watching you."

Henri lowered his eyes. "Forgive me, Vincent."

Vincent took Henri's trembling hands in his own. "It's okay. Now I understand why you seemed distrustful the last few days. Did you tell Pierre or Konrad? Do they know you're here?"

The boy shook his head. "I didn't tell them anything. No one knows."

For the first time, he looked around. "Is this a dungeon?"

"In theory, no."

"Are those scoundrels going to let us die here?"

"They might be counting on it, but we're not going to let them get the better of us."

Vincent stood up and began to snuff out most of the oil lamps.

"We have to save light, otherwise not only will we be imprisoned, we'll also be in the dark."

The Nail got up as well, walked straight to the grate and grabbed it. He shook it with all his might, but it was no use. This time, he had no trouble identifying with the imprisoned hero in his book.

Vincent walked over to him to study the lock and the bars. "Look at that. That's good workmanship. We'll never manage to pick that. We have to find another way out."

To minimize the dire reality of their situation, he tried to adopt a controlled tone. If he had been alone, Vincent would probably have exploded with anger and fear. But he had to control himself to keep Henri from losing hope.

He turned to listen for noise coming from the cellar's first rooms and the stairs, but heard only the echo of his young sniffling cell-mate. Minguier's men had probably left the house, abandoning them to their fate. They would come see the result once the deadline had passed. Henri sniffled again.

"Wipe your nose, please."

"Why? We're done for."

Vincent grabbed him by the shoulders and looked him in the eyes. "As long as the heart beats, anything is possible. I'm talking to the future doctor in there. Would you throw a dying man into the grave while he was still breathing?"

The boy shook his head, wiped his nose on his sleeve and asked, "Is this the room you were drawing in all those diagrams?"

"The very same."

Henri raised his chin toward the back of the room. "And that's supposed to open?"

"Indeed.

The Nail approached the wall. He stood defiant before it a moment, then suddenly started kicking it, more and more, and soon began punching it as well. He hit harder and harder, faster and faster, until he was howling with rage.

Vincent didn't stop him. Henri lost control, unleashing his aggression in the process. Gradually, however, his blows grew less violent, and the Nail eventually stopped of his own accord, out of breath.

"I hadn't tried that approach yet," murmured Vincent.

His young companion remained unmoved. He turned around and leaned against the wall. His fingers were bloody, but he paid them no mind. In a hoarse voice he said, "They'll be back in a few hours. Why would you manage to open this passage in so little time, when you haven't been able to for weeks?"

"Because I'm going to try again, and this time might be the one. And now you're here."

Ironically, even though Vincent would have given anything to keep the boy out of all this, he was happy to have him by his side. After a brief moment of guilt, he decided that being ashamed of his misplaced joy was useless, because it did nothing to change the situation.

He pointed to the wall Henri was leaning against.

"You won't beat it by turning your back on it. You wanted to learn the rules that make for a good secret passage. Well, this is an excellent opportunity. Think of this as field work."

"More like hard labor."

"What is the first rule again?"

The boy grumbled and sent soil flying with a kick. "The best passage is one nobody suspects exists."

"Very good."

"Well, that got us far. We know it's there, so what?"

"The second principle allows us to go further: 'A passage must play on the illusions of the person looking at it.'"

"What does that mean?"

"We all create images of things, according to what we've been taught, or according to our own experience. Often we stop at that. When people see stone—or what appears to be stone—they conclude that it's solid and impossible to penetrate. When they're confronted with a seemingly smooth surface, they don't expect it to contain a hold or an opening. We rarely go further than our assumptions. That's how the human brain works. As soon as it believes it has understood something, it stops thinking. A good passage also hides behind preconceived notions."

"And what does that mean for this one?"

"Not much," sighed Vincent, "because I've already been around the place a hundred times in every direction. I investigated the pillars, the ceiling arches, the joints, who knows what else."

"So we're trapped like rats?"

"Not exactly. It just means that this passage doesn't play on our illusions."

Henri began to rummage around in the piles of old furniture. He pushed them roughly aside and away with his foot. He was hoping to get lucky and find an iron bar or an abandoned tool he could use on the bars.

Vincent sat on a broken crate near the entrance and watched him. He thought of the time passing and avoided thinking about what would happen if he had still found nothing when Minguier and his brutes returned. He did all he could to chase away the horrible images that came to him. However he wasn't thinking of his own suffering, but of what might befall Henri.

Continuing his search, the Nail called out, "And the other rules? What are they?"

Lost in his dark thoughts, Vincent didn't immediately respond. Eventually he said, "'The passage must always be triggered by unexpected means.'"

"Like a secret button, a rose that turns, like at our place, or a pivoting chandelier?"

"Something like that."

"But there's nothing here, not the slightest contraption that we could pull or shift."

"I know. And believe me, I've pushed every square inch of these damn walls."

Henri dropped the shelf he had picked up. As it fell, it knocked over a pile of boards that collapsed with a dusty thump. He pointed to the bottom of the freshly revealed wall. "Why is this stone sticking out?"

Vincent shook his head. "Nothing sticks out."

The Nail bent down and insisted. "Come see for yourself."

Vincent got up with perfunctory calm. "I've spent entire nights scrutinizing this cellar. I know for certain that nothing..."

He froze when he saw the small stone, no bigger than a cobblestone, protruding from the wall.

"Good Lord!" he exclaimed, dropping to his knees. "I swear this wasn't there before."

"Pull it, or press it!" The boy was hopping up and down with excitement.

"Let's not be hasty," said Vincent to calm him. "It could be a trap." He didn't dare touch it. "By all the saints in heaven, how did this thing appear out of the masonry? And why now?"

Cheered by the discovery, Henri began searching the rest of the room. Planks of wood went flying as he vigorously removed anything that got in his way of verifying the other walls. Suddenly he cried out, "Here's another one!"

Vincent hurried over. "Directly opposite the first one." He let out a small cry of excitement. He closed his eyes and concentrated. "Damn it, what could have made these two stones move? What is different about this room? What did we change?"

He opened his eyes and hurried to the door. "The grate! It's closed and locked, which it never was during our nights of investigation!"

He began frantically examining the edge of the door, but the fit was too snug in the stone frame for him to detect anything. "There must be a rod or a pawl that controls the stones' movement."

He returned to their initial discovery and got down on all fours for a closer look. "Bring me a lamp, please."

Henri complied and returned with one of the oil lamps, which he placed near the wall. Vincent brushed his fingertip along the protruding stone. He hesitated.

The Nail kneeled by his side. "You're cautious?"

"Always."

"If we press on the right stone, the secret room will open, and if we press on the wrong one, everything will collapse around us?"

"Nothing so outlandish. But it could be a double trigger."

"A what?"

"A mechanism designed to be operated by more than one person. Some ancient caches were equipped with this type of system."

"Why?"

"To prevent a single individual from having access to the contents. Most of the secret compartments in the Egyptian temples could only be unlocked by two priests. Some things are too important to be left within the reach of a single mortal."

"But..."

"Let me think, please." Vincent sat down cross-legged, his head in his hands.

"This changes everything. The creators made sure that the gate had to be locked for the passage to be opened. It was an additional protective measure. Therefore this room is a kind of antechamber."

He got up and stood in the center of the room, and continued with his line of thought. "The passage is never directly accessible from the cellar. One must first be safely locked in here. It's impossible to rush in from upstairs in one go."

He took three steps and stood before the wall. He whispered to it, "I'm beginning to understand you. But that still doesn't tell me how you move."

He turned around. "Henri, help me. We have to clear everything away from the walls. Let's pile it up against the grate. If Minguier and his henchmen return, we can't let them see what we're doing."

The Nail immediately rushed forward and set to work.

41

Vincent positioned himself in front of one of the protruding stones; Henri stood before the other. The entire underground room had been swept clean. Anything lying about had been piled up against the grate, which had completely disappeared behind an accumulation of assorted debris.

"Ready?" Vincent asked the Nail.

"Whenever you are."

"I'll count down to zero from three, then we do it."

The boy agreed. Vincent placed his palm on the stone. He had no idea what would happen once he tried to push it back into its slot, but it was the only movement possible. He took a deep breath and called out, "Three, two, one... zero!"

The two companions pressed the stones simultaneously. The fluidity of the movement surprised Vincent; nothing caught as the element slid perfectly into the wall. He accompanied it to the very end.

The two stones had regained their places; they no longer looked any different from the others. Vincent and Henri exchanged looks. Nothing moved in the total silence.

The Nail said in astonishment, "Do you think they..."

He was interrupted by a dull thud, followed immediately by a rumbling, accompanied by a tremor that shook the very foundations of the vaulted room. Something had just been set in motion.

Vincent watched the back wall, expecting to see it disappear in one way or another, but the masonry remained in place.

Now the muffled sound of a chain or a rack and pinion filled the room. It was impossible to tell where it was coming from, as diffuse as it was. Suddenly, the floor began to vibrate, causing the dust on the beaten earth to twitch. The flames danced, and one of the still burning lamps fell over and went out. Vincent dove to grab the other.

"Hold on, Henri!"

In a panic, the boy rushed toward his friend. "We never should have pressed them! Everything is collapsing!"

Vincent caught him as he went flying and pulled him close. To steady himself, he leaned against the neighboring wall. To his great surprise, it was completely immobile; the wall was not trembling. He looked up and checked the arches; no dust fell from above.

"No, my boy. I don't know what's going on, but it's not collapsing."

The floor began to vibrate more intensely. And now it was beginning to tilt! Near the grate it remained at the same level, but near the passage it began to slant downwards. Vincent slid away from the wall. Some debris began to slide along with him. The lamps skidded and rolled, while Vincent held tight to his. The slope grew steeper.

"The floor is slipping away!" cried Henri.

"No, look: it's sinking and showing us a path."

Like a drawbridge, the floor continued to shift, revealing an opening located beneath the presumed location of the passage.

"Actually, the wall couldn't move," said Vincent in admiration. "It's the floor that descends to open the hidden passage below."

He stood up, careful not to lose his balance, and reveled in his discovery.

"Do you realize what this means, Henri? The solution was right under our feet! This secret opening was playing on our preconceptions after all!"

He watched in fascination as the floor transformed into an access ramp. The incline gradually revealed a narrow arch that became an opening marking the entrance to an actual corridor.

"The people who designed this device were geniuses!" he cried. Vincent forgot his fear as he marveled at the secret passage. He would have liked for Begel and Robert-Houdin to be with him to share in the incredible discovery.

As Vincent's enthusiasm grew, the Nail's confidence returned.

The ground seemed to have stabilized. Vincent ran down the slope to the now unobstructed corridor entrance. He ran his hand along the stones of the arch and murmured in gratitude, "Thank you, thank you! I much prefer this beyond to the other one. I will not betray your trust."

"You talk to walls?" said Henri in surprise.

"I talk to anything that moves me."

Vincent cautiously entered the pitch black passage, where a muted silence reigned. He immediately felt a violent cold draft. He stopped and focused. As fascinated as he was by the access mechanism, something troubled him.

"How could a single man, even a rich one, even an alchemist, design and carry out such a device? He would have had to have access to extraordinary knowledge and exceptionally skilled craftsmen who truly mastered secret architecture."

"Maybe he knew some?"

Vincent held his lamp out toward the darkness and the unknown. "It's time to find out if there's a treasure hiding in there."

Henri made as if to run, but his mentor stopped him.

"Not so fast. There might be traps ahead."

Discouraged at the thought, the boy fell in behind Vincent, who advanced warily. The light now illuminated the beyond. There was neither a buried room nor a secret compartment—and certainly no treasure. He peered into the dark, narrow corridor; it was cut from the stone and extended much further than what was visible to him.

Another muffled clang rang out, this time closer and more powerful. Henri clung to Vincent and cried out, "The floor is rising back to its original position!"

Vincent hesitated. He faced a critical and urgent choice: should they turn back or continue on? Was it better to haggle with killers over their discovery or risk everything and bet that the passage led to escape?

"What do we do?" asked Henri in a panic.

It would have been nearly impossible for them to drag themselves up into the opening, which grew narrower as the structure rose.

Vincent's instinct told him to continue. In the time it took him to think it, the alternative disappeared: the passage had closed behind them.

When silence settled again, Vincent felt Henri trembling against his back. They had only a single lamp, and the flame, despite the protective glass, burned with difficulty in the rushing air.

Vincent suddenly doubted his choice. He didn't know if they were standing at the foot of a tunnel that would take them toward the light, or on the threshold of their tomb. Perhaps Minguier would have proved less dangerous than what now awaited them.

Just as he was hoping to see the sun again, a terrifying roar resounded in the tunnel, an animal cry that made his blood curdle. The deafening, inhuman roar drew nearer. It was the roar of a monster ranting with centuries of pent-up hunger.

42

The bestial roar grew ever more violent as it approached. Henri's and Vincent's eardrums were splitting. The Nail had covered his ears with his hands to protect them, but that did nothing to diminish his terror. His legs grew weak. Just ahead of him, Vincent was struggling to stay upright in the powerful wind. It was difficult for him to keep his eyes open; the fast-moving air quickly dried them. He used his body to shield the lamp as best he could. If it went out, they would be plunged into total darkness.

What kind of abomination could produce such a terrifying howl? The answers were not of this world: Henri imagined a creature escaped from mythology, or a dragon wrenched from a dream. He trembled at the thought of it, and his mind raced. He could already envision a Minotaur, furious at seeing trespassers in its lair. Vincent was also bracing for the worst; he knew that no matter what it was, his knife would be useless against it. He peered into the tunnel, fearful of what might suddenly appear there. If it had still been possible, he would have turned back without hesitation. Even the worst assassin frightened him less than this prehistoric bellowing.

Henri fell to his knees. His body twisted with fear and the icy wind. He began screaming, but the howling of the beast drowned out his cries of distress. Realizing just how petrified the boy was, Vincent crouched down in front of him. He was ready to shield the Nail with his body so the boy would have a chance at survival; never mind if he were devoured in return.

Meanwhile the beast kept its distance; its anger did not seem to intensify. The monster seemed to hold its position; it was most likely lurking around the bend in the tunnel. Was it too large to fit through the narrow passageway? Would it be restrained by a grate or iron bars? Its fury gradually waned to a roar. Vincent decided to continue forwards and evaluate the threat.

He flattened himself against the limestone wall and took a few breathless, careful steps, wondering if the creature could smell his scent or if it would react to the glow of his lamp. Henri had remained behind, prostrate on the ground, huddled against the stone.

As Vincent slowly moved forward, it seemed to him that the beast retreated in equal measure. Seeing his partner's light fade, Henri realized that he would soon find himself alone in the darkness. With a jolt, he jumped up and caught up to Vincent, grabbing his jacket.

Vincent's senses were on high alert, evaluating every parameter in the hostile environment. Nothing escaped his notice, not the minor variations in the tunnel's shape, nor the slope or the traction of the ground. Any incongruous elements could indicate traps.

The monster didn't charge; the situation was more and more intriguing. Vincent didn't hear the scraping of clawed paws trying to force a way in, or the whistling of a gigantic forked tongue. The roar had given way to a wail, changing without interruption. Sometimes it sounded far away, other times much closer, but nothing else happened.

The corridor that stretched out before Vincent took another turn, more pronounced than the previous one. Breathing deeply to give himself courage, Vincent followed it and froze. A few yards in front of him, in the light of his less and less wind-battered lamp, long vertical streaks gashed the tunnel wall. The draft waned. He took a careful step forward. The lamp drove back the darkness and enabled him to better discern tall notches in the wall, similar to narrow arrow slits. He counted no fewer than six.

Henri tried to hold him back by grabbing at his clothes. "Don't go there! It must be a trap!"

The icy wind had almost abated, and the bloodcurdling howl was no more than a distant whine. Had the beast fled?

When he reached the openings, Vincent felt nothing more than a light breeze on his face. What remained of the draft penetrated the tunnel through the curious fissures. Raising the lamp for a better view, he could make out in the gaps suspended tubes and strange strips of metal arranged diagonally. They were of all different sizes and crafted from an alloy that resembled copper covered in greenish oxide. The manner in which the air holes were carved caught Vincent's attention; he began to understand what was happening. After all, they had only *heard* the monster.

He motioned Henri to join him. "Look. I'm beginning to think the beast was just an illusion."

He pointed to the slits, carved into whistles, the plates, and the tubes. "The breeze filtering through these ingenious wind instruments produced the monster's voice. These hanging slats are probably some kind of reed. Our imagination did the rest."

"There's no dragon?"

"Just the ones in our minds. There's only sound, air that becomes a combination of different notes when it travels through these openings."

"Why did it stop?"

Vincent looked behind him.

"Probably because the passage closed. The phenomenon must be triggered by an indraft created when the passage opens. The tunnel acts like a giant clarinet, producing its horrifying music. It's a rather clever way to terrify unwanted visitors!"

The boy laughed nervously and tentatively reached a hand into one of the slots to touch a suspended tube. "They wanted to scare us to death."

"They succeeded. Whoever 'they' are. Come on, we're not out of the woods yet."

43

Walking single file, the two travelers had been on their underground journey for some time. With each new bend in the tunnel, they hoped to finally discover a route to the surface. But for the moment the narrow passageway wound along, offering no other option but forward. For Vincent it was enough that they hadn't yet been confronted with a trapdoor or a dungeon, or even a fork branching off into several directions, which would have seriously complicated their situation.

Despite Vincent's efforts to keep the conversation going, the signs were clear: Henri's responses grew increasingly vague and his steps dragged.

The Nail stumbled and asked again, "How much lamp oil do we have left?"

"Not much." The reservoir was almost empty, and Vincent had no other choice but to prepare his young companion for what awaited them.

"We might have to continue in the dark."

Henri was immediately discouraged by the thought. "We'll never get out of here. They'll find our skeletons a thousand years from now," he moaned.

"Don't be dramatic. We've already escaped the hound from hell that we imagined earlier. If the lamp goes out, we'll continue more slowly, but we'll keep going all the same. The air is breathable. There's not a trace of mold anywhere. There's a good chance this passage leads somewhere."

"Do you think it's an old quarry?"

"I'm not sure. The corridor is too narrow to be part of mining activities, and there's no trace of extraction. Plus, judging from the cut marks in the walls, whoever dug it worked slowly and gradually, using a chisel. The Romans worked like that, but techniques have evolved since then."

"Could it just be an ancient underground corridor?"

"That's what it looks like."

"Leading where?"

"The answer must be at the end, and I'm as curious as you are to get there. Perhaps it was an escape route, like the ones we've built for some of our clients. But it seems increasingly clear to me that this colossal task, combined with the mechanism that hides the entrance, could not have been the work of a single man. It would take damn good organization to build all this. And a damn good reason, too."

As the tunnel sloped up into a curve, they arrived at the foot of a pile of rubble. The ceiling had collapsed and the volume of earth and rock fragments that had fallen almost entirely blocked the passage. Roots dangled from the gaping vault. Vincent held the light up to the imposing heap from different angles, trying to gauge its size.

"A trap?" asked Henri.

Vincent shook his head. "Just an ordinary structural break. Ground movement, or the work of time. The good news is, the presence of vegetation indicates that we're nearing the surface. The bad news is, to continue, we have to slip through that tiny hole up there, between what's left of the ceiling and the mound of earth, without causing anything else to fall. If you prefer, you can wait for me here. I'll hurry up there and see what awaits us on the other side."

"We stay together! I'm going to go crazy if you leave me behind. I prefer to follow you into hell than stay here alone!" protested Henri.

"As you like," Vincent yielded. "Let's go to hell together then."

He began to climb the rubble with care; stones and earth rolled under his feet. Finally, he crawled into the small open space. The roots that had grown into it clawed at his scalp and scratched his face. They were so dense, he had to protect his mouth and nostrils with his hand, as he inched along on his elbows. His lamp barely fit through the space; he had to tilt it, praying as he did so that it wouldn't go out. He cleared a path with one hand and wriggled his way forward with difficulty.

Hindered by the debris that rained down with his every movement, he just barely managed to make his way, careful not to get caught on anything. The unstable material still hanging above them posed a threat: a new landslide could bury them.

Vincent sniffed the air: it was humid. As he made his way with difficulty, he thought he felt a very gentle breeze against his dirt-stained face.

"Are you still following me?"

"Right on your heels. Please, don't stop, I don't want to end up buried alive."

Sparing no effort, Vincent finally came out on the other side. He let out a sigh of relief as he struggled to extract himself from the bottleneck, steadied himself, and checked his lamp before beginning the descent down the other side of the heap.

No sooner had he set foot on the tunnel floor than he jumped as he felt something run between his legs. He swore.

"What's happening?" cried Henri, who was on the edge of panic.

"Everything's fine, just a rat on the run." He heaved a sigh and added, "Would you believe it? I'm happy to see him. It's a good sign. If he's wandering around in here, it means there must be a route to the surface."

Vincent extended a hand to his young friend, who made his way out as well. The Nail dusted himself off and began rubbing at the traces of dirt staining his clothes.

Vincent jiggled the lamp in front of his face, indicating that the reservoir was almost dry. "Let's get going fast."

Henri followed him as best he could.

Two bends later, his already faltering courage was abruptly reduced to nothing: a burrstone wall blocked their path, making it impossible to go any further. They had walked and crawled for hours to end up in a cul-de-sac. This time, they both gave in to discouragement.

"If we ever get out of here, we will always be able to tell the story of the worst night of our lives," fulminated Vincent.

Henri moaned and slid to the ground. He closed his eyes, exhausted. The sight of the weakened boy spurred Vincent to action. No, he couldn't give up; he wouldn't abandon Henri. Raising his lamp to take advantage of the last flickering light, Vincent began to examine the obstacle.

"These stones don't look very old. I bet they were laid at most a few years ago, as if this tunnel had been intersected by a more recent construction."

Suddenly, in a niche high up on the wall, Vincent came face to face with a rat. He had just enough time to catch a glimpse of his muzzle and his little glistening eyes. They each frightened the other, and the creature scurried back into its hole. Vincent burst out laughing, so hard that Henri thought his companion may have slipped into madness.

"What's wrong with you? There's nothing funny."

"But there is! This wonderful specimen! On your feet, Henri," he said, studying the opening through which the rodent had slipped away. "Our little friend will show us the way. I'm going to need your help."

He opened his knife and began hacking at the joints. At that very moment, the lamp began to flicker. A few seconds later, it went out—for good.

44

Darkness. A scream. Henri could see nothing. He spun around in circles, in complete panic. The threat was very close, he could feel it. The boy wanted to run away, but every door he tried opened onto walls. He was trapped. The thing would catch up with him soon. He could already hear it breathing. When he turned around, it was upon him with its huge, gaping maw.

Henri cried out—and awoke in a sweat. A nightmare, it was only a nightmare.

At his bedside, Vincent murmured a few words of comfort. The Nail, distraught, barely heard them; to reassure himself, he grabbed Vincent's hand and squeezed it hard. His breathing gradually returned to normal.

After pulling the blanket up over Henri's shoulders, Vincent waited a few minutes to be sure the boy remained well covered. Although only his head poked out, he still shivered. Vincent put a palm to his burning forehead. He had a fever; there was no doubt about that. The boy had not been able to warm up since their return home. A rubdown with hot water and a bowl of broth by the oven had not put an end to his shivering fits. He was probably in for a bad cold, but it was hardly serious, especially compared with the danger he had faced mere hours earlier. Luckily he was now safe.

When, in the early morning, the two friends finally escaped their underground hell, they ran home as fast as they could; despite their fatigue, despite the danger, like exhausted wolves incapable of marking the slightest pause before racing back to their den.

After scratching away for hours in the dark, and loosening stone after stone, they finally managed to clear a passage through the wall, into the sewers. While the odor that greeted them was repulsive, it also bore the sweet smell of liberty. Reenergized by the prospect of finally finding a way out, it didn't take them long to locate the iron ladder that led to an opening above ground, even groping their way in the dark.

The fresh air and familiar urban surroundings had a redeeming effect on them. What had seemed utterly ordinary the day before now appeared extraordinary: a street in the dawn light, a cart passing, a cock crowing, the play of early morning sun in the tree leaves.

Vincent and the Nail washed themselves at the first fountain they came across, and tried to remove the disgusting muck and foul odor clinging to their skin. In the cool morning, surrounded by horses left to quench their thirst before starting the work day, they splashed themselves with generous amounts of icy water. They were so dirty that even the animals kept their distance, in what might have been taken for disdain.

Soaked to the bone and shivering with cold, the two survivors headed for Montmartre as fast as their remaining strength allowed.

Once they reached home, they had to explain everything to the others, who were worried and ready for battle. Their companions could never have imagined the ordeal they had endured. Thrilled to see them alive, they didn't for an instant think of reprimanding Henri for recklessly following Vincent, or of rebuking their leader for carelessly venturing out at the mercy of Minguier.

Calm had finally returned to the house, but Vincent could not bring himself to leave the Nail's side. The boy seemed exhausted; dark circles rimmed his eyes, which he focused on Vincent. Standing at the foot of the bed, he contemplated what remained of his knife, now worn down to the handle.

"Not good for much anymore, is it?" joked Henri.

"Nothing at all," smiled Vincent. "That's all right. I'll buy another one."

"Can I keep it? As a souvenir?"

Vincent folded it and set it on the bedside table.

"It's yours."

He crouched down next to the Nail. "You really need to sleep now. You must regain your strength. Set your mind at ease; we're standing guard."

As he was about to leave, the Nail called out, "Vincent!"

The leader turned around. Henri's eyes shone with fever and he could hardly contain his emotion when he said: "Thank you for saving my life."

Vincent winked at him. "Don't thank me. I wouldn't have been able to open that passage without your help. If you hadn't been there, I would probably be dead right now."

"You were right. We just needed to try one last time."

"Remember that when you find yourself about to give up."

"You know," added the boy softly, "don't tell the others, but I've never been so afraid. When they grabbed me, threw me in that dungeon. And that horrible screaming wind. I really thought I was done for."

"Fortunately, it's all nothing more than a bad memory this morning."

"Vincent, have you ever felt like you were going to die?"

Vincent hesitated. "I've seen death up close. But it wasn't coming for me."

"You don't feel the same afterwards, do you?"

"You can say that again. And now, sleep."

Henri closed his eyes and sunk back into his pillow. Vincent stood motionless and thoughtful, contemplating the boy's face, calm at last. The Nail was right: no one is ever the same after a brush with death. The question is whether you continue on stronger for having survived, or more fragile because you know it will be back.

The Nail finally fell asleep. His hand hung limp over the side of the bed. Vincent placed it gently under the covers. It had been a long time since he himself had been able to fall asleep so quickly.

As he left the room, a gunshot rang out—he swore it came from behind the house.

45

Konrad closed one eye to adjust his aim and pulled the trigger. The shot rang out, and the chipped tile balanced at the other end of the old grain depot blew to pieces. The explosion frightened a couple of turtledoves, who flapped their wings and fled.

Vincent sprang from the boardinghouse like a jack-in-the-box, brandishing a club.

"Are we being attacked?"

"*Mein Gott*, no! I'm practicing. In case those *Schweinehunde* show up."

Perched atop a pole near the carpenter, Pierre called out to his brother, "I thought you were in bed. You haven't slept after the night you had?"

"I was with Henri. He just fell asleep. Luckily he drifted off before you started shooting, otherwise he would have been scared stiff again!"

Konrad strode over to the far side of the depot. With the back of his hand, he swept the debris from the old shelf and set up a new tile. He came back and held his gun out to Pierre.

"Your turn. Be careful, it tends to shoot a little low."

Pierre jumped down from his perch and firmly planted his legs in position. Try as he might, his hands still trembled. But it wasn't resolve that he lacked. When the shot fired, he jumped in surprise; the bullet flew past its target and struck a beam, shattering the wood.

"Not bad," said the German. "But you have to remain steady. You shouldn't fear your own revolver. When you decide to use it, it will be your best friend, and it could save your life."

"That's easier said than done, Konrad! I'm not used to shooting."

The carpenter scratched his beard. "The way things are going, you'll have to get used to it."

"Yeah. In the meantime, I'm going to watch you a bit more."

Pierre handed him the revolver and turned to his brother. "So, you were able to open that passageway after all."

"I only managed because I had Henri and luck on my side."

"I'd have liked to see the look on Minguier's face when he came back. He must not have expected to find your prison empty."

Both brothers chuckled.

"I'll bet he was very annoyed!" exclaimed Vincent. "Especially since he has no way of knowing how we got out. Unless he locks himself inside, which he would have no reason to do, he'll never work out how to trigger the mechanism."

"He must think you disappeared without a trace! He'll suspect a magic trick."

"I'd really like to know what he's going to do."

"He'll send killers after you, that's for certain. He must be furious!"

The thought of Minguier angry was not displeasing to Vincent, but the potential consequences worried him.

"He'll end up coming here..."

Konrad fired again, pulverizing the tile. "Let them come," he said, determined. "We'll give them the welcome they deserve."

"Did Minguier really think he would find the alchemist Nicolas Flamel's treasure?" Pierre asked in astonishment.

"He was convinced of it. His eyes glittered with desire at the very mention."

"He's going to think you took it with you."

"I don't care."

Konrad walked over and held his gun out to Vincent. "Do you want to try? It might be useful."

"Another time. Right now, I absolutely must go out. I know what you're going to say, but risking a trip outside is no more dangerous than waiting around here for them to burst in on us. You stay here and keep watch. There's a good chance that our Italian friend and you, Konrad, are believed to be dead. Take that as an opportunity to have a drink and relax. It's not every day that death buys you a round."

46

Before going out, Vincent had traded his black craftsman's attire—a canvas jacket and trousers—for more ordinary clothes that would let him blend into the crowd: gray trousers, a white shirt, a vest, and a long loose coat. To avoid drawing attention, he even resigned himself to wearing an old bowler hat that he found in a cupboard. It itched from the moment he put it on.

For lack of practice, he forgot at first to remove the hat when he presented himself at the annex of the Paris prefecture where the special investigation services were located.

He greeted the officer on duty and asked to see Inspector Clément Bertelot.

"Do you have an appointment?"

"No, but I know him personally, and it's important. My name is Vincent Cavel."

The man wrote Vincent's name on a piece of paper, then pointed to a bench in the hall. "Wait over there. I'll inform him."

The entrance hall was a hive of activity, a nonstop procession of men coming and going up and down stairs and in and out of doors leading to different departments. Although they all wore civilian clothes, Vincent was able to distinguish the agents from the visitors: they had a slight stiffness about them and a gaze as keen as it was furtive. Many of them stared at him as they passed; some escorted handcuffed individuals.

Clément finally came down a set of stairs to meet him. "What fair wind blows you in here, old friend? Something good, I hope?"

"More like a whirlwind. I need to speak with you."

"We're rather on tenterhooks here, between spies and groupuscules taking advantage of the Fair to have a field day. If you could—"

"I only need a few minutes. It's serious." Vincent's tone of voice and his expression immediately convinced the police officer.

"Follow me to my office."

Inspector Bertelot led his childhood friend through a warren of stairs and corridors capable of confounding even the best of navigators. Floors and departments were a tangle of feverish activity; all around them, men hurried along, clutching files, talking, or calling out to each other from different levels.

"Looks like you're swamped."

The inspector nodded. "Anyone would think the world's degenerates had all arranged to meet in Paris! They're taking advantage of the Fair to intensify their activities. Between thwarting assassination attempts, officials who call us up for nothing, and madmen ready to do anything for attention, we don't get much sleep these days. On Tuesday, we actually had two instances of a new kind of theft in the same day. Hold on to your hat: one from the private coffers of a branch of the Banque de France and, several hours later, the same kind of operation in a parish archive. They swiped the registers, but left highly valuable illuminated manuscripts. It makes no sense."

He cast an inquiring glance at Vincent and added, "You don't look so good yourself. This is the first time you've come to see me here."

"I had to."

When they reached the third floor, Bertelot pointed to a half-open door. "Please enter."

The office was cramped and cluttered with stacks of files that were difficult to avoid bumping into. On the walls hung lists and annotated maps of neighborhoods in the capital.

"Have a seat and tell me what brings you here."

Vincent got straight to the point. "A man tried to kill me and the kid I look after."

"Good heavens! A murder attempt. Did you alert the police?"

"The case is as unusual as the criminal, so I preferred to speak to you. He held us prisoner and threatened us. He was ready to kill us, but we managed to escape. I don't know what he's up to, but I'll bet you anything he runs in occult circles."

The policeman nodded his head. "They're turning up everywhere. Apparently they're in fashion."

"He mentioned a 'new power' capable of bringing down political authorities. I thought that might fall within your jurisdiction."

"An anarchist?"

"I don't know. But he's certainly not a penniless revolutionary. He's an industrialist, and a rich one at that. He has a beautiful mansion on Avenue Malakoff. He's even presenting at the World's Fair. His name is Alfred Minguier."

Clément jotted down the name. Suddenly he stopped and frowned. "Minguier, did you say?"

"That's right."

"Just a moment, please."

Clément got up. "Jaubert!" he called out.

"Yes, boss?" came a distant voice.

"Bring me the activity register."

"Right away!"

Bertelot came back and sat down at his desk.

"I feel like I've seen that name before."

"Is he under surveillance?"

"Not that I know of, but I may have seen something in the most recent reports."

A man entered without knocking, greeted Vincent quickly, and held out a bound volume to his superior.

"Thank you, Jaubert."

Inspector Bertelot skimmed several pages, then focused his search by running his finger down the list of the latest cases, finally coming to rest on a single paragraph. "Minguier! That's what I thought. Alfred is his first name. 'Businessman, manufacturer of welded link chains for various land-based and maritime uses,' residing indeed in a well-to-do neighborhood."

"That's him."

Bertelot frowned. "We're not going to be able to question him, let alone arrest him."

"Does he have political protection?"

"Even more ironclad than that—he was found dead this morning, in his home."

Vincent took in the news; then his eyes widened. "Are you informed of all deaths?"

"Of course not, but I see here that 'his butler called the police, stating that his employer had been assassinated by masked men who forced him to drink poison.' Since he's a high-profile individual, we took over the case."

Vincent couldn't get over what he was hearing. "Minguier. Poisoned."

"Stone-dead. Whatever he did to you, he won't answer for it."

Vincent slumped back in his chair, incredulous. "Even so, life is strange. Everything pointed to me as the corpse and he the survivor. In a matter of hours, the roles have been reversed. Are you going to investigate?"

"We have no plans to. We don't have enough staff. And the comments attached to the report indicate that besides the remarks—incoherent as they were—of his manservant, there's nothing suspicious about the case. Your man probably died of natural causes."

"That, I don't believe."

"When did you last see him?"

"Last night."

"Gosh, divine justice works much faster than ours!" Clément laughed at his own joke.

Vincent told himself that his friend's casual reaction to his misfortune must be due to the regularity with which he was confronted with the worst kinds of crimes.

"My dear Vincent," added the inspector as he stood up. "I must now return to other cases. Say hello to Pierre for me. Let's try to get a drink together one of these days. There are some excellent establishments opening up."

"Why not?" Vincent responded mechanically. He was already thinking of the implications Alfred Minguier's brutal demise would have. It would not clarify anything—quite the contrary.

47

Keeping watch from one of the first-floor windows, Eustasio signaled to Konrad and Vincent to join him quietly. Taking care to remain hidden, he pointed to the street below. "Come have a look."

He pointed out a man on the opposite sidewalk dressed in a coachman's uniform.

"I noticed him yesterday morning. He hasn't moved since, and he even spent the night there. I'm certain he's watching us."

"I can't make out his face from here, but he's dressed just like the man who bumped into me," grumbled Konrad.

"There are quite a few of them who wear that uniform," said Vincent. "In theory he's there to protect us, and he's come at a good time. I have something to tell him."

"You're going out through the front door?" asked Eustasio in surprise.

"I won't be long. Stay hidden. Konrad, please cover me with your weapon, in case I'm mistaken about his identity."

Vincent slipped into his ordinary-looking clothes and exited the house. Weaving his way between carts piled with sacks of coal and a barrow full of kegs, he jogged across the street and headed right for the coachman, who seemed uncomfortable with being approached directly.

"Excuse me!" Vincent called out. "I imagine you know who I am?"

The man lowered his face beneath the brim of his hat and turned away, refusing to engage in conversation. Vincent waited for a few curious pedestrians to pass them. Pretending to look elsewhere he said, "If you work with Charles, go to him quickly and tell him we need to talk. It's urgent. Something important happened last night."

The man looked up at him. He stared at Vincent pointedly, as though trying to evaluate the sincerity of his words.

"It's very urgent," insisted Vincent. "I'm risking my life just by coming out to see you."

The coachman still said nothing, but raised his arm and signaled with his hand.

Vincent looked around. "Who the hell are you signaling to?"

The man still didn't speak.

"I'm warning you," said Vincent, "my friend is armed and he has you in his sights."

The coachman remained unmoved. A fiacre quickly arrived and stopped when it reached them. The driver invited Vincent to get in, but he stepped back, raising a hand in refusal. "Easy, friend! I'm not going anywhere unless I know with whom and why."

Charles's face emerged furtively from the cab window. "Hurry up, if you don't want to end up like Alfred Minguier!"

48

In the heavy early morning traffic, the fiacre advanced at the even pace of the horse's trot. As soon as he was seated, Vincent began to question Adinson.

"Did you order Minguier's execution?"

Charles was hurt by the question and fiercely denied the accusation. "Of course not. Are we such strangers that you believe we could be assassins?"

"Then how did you learn of his death?"

"You're not the only one with police connections."

"So you know there won't be an investigation? His butler may have cried poisoning, but law enforcement doesn't care."

"That is convenient for us. The fewer people who get involved in this affair, the less trouble we'll have. Even so, the witness's days are certainly numbered."

Vincent watched the streets go by though the window of the cab door. "We aren't going to the underground chapel?"

"Given the turn of events, it is no longer safe enough. We're going to my home, but you won't find the area completely alien."

Vincent didn't respond. He wanted clarification about a far more pressing subject. "Last night, Henri and I almost died. Weren't your coachmen supposed to guarantee our safety?"

"We were preparing to intervene on Rue de Montmorency when we were informed that the house was empty and you had returned home."

"You were preparing to intervene? What time did you intend to show up? While you were dilly-dallying, Minguier and his henchmen had all the time in the world to do away with us!" Vincent's words caught in his throat.

"Sending men in too early would have provoked a hasty confrontation, when we didn't know what you were doing."

"We were lucky to get out," said Vincent accusingly.

"Why did they let you go?"

"They didn't. They locked us up, but Henri and I managed to escape through the hidden passageway."

Adinson leaned forward with sudden interest. "So you managed to get past the wall?"

"Yes, my dear sir, and it was absolutely wonderful!"

Charles's eyes glittered with mischief. "Are you going to tell me about it?"

Vincent nodded and added, "I'm sure you and your friend Robert-Houdin would have loved it."

The fiacre slowed and turned to enter a tall carriage gateway whose immense doors had just been opened. The carriage entered a large interior courtyard that rang with the hammering of horseshoes. Once it had pulled to a stop, a coachman opened the door.

Vincent paused at the bottom of the steps. The buildings seemed familiar, but it was the enormous front stairway that suddenly brought back forgotten memories.

He recognized the place; he had been here before. He had been much younger then, and the courtyard had not been jammed with carriages as it was now. As Vincent's memory came back to him, a powerful emotion arose within. Seeing him dumbstruck, Adinson smiled and invited Vincent to follow him.

49

Vincent made his way through the carriages and the men in coach-man's dress bustling about them, all the while scrutinizing the elegant pale stone buildings.

"Jean-Eugène Robert-Houdin lived here. I only came a few times, but I remember it very clearly." Carried away by his memories, he no longer knew where to look and turned his head every which way. "Heavens! I was so impressed! The first time I came, it was to present a project I was hoping he would include me in."

"A rigged staircase he needed for his future theater."

"How do you know?"

"He was delighted with the device you proposed and spoke to me about it."

Vincent pointed to the central building. "That's where he lived, but there weren't all these carriages back then."

"I took over his lodgings and have spread out a bit." Adinson gestured to the courtyard with a sweeping motion. "This all belongs to us now. A veritable little fortress in the heart of Paris: officially a transportation company with hansom cabs, long-distance stage-coaches, and mail coaches. Incidentally, it's the largest private team of coachmen."

"Why coachmen?"

"That was Jean-Eugène's idea; I expanded on it with my research companions. Regardless of time or place, no one is surprised to see coachmen. Their uniform associates them with a simple function that people can easily identify. No one asks any questions about them; everyone thinks they know who they are and what they do. The coachmen's appearance enables them to blend in anywhere without drawing attention—which is exactly what we need. I will show you their quarters if you're interested, but first we have work to do."

Vincent was overcome by an even stronger emotion as he entered Robert-Houdin's former residence. The immense entrance hall hadn't changed, and it reminded him of the young man he had been some years earlier. The magician had created the decor using enormous posters of his most famous acts—Sawing Through a Woman, The Surprising Handkerchief, The Royalist Guillotine, The Marvelous Orange Tree, The Prince of Smoke, and his masterpiece, The Flying Specter—and objects related to his illusions. The imposing Egyptian sarcophagus covered in hieroglyphs still dominated the center of the room, near a pillory with rusted irons and a stuffed lion with glass eyes and lips pulled back to reveal terrifying fangs. In the back still hung a sumptuous set of full-length black velvet curtains trimmed with silver braid, like those draped from church pediments at celebrity funerals. A taste for irony had prompted Robert-Houdin to have his own initials embroidered on them, as was custom for the deceased. The gothic, mysterious spirit of the place had lost none of its enthralling beauty.

"You kept everything."

"You're about to see just to what extent. Jean-Eugène's office is now mine. Come."

As he crossed the threshold, Vincent was overcome by a strange feeling, as if he were journeying back in time to return to his beginnings. There he was, immersed once again in the magical world that had awoken him to his vocation.

Although time was of the essence, Adinson knew he must give Vincent a few moments to rediscover the building on his own terms. Vincent advanced timidly, as though he were still that young man visiting a place where everything intimidated him. His gaze traveled from point to point, following only the logic of his growing curiosity. With every fiber of his being, he felt that he was in his element here. Inwardly, he realized to what extent the creative space he had built in the boardinghouse cellar was rooted in the same spirit, though it was neither as opulent nor as chock-full as this one.

He approached the table and touched a blotter on which sat a porcelain inkwell and quills ready for use. "It's as if he were going to come back at any moment."

"Sometimes I wish he would."

Adinson continued on.

"You live at the heart of his work," murmured Vincent.

"I see his office as a sort of museum. I have the utmost respect for it, so much that I don't let anyone else clean it. I maintain this room myself. But I don't work here, no more than he did, actually."

Vincent raised an eyebrow. Charles teased him mischievously. "Did you really think someone as complex as Robert-Houdin would be satisfied with an office accessed by a simple door?"

"You mean..." Vincent spun around. "A secret passage?"

Adinson nodded knowingly. Vincent's interest was piqued; he began to examine the room, starting with the floor. "Perhaps a hidden trapdoor, like the ones on the stages where he performed?" he said, thinking out loud.

The thought of having to find a concealed passage created by the master himself, for his own use, excited Vincent enormously. Just as he was getting caught up in the hunt, Adinson was obliged to rein in his enthusiasm.

"I'm terribly sorry, Vincent, but we don't have time. Unfortunately you won't have the satisfaction of discovering it for yourself—though I know you are capable of doing so—but you will be one of a privileged few to know of its existence, for besides Robert, who shared his secret with me, no one else knows about it."

Adinson walked toward a map cabinet standing under a large painting of three Greek scholars contemplating a supernatural glow in a stormy sky. The rather thin drawers, intended to hold blueprints and geographical surveys, ran the entire length of the cabinet. Adinson beckoned to Vincent to join him.

"Open it please. I'm sure you'll appreciate his incredible attention to detail."

In one of the drawers, Vincent discovered blueprints for stage mechanisms. The next held maps of the Austro-Hungarian Empire and other European countries.

Adinson signaled to him to watch carefully. He closed the drawers and, with one of his feet, pushed the cabinet baseboard, while simultaneously grasping what appeared to be nothing more than an ordinary piece of edging, activating it like a small lever. When he pulled, a click signaled that a mechanism had been set in motion. Adinson stepped back, and Vincent followed suit.

The cabinet sprang to life before them. The various storage spaces opened by degrees and with elegant fluidity, as though enchanted, to form a mahogany staircase, each drawer now one of the steps. Thus arranged, they laid a path to the top of the cabinet, right up to the foot of the painting. There was something magical about watching the cabinet, diverted from its original function, transform to accommodate an entirely different purpose.

Once each element had settled perfectly into place, the mechanism drew to a halt.

"Isn't it marvelous?"

"If I weren't already trying to do so, this marvel would surely make me want to follow the path forged by Mr. Robert-Houdin."

Adinson climbed to the top of the rigged cabinet as though it were an ordinary stair landing. He now stood at the right level to shift the base of one of the lamps that framed the painting and pressed a combination of gilded motifs on the frame. Now unlocked, the large painting pivoted and swung open like a door.

Adinson gestured toward the secret room, which was now revealed. "If you don't mind."

Captivated by the device, Vincent climbed the ingenious staircase and entered a space unlike any he had ever encountered.

If the office was a metaphor for Robert-Houdin's official image, Vincent felt that in crossing the threshold of this secret room he was venturing into the intimacy of the man's brain. It was a kind of eccentric storeroom, a bountiful chaos structured by massive beams from which hung a multitude of objects, including the famous "specter" the magician terrified entire audiences with by making it fly through the air. The rough timber walls were entirely covered in mechanical elements, sketches, archive cabinets, and rows of carefully labeled boxes. Instead of a chair standing in front of the workbench piled with tools and dismantled clock mechanisms, there hung an armchair suspended like a swing. The space was as enchanting as an attic stocked with treasures, as welcoming as a hidden treehouse, and as mysterious as a magician's den crammed with tricks. It was easy to get lost in what appeared to be chaos, but which certainly had not been to its inventor.

Charles pushed a lever behind them. Outside, the drawers regained their places and the painting closed once more. No one would ever suspect they were there.

"Since Jean-Eugène's death, I have always come alone to this place," Adinson confided with emotion.

"Would you prefer to keep it that way?"

"Most definitely not. I am convinced, as are you, Vincent, that only shared experiences are worth the effort. I am truly happy that you are here."

"Thank you for the honor, Charles."

"Let us hope that Jean-Eugène's spirit and the wonder that his hideaway provokes in you will give us the inspiration and the strength for the harsh battle that lies ahead of us."

50

Vincent filled out his sketch so that Charles was sure to understand the configuration of the space and the principle of the tilting floor. Settled in the armchair suspended in front of the workbench, Adinson still seemed disappointed.

"So there was no treasure hidden behind this passage?"

"None, just access to a tunnel equipped with these tubes and these vibrating slats that, by the wind's effect, produced a howling worthy of the most terrifying monster drawn from myth."

Adinson rubbed his chin thoughtfully. "Whoever built this device went to a lot of trouble. Do you have a hypothesis about where it leads?"

"None."

"Did you notice symbols, emblems of chivalry, or signs of secret societies on the entrance arch or elsewhere in the passage?"

"Not the slightest mark."

Charles bent over the sketches and thought out loud. "So this underground passageway was intersected by the installation of a sewer tunnel. Whoever did the work was certainly unaware of what they were destroying."

"Workers assigned to new projects in Paris must regularly encounter old quarry galleries. Whoever dug this sewer probably thought that's what it was."

"There you have a perfect example of the dangers confronting these places. This is exactly the kind of unconscious massacre that urban development causes."

"To be precise, the sewer pipe merely intersected the tunnel."

Adinson's eyes lit up. "Which means if we begin on the other side of the pipe..."

"... there's a good chance that we can continue exploring to the final destination!" said Vincent, finishing his thought.

The two men were delighted at the idea, but Adinson's face quickly fell. "Minguier's men may have discovered the entrance to the tunnel in the cellar of Flamel's house. They could very well reach the same conclusion that we have and get a head start on us."

"That's unlikely. Even if they decided to break down the wall that they have always believed moves, they would only find backfill. There's no way they could imagine the path lies below."

"Then we're a step ahead of them."

"When he locked me up, Minguier mentioned 'the true powers that govern the world.' He referred to, in his own words, occultism and magic."

"Perhaps he belonged to one of those sects eager for treasure and supernatural powers? However, his organization is more formidable than the usual groups of eccentrics who disguise themselves as great priests and hold black masses—they don't go so far as to eliminate their own members by such violent means."

"They killed him after our escape, to make him pay for his failure."

"It's also likely that they wanted to prevent him from being interrogated by the police, since you would have been quite capable of identifying him. They clearly leave no trace."

Adinson paced as he thought. "Tell me, Vincent, did it occur to you that this secret access route, which uses air as artifice, could be the labyrinth entrance connected to wind?" He nodded toward Ignatius of Loyola's account, lying in its open coffer on the table near Vincent's sketches.

Vincent acquiesced. "I only made the connection once we got out."

"Did you notice anywhere this engraved key could have been used?"

"Not at all."

Charles gave a slight push that set the armchair rocking. He kept his pensive gaze on the sketch of the tunnel Vincent had drawn. Suddenly he turned toward him and asked, "What would you say about going back underground to see just where this passage leads?"

51

The cool water running over his face felt so good it was like bathing in the fountain of youth. That he was alone also contributed to his feeling of calm. Bare-chested and dripping wet, Vincent took a moment to breathe. He closed his eyes and exhaled slowly, emptying his lungs entirely, then inhaled again. He did this several times, his sense of serenity increasing with each cycle. He concentrated on the beating of his heart. For at least a few moments, he mastered his own rhythm, unconstrained by any pace but his own.

He pushed aside the images clamoring for attention in his mind: the floor tilting; Henri terrified; the rat's long whiskers; Robert-Houdin's secret office, where Charles smiled as though they were arguing over a game of chess. In that den, as he told Charles what he had experienced, Vincent finally realized that, despite the circumstances, the discovery of the secret passage under Nicolas Flamel's house had offered him a clearer glimpse of eternity than ever before. Neither the fears conspiring against him, nor the uncertainties weighing on their future had succeeded in robbing him of that intoxicating feeling of transcending it all.

Vincent dunked his face in the porcelain basin again. His hands traveled over his own features, as if he needed to rediscover them. He was changing in so many ways that at times he feared he wouldn't recognize himself. But his appearance stayed the same; the transformations taking place were deep within.

He cupped some water in his hands and doused himself one last time. He savored these fleeting moments, delighted in them like rare little pleasures that his trials and tribulations had not yet managed to destroy. He needed these tiny quivers of absolute purity to remind himself that he was still alive and that his existence did not boil down to being prisoner in a nightmare. Then he remembered: while he was diving into a world he knew nothing about, most people were going about life as if nothing had changed.

Vincent examined his reflection in the mirror. He grasped his jaw to stretch the skin of his neck; he was probably going to have to grow a mustache to change his appearance. Then he would look like most other men. Perhaps even grow a little beard. But how long would that thin disguise protect him?

He grabbed the piece of cloth that he had placed near the basin and wiped his neck first. He took unusual care, drawing out the moment of calm as long as possible; he knew that reality would soon take hold of him once more.

He heard Gabrielle upstairs; her laughter mingled with Pierre's voice. They were frolicking around. The two of them shared something that grew stronger each day; strong enough that when they were in their own little world, they could forget the lurking threat.

Vincent opened the door and listened. He leaned on the doorframe, one foot on the landing. Judging by conversations and reassuring sounds of everyday life, it was hard to believe the boardinghouse was under siege. Gabrielle once said that people just carry on with their lives; she was right. Henri's voice suddenly stood out from the rest. He was insisting that Konrad teach him to shoot. The German and the Italian burst into laughter; the carpenter told him that there was only one weapon in the house and that it was better if he were the one to use it. Eustasio spoke of caution. What an odd word given the situation.

Vincent would have liked to surrender to the cordial atmosphere. He enjoyed being witness to it, even if he couldn't participate in it. He often felt like he was the only one to realize the true extent of the danger. Begel often joked that no one equaled him when it came to detecting what was amiss. Was it a talent or a curse? Either way, it didn't reduce the burden.

More than anything, he would have liked to be able to tell himself that those he cared so much about were by his side, at peace, with enough work to meet their needs, and enough dreams to carry them forward. But he couldn't. Even if he refused to accord it too much importance, a faint voice kept telling him that the odd little family he had built was in danger and that he couldn't necessarily save it. Throwing himself into battle remained his best chance at doing so.

52

Paris had become a kingdom of shadows. The last gas streetlights had been extinguished; the night owls had gone home and the cesspit workers would not arrive until later. As for the delivery men, they wouldn't restock the surrounding markets until five o'clock in the morning.

But the calm that hung over the neighborhood was an illusion. Vincent had no trouble locating the sewer hatch through which he and Henri had escaped, but this time he had come with backup: Charles and two of the men who had searched the floor of the Saint-Pierre de Montmartre church with him. To avoid any unpleasant surprises, coachmen had been dispatched to strategic points on the surrounding streets. About twenty of them stood guard at the intersections, ready to sound the alert or step into action. Fiacres had been positioned nearby, prepared to evacuate Charles and his team or to call the troops back in the event that things took a turn for the worse.

The two burly men quickly raised the hatch and invited Vincent to descend. Despite his waders, he paused. It wasn't the fetid water that repulsed him, but rather the idea of returning underground. The feeling of entrapment oppressed him, and he wasn't thrilled at the idea of experiencing it again.

"Come now, quickly," Charles urged him, "a police patrol could appear at any moment."

Steadying himself on the rim, Vincent slipped into the hole and disappeared. After wrapping a scarf over his nose in an attempt to shield himself from the odor, Charles followed suit. The two others joined them, carrying their tools, and closed the heavy hatch above them.

The four men found themselves standing in the sewer main, surrounded by the repulsive water that flowed by and reached halfway up their waders. They turned the lanterns up as bright as they would go.

"This way," said Vincent, indicating the direction. The small group set out against the current.

"How far?" asked Charles.

"It's hard to say. We were moving in the dark."

They walked the sewer tunnel in silence. After several minutes, Vincent came upon the wall he and Henri had escaped through, on the right. "That's where we came out."

Upon seeing the small opening they had created by removing a few burrstones, he said, "When I think back to the time and effort it took us to clear that minuscule passage..."

Charles was already investigating the opposite wall, looking for the best place to break through. "Let's start here, up high, please," he instructed the workers.

One of the men set upon the masonry with a pick. His blows soon dislodged a stone, which fell behind the wall with a dull thud.

"It's hollow," said Charles with satisfaction.

"It's faster when you have something besides a knife to work with," said Vincent ironically.

As chunks of stone fell one after another, Charles held his lantern up to the wall, trying to get a glimpse of the other side. "The tunnel continues just as we hoped!" he exclaimed enthusiastically.

Once the passage had been sufficiently enlarged, one of the workers squeezed through it, followed by Vincent, then the others. Vincent immediately noticed that the air was drier in this section. An odor of dust hung undisturbed by any breeze. Charles was already examining the chisel marks on the walls. "The incisions were made with pointed tools," he said.

One of Charles's men held a lantern out to Vincent and suggested he lead the way. The men's shadows danced on the walls. The foul odor of the sewer diminished as they continued on. As they made their way silently forwards, brief images of what Vincent had gone through with Henri surfaced in his mind and overlapped with reality.

He faltered. Noticing the change, Charles asked, "Is everything all right, Vincent?"

Vincent shuddered and pulled himself together. "Everything is just fine," he said with resolve.

They inspected the walls and the arch for signs or inscriptions. The ceiling dipped at times, forcing the men to stoop to avoid hitting their heads.

"This is odd," said Charles in surprise.

"What is?"

"This long tunnel. It's too narrow to accommodate anything other than men on foot, without any shafts or staircases. Why go through all the trouble to build it?"

"I don't know about this passage," replied Vincent, "but the first civilizations added many detours to purposely lengthen access routes to the most secret sections hidden in their temple foundations. Evidence of this has been found in Mesopotamian and Egyptian monuments, and even in a network of recently discovered grottos in Greece."

"To what end?"

"Archeologists think that the goal was to confuse unwelcome visitors, but especially to discourage the least determined among them by creating a sense of unease. Their increasing anxiety and the feeling of oppression was often enough to convince them to turn back. Passages were not shortened until other means to block them were developed. Impassable doors, metal grates, and even complex locks are actually only a few centuries old."

"Then that would support the idea that this tunnel is very old."

"The evidence suggests so."

Charles continued his line of reasoning. "If this tunnel was dug only as a means of passage, whatever it leads to must be of great importance, given the incredible amount of work it would have required."

"As great as the power of those who used it. I wonder if the alchemist Flamel participated in its construction, or if he only built his house above it in order to control the access."

Several yards later, Charles remarked, "It seems to me as if the tunnel is sloping downward."

"We're descending, there's no doubt about it."

"How far below the surface do you think we are?"

"It's impossible to say without a reference point. At the very minimum we would need knowledge of geology. We're still traveling through the limestone layer, but I don't know how thick it is in this neighborhood."

"Can you tell where we are in relationship to the city above?"

"I've been keeping loose track by counting my steps. I assume we headed north-east, but if you keep talking to me, I'm going to lose count."

The four men fell silent and continued walking. With each inhale, Vincent felt the humidity level rising rapidly. Soon the tunnel sloped more sharply downward. From this point on, the floor was sculpted in long successive steps and landings that grew shorter as the gradient increased. The tunnel turned a curve and the rock grew slick.

"Watch out, it's slippery," said Vincent.

Charles nodded and steadied himself by running a hand along the wall.

At the end of the turn, Vincent stopped suddenly. The tunnel seemed to have broken off; it plunged into a brackish pool and disappeared, making further progress impossible without going under water.

Vincent stepped forward cautiously and raised his lantern to be sure of what he was seeing. Indeed, the entire tunnel plunged into the liquid; there was no other route. He crouched down and smelled the standing water. No suspicious odors alerted him. He reached out a finger; the liquid was cool and fluid. He raised his head and tried to identify what could have caused the tunnel to change course.

Charles joined him. "A landslide?" he asked.

"Possibly, but I don't see any fracture lines in the rock, signs of infiltration, or traces of collapse. Given the impressive setup I witnessed in the first section, I wonder if it isn't all intentional."

"They simulated a breach in the rock and a flood to make it appear as if the passage stops here?"

"It merits consideration."

Vincent slowly entered the water. Cold gripped him through his waders. He felt around with his foot. "The ground is smooth and very slippery. I feel a layer of silt."

The workers offered him their support from the shore. Vincent ventured further out, gripping their outstretched arms as best he could. Underwater, the plunging incline mirrored the curved ceiling. The tunnel hadn't been crushed: it had purposely been dug to be submerged.

Vincent retraced his steps, and the others helped him back onto dry land.

"What do you think?" asked Charles.

"I don't really know," he said, shaking his boots dry. "The first illusion protecting the tunnel was connected to air; this one could be tied to water."

"Then we are at the entrance to the labyrinth," Charles promptly concluded.

"It's too early to be certain."

"But we've already encountered two elements mentioned in Loyola's account: air and water."

"It's possible."

"You don't seem convinced."

"I saw how masterfully the air vents that produced the fake howling were constructed," he said, the mere mention of them sending shivers down his spine.

"Well then?"

"The creators were clearly ahead of their time on many fronts, so it makes me wary to see this tunnel plunge into a pool of water. If they didn't succeed in scaring us off with their monstrous roaring, what hex do they have in store for us here?"

The four men considered the obstacle doubtfully.

"Still waters run deep," said Vincent thoughtfully.

"How do we find out what it's hiding?"

"By diving in."

53

As Vincent finished removing his clothes, one of the workmen insisted, "You should let one of us go. It might be dangerous."

"It most certainly is, but I'm the most capable of determining whether or not there's a way through. Thank you for your offer."

He handed his clothes to Charles.

"Be very careful. Don't take any risks. If you have the slightest doubt, don't force it. We'll find another way," Charles said with a hint of concern in his voice.

Stripped down to his long underwear, Vincent winked at Charles. "Are you sure? Don't you want to know where this tunnel leads?"

"Of course."

"So do I, and I'm going to find out."

He tested the temperature with his toes and frowned. "It seems much colder when you're about to go for a swim."

He entered the water, supported by a workman who offered an outstretched arm to keep him from slipping. Step by step, Vincent made his way slowly forward. He considered the fact that the liquid might contain a toxin and that the floor could be riddled with traps. He even kept an eye on the arch above him; motionless as it was, the mass of rock appeared no less threatening.

Vincent felt as though he were entering a gaping mouth, an open maw that could brutally snap shut on him at any moment. The water now came up to his chest. There was no one to support him as he made his way alone. Although he knew how to swim a bit, this was of little comfort. The cold water forced him to breathe rapidly, as if it were squeezing his ribs. He scouted around on the floor with his foot, hoping to anticipate any unpleasant surprises.

"Do you feel anything?" asked Charles.

"Nothing special."

Now submerged up to his neck, he could barely touch the bottom and paddled with his arms to keep his head above water. He moved from wall to wall, feeling for a protrusion or a snag, but he found nothing there or on the floor.

He continued on. If he went much further, he would be completely submerged. His companions watched from the shore, never taking their eyes off of him. Their anxiety was palpable.

"It's deep," he called out, "but the water doesn't seem dangerous. I'm going under."

Charles protested, but Vincent was determined. He took a deep breath, held it, and disappeared. It would have been no use opening his eyes; the water was too murky and it was too dark. He dove deeper. The walls he felt under his fingers were exactly like those in the tunnel: chiseled, but covered with a thin layer of sediment.

The submerged section presented no trace of a rockslide or breaks in the stone. Despite his instinct urging him to return to the surface, Vincent forced himself to remain calm and keep his eyes closed. He swam forward in the sunken tunnel. He was starting to feel the oxygen deprivation; his temples throbbed to the beat of his heart. He had no idea how far he still had to go.

Suddenly his hand caught on something: an iron bar, solid and very resistant, despite the blisters of oxidation he felt as he ran his hand along it. His other hand encountered a bar as well. He had found a grate. It made him think of the one he had been imprisoned behind in the cellar. A spasm reminded him that he was running out of air. He had only just made a discovery, and here he was, forced to surface for air. He turned around, swam with a few chaotic strokes, and emerged with a violent inhale.

Charles called to him and asked him to come back out. The workers reached out their hands to pull him out of the water, but he didn't take them. "I found a grate," he panted. "I'm going back in."

He inhaled and dove once again. He touched the bars, feeling around the edges. The grate entirely blocked the submerged tunnel.

He tested the edges for a lock, blindly searching for hinges or a means of lifting the grate, but he found nothing that told him anything about how it opened. His movements demanded more and more effort. He was nearing asphyxiation; he had to turn back again.

This time, he resolved to reach dry land, swimming and crawling his way there. His dive had demanded a great deal of energy.

"The tunnel continues," he said, breathless. "But the passage is blocked by a grate, maybe a portcullis."

"Don't force yourself, Vincent," said Charles decidedly.

One of the workers spoke up. "I'm a strong swimmer. I have good lung capacity. Tell me what I should be looking for."

Vincent stood up and said, "A means of opening or raising that grate. I'm not convinced it's fixed. There is no way this tunnel was dug to lead to a dead end."

He had difficulty catching his breath. The man undressed and entered the water without hesitation; he began swimming right away to avoid slipping. "If I find something, I'll come back and describe it to you, and you'll tell me what to do."

Vincent acquiesced. The man took a spectacular inhale and dove.

54

Vincent had nothing to dry himself with, so he dressed in his clothes, which clung to his skin. His jaw trembled and he was shivering, but he was too preoccupied to care. He peered at the water in the lamplight. Small eddies troubled the surface along with the occasional bubble.

"If he takes too long, I'll go in after him," said Vincent.

"Don't worry. Baptiste knows what he's doing. He has a good set of lungs," the other worker reassured him.

It was true: the fellow soon resurfaced in a spray of water.

"Well?"

"Nothing. No lever, no handle, but maybe with our crow bar..."

His companion hurried to pull the tool from his satchel and held it out to him. Vincent warned him, "The iron didn't appear to have a weak spot."

"I'm going to try to use the bar as a lever against the floor to lift or push the grate."

"Be careful."

In response, the man raised his hand, filled his lungs, and dove again.

For those waiting in the silent tunnel, the seconds stretched out and seemed very long. Now and then a few ripples betrayed the movements of the underwater explorer.

The man would not be long now. They were expecting to see him return at any moment, when a sudden jolt shook the tunnel. Charles steadied himself against the wall; Vincent nearly slipped. The dull thundering continued, and the water began to froth. It rose rapidly, agitated by increasingly powerful eddies. The pool had become a raging sea. Charles and the worker stepped back, but Vincent didn't move. "Good God, what is happening down there?"

Suddenly a crack appeared in the ceiling. Fine dust fell, then a fragment of rock.

"He has to come back," cried Vincent. "He's going to be crushed! I'm going in."

Before Charles could persuade him otherwise, a more violent eddy expelled the diver's body. Like a maw rejecting its prey's carcass, the liquid mass vomited the man up. He floated face-down in the water, motionless, arms and legs spread.

The bubbling gradually lessened and the dull thundering faded, but the water level did not drop. Reddish whorls spread around the unfortunate man.

"Baptiste, Baptiste!" repeated his companion, who tried to revive him after hauling him out.

The poor man's body was covered with many bloody gashes. Given the number and depth of the wounds, the diver didn't appear to have succumbed to the quake but rather to have been riddled with spikes.

His companion could not accept his death. He gathered the body into his arms and wept. Charles placed a hand on his shoulder and spoke softly to him. The man shook his head, but Charles managed to calm him and convinced him to set the body down. "It's too late. I'm sorry," he said.

Vincent closed the dead man's eyes. The water, which was still again, was higher and murkier than before. It was tinted with the blood of its victim. Vincent peered at what remained of the tunnel as if he were scrutinizing a murder suspect.

"Poor boy," murmured Charles. "Did he set off a trap, or is the structure so old that it collapsed as a result of his actions?"

"We'll never know what killed him, but one thing is for certain: this passage is no longer accessible."

Charles acquiesced and stood up, hanging his head. "We must bring our friend's body to the surface."

55

Darkness blanketed Paris as the convoy of fiacres full of men drove at breakneck speed. Traveling at full tilt, the carriages headed up still deserted streets and boulevards with a clattering of wheels on cobblestones and the cracking of whips as the coachmen kept their horses at a gallop.

In the lead car, Vincent observed their progress anxiously. Unfortunately it was too late for the worker who had met a mysterious end in the tunnel, but Vincent didn't have a second to lose.

When they reached the surface carrying the body of the unlucky man, terrifying news awaited them. One of the coachmen assigned to protect the boardinghouse came to inform them that an attack had taken place there. All available men had been dispatched.

The animals struggled but did not slow. Rue de Rochechouart was straight enough for them to maintain their pace. Charles tried his best to remain calm so as not to increase his companion's distress.

Vincent grew more impatient as they drew nearer to Montmartre. The worst scenario he could have imagined had come to pass. Gabrielle had been right: Minguier's accomplices hadn't lost any time seeking them out. The scoundrels hadn't even waited for them to venture outside. After a series of devious attacks, their new strategy seemed to be attacking head-on and violently.

As their horse poured all its strength into reaching the north side of Montmartre, Vincent joined his hands and, without realizing it, began to pray. He had never done so except at his mother's command. This time it was different. He didn't know to whom he addressed his prayer, but he hoped that someone would hear it. He needed help, not for himself, but for his loved ones. He prayed that the coachmen had arrived in time; he prayed that Konrad would hit his target, that Eustasio would be able to protect Henri, that Pierre and Gabrielle would get away.

Just as the convoy hurtled from Rue Custine onto Rue Caulaincourt, Vincent saw an ominous red glow in the distance. He gripped the door. As they approached at full speed, he could make out a billowing column of smoke, carrying swirling embers toward the stars. Vincent leaned out of the carriage for a better view. He dared to hope that tragedy had struck somewhere other than his home, but the sight before him left no room for illusion.

The boardinghouse was in flames. The street was crammed with red fire carriages. The heat was palpable, even from a distance. The firefighters were busy spraying the fire with their hand pumps, but the jets of water seemed puny compared to the size of the blaze. Even the steam pump brought in as reinforcement could not overcome the flames.

The carriage was still moving when Vincent jumped down and rushed toward the fire.

The inferno devoured the house in a terrifying roar. Every floor was engulfed in flames; they escaped by what was left of the windows, licking up the facade. He watched as a section of flooring on the first level collapsed with an infernal crash.

Vincent made his way through the group of neighbors who had crawled out of bed to watch the disaster with alarm. The firefighters knew that the building was a lost cause; all they could do was spray the neighboring homes in hopes of keeping them from going up in flames as well.

Vincent didn't care about what was burning; he was distraught with worry for his loved ones. Feverishly he scanned the crowd, looking for them. He was surrounded by stunned faces, none of them familiar. He wasn't going to stand around waiting for more bodies; he would tear his loved ones from the inferno himself. Neither the heat nor the danger would stop him. He rushed forward and crossed the cordon, dodging the firefighters. Holding tightly to their hoses, they yelled at him, "Get back! You'll be burned alive!"

"Get out of here!"

Vincent didn't listen. He shouted at the top of his lungs, "Pierre! Henri!"

His voice was lost in the whistling and cracking of the flaming house. His eyes filled with tears. The smoke prevented him from breathing; the heat burned his skin and his lungs. Against his will, he stepped back. He didn't know what to do or where to go. Disoriented, he retraced his steps before dashing once more toward the house in desperation. He could make out nothing. He no longer recognized their house. On the top floor, where Henri slept, the last shreds of curtain dissolved in the burning wind.

A firefighter grabbed Vincent by the arm. "Don't stay here. The gable may collapse!"

A coachman appeared and took over. "Let go; I'll take care of him. He lived here."

The firefighter released Vincent with an encouraging pat on the shoulder. Distraught as he was, Vincent was incapable of putting up a fight. His strength had dissolved. He turned one last time toward what had been his home, tortured by the gruesome fate that had befallen his only family.

The coachman guided him behind the growing crowd. For Vincent, it was all over.

Suddenly he felt an arm embrace him, then another. A voice said his name. "Vincent!"

It was Pierre! Vincent couldn't believe it. Pierre was alive! So was Henri! The boy threw himself at Vincent, who took both of them in his arms. They returned his embrace warmly. Konrad and Eustasio were there too, and Gabrielle!

Vincent looked at each of them, unable to believe his eyes. Was it really them, or was it their ghosts haunting him already, reproaching him for abandoning them? He was suffocating from the smoke and the emotion. He looked at them each in turn. As he slowly realized they were really there, alive, in front of him, he began to cry uncontrollably. He stumbled from one to the other, touching them again and again. He embraced Gabrielle last, holding her close in silence.

Charles joined them. Although Pierre had never met him, he recognized the man right away. "We owe our lives to your men, sir."

"I am pleased to hear that."

The two men shook hands.

"No victims?" asked Adinson nodding to the burning building.

"It was a close call."

"What happened?"

"We were sleeping," recounted Pierre, "when some strangers threw flaming bottles through the windows. The fire caught immediately and spread very quickly. If the men watching our house hadn't sounded the alarm, we would most certainly have been trapped upstairs by the flames."

"My God!"

"When we came downstairs," added Konrad, "it was already impossible to breathe in the stairwell and the steps were on fire."

"One of your men risked his life to get us out of bed," added Pierre. "I didn't even wake up."

The crowd parted to let a few more fire carriages through as backup. A brigade chief yelled to anyone who would listen, "Bring water, form a chain with buckets, otherwise the whole street will go up in smoke!"

In a panicked commotion, the bystanders began moving about and organizing themselves, gathering every imaginable container—buckets, jugs, pots, bowls—and formed a long chain starting at the fountain on the corner of Rue Lamarck.

Charles asked the coachmen, "Who among you was present when it happened?"

"I was, sir," one of them replied.

"How many arsonists?"

"Five. Three in front and two around back. Given their weapons and their method of operation, they surely intended to drive out the occupants using fire, then kill them as soon as they got outside. We intervened. They didn't expect to find us here. We had the element of surprise on our side."

"And where are they now?"

"Four are dead, and we have the last one, wounded but alive."

"Make sure he doesn't kill himself. That is essential. We have a few questions to ask him. In the meantime, everyone who lived in this boardinghouse must disappear for a time. I will send them where no one will be able to find them. Quietly ready a car."

56

Pierre was awakened by daylight filtering through his eyelids; he rolled over, determined to fall back asleep. That night he had dreamed dreadful dreams. He pulled the cover up to protect himself—and felt his feet sticking out. What a state his bed must be in! Half-asleep, he heard the distinct sound of birdsong, as well as a few distant voices; but the most surprising of all was the occasional wooden creaking, like the sound made by timber framework warming in the sun. His subconscious did not recognize his usual environment, and his brain set in motion. The air was cool; his exposed feet confirmed as much. He was bathed in light. He might even be lying outside.

Pierre opened his eyes with difficulty. He saw a small room made of wood: he was lying in a caravan! At the sight, he woke completely, as everything came back to him with brutal force.

He sat up, assailed by images: the boardinghouse in flames; the coachman guiding him through the smoke; Gabrielle's composure when he woke her; the fire spreading through the house; reuniting with his brother; then the flight from Paris to an improbable location where strange people laughed and drank, danced, and embraced in an ambiance that seemed surreal. None of it had been a dream.

Pierre swung his legs over the edge of the narrow bunk and sat on the edge. He held his head in his hands to keep it from exploding. Then he got up, bumping several times against the narrow caravan, which swayed when he moved. Finally he stepped out onto the shaky wood balcony and shielded his eyes with his hands. He had difficulty adjusting to the early morning light.

His faded blue caravan stood on a hill with a half dozen others, overlooking a strange complex of shanties built around a vast central square. The tables scattered at random, the chairs strewn higgledy-piggledy, and the beer steins standing here and there suggested recent intense activity, but the area was completely deserted. The refreshment stalls had been left in disarray, with sideboards supporting casks and bar counters still covered with pitchers and glasses, as if whoever who had been drinking there had suddenly disappeared. Pierre barely recognized the boisterous square he had crossed in the middle of the night just hours earlier. What had become of the ebullient crowd through which their escort of coachmen had been forced to cut a path?

In the distance, beyond the caravans and the bordering woods, Pierre could make out the tip of the Eiffel Tower. Judging by the sun's position, they had been evacuated to the countryside somewhere south of Paris. The events of the previous night slowly came back to him. He cast a glance at the neighboring caravans. Loud snores arose from the third in line: they were definitely coming from Konrad. This morning, Pierre was happy to hear them.

In the other direction he saw a tall, green-eyed bald man looking at him. The huge man was seated comfortably, with his legs outstretched and his feet propped on the railing.

"Did you sleep well?" asked the big fellow.

Pierre didn't know what to say. He had never seen this man, and he didn't recognize him. He was a giant, and his arms were tattooed with patterns that intimidated Pierre: a cross, flames, a boat, a naked woman with a flower for a face, and a skull—an odd mix indeed.

The stranger stood up. He was even taller than Pierre had imagined, and the young man wondered if he should flee or offer his hand, but the giant turned away and bent in half to enter his caravan. Pierre was still wondering what to do when the man returned almost immediately with two metal cups and a dented coffee pot with chipped enamel.

"Coffee? I make it Turkish style."

Pierre nodded in thanks and took the hot cup. The man raised his as if in a toast and swallowed the coffee in one gulp. Pierre pointed to the deserted square below. "Wasn't there a party here last night? Where are all the people?"

The giant shrugged his shoulders. "At this hour, God only knows what they're doing. But they'll be back this evening."

"Where are we?"

"Here, my boy, we don't ask questions. I'm not going to ask you why you and your gang arrived in the middle of the night, covered in soot and guarded like the great sultan's virgins. And you won't ask me or anyone you encounter any questions either, no matter how surprising they may seem. And believe me, you're going to meet some strange characters. So you and your friends keep the peace and nothing will happen to you."

"Understood. Still, I should warn you that we are being hunted by murderers who don't think twice about killing or burning down houses."

The man was unmoved. He drew close to Pierre, who took a step back. But the man was so tall, Pierre was forced to look up to continue to meet his gaze. "I don't know your story, and I don't even know your name, but I can guarantee you that no one will make trouble for you here." The giant bent down and added, "I escaped a labor camp six years ago and no one has ever managed to capture me."

"Please note that I didn't ask you any questions."

The man smiled and tilted his chin toward the caravans.

"The people who wind up here all have a genuine need to escape the world. There's a good reason these cabins are nicknamed 'the embassies.'"

"The embassies?"

"A small piece of land that doesn't belong to the surrounding country; an island in the ocean. I'll say it again: you're not in danger here."

Pierre took in the view and sipped his coffee—and choked on it. It was awful; too sweet, definitely too strong, and full of grounds.

"Turkish style," laughed his new friend. "By the way, my name is Victor."

One of the caravans began to rock. Someone was moving around inside. Vincent soon appeared on the threshold, also blinded by the morning light. Luckily the handrail stopped him; otherwise he might have tumbled all the way down the hill. Pierre read in his brother's face the same disbelief that must have colored his own upon discovering their whereabouts.

Vincent blinked his eyes, then spotted his brother and the giant, who waved to him.

"Up already, Pierre?"

"The sun got me out of bed."

Vincent rubbed his face to chase away the last of his sleep.

"The washroom is back there, on the river bank. The biggest in Paris! There's no hot water, I'm afraid," the giant murmured. "Do keep one thing in mind though: never cross the river; our territory only extends halfway across. The other side belongs to the bohemians, and they don't like to be disturbed."

"Got it," replied Vincent.

Pierre walked over to his brother. "Do you know where we are?" he asked under his breath.

"Safe, according to Charles. After what we've been through, that's all that matters. Last night he entrusted us to this big fellow."

"It's an odd place. This fellow is odd too. Whatever you do, don't drink his coffee."

"Right now, Pierre, everything is odd. Let's be happy we've survived, as we wait for something better to come along. You're going to stay here and prepare with the others. Don't leave camp. I must find Charles."

57

Before he entered the cell, Adinson made a final appeal to Vincent. "However angry you are at this man, do not let that dictate your behavior. We are not here to punish him, much less to take our revenge. Our only objective is to get answers. Whatever happens, don't forget that."

Vincent nodded without much conviction. Adinson squared his shoulders and opened the door.

The walls of the small room were bare and windowless; the prisoner lay on his back on a straw mattress with his wrists and ankles tightly bound. Two men silently kept watch over him. On a table nearby were sharp tools, a dagger, and jars of water. A hangman's knot hung from the ceiling, directly in front of the prisoner. Everything had been arranged to make the captive think he was going to be tortured. However, the only discomfort he'd suffered up to that point was a ladleful of cold water in the face each time he fell asleep.

Charles walked toward him. The man did not seem particularly afraid; he even displayed a hint of bravado. He turned to look at Adinson and didn't even flinch as he watched him approach.

Charles launched into his interrogation. "Who do you work for?"

"I don't know anything," replied the man coldly. "I was paid to do a job, and that's all."

"Burning down houses to kill people is not a job. I'll ask you again: whose orders were you following?"

The man didn't even bother to respond.

"Your accomplices are dead," continued Charles. "You are the only survivor. Your methods indicate that you are not amateurs. So if you want to make it out of here, I suggest you tell us what you know."

"Make it out?" snickered the stranger. "If I talk, they'll kill me, and they don't mess around."

"Who are you referring to? Who are these people?"

The prisoner stared hard at him. "You have no idea what they are capable of. They're everywhere. We failed, so they'll send other men who will succeed."

Despite being in a position of vulnerability, the man still seemed to feel a sense of pride, even impunity. How could he? How could he still believe that he had the upper hand when he was alone with four men who were equipped with tools, each of which could take his life? Vincent clenched his fists. Hard as he tried to keep Charles's warning in mind, he could not remain impassive before the provocations of the man who had wanted to kill his friends.

He walked calmly toward him. Something told Vincent that this good-for-nothing would not talk if all they did was ask him questions. He scrutinized and studied him. The other man behaved like a venomous snake about to be captured. Vincent did not intend to take revenge or punish the man, but he was going to make the arsonist admit everything he knew, all the same.

Charles continued. "Do you realize the danger you're in?"

The man was impassive. It almost seemed as if Charles's questions encouraged his behavior. After all, his captors didn't know anything. Their ignorance probably made him feel in control.

He stared at Adinson coldly. "You caught me; good for you. You're going to hurt me, and it will probably kill me. I don't care. The forces I belong to will make you pay for it sooner or later. You have no idea what you're up against."

The man gestured toward the instruments of torture on the table. "Is that all you have? Those are your weapons?" He sighed scornfully. "You want me to tell you what I know, so I will. It can be summed up in a few words: the ones I serve will soon be your masters, and my death won't change that."

Vincent couldn't stand it anymore. With one stride he was upon the man and grabbed him by the throat. "Here, your masters can do nothing for you, and if they were as powerful as you say they are, they would have come for you. But I don't see anyone to save your skin or spare you from the rope."

Charles joined him. He held his open hand up to the criminal's face. "I would add, my friend, that you know nothing of our powers."

The moment the words were out of his mouth, his fingers burst into flames. Vincent stepped back; the prisoner panicked. Adinson calmly savored the effect, and waved his fiery hand close to the prisoner's face. The man's expression had radically changed: his eyes were no longer full of disdain, only terror.

"You see," murmured Charles. "You don't know who you're dealing with either."

The man struggled against his bonds to escape Adinson. His breath quickened. He turned his face away, twisting to avoid the flames that licked at him. "Leave me alone!" he begged. "It's impossible! Only the Mage is capable of such enchantments."

Charles bent over him, taking his time. "The Mage?" he asked, waving his miraculously flaming hand in front of the prisoner.

The man's attitude shifted suddenly. He no longer looked away; his gaze had become that of a fanatic. "It's you! You're the Mage! You put me to the test to see if I would betray you, but I've said nothing, I swear! *Aurorae sacrum honorem! Aurorae sacrum honorem!* I would die to serve you!"

Adinson's burning fingers were reflected in the prisoner's distraught eyes. "I'm sorry, you pathetic scoundrel, but I'm not your Mage. And let me tell you a secret that ought to make you tremble: I can read your mind, whether you like it or not."

The man let out a strangled cry and his confidence drained away. All hope of surrendering to the one he worshiped had just dissolved. He cursed Adinson. "You're the devil!"

"It doesn't matter what you call me, you will obey me in the end."

Consumed by panic, the man grew agitated and began to scream. He struggled against his bonds until they tore his flesh. His face grew scarlet, and the veins of his neck and forehead bulged under the surface of his skin. Suddenly his body went limp and motionless, and his head rolled to one side.

A guard checked his eyes and pulse. "He fainted."

Charles hurried to the jar of water and plunged his hand in it. "As I live and breathe!" he exclaimed. "I don't know how Jean-Eugène managed to hold out so long during his shows."

Vincent applauded the performance. Adinson groaned in relief. He pulled his cooled hand from the water and removed the flesh-colored glove that protected it from the flammable syrup.

"My jacket sleeve is ruined," he grumbled. "And this damned glove doesn't block the heat as well as he assured me it did!"

Amused, Vincent said, "Tell me, Charles, I'm not the only one who thinks you're the devil. Do you have something to confess?"

58

Vincent shifted a board in the fence and slipped through behind his brother. His throat tightened: he dreaded what he was about to see.

For the moment, judging only by what he saw around him, he might still believe that nothing had changed; but it was only an illusion. And he knew it. The old grain depot might look the same, but a powerful odor of smoke hung in the air.

Out of habit, the two men left little evidence of their passage behind them. But that didn't matter today.

When they arrived in the garden side by side, they froze, transfixed by the same sight. The back gable of the boardinghouse was still standing, but it was all that remained of their former home. It was blackened and stripped down to its skeleton, like a carcass gnawed to the bone. The roof, walls, and floor had collapsed or gone up in smoke; the windows were nothing more than gaping rectangles framing a perfect blue sky.

The birds were singing. Their joyful chirping seemed somehow incongruous with the devastation. At that moment, Vincent envied their ability to simply accept things as they were. They knew how to adapt to any circumstance. All that mattered to them was remaining faithful to their nature: if it rained, they took shelter and waited. If they sensed danger, they moved away from it. If the storm destroyed their nest, they rebuilt it. As long as they had the strength to, they continued at all costs. This morning, they twittered away. In a few days, when the walls had cooled, they would alight there, and eventually nest in the gaps.

As he examined the ruins of his house, Vincent wondered if a man would be capable of living by the same principles. Were they proof of profound wisdom or of absolute powerlessness to enact change?

Most of the vegetation was scorched, evidence of the inferno's alarming heat. Pierre moved through the burnt grass, incredulous at the sight before him. Around them were nothing but ruins. The brothers did not speak, but the looks they exchanged spoke volumes about their distress.

The back door had collapsed. Knowledge of the mechanisms was no longer necessary to open it—one step over it sufficed. Pierre showed his brother the heavy load that had collapsed in the hallway. Had the fire destroyed the trap, or had it been triggered by one of the killers trying to get into the house? His crushed, charred body might be underneath it. Neither of them wanted to see for certain.

Vincent ventured into the hallway, which was blocked by an unstable tangle of charred beams. He climbed carefully over piles of scorched debris, bits of plaster, pieces of metal deformed by the heat, and ashes. The dearth of remains testified to how violently the fire had blazed. The brothers made their way with difficulty through the hellacious scene, where some of the rubble still lay smoking.

The kitchen was now open to the sky. Only the stone walls and the large iron stove had resisted the raging flames. Even the sink had collapsed in on itself. Nothing remained of the table and chairs. The vase that Gabrielle liked to fill with flowers was no longer there, nor was the shelf on which she placed it. Pierre bent down and picked up a fragment of broken plate: it may have been the one he used when he tasted the young woman's first pastry.

Vincent was already waiting for him in front of the chimney—this is what they had come for.

They cleared away the pieces of blackened wood that might prevent the wall from moving. Would it still work? In what state would they find their cellar? Vincent placed his hand in the hole left by the missing brick. Everything was covered in soot, and the walls were still warm. He triggered the mechanism. With a scraping that sounded rougher than usual, it did what it was built to do. The wall shifted, although they had to help it along at the end.

The men entered the passage, carefully closing the wall behind them. They descended the stairs, prepared for the worst. They expected a shock, but couldn't imagine just how big it would be.

When they reached the bottom of the stairs, they were astonished to find their den intact! They couldn't believe their eyes. The disaster that had ravaged the boardinghouse had spared the underground portion. Everything was where it should be. The venerable medieval cellar had been perfectly preserved, while nothing remained of the more recent house above. Nothing in the workshop betrayed the tragedy that had unfolded, except perhaps for the slightly warmer temperature.

Incredulous, Vincent wandered at random, as in a dream, walking from one workbench to the next. Pierre had to touch objects to convince himself he wasn't daydreaming. He placed a hand on Konrad's vise, picked up the pyrite on the central table, hefted a metal pendulum that he hadn't completed. "You always said," he murmured, "that this was the safest part."

Vincent headed straight for a large chest and opened the doors. There was the automaton house built by Robert-Houdin that the watchmaker had left to him. He removed the protective velvet cover and carefully wound the handle on the side.

It made the same clicking sound that it always had: steady and reassuring. Since the very first time he heard it, Vincent had always appreciated this familiar sound of a mechanism carrying out the function it was designed for. Each cog that turned, each pawl that engaged, carried the promise that things were going to take place as planned, within the allotted time—an ideal vision of control that life never allowed.

Pierre walked over to his brother. He had not often seen the little marvel in action, but he knew what it meant to Vincent. He sat down on the floor, like a child about to watch a performance.

When he had finished winding the spring, Vincent engaged the mechanism and sat down next to his brother.

The woman hung out her laundry, the man put on his hat, and the cat scampered across the roof between the two chimney stacks. They hadn't changed; their lives had stayed the same. The sudden appearance of the dancing flames had a strange effect on the two brothers that morning. In them Pierre saw flashes of the catastrophe he had survived. His eyes filled with tears, and he was overwhelmed by memories of the tragedy that the animated scene awakened. Vincent's response went deeper. He stared at the wavering flames; he watched the fire carriage arrive and the long ladder unfold. This mechanical wonder held great meaning for him; it was a souvenir of the masters he admired, a tangible bond to an increasingly distant past, and the embodiment of the feeling that had led him to become the man he was.

The flames disappeared, and the carriage retreated. The worst was over. The miniature building bore no trace of the accident that had just taken place. The woman and the man returned to their activities as though nothing had happened—so did the cat. Reality was quite different for Vincent and his loved ones.

The two brothers continued to sit in silence after the automaton had completed its cycle. Vincent gradually let himself be overcome by an emotion that flooded over him. For the first time, the automaton's magic had not worked on him. For the first time, he looked at this little masterpiece and saw nothing more than an ingenious—but meaningless—mechanism. It pained him. It was a farewell to a piece of himself and it left him grieving for a bygone era. No doubt he was too old for such illusions. He knew too much now to be satisfied with simple distractions. Suddenly he thought of the secret passage in Nicolas Flamel's residence, the submerged path that had cost a man his life. Those mechanisms weren't just for show. They were much more than a bit of sleight-of-hand intended to entertain.

Vincent stood up. With deference and tenderness, he slipped the velvet cover over the automaton once more and closed the chest doors. The little performance had given him another spark after all: in watching it for the last time, he had accepted the need to bid farewell to his past in order to prepare to face the future.

59

The first rickety carriages appeared late in the afternoon, arriving from all directions to converge on the countryside as though they had been invited to a secret meeting. They came by the main road and by the hilly dirt paths that wound through the surrounding fields, orchards, and woods. They were as different from one another as enemy animal species that had agreed to a truce so they could slake their thirst at the only watering hole in the desert: a sacred rallying point, anticipated and respected by all. Impossible to categorize or describe, the strange teams all displayed equal enthusiasm for gathering there. Fair carts and traveling attractions parked at random; the first to arrive were the closest to the square, creating a kind of temporary city around the refreshment stands at its center.

Men and women in various states of extravagant dress—or undress—gradually filled the tables. They hailed and greeted each other, already raising their glasses. It was difficult to say whether they were servers or clients; from one minute to the next, they could be found behind the counters hard at work or sitting sipping like princes. It quickly became clear that there were no customers or proprietors here, no kings or slaves; everyone graciously alternated roles according to the situation. There were no spectators, just acrobats of all stripes presenting their own acts or recounting their adventures to others who, in turn, would do the same.

Leaning against his caravan, Konrad observed the activity from the crest of the hill. He could never have imagined that such a place existed. He and his companions had definitely driven through it last night on their way in, but they had been in no condition to realize just how unique it was. Fortune tellers, jugglers, dwarves, and bearded ladies conversed and laughed together. These odd characters, street performers, and minstrels mingled with hucksters, preachers, and other charlatans. After all, they practiced nearly the same profession: they made their living off of the average person's desire to be entertained or to believe, in exchange for a few coins.

Konrad tried to study each of them, fascinated and amused by this tribe of performers whose existence he had never even imagined. The German had been surprisingly quiet since the fire in the boardinghouse. Usually so quick to give his opinion, he now remained seated, only moving if he was prompted. At the boardinghouse, he had been the burliest by far, and his status as a deep-voiced colossus was a self-evident fact that everyone respected. But here, he looked almost like a child compared to the giant that watched over them from the neighboring caravan. Many of the certainties he defined himself by had been called into question over the last few days.

People continued pouring into the central square. The joyful chaos only fell into place once the first musicians arrived. They set the rhythm. But contrary to custom in more formal establishments, they didn't perform on a stage; instead they remained scattered throughout the square, wherever their desires and encounters led them. Occasionally they responded to or riffed off one another from a distance, backed by the guests, who took up the popular refrains in spontaneous chorus. Some even stopped playing to drink a tankard of beer or converse, but there were always enough of them strumming away together to keep the atmosphere lively.

Henri emerged from his caravan, stretching. He yawned, then remarked on the intensifying activity below. "What's going on?"

"I don't know," replied Konrad, "but it's worth a look."

The Nail leaned on his railing and discovered to his astonishment the surprising group of individuals that continued to grow and spread out as evening fell.

"Looks like the same people that were here last night. But where were they during the day?"

Victor the giant joined in the conversation. "They were in Paris," he explained, "earning a living. Some are still there and will arrive later."

"I'm not sure what goes on around here is appropriate for a young soul," Konrad warned Henri.

"I'm not a kid anymore," retorted the Nail. "You know, I've seen a naked woman!"

Konrad turned to him with curiosity. "Well done, my boy! And when did this miracle take place?"

"This afternoon, by the river, out back. The girls were bathing there."

Konrad was amused to see the boy blush. The activity below drew their attention once again. Hundreds of small lights now dotted the strange and teeming square. In the darkness, each of the lanterns lit a face, a scene, or an event in the curious kaleidoscope of performers: a woman performed a card trick for a pair of identically dressed harlequins; two men danced tenderly entwined, encouraged by women whose lingerie was visible even from such a distance; a one-armed man led his horse to a table and ordered it a bowl of beer.

Victor the giant drew nearer to Konrad and said, "Quite a show, isn't it?" The German nodded his head in agreement.

"I arrived years ago, and I'm still surprised when night falls," confided the guardian of the embassies. "Whether it's raining, snowing, or windy, they all turn up and the circus begins again. You won't always find exactly the same people; some only come occasionally, but there's always enough of a crowd to keep from getting bored."

"Who are these people?"

"They're the ones that Paris only tolerates to entertain its residents. During the day, they stand on every street corner, in the squares, outside of train stations, and at the foot of churches. Thanks to this band of miscreants, the townspeople awaken their wildest instincts and their childish dreams. The bourgeois love their tricks and toss them a few cents. But when evening falls, no one wants to see them linger in their neighborhood. Considered pleasant enough attractions in the light of day, they become thieves by moonlight. As soon as evening falls, they are chased beyond the city walls."

Konrad remained thoughtful. "I never stopped to wonder what became of the peddlers after they packed up their stands."

"Some find makeshift shelter in the city, but many come here. The police have come down even harder on them since the Fair opened. These marginal creatures don't fit in with the image the capital wants to project. So in the evening they gather together, practice their acts, and share the tricks of the trade that can't be learned in any school."

"It's certainly not like the World's Fair," said Henri, "but I like it."

"Here, there are no futuristic inventions or machines," said the giant, "just men and women. No beautiful clothes or superficial manners, just the truth of what we are: human, liberated and unadorned. All that matters is what you can do, and the effect it has on others."

Konrad spotted Pierre, who had finally returned, without Vincent. The carpenter placed a hand on Henri's arm; the boy's attention was focused on the young women dancing, whose petticoats went flying as they kicked up their legs.

"Tell Gabrielle: I'm going down to meet him."

60

The prisoner's attitude had changed dramatically since the appearance of the flaming hand. Now he seemed to fear everything and everyone. Two guards dragged him along, tied to a board, his head covered with a canvas sack. Over and over he begged, "Release me. Where are you taking me?"

Neither man responded. They carried him through the corridors to a much larger room that had been prepared for the next interrogation. The captive, still bound, was propped in a sitting position and kept motionless in the silent room. He turned his still covered head wildly in an attempt to pick out sounds.

Silently Adinson drew near the man and whispered in his ear, "Your fate is about to change."

Recognizing the man with the diabolical powers, the prisoner shuddered and cowered in his bonds. He moaned the pitiful wail of a terrified animal. Vincent hung back. He hardly recognized the man who had put up such resistance just a day earlier. How could this pathetic lout have appeared so dangerous?

"What are you going to do to me?" he said in a trembling voice, panting under the hood. Suddenly Charles whipped it off his head. The prisoner squinted, then glanced around in panic. His gaze came to rest on Adinson. "Have mercy on me! I don't know anything!"

Every movement Charles made frightened the man: more than anything, he was afraid of becoming the target of yet another enchantment. Adinson took his time. "Are you sure about that?"

"I swear on my father's grave!"

"Show some respect for his memory; I doubt he would approve of the crime you have committed."

"You can read my mind, I don't care. You'll see that I don't know anything."

"Then you are of no more use to me." Adinson stepped back, and with a theatrical gesture, tore the veil off a magnificent guillotine.

The prisoner was paralyzed. "You're going to execute me!" he yelped.

"Isn't that what you intended to do to innocent people? What did they do to deserve that?"

"We were ordered to do it!"

"So you obey without knowing why?"

"They were enemies of our cause!"

"A cause you don't know much about."

"Please, release me. I'm no one, I just follow orders!"

The man closed his eyes and intoned, "*Aurorae sacrum honorem, Aurorae sacrum honorem.*"

Charles slowly circled him, like a wolf about to finish off its dying prey. "Yesterday you were a glorious soldier serving an absolute power capable of reducing us to ashes, and today you're nothing but an insignificant cog in an organization you know nothing about."

Charles motioned to one of the guards, who placed a cabbage on the guillotine platform, then stepped back and stood ready to activate the killing machine.

The prisoner stared at the instrument of death. At a nod from Charles, the man pulled the cord, freeing the blade from the crossbar. With a sinister whistling sound, the metal plummeted toward the cabbage and sliced it cleanly down the middle, sending the two halves flying.

The prisoner closed his eyes. His entire body trembled. Charles came to stand before him again. "Since you have nothing to tell me, I have no use for you."

"Please, I'm begging you, have mercy!"

One of the guards hoisted the blade to the top of the frame. As it traveled up the grooves, the metal made a screeching sound that would have caused even the innocent to tremble. The safety latch rearmed with a click.

Satisfied, he proceeded to help his colleague. The two men firmly grasped the board to which the miserable prisoner was bound and carried it to the scaffold. The poor devil struggled against his bonds, but it was no use. The more he flailed about, the deeper they cut into his skin. Contrary to charitable custom, he had been placed on his back—giving him a full view of the blade plunging toward his neck.

As they attached him to the platform, he cried out, "No! For the love of God!"

"Do not appeal to that which you have betrayed in the face of your demise."

The guards stepped aside, and Adinson took hold of the cord. The condemned man sobbed, hiccupped, and choked on his tears. Charles held his gaze. As he prepared to pull the release, the man screamed, "I know things!"

"Don't pretend, my friend. I think you've told me everything. There's no point in drawing out this painful moment."

"Wait! I've only seen the Mage once, but I don't remember where it was now."

"How unfortunate for you."

"It was in a cabaret, but it was only a cover. He receives visitors there."

Charles grasped the cord firmly. "Don't worry, we'll find him. Rest in peace, and may the Almighty forgive you."

The cord grew taut. The prisoner panicked and screamed, "Le Chat Noir! It's at Le Chat Noir!"

Adinson pulled the cord sharply; the blade fell. Wild-eyed, the man watched the heavy blade release and race toward him. He let out a horrible cry—that continued long after the rigged blade spared his life.

61

The river wound between grassy banks lined with wild apple trees. As night fell, the birds quieted, giving way to the crickets. Reedbeds waved gently in the evening breeze; the wind set their dry leaves gently rustling. The bucolic setting and the sound of flowing water formed a peaceful backdrop. It promised to be a mild spring evening.

Gabrielle had preferred to wait until the area was deserted to bathe there. Pierre escorted her, maintaining a respectful distance; he was happy enough keeping lookout.

The night was illuminated by the huge bonfire the bohemians had lit on the opposite bank. Their silhouettes stood out against the glow of the dancing flames. Inaudible conversations and the sound of a violin being tuned drifted up from their gathering.

Gabrielle found a quiet spot among the high grass where she undressed and hung her clothes in the low branches of a tree. Pierre heard the sound of rustling fabric, but scrupulously avoided looking in her direction.

The young woman, now bare-skinned, entered the river. The cool water elicited a small cry.

"Are you all right?" asked her young admirer.

"It's going to be an ice bath, but I don't care. I can't wait to feel clean. I can't stand this soot anymore."

Pierre heard her slip into the water. He could make out the movements of her arms and her hands playing in the lapping water. Just imagining her made him blush. The young woman relaxed, though the cold water took her breath away.

"The river is deeper than it appears," she said. "I can barely touch the bottom."

"Watch out for the current."

She plunged her head under the water for a moment and surfaced panting. Then she began to rub her body briskly to fight off the cold that made the hair on her skin stand up.

"Tomorrow," she said, "I'll wash my clothes. I don't even know if the odor of smoke will come out. Anyway, they're all I have."

"The first chance we get, we'll buy you new ones."

The young woman ran her fingers through her long loose hair to untangle it. "When I think of the beautiful blue and white dress you bought me," she sighed, "it makes me sad. I only wore it once. I really wish I could have saved it from the fire."

"We're safe and healthy. That's all that matters. I'll get you another, even more beautiful, dress."

It wasn't so much the dress that the young woman lamented, but what it symbolized. It was the first gift Pierre had offered her, and for someone who had received few gifts, it was important. She had been deeply moved by the surprise, even more so because Pierre had not tried to profit from his generosity.

Up until that point, Gabrielle had learned that gifts always came with strings attached—especially when they were offered by men—and that the price would have to be paid sooner or later, in one way or another. So she had grown accustomed to managing displays of "generosity" that involved exchanges, interests, or power relations—never feelings. When the young man had brought her the dress wrapped in elegant white tissue paper, she had not felt immediate delight; she feared the offering was the first step toward a request or even a demand. Then, as the days passed, she saw that Pierre's behavior toward her had not changed; she had come to understand that his gesture had been as affectionate as it was unconditional. That's when she really began to see him differently. Each day she grew more attached to the dress as proof that sometimes men are capable of acting without expecting anything in return. By comparison, everything else she had lost in the fire mattered little to her. She had often found herself with nothing, enough to know that possession or loss—of an object, in any case—changes little in one's existence.

Hearing the splash of a dive, Pierre grew worried. "Do you know how to swim at least?"

"Not really, but I'm staying near the bank."

Through the reeds, Pierre couldn't help noticing the young woman's silhouette. Her dripping skin glowed in the golden light of the campfire across the river.

"Gabrielle?"

"Yes?"

"I've been wanting to ask you a question, but you must promise to tell me the truth."

"Why would I lie to you?" She made a few movements to stay warm.

"I want to know if you're happy with us." He hurried to add, "Despite everything that's happened."

The young woman took a moment to think. "Happy with you?"

"Usually we lead a calmer life. But at the moment... So I was wondering... I don't want you to be afraid."

Gabrielle moved closer to shore and tossed her long wet locks behind her head. "How can you expect me not to be afraid? I'm no different than you. The situation would make anyone's blood run cold. You elude death on a daily basis. I nearly saw you get killed. They set the house on fire and left us with nothing."

Pierre hesitated to ask her the only question that really mattered to him. The stakes were so high.

"Why are you asking me this?" she asked in surprise.

Lacking the courage to respond, the young man decided to confide in her instead. "I'm scared too," he declared. "That's true. But what terrifies me the most is the thought that you might want to leave."

He paused, searching for the right words. "Every day, I do everything I can to make you want to stay. Obviously that doesn't carry much weight compared to what we've been through. But the fact is, if you leave, I'll miss you terribly. To be honest, I can't imagine living without you."

She laughed. At first Pierre thought perhaps she hadn't understood. How could she laugh when he was opening his heart to her? "I'm not joking, Gabrielle."

"I know that, Pierre." She turned her face toward the starry sky. "You know," she said, "life has never been easy for me. But I've never experienced the kind of violence you have to contend with. Yet, whatever you're going through, I realize that the problems and the dangers are external, not within. This is the first time I've lived with a group of people who aren't all wondering what they're going to steal from each other. When I see how you live, I understand what it means to count on someone else. For the first time, too, I feel like what I do is appreciated; I believe I'm respected, that I'm cared for. So whatever we have to endure, I will always be better off with you than anywhere else."

"You're not going to leave?"

The young woman seemed surprised by the idea. "I don't intend to, unless you ask me to. And I would be sorry to go."

The young man's heart lifted and beat faster, as if it were going to take flight. He was certain if Gabrielle stayed, then he could handle anything. For her, he would face any fear. "No matter where we live next, you'll stay with us?"

"With the group, or with you?"

The question forced Pierre to confront the reality of his feelings. Even though his answer was obvious, to admit it would force him to reveal so much about himself that his shyness made it impossible for him to do so. He tossed a pebble into the water. There are some words that must be said, even though we worry how they'll be received. Yet he murmured, "If you only knew what I want for you, for us."

Over the high grass, the young woman sent a large spray of water in his direction. Pierre was shocked, as much by the cold as by her uninhibited gesture.

"I heard you," she called.

Caught in the act of showing his affection, Pierre remained silent. But not Gabrielle. "Do you really think I don't know what you want for the two of us?"

Pierre panicked. He was incapable of logical thought. Gabrielle sent another splash his way and murmured, "Come. Come to me."

62

Charles pointed to the Rue des Vertus, located at the center of the city map spread out on his desk, and indicated a specific block of houses.

"If your estimation of distances underground is accurate, the passage that collapsed on our unfortunate companion should be located somewhere under this group of houses here."

Vincent thought for a moment. "What's over there?"

"Rather run-down housing, a few stores, and a factory that manufactures enameled metal kitchen utensils. It's quite possible that the people who live in the area are completely unaware of the tunnel winding beneath their feet."

Vincent scratched his nascent beard, which he was having a hard time getting accustomed to. "No one could imagine something like that," he conceded. "The inclines we encountered during our exploration suggest that we must have descended well below even the deepest cellars." He paused. "Do you know what troubles me most about this tunnel, Charles?"

Adinson shook his head.

"Ordinarily, a secret passage follows its own logic, one rooted in the purpose it serves and the culture of whoever created it. But the one in question calls upon knowledge and means that far surpass the resources of each of the communities that might have built it."

"In other words?"

"It has the purity of passages designed by clergymen, but is more devious in nature, and deadly even, which goes against their principles. It's brutal enough to have been conceived by bandits, but they never would have been able to add such complex security systems. It could also have been built by occult devotees, but it draws on branches of science they don't usually dabble in, and we found none of their symbols, which they abundantly disseminate. Either it's an exceptional combination, or I'm missing something. It's as if whoever designed it decided to pick and choose only the most effective methods. If only we knew where it led."

"I spoke to my companions about it. A few of them can offer us precious aid, and set right to work. Loyola's manuscript and the etched key are being examined at this very moment."

"I'm eager to hear their conclusions."

"One of our historians has already signaled a fact that, in my opinion, seems to be of the utmost importance."

"Really?"

"In his study of the history of Flamel's house and Rue de Montmorency, he discovered a significant piece of information: there is a very good chance that the alchemist's property, old as it is, was not the first building to be erected on the site."

Vincent hung on Adinson's every word.

"It appears that before the first houses were built, prefiguring the street as we know it today, something entirely different occupied the site. Flamel's home was built in 1406. According to our researcher, a compound—perhaps attached to a hospice or even a small garrison—was located there at least two centuries earlier. The surroundings were far less urban at the time and practically lost in the middle of fields and woods."

"A hospice or a garrison? They're hardly the same thing."

"Whatever it was, it turns out there was a sepulcher located there, one large enough to be listed in several inventories and notarial acts of the time. I don't mean a simple gravestone; it was at least a vault or a chapel."

"Do we know who was buried there?"

"Not exactly, but at the time, the plot belonged to Enguerrand de Tardenay, known for his participation in the third Crusade, for which he ensured supply operations in the region of Saint-Jean-d'Acre."

"Was he connected to the Knights Templar?"

"His name appears in none of the dignitary registers, but given his position in a region where warrior monks were present in large numbers, there is no doubt he was close to them."

Vincent tried to connect this information to what he already knew. "This is certainly an excellent piece for our puzzle. It would support the idea that Nicolas Flamel moved there to claim, or to protect, the underground entrance."

"How would he have known about it?"

"Whether he is considered a true alchemist, a skilled real estate negotiator, or the lucky discoverer of a treasure, those who have studied his story agree that he was initiated into the mysteries of occult knowledge."

"That doesn't tell us why an entrance was hidden in the sepulture prior to that."

"Concealing a secret entrance in a final resting place was a relatively common practice."

"Like in Egyptian tombs?"

"Not exactly. The devices used in the tombs of the Egyptian rulers existed only to protect the eternal rest of the deceased and the riches left for them for the afterlife. Their funerary monuments were essentially safes. It was only much later, during the first revolts in the Roman Empire, that vaults were used by conspirators, the oppressed, or fugitives as hideouts or secret passages. For a while, their sacred nature kept the authorities from flushing the persecuted out. At the time, no one suspected that anyone would take refuge with the dead, in places heavy with superstition. And so people who had no other choice began to gather in vaults, and to hide there, as the first persecuted Christians did. The phenomenon grew with the development of the catacombs. Over time, many came to understand that sepultures were monuments that could not be destroyed easily. Mausoleums were reputed to last longer than utilitarian buildings; what was concealed there was meant to be protected for all eternity."

"Yet today," remarked Charles, "entire cemeteries are displaced. Holy Innocents' Cemetery was emptied to create Paris's Les Halles marketplace."

"That's a very recent practice that doesn't apply to our case."

This comforted Charles. "Therefore it is plausible that the tomb protected the tunnel entrance before Flamel's house replaced it on the same site."

Vincent acquiesced. "The dates match. But we must hope that it wasn't the only entrance to the labyrinth, because the collapse of the deepest section made it impassable."

"Unless it was to be dug again…"

"I wouldn't bet on it. Work of that scale would potentially destabilize the foundation of the constructions above, require too many resources, and offers no guarantee of a result. We're better off looking elsewhere."

"If other routes exist, logically their entrances would be protected in buildings from the same period, around the thirteenth century."

Vincent nodded in agreement. Charles's face fell. "Do you know how many possibilities that represents in a city like Paris?"

63

Evidently the horse tolerated the beer better than the juggler, who missed every one of his tosses after the second tankard. His wood pins fell to the ground all around him, to the great amusement of his acrobat friends, who leapt aside to avoid taking one in the head. They roared with laughter as they applauded him. The show wouldn't earn him the scantiest sum, but that didn't matter; they were having a fine time together.

Konrad had taken a seat at one of the long tables amid the festive activity. He found the atmosphere all the more charming because it wasn't prompted by any obligation to entertain. It arose from the guests' very nature.

The carpenter was seated between a talkative mime artist and a silent fortune teller. Many questioned him with a look, curious to know what trick this big bearded man might have to offer. So he began to sculpt a small animal out of a piece of wood with his knife. He started with a pony, which he gave to a belly dancer. Hardly shy, she kissed him and mussed his hair, pointing out with a few words and many gestures that the animal's delicate appearance contrasted with the size of the hands that created it.

Konrad had come down from his caravan in the late afternoon to take his mind off of things, of course, but even more so to avoid being duped as he had been the previous day. There was one rule in the camp that had left him starving for hours: just one meal was served each day—dinner. There was no lunch at noon. Besides, there would be no one there to share it with; everyone went to the city to entertain its residents. Only Henri, who had become a favorite of young and not so young women alike, had been granted the privilege of a crust of bread, after complaining how hungry he was.

As soon as the dinner cry rang out, Konrad literally threw himself on his bowl of boiled rabbit and turnips. Neither he nor his companions were asked to pay. They were given room and board, because even though no one was supposed to ask questions in the camp, everyone knew they had nothing left. Generosity is a common practice among people of modest means.

With his plate empty and his glass soon to be as well, Konrad busied his hands by sculpting another little figurine, this time a rabbit. He prepared the body; then with the tip of his blade, he perfected the curve of the fluffy tail, blowing it clean of wood shavings.

Just then, between the bustling tables, he noticed a carriage stop at the entrance to the camp. Vincent stepped down out of it. He walked through the gathering, hardly paying attention to the colorful characters he encountered.

He sat down across from the German, looking gaunt. "Did you eat?" asked Konrad.

"No, but I'm not hungry, thanks. I am thirsty, though."

Konrad slid his glass toward his friend. "You should eat," he advised him, "because you won't get another bite until tomorrow night."

"Who knows where I'll be then." Vincent swallowed the wine in one draught.

Konrad sensed his weariness, and what he had to tell him wasn't going to raise his spirits. "I prefer to tell you straight away: Eustasio left."

"What do you mean, 'left'?"

"He went to be with his countess."

Vincent's shoulders slumped. "You weren't able to stop him?"

"I tried, but it was a lost cause. Put yourself in his shoes; he hadn't seen his sweetheart since he got back to the boardinghouse. I told him to wait until you got back, but there was no reasoning with him. He was dying to see her. There's nothing I could do about that."

Vincent sighed. "I can't blame him. I think he and Madame de Vignole are sincerely in love. Let's just hope nothing happens to him on the way there."

"No one will recognize him dressed in those clothes he got from a peddler—maybe not even his beloved!"

"Did he say when he intended to return?"

Konrad shook his head. He placed his rabbit on the table to see if it stood level. "Since we're on the subject of love," he murmured, "I believe your brother and little Gabrielle..."

Vincent smiled. "Good for them. In the meantime, they won't worry about all the rest. It's spring, after all."

Over the carpenter's shoulder, Vincent spotted Henri near the caravans. The boy was leaping around Victor like a kid goat. He took a running jump and swung on the giant's outstretched arm as if it were a crossbar. They laughed together.

With his expert blade, Konrad refined the rabbit's ears. "Are you growing a beard, like me?" he asked his friend.

"More like someone who's trying to hide. Mine will never be as handsome as yours. The ladies make no mistake there."

He discreetly motioned to a young woman who hadn't taken her eyes off Konrad, who blushed, to Vincent's surprise.

"She's one of the dancers. I gave my first carved animal to her friend earlier; she's probably hoping to get the rabbit."

The German motioned that it would be for her, while smoothing his beard. The young lady was elated.

"Pierre told me you went to the boardinghouse this morning. He didn't go into detail, but from his voice I gathered that it wasn't a pretty sight."

"A sad heap of ruins and ashes."

"What do you intend to do?"

"I have no idea."

"We could move and set up shop somewhere else. With our nest egg, we could even build a house. What do you think?"

Vincent sighed. "My poor friend, look around us. Look where we are. You were all nearly burned alive. Each day brings its share of conspiracies and mysteries. I admire your spirit, but as for myself, I'm unable to make the slightest plan. All that matters to me is to survive each day, hoping that the next will unfold under more auspicious circumstances."

"Are they going to come after us again?"

"I have no doubt about that. I think that taking your distance from me would be a good first step in protecting yourselves."

"Are you joking? There's no way we're splitting up."

"I don't like it either, but I don't see any alternative. Minguier so much as admitted it. They're using you to coerce me. By taking our friendship hostage, they control me. If we separate, I hope they will leave you in peace."

Konrad grunted. He shook his head and huffed and puffed like a bull wondering whether or not to charge. "Vincent, you came for me. I can still see you entering that workshop in the east where I was stagnating. You trusted me. Even better, you restored my self-confidence. I've followed you all these years. I've approved of every one of your decisions. The fact is, you are the most capable of making the right choices for our team. You've proven it. But not this time." Konrad looked down. "Do you remember when you asked me what I wanted most in the world?"

"Of course."

"I know you asked each of us that question. We talked about it when you weren't around."

"Did you find the answer?"

"Would you believe it? The answer came to me, by surprise but crystal clear, as I watched our house burn."

"What is it?"

"What I want most in the world is to go back to living as we were. It doesn't matter where, but it has to be with the same people, maintaining our shared spirit. I want us to continue to work together, to live and to dream together. So much the better if each of us falls in love, like Pierre and the girl. That won't change what binds us. Because I'm certain of one thing, my friend: you, me, your brother, even that wild cat Eustasio and the kid Henri are worth more when we forge ahead side by side. Each of us is a boon to the others. You're the one who showed me that, and it will probably remain the greatest achievement of my miserable existence. So ask me to make any sacrifice to preserve it, but don't ask me to do without it. I don't care about being sensible. Whatever happens, I'm staying with you."

64

The immense figure of a cat presiding in the center of a shining sun that stood out from the building's facade left no room for doubt. The felines adorning the large lantern like gargoyles only confirmed it.

Vincent must have passed the two-story, ivy-covered building twenty times, pacing back and forth on the opposite sidewalk. To avoid attracting attention, he limited himself to brief glances and never stopped in front of the building.

Le Chat Noir cabaret had a reputation known even to those who never patronized it. Its shadow plays drew crowds, but even more popular were its singers, who condemned the scandals of the Republic by mocking its politicians. The cabaret's originality and impertinence guaranteed that the powerful found it as appalling as the people found it delightful. Ministers and those close to the halls of power who had tried to silence the satirical voices received little for their efforts, giving them tremendous publicity instead. The cabaret's move four years earlier from Boulevard de Rochechouart to Rue Victor-Massé had in no way diminished its success, quite the contrary. The fact that Aristide Bruant had stayed at the original address with the artists and bad boys who had first popularized Le Chat Noir did nothing to weaken the relocated cabaret's success.

When the captured arsonist had cited this hub of Parisian life as the headquarters for the one he called the Mage, Vincent at first suspected him of spouting nonsense to talk his way out of captivity. But the fact was, as he lingered outside the building, certain elements seemed suspicious to him—starting with the appearance of certain "clients." Merry groups and charming couples hurried in, but so did other visitors with far less pleasant faces. The rascals didn't look like they had come to listen to singers, and even less so to see the shadow play.

Vincent couldn't contain himself. He couldn't learn anything more from the outside, and he had to be certain. He adjusted his hat and crossed the street with a determined step. Other clients were already standing under the porch, with its small pointed roof.

When he was just a few steps away from them, a coachman coming from the other direction pretended to bump into him. "Don't go in there. If they recognize you, they'll kill you. It's our job to investigate," he whispered.

"The last time I let someone else venture into troubled waters, he died," replied Vincent in a low voice.

It took him several moments to adjust to the relative darkness inside the cabaret. People spoke loudly; the tables were full of men and women, some of whom were clearly feeling the effects of over-indulgence. Poets, writers, journalists, actors, and musicians, prominent individuals and the more discreetly wealthy sat side by side with ordinary people; lawful couples rubbed shoulders with gallant lovers and their lady friends—women whose morals were so loose they were known as "the horizontals." Vincent scanned the merry gathering, ready to detect the slightest feature or detail that might give him a lead.

The exuberant decor was crammed with a multitude of extraordinary objects of medieval or esoteric inspiration. Works by Caran d'Ache and Adolphe Willette were framed by hanging ropes, chains, instruments of torture, chastity belts, and other curiosities with more or less scandalous connotations.

A server in a short black jacket with a starched white napkin draped over his forearm intercepted Vincent. "If you're not expected at a reserved table, then it's full. Unless you're here for the shadow play or the singers?"

"Yes, I came to see them."

The man pointed to the stairs leading to the upper floors and headed off with his pitcher of fake absinthe.

Vincent thought quickly as he climbed the stairs. Each step he took drew him deeper in. If the situation were to get out of hand, he would have to retrace his steps in order to escape. Of this he was well aware.

Although the staircase afforded him a sweeping view of the ground floor, he didn't recognize any of the shifty characters he'd seen enter.

He noticed that among the multitude of accumulated objects, talismans, good-luck charms, and other amulets were frequently displayed. To anyone capable of reading between the lines, occult influence and mystical symbolism were obvious in the decor. The cabaret may have been named for the black cat on the facade, but the fact that the animal stood before a shining sun with rays resembling the dawn could easily contain a hidden meaning. The establishment was not far from openly celebrating a "sacred dawn."

When he arrived on the first floor landing, Vincent heard laughter from the theater; a booth in front of a curtain marked the entrance. A nasal voice mocked the expenses incurred for the World's Fair while clinics for the battle-scarred of the War of 1870 fell into ruin.

The ticket seller was poised to accept Vincent's coin and let him in, but Vincent kept his hands pointedly in his pockets. In a low voice he made up a reason to enter the theater. "I'm supposed to meet a friend, but I don't know if he's in there or upstairs."

Suddenly suspicious, the man grudgingly allowed him to take a look. The room was nowhere near full and Vincent didn't see any of the people who had caught his attention there, either.

The ticket seller looked at him askance. Vincent made up his mind and rushed upstairs to the shadow play. This time it would be all or nothing, he was certain of that. After noticing nothing strange on the first floors, he was either going to find something now, or be forced to conclude that he had been imagining things.

When he arrived on the upper level, he paid the entrance fee and slipped into the dark room. The only light came from the glow of the stretched canvas; zinc silhouettes moved behind it. A deep voice rolled its r's as it recited the dialogue, while a pianist sitting in the dark accentuated the dramatic effects.

The audience seemed captivated by the story of a young pauper who makes a deal with the devil. For the best view of the show, Vincent slipped into the last row.

The spectators watched attentively. There were no couples or merry groups among them. "Serve me loyally and you will be the most admired among men!" declared the devil, opening his arms in a gesture of omnipotence.

The sets glided smoothly behind the canvas, creating an illusion of real movement in the action, while a skillful play of colored lights drew attention to the puppets. The effect was most successful. For a moment, Vincent forgot why he was there.

The devil's eyes lit up in a phantasmagoria of blazing colors. He thundered, "Who among you would also like to see his dreams become reality? What are you prepared to do for that? Who has the courage to join me? You, there, in the back?"

Vincent started in surprise. One might have thought the devil had just addressed him personally. The staging was very convincing in any case. Amused, but slightly uneasy, Vincent glanced around at the others who, like him, were seated in the last row. He saw only one person, a man. Suddenly Vincent froze. The stranger seated just a chair away from him was playing with a thin leather cord.

Although Vincent rushed toward the exit as fast as he could, he already knew that he would never reach it.

65

Vincent was blindfolded and seated in a strangely comfortable arm-chair. Only his hands were bound, and although he'd been captured unceremoniously, he hadn't been hurt in any way.

He had probably been the only person actually watching the shadow play, for when he tried to run away, the faces all turned toward him at the same time. He had recognized many that he was in no hurry to see again.

Someone removed his blindfold; he blinked. The man with the leather cord was standing near him. Two of his accomplices kept their distance and stared at him as though he were a strange animal. He was seated in the center of some kind of luxuriously furnished courtroom. Two gilded thrones were perched side by side on a small platform in front of him. The room was lined with two rows of empty seats crowned overhead with many pennons bearing strange crosses against the background of a burning sun. Clearly the room had not been built for the mysterious function it now fulfilled; it appeared to be a preexisting room that had been reconfigured. The wood flooring and walls visible behind the ostentation were reminiscent of a craftsman's workshop. What might have been made here before it was turned into this caricature of a temple?

Although Vincent had been blindfolded after his capture, he had noticed that he hadn't been led up or down any stairs. Logically, then, the room was located on the same floor as the shadow theater, perhaps in a building adjacent to the cabaret, which served as a facade.

The man with the cord moved to face his prisoner. "It took us a while to catch you." His voice was calm, almost friendly, so much so that it left Vincent perplexed.

"The Mage was right: you're clever. He predicted that we wouldn't have to chase after you, and that you would end up coming on your own. We were waiting for you. The show was planned just for you. Did you enjoy it?"

Vincent said nothing. The man continued. "My name is Joshua, and as surprising as you might find it, we'll probably be working together very soon."

Vincent raised an eyebrow and couldn't help responding. "Working together? Are you joking?"

The man smiled and began to pace. "You think we're different, is that it? You think I'm a monster and you're a good guy?"

"I don't kill people."

"I bet you'd be ready to if it could save the ones you love. Isn't that so? Be honest with yourself. Perhaps at this very moment you want to go for my throat?" The man tried to catch Vincent's gaze, but he looked away.

"However, you're right: we're not quite the same. I'm not fighting to protect my clan. I'm not devoted to a handful of mortals, but to ideals that could save many more people."

"*Aurorae sacrum honorem...*"

"Exactly." Joshua paused and sought Vincent's eyes once more. "Do you approve of this age we're living in, Vincent? Do you like what it does to men like us? Do you condone its values?"

Vincent raised his head and held the man's gaze, but said nothing.

"You don't need to answer. I've been following you long enough to know who you are. I've had time to observe you, to study you, and even to understand you. I probably know more about you than those friends you'd be ready to kill me for."

Vincent tried to remain calm, but the tenor of the conversation was drawing him into unexpected territory. Things would have been simpler if the man had mistreated and threatened him as criminals did. Joshua stopped pacing.

"I've been walking in your shadow for some time. Don't hold it against me; it was necessary. I saw you celebrating with your companions. I was there when you hesitated just before meeting with your clients. I even heard you speaking beside that watchmaker's grave."

Vincent was shaken, but controlled himself.

"Believe what you wish," added Joshua, "but we are more alike than you think."

"What do you want from me?"

"For you to do what you do so well. Nothing more, nothing less. Penetrate these passages that we cannot enter, decipher them so that we may continue our progress."

"If I refuse or I'm unable to, I'll end up like Minguier."

"He was just an idiot," replied Joshua, "who entertained himself with ideals, like a child playing at being a knight with a wooden sword. He may have claimed to be a part of a grand scheme, but nothing mattered more than his own petty interests. I had my eye on him. He thought he was cleverer than us."

"Meanwhile, you eliminated the man who served you."

"Minguier's case was like a couple that marries without love: when the contract isn't respected, it terminates of its own accord. It's as simple as that. When he was no longer of use to us, he was removed."

"How will my fate be different?"

"You are of another caliber. I told you, I've come to know you. You follow your own path, you keep your word, you experience doubt. And even more importantly, you are capable of thinking beyond your own needs. We don't want to employ you, we want you to join us."

"'We'?"

"A fellowship of men and women from all backgrounds working to prevent the decline of our civilization. A Sacred Dawn to save humanity's future from devolving into what you see in the shop windows. We believe that nothing presented to us as progress truly is so, if it is for sale."

"That's a nice manifesto, but that's not what Minguier told me. He described you as a new power ready to do anything and capable of overthrowing political systems."

Joshua shook his head disapprovingly. "Clearly he understood nothing. We don't just want to overthrow them, we want to transform them."

"Why are you looking for Nicolas Flamel's treasure?"

"Because to achieve our goals, we need resources. Our brothers and sisters give us what they can, but few of them are wealthy. The Mage came up with the idea to recover abandoned treasures. By definition, no one is using them anymore. We don't steal; we collect what is presumed to no longer exist."

"So you're chasing after gold."

"For now, but that's not our only goal. Like Flamel, we associate material wealth with spiritual wealth. He was a philanthropist who helped the impoverished by providing them with room and board and employment. Our ambitions overlap with his, but we are raising them much higher. The Mage's vision presages a world in which no one will beg, because it will no longer be necessary. Everyone will have found their place in a reimagined society."

"Of which your Mage will be master, of course."

"More of an enlightened guide."

Vincent was struck by the man's conviction. While certain aspects of the message might seem appealing, Vincent also remembered that these proponents of a perfect civilization had attempted to murder several members of his team, before setting fire to their house.

"Do I have a choice? What do you intend to do if I refuse to help you?"

"We will continue to act in the name of what we believe. It will be more difficult without you, there's no denying it. The very possibility that you could stand in our way would force us to destroy you. You cracked the secret of Flamel's cellar. We didn't. If you tell us what lies behind it, if you hand over everything you found there, we will show our gratitude. Otherwise..."

There was nothing ambiguous about the threat. Vincent needed to buy himself some time. "I need to think about it."

"Impossible. Our meeting with History will not afford us the luxury of waiting. The world is watching Paris. The moment is uniquely opportune, and destiny waits for no man. Don't be late."

"I don't know anything about you."

"Once again, the Mage predicted your response. So that you might understand our fellowship, he is offering you the chance to experience the Sacred Dawn deep within yourself. You are fortunate. Prepare yourself, for the time has come."

66

Joshua used his knife to slice through the cord that bound Vincent's hands.

"The Mage doesn't meet with prisoners. All appear before him as free men."

"Free to leave?" retorted Vincent ironically.

"If that's what he decides, yes."

Vincent rubbed his wrists and felt his circulation return.

"Don't take this meeting lightly," warned Joshua. "When I was in your position, it changed my destiny. Don't provoke the Mage, and don't lie to him; he'll know. He can make the dead speak; I've seen him do it. He has the power to intensify your experience of life or to destroy you. I've seen him cause those who doubted this to succumb without even laying a hand on them."

Vincent grew increasingly intrigued by the devotion tinged with admiration that Joshua showed for his master. He was almost eager to discover the man who had inspired it.

He didn't have to wait long. Four women in long white robes entered the room. Joshua invited Vincent to stand. They were very young and very beautiful, and walked with the same slow rhythmic gait. Their white attire was embellished with red and gold ribbons. One carried a crystal carafe and glasses on a platter, another clutched a thick and obviously ancient book to her breast, the third held a wood coffer, and the fourth woman displayed some kind of monstrance containing a fragment of something that Vincent could not identify.

Moving with the solemnity of a religious procession, the young women positioned themselves at the four corners of the dais where the thrones stood. Vincent expected to see a carnival king enter with his queen, but instead four men appeared. They were very tall, muscular, and dressed like gladiators, and they wore the same leather masks that Vincent had seen in the cellar of Flamel's house. They were so big that at first he didn't notice the two individuals between them. But when he did see them at last, he was intrigued by their appearance.

Their heads were shaven and they were dressed like ancient priests, in very simple robes, one black and the other white. Most surprising of all was their resemblance to one another: they were as alike as two peas in a pod, and while their gait suggested advanced age, their features appeared much younger. Vincent thought to himself that the Mage's court had some strange disciples, until the twins seated themselves on the thrones.

Joshua bowed respectfully. "Which one is the Mage?" Vincent asked quietly.

"'They' are the Mage."

Vincent had not forgotten that he was being held captive, or that these two wielded the power of life and death over him; but, oddly enough, he was not afraid. The pageantry, the theatricality, and even the appearance of the two individuals reminded him more of a Greek play or a simulacrum of Mass than a meeting that could change his life.

The twins' features were identical in all respects. With their smooth skulls and fine-featured faces, they might even have passed for women. This ambiguity extended to their robes, which seemed equally inspired by Roman togas and Greek tunics. It was impossible to guess their ancestry; one might easily think they were from Asia or the Middle East. That it was impossible to identify them by their physique or their gender gave them an aura that was at once unsettling and fascinating. In a most extraordinary way, their pale eyes moved in tandem, as if they were commanded by a single brain.

The twin in white spoke first. "I am pleased to finally meet you under conditions favorable to dialogue."

The other twin continued with disconcerting fluidity. "I know all that you are capable of bringing to our fellowship, and although

I am certain I can offer you much in return, I am the one most in need of your talents."

The twin in white continued without pausing. "I understand my error in allowing those who would use you by force to go astray. You are not one to bend. The time has come to ask for your forgiveness and try to persuade you."

Vincent felt uneasy in the presence of these two individuals, who referred to themselves as "I" in identical voices. The twins behaved as if they were one person. The encounter had a strange result: Vincent didn't know which one to look in the eyes. In fact he no longer knew which of the twins had said what, as if everything in their behavior intended for them to be seen as one.

"You have questions for me," declared the twin in white. "Ask them without fear."

"Can you read my mind?"

"Not the way you imagine," replied the twin in black. "I am not a circus freak. I cannot extract your thoughts from your mind, but when we converse, I am sensitive to the degree of truth in your words."

The other twin added, "Let us say that I perceive with particular acuity what is commonly referred to as sincerity."

"Yet I was led to believe that you had the power to make the dead speak," Vincent replied.

The two became immobile. They froze, motionless, as if their minds were taking the time to synchronize through an invisible connection before responding. When they began to move again, with perfectly identical gestures, they resembled automatons.

"Why is that important to you? Would you like to contact the dead?" If this possibility had seemed credible to Vincent, he would certainly have been interested; but he remained unswayed from his inquiry.

"Instead of counting on me to open Flamel's passage, why didn't you call up his spirit to reveal the secret?"

The Mages had such identical smiles that the phenomenon became disturbing. "Doubt as much as you wish, but do not mock. Liberate yourself from scorn, or it will forever prevent you from seeing what you do not know," replied the twin in the black robe.

The Mage in white added, "I can indeed enter into contact with certain deceased individuals, but in order to do so, I must go through a living relation, someone they would have been close to. There is no longer anyone alive who had direct contact with Nicolas Flamel. That is why it is impossible for me to obtain the answers I seek."

The excuse was irrefutable, but Vincent still wasn't convinced.

"However, you still haven't answered my question," remarked the twin in black. "Would you like to contact loved ones who have passed on?"

Although Vincent was still skeptical, this time the question stirred something in his heart. In spite of himself, he thought of his father, of Étienne Begel, of Mr. Robert-Houdin. He tried to contain the overwhelming emotion provoked by the idea of speaking to them again, and he was not about to pour his heart out to these people.

"I sense your uneasiness," said the twin in white. "I see it clearly. Your spirit is not at peace, I can feel it... and this fragility seems to be rooted in your past."

"Or rather in an aspect of your youth that you were deprived of," finished the other.

Vincent looked from one to the other in disbelief. The twin in white continued. "Are these souls that haunt you of no help today?"

The last time Vincent had felt so shaken was when Charles had evoked the secrets of his father's death; but that had been a very different situation. Adinson had known about the event through entirely rational means and had not tried to dramatize them. These two bizarre individuals were of an entirely different breed. In their effort to destabilize him, they could very well try to exploit whatever information Joshua had managed to glean, if only from what he had said during his visit to Begel's grave. Vincent hesitated. Even though he didn't enjoy playing with his most private feelings, he was ready to take a chance, to see just how far they would go.

"I do have one question..."

67

Vincent was taken to what his jailer himself referred to as the "spirit chamber." No one bound his hands or blindfolded him this time, but three guards nevertheless stood near Joshua to discourage any attempt at escape. Outnumbered four to one, Vincent wasn't going to attempt anything, especially since he wasn't sure he could find his way out.

"You are privileged," Joshua explained. "Few receive the honor of a one-on-one meeting with the Mage. I, myself, have only attended group séances."

He led Vincent onto a kind of wooden bridge that compensated for the difference in height between two adjoining buildings. In this way, they passed from one building to another through the walls, moving away from the cabaret. As Vincent made his way through the hidden portion of the fellowship's lair, he saw that it had been built over several floors, probably spread across multiple buildings in the same neighborhood. Some passages even meandered beneath the rafters. His best chance at escape might be through one of the openings, should the opportunity arise.

After winding along for a time, the prisoner and his guards came out into a vast attic, probably an old granary or drying room. In the center, a more recent dome-like structure had been erected. A studded wooden door, low and thick enough for a prison, marked the entrance. The Mages' entourage and the two young women bearing the book and the monstrance had formed a line on either side of the door in a sort of honor guard. Joshua invited Vincent to enter and stepped aside.

"You're not coming?" asked Vincent.

"What is said in the secrecy of the chamber concerns you alone."

Vincent stepped forward cautiously. As he walked between the guards, their inquiring gazes weighed heavily on him. Their impressive musculature provided a clear idea of the violence they would be capable of unleashing at the slightest error.

Vincent lowered his head to walk through the door frame and stepped into a long corridor made entirely of wood and reminiscent of a ship's passageway. The heavy door swung closed behind him.

At the opposite end there stood another opening, haloed with an orange glow. Vincent stepped through and came out into a small round chamber with a low cupola ceiling.

The two other young women stood behind the Mages, who were seated at a round table with a black marble top inlaid with a triangular geometric pattern made of jade. Each twin sat at one of the points. A large silver metal ring was lying on the table.

The circular room was lit by altar candles placed at regular intervals around the perimeter, and the walls were covered in copper plates riveted together to form a sort of tank, that muffled even the sound of Vincent's footsteps. The woman with the carafe moved a panel located behind him, and suddenly the entrance was no longer visible.

The Mage in white invited Vincent to take a seat at the triangle's third point. He and his double in black took the ring in their hands, gripping it firmly as they closed their eyes.

Vincent scrutinized each of their gestures. Their solemn bearing, the extreme slowness with which they executed their movements, and their strange garments from another time all reminded him of the theatrics used in magic shows and spiritism séances. He was quite familiar with these tricks, pseudo-rituals intended to condition the audience into leading themselves to believe that they are about to witness something extraordinary. While neither the decor nor the behavior fooled Vincent, the twins still troubled him. They were a mystery in their own right. How were they able to breathe in unison, even with their eyes closed? Their chests rose in exactly the same rhythm and at the same time. Now that he was close to them, Vincent also observed that their perfect complexion was not the result of makeup. Their completely hairless skin was incredibly smooth.

"Take the ring. It will be our link. Then close your eyes," announced the Mage in black.

Vincent obeyed. The sensation surprised him. Contrary to the usual experience of touching metal, he felt an initial intense heat that gradually waned. It seemed to him as if the Mages' hands were alive with minuscule, very rapid vibrations that traveled to him through the object.

"We're going to practice spiritism, are we?"

The twin in white finished breathing in before responding. "Do not try to connect what you are about to experience with what you believe you know. Our actions may resemble those made by the impure who imitate the messengers of souls, but we are not of their ilk. I asked you to close your eyes. Then tell us what spirit you would like to contact."

Vincent closed his eyes. He tried to control his breathing, but a creeping feeling of vulnerability prevented him from doing so.

"I wish to communicate with the man who initiated my vocation. My benefactor's master." He purposefully used the term "master" to imitate their vocabulary. The Mages remained motionless.

"Must I name him, or invoke him in some manner?" he asked.

"That is not necessary. We need to feel what connected you above all else. Define him rather through why he was special to you."

Vincent thought a moment, choosing his words with care. He must not make it too easy for the twins to identify the man he was referring to. Information that was too precise would enable them to use what Joshua or his henchmen might have told them. Although he remained wary, the exercise forced him to venture into the heart of his true feelings to define who Robert-Houdin was to him.

He concentrated. "He taught me to see 'beyond,' and never to believe any wall impenetrable." He paused. "He taught me that behind every dead end lies a passage leading to the truth."

"A wise man. I feel his presence very strong within you. He accompanies you in all your actions."

Which of the twins had spoken? Vincent couldn't tell if the voice had come from the left or the right. The comment, though relevant, was still general enough to describe any protective figure who had awoken a vocation. His response was vague, but sincere. "I think of him every day, each time I must make a choice."

Vincent was surprised to hear himself declare this absolute truth in an exchange that he suspected to be shot through with deceit. He heard the Mage speak in a calm, level voice.

"You are committed to continuing his work, including—more recently—the most personal aspects. The most secret. He knows it. I sense that you recently joined one of his friends in this quest. The presence of a mutual friend is perceptible and draws you even closer together."

Vincent was disturbed, both by the accuracy of the observation, which went so far as to mention Charles, but also by the fact that, once again, he could not say which of the two had spoken. Unless they spoke together?

The Mage went on. "You recently discovered an aspect of his personality hitherto hidden in the shadows. It enlightened you, didn't it?"

Vincent now felt a strange heat enter his body, as if a warm stream were flowing from the twins' hands through the ring and into him; a lava spreading, capable of turning him to stone. How could these two beings speak the truth about one of his most privately held feelings? No one but he could know about it. No spy could have guessed that.

His hands remained glued to the metal; he couldn't tear them away. His arms felt so heavy, he could no longer lift them. He opened his eyes. The Mages and the young women kept their eyes closed. He was the only one to see. He was overcome by dizziness, coupled with a new fear: that the psychic power of these two beings would shatter his very conception of reality. If this was not a hoax, then his perception of the world would be forever altered. He took deep breaths, beset by the loathsome feeling of losing control.

"Do not fear," murmured the Mage. "What you are discovering will frighten you, but no more than the first step toward freedom. Leave the comfort of ordinary knowledge. The unknown challenges us, but in doing so it reveals new horizons. You must abandon your preconceptions and simply let yourself be guided by what you feel deep within."

The twins were in fact speaking with one voice. Their lips moved simultaneously. It was inhuman, terrifying, prodigious. It couldn't be a trick. Even Robert-Houdin would have been transfixed. "A man can access the universal through that which he feels most intimately. What would you like to learn from the one who is no more?"

Vincent was shaken. He found his most solid convictions wavering. He had planned to ask a trick question to catch them in their own trap and unmask them, but suddenly another possibility presented itself to him.

Could these two beings really be capable of putting him into contact with the spirit of Jean-Eugène Robert-Houdin? Wasn't that kind of belief just a boon for peddlers of illusion who profited at the expense of the hopeful? Talking to the dead; obtaining responses they couldn't give before dying. The idea was so mind-bending that it could fundamentally change everything about humans, down to the very way they live their lives. To contact Robert-Houdin. To speak with him? Having the privilege of a final conversation after his absence. What would he ask him?

Unless he would rather speak to his father. His mind raced and it made him feverish. Yet, he didn't really have anything to ask him. He just wished he could talk to him, and, most of all, hear his voice.

"Your connection is growing muddled. Do not distance yourself from the one you wish to address."

Vincent closed his eyes. He began to panic. He was torn between the power of the experience and his distrust of those who made it possible. He must not let down his guard, and yet... The truth about who he was had never been so exposed. What stroke of fate had determined that it was to take place in front of people who threatened to destroy him? After trying to annihilate his world, could his worst enemies offer him another?

He spoke without the slightest calculation. "During the brief time that I had the privilege of studying with him, I often saw him question or doubt himself, but he always managed to overcome his uncertainties."

The Mages interrupted him. "It is not us you must address, but him. He is listening."

Vincent was overcome. The sorrow he felt when Robert-Houdin died still lay within him; ever more tears waiting to flow.

"You left so quickly," he murmured in a broken voice. "You still had so much to teach me. You had many of the answers that I'm looking for, and that I doubt I have the strength to find. Please, tell me what I should do!"

Vincent suddenly broke out in a sweat; his fingers were burning and his throat was dry. He didn't want to open his eyes, or do anything that might cloud his message.

The unified voice of the twins rang out in the perfect silence. "What I know is within your reach. Walk on Austria-Hungary and follow the three wise men up to heaven. The phantom will show you the way."

Vincent began to tremble. The answer, as nonsensical as it sounded, made sense to him. He understood snatches of it. One thing was absolutely certain: the Mages could not have invented it. While the end of the mysterious statement remained unclear, the beginning indicated without a shadow of a doubt the rigged entrance to Robert-Houdin's secret office. There were indeed maps to climb, including one he had seen of the Austro-Hungarian empire, to join the trio of Greek scholars contemplating something glowing in the sky. As for the phantom, it could be the specter the magician used in his shows, and that now hung from the ceiling of his den. But how could the accessory help him?

The twins let go of the contact ring. The sudden rupture caused Vincent to moan despite himself. He suddenly felt as though he were being drained of all his energy. He let go of the ring. His heartbeat slowed—he hadn't realized how wildly it had been pounding—until it beat almost too slowly, listlessly. He wiped his dripping forehead on his sleeve. After the sensation of supernatural heat, he was now chilled to the bone, except for his hands, which burned more than ever. He looked at them aghast, almost expecting them to catch fire before his eyes. He was shocked by what he had just heard, but even more so by the way he had learned it.

"What did you do to me?"

The twins were perfectly calm; not a drop of sweat pearled on their temples. The one in white replied, "We enabled you to obtain the response to your question. Isn't that what you wanted?"

Vincent stumbled over his words. "This power, this talent that you have..."

The Mage in the black robe murmured, "Join forces with us. If you help us, we can guide you on the path of the spirits. Find the riches that will serve our cause. Open what is closed to us in this world. We will do the same for you in the next."

The Mage in white motioned to the young woman to bring the drink. She filled three glasses with a liquid that looked like water.

Vincent's mouth was dry; he was dying of thirst, but he was wary of what the glass might contain.

The twins drank theirs. Convinced he wouldn't be poisoned, Vincent hurried to swallow his.

The cool sips slid down his throat, but they didn't seem to quench his thirst. He did not feel normal; his vision blurred. Was it a side effect of what he had just experienced, or was it a new enchantment? He suddenly felt himself grow heavy, as though his body were being filled with lead.

Vincent lost control of his arms and legs. His body suddenly weighed a ton. He abruptly collapsed.

68

A shudder tore Vincent from his torpor. An initial conscious thought formed. As an arm tried to encircle him, Vincent reared up and thrashed about. Like a wild animal, he lashed out violently at the air to escape the grip. The arm withdrew like a moray eel. A voice thundered, "Calm down! No one wants to hurt you!"

Vincent fell back and surrendered. He didn't have the strength to fight anyway. He recognized the voice and tried to open his eyes.

A blurry figure bent over him. Another moved in the background. He concentrated, trying to make it out and murmured incredulously, "Charles?"

"Are you so confused that you don't recognize me?"

Adinson helped Vincent as he tried to sit up.

"Easy, my friend. Take it slowly. Let yourself come to first. I don't remember ever seeing such troubled sleep."

Vincent saw he was in a bright room with rows of iron beds and wooden night tables. "Where are we?"

"In the dispensary of the coachmen's brigade.

Vincent winced. "How did I get here?"

"We picked you up at the foot of the Tour Saint-Jacques, unconscious. The police took you for a wandering drunk. You were in quite a state."

"A drunk? How did I end up there?"

"I was rather hoping you would tell me."

"It's true, I am thirsty."

"You won't get anything but water here," teased Charles, signaling to a man to bring something for Vincent to drink.

"One of the coachmen saw you enter Le Chat Noir, where you then disappeared. Our men mingled with the clientele in search of you, but they discovered no trace of your visit."

Vincent stared at his palms and touched them hesitantly. This strange behavior intrigued Adinson, who continued all the same. "What happened? I imagine you discovered something, to have stayed so long. What happened to you?"

Vincent tried to bring some order to his confused thoughts. He raised a hand to his forehead in an attempt to calm his growing migraine and repeated Charles's words. "Le Chat Noir."

The meeting with the twins suddenly came back to him. "Actually, I discovered someone. The fellowship of the Sacred Dawn. Does that mean anything to you?"

Charles thought for a moment. "No, nothing. It sounds like a sect."

"It's probably much more than that. Would you believe it? I met the man who stabbed Eustasio and who most likely orchestrated the other attacks. He's a pretty nice guy, incidentally."

Adinson frowned. "Vincent, are you quite all right?"

"But the most impressive are the Mages. When they speak, it's truly magical! A single entity sharing two bodies; it's enough to make you think you're seeing double."

"Did you drink?"

"Not a drop. I don't believe I've ever been as conscious as when I was seated before them."

Worried, Adinson checked to see if Vincent's pupils were dilated. Vincent continued his incoherent confession, then sat up abruptly, pushed Adinson's hand away, and looked him in the eyes. "Charles, do you believe it's possible to communicate with the dead?"

Adinson was disconcerted by the question. "Some people say it's true, but as far as I'm concerned, I'm the only dead man I speak with."

Vincent shook his head sharply. He seemed perfectly conscious. "I'm not joking, Charles."

"I'd have preferred you were. What a question! What are you talking about? Were you witness to black magic or occult practices? In theory, God is the only one mortals may speak to after death."

"I'm not certain of that."

"You're raving. Tell me what happened instead."

"I had an impossible, unbelievable encounter."

"I'm curious to know more. Don't leave anything out."

"You know, Charles, I don't think I escaped. I would even bet they let me leave."

Charles stiffened. "Are you aware of what you're saying? After trying to kill you, they had you at their mercy at last, but in the end decided to release you?"

"I'm as surprised as you are, and yet, that's probably what happened. The way they do things is unsettling, and I admit that some of their beliefs caught my attention."

Adinson showed signs of annoyance. "You're not yourself. Did they drug you, or beat you? You don't appear to have been mistreated."

"They didn't harm me. We talked, they gave me their point of view, and they let me go."

Vincent's distant gaze worried Adinson. "It must have been a fascinating conversation, to keep you busy for two whole days," he said.

"Two days?"

"Fifty-four hours to be precise. That's how long you were gone."

"I could have sworn it all lasted less…"

Vincent's mind began to race. Suddenly he grasped Charles's arm. "I don't remember anything about the last two days. However, there's something we can clear up right away to determine whether or not I've gone crazy."

69

Vincent pressed Charles to show him the way. He could barely stand, but that didn't slow him down. He stumbled and bumped into hallway corners, and at times he had to put out a hand to steady himself on the furniture to keep himself from collapsing. But nothing was going to stop him.

On the way, Charles reassured the coachmen, who were alarmed by the strange duo's agitated state.

"Will you tell me what is so urgent?"

"You'll see in a moment. Otherwise, you can always have me locked up."

"Vincent, you're frightening me. I don't recognize you."

"I'm frightening myself. What if I told you Robert-Houdin had spoken to me?"

"Excuse me?"

"Quite simply: your friend spoke to me."

This time it was Charles who stumbled. "Pure madness," he said. "The members of this sect fooled you. You received the best training; you know how easy it is to fool even the sharpest of minds."

"That's what I thought. And then..." Vincent began to flag.

"And then what?"

"It was so strange, so real that I need to be sure."

"To be sure? But to be sure of what?"

The two men crossed the courtyard and rushed through the entrance to the magician's former residence. Vincent strode across the hall and entered the office, begging Adinson to hurry, and then carefully locked the door behind them.

Charles went directly to the mapmaker's cabinet and activated the mechanism. The steps shifted into place; he raced to open the passage behind the painting and, out of breath, invited Vincent to slip into the secret chamber.

"Here we are. I hope you will be able to put your mind at ease. I'm exhausted."

Vincent entered and murmured, "I walked on Austria-Hungary. I followed the three wise men up to heaven."

He walked into the office without a moment's hesitation and stood beneath the phantom hanging from the rafters. The wire structure was there, suspended in the air and shrouded in diaphanous veils that had once created a supernatural aura as they skittered above the crowds.

Vincent observed the object from every angle and spoke to it. "So you're supposed to show me the way. 'What I know is within your reach. The phantom will show you the way.'"

"You seem quite agitated, my friend," said Adinson, perplexed. "Perhaps it would be sensible to consult..."

"First I want to know if these Mages are the world's best charlatans, or if they possess an extraordinary gift."

The phantom's arm seemed to point directly in front of him. "Charles, have you moved the Flying Specter since you inherited this office?"

"Never. Why would I do that?"

Vincent said nothing; he tried to identify what the slender figure was pointing to.

"It looks as if it's pointing to that partition, there, between the two shelves..."

Adinson lost his temper. "I don't understand any of this! You sound insane. You made me rush all the way here without explanation. You talk to the phantom. Worse, if I can believe my ears, you think the people who tried to kill you were courteous. You even seem to like them. Good heavens, did they indoctrinate you?"

Vincent walked over to the boards that formed the partition and replied, "Are we such strangers to one another that you think I could betray you?"

He began to probe the wall, which appeared to be solid. Charles joined him. "Are you in your right mind when you say Robert-Houdin spoke to you?"

"We'll know soon enough. If it was him, he spoke to me through the Mages' voices."

"Are they mediums?"

"There's only one way to find out. He gave me a clue. If it's authentic, we'll know for sure."

Vincent kept probing. He went up and down, looking everywhere, even past the beams that framed the partition. He ran his hands meticulously over the wood and knocked on the wall under the joints.

Nothing. There were no notches, nor the slightest protrusion that might be used to open a section of the wall. Leaving nothing to chance, he knelt down and tried to remove the baseboard.

As he leaned into the floor, a slight movement in one of the floorboards caught his attention. Feverishly, Vincent tried to pull at it; he was feeling around the cracks when he suddenly felt it shift.

He exchanged a look with Charles and tried to slide the board out. With some difficulty, he managed to shift it an inch or two. The wood, which hadn't been moved in years, did not give way easily, but Vincent kept at it and the opening finally appeared.

Charles was dumbstruck.

"Did you know this cache existed?" asked Vincent.

"I assure you, I had no idea."

"Then only Robert-Houdin knew about it."

Vincent slipped his hand into the newly revealed space and brought out a small packet, which he placed on the desk. From a rolled-up cotton sack he pulled three similar notebooks bound in black leather.

Charles took one and flipped through it. Recognizing his friend's perfectly formed penmanship, he was overcome with intense emotion. A quick inspection revealed that all the notebooks were written in the magician's hand.

"My God. I'm certain I saw Jean-Eugène writing some of these pages. He always had his notebook with him. No one, not even his wife, was allowed to touch it. I didn't know there was more than one.

When I moved in, I searched the archives, but, finding nothing, I assumed the document had been lost forever."

The volume Vincent was skimming through contained notes, thoughts, and ideas about problems Robert-Houdin had been confronted with. He happened upon a list of secret passages created for a variety of high-profile clients, followed by out-of-sequence diagrams for acts of illusion and trigger mechanisms. The motley collection was peppered with short summaries that appeared to be related to the research he had carried out with his cohorts.

Vincent stopped on one paragraph in particular. "Charles, were you aware of an affair related to a reliquary unearthed in a chapel near the former Holy Innocents' Cemetery?"

"Yes, I remember it very well. The structure was spared when the graves were exhumed, but several years ago new construction doomed it to oblivion. We cross-checked the archives and discovered that the precious monstrance had been buried to protect it from the revolutionaries."

"Robert-Houdin mentions it here, and it's not the only passage that refers to your discoveries."

"But what did you ask that would make him reveal their location?"

Vincent looked up from the text. "I said that I regretted that he hadn't had the time to teach me all that he knew. I told him that I was lost."

He paused. "Speaking through the mediums, he told me that his knowledge was within my reach and where to find it."

"Good heavens," murmured Adinson. "I don't know what I find more upsetting, the fear or the pleasure. I'm so pleased at the hope that he is still present somewhere above us, and so appalled that our adversaries were the ones who revealed this to you."

"I am as well."

"This experience must have unsettled you."

"Profoundly."

"Perhaps that demonstration convinced you...?"

Vincent detected apprehension in Charles's tone. He also perceived everything that it implied.

"The séance was deeply moving, I won't deny it. This sign from my master—from your friend—has me questioning myself deep down and is likely to haunt me for quite some time. But Robert-Houdin was not one of them. I think that today he would be one of their targets as well. This fellowship is looking for treasures, like we are, but not for the same reasons. Robert-Houdin, Begel, you, and your circle seek to protect them, and that's what I've committed myself to doing alongside you. These people themselves admit that they wish to use these treasures to increase their strength. They don't care about what they covet; they only want to use it, to draw power from it. If I had been on my own when I met these Mages, I probably would have been bewitched and perhaps even tempted to join them; but I met them after training with men whom I never once saw give in to corruption, and after meeting you, and I have my family. As fascinating as their gift may be, it doesn't mean they're using it to honest ends."

Charles gathered up the notebooks and handed them to Vincent. "You must study these notes."

"You must want to read them as much as I do."

"You are the most capable of identifying what may be of use to us."

Vincent accepted them with respect. "Thank you, Charles."

"Make haste, my friend, for the time it took us to find you gave them a two-day head start."

70

Vincent hadn't managed to sleep past the first rays of dawn. As he left his caravan at daybreak, he encountered only Victor, the giant who seemed to keep watch day and night. Absolute calm hung over the camp. The colorful troupe had already left for the capital, where they would bring the streets to life later that morning.

On the meadow still laced with dew, rabbits formed a circle that was quickly broken up by two stray dogs. The river flowed calmly below.

The guardian of the embassies hailed Vincent, who had walked to the top of a neighboring embankment to be alone. Vincent sat down on a stump and leaned against a tree. He kept an eye on the camp as he warmed himself in the first rays of sunlight. There, he began to analyze each line of the notebooks, which he had exhausted himself reading the night before.

Page after page, many things fascinated him. He held in his hands the information that Jean-Eugène Robert-Houdin had considered to be the most important. He was never without his notebook, and in it he inscribed everything he deemed essential. But Vincent also felt like he was entering his mentor's most private thoughts. His remarks and comments revealed how his mind operated. It was like diving deep into the workings of his intelligence. The style was direct, without embellishment, and the sole objective was to advance his reasoning and clarify his thoughts. Overall it was so spontaneous that at times Vincent thought he could hear the magician's voice.

Had Robert-Houdin left this private legacy to someone in particular? Charles's name stood out in Vincent's mind, but a moment later he began to muse that his master might have considered leaving it all to him. Yes, to him, the young apprentice. Vincent still defined himself that way in relation to Robert-Houdin's genius. As an apprentice. Was he worthy of it now?

Each page brought its share of surprises and demanded his utmost attention; the collection's only logic was chronological. Jean-Eugène Robert-Houdin had begun roughly around the same age as Vincent had, and had continued to the end—his last note was dated just days before his death. That's where Vincent began reading. Robert-Houdin must not have suspected that his death was imminent, for he only mentioned an upcoming journey and two inventions to modify.

In the paragraphs related to preliminary studies for secret passages, he regularly mentioned Étienne Begel: "Consult Étienne to verify the feasibility of a reversible mechanism," "Ask Begel's advice about what metal to use." A quick sketch of each project outlined its operation and opening contraption. Four or five small crosses were drawn in the margins; devices with only three were crossed out with what sometimes seemed like a furious hand. It didn't take Vincent long to work out that the crosses were ratings that enabled Robert-Houdin to determine if his idea respected each of the five principles that governed the best secret passages. Clearly he only built the ones he was completely satisfied with—yet more proof of his exacting nature.

The following page openly addressed the day-to-day affairs of the research group he belonged to—the one Adinson was now part of. There, Robert-Houdin described their meetings. No names were ever mentioned; each member was identified only by function, such as archivist, investigator, physicist, architect, mathematician, theologian, historian, and several mentions of a devil's advocate. This last moniker intrigued Vincent.

The various dossiers referred to more than thirty treasures that were found and saved from looting or destruction. In this way, symbols of forgotten powers, relics, invaluable texts, and of course wealth in the form of gold or precious stones were safeguarded.

A few passages, however, mentioned unsolved mysteries, including one that the research circle had finally given up on and that reminded Vincent of the difficulties he had encountered in trying to open the tunnel in Flamel's cave. It mentioned a shipowner who had disappeared mysteriously in the Mediterranean; his unusually thick-walled home hid secret rooms, yet it had been impossible to find their entrance.

Within this eclectic collection of mysteries, projects, and questions, Robert-Houdin even showed an interest in historical events or strange news items that he suspected might conceal a mystery, like the case of the journalist who was murdered after announcing a forthcoming sensationalist piece on a fake Egyptian mummy racket.

A shadow that suddenly blotted out the sun tore Vincent from his thoughts.

"You're up early to study and you already look worried."

He hadn't heard Gabrielle approach. Against the light, her long hair filtered the sun's rays gloriously; a saint magnified by the aura of stained glass. Vincent closed the notebook.

"Have I come at a bad time?" asked the young woman.

"Never, but I see that even in an empty field you manage to appear without warning. You have a gift."

She laughed as she stretched and breathed in the fresh air. "Last night I heard you speaking with your friends. I didn't want to interfere, but I was surprised that none of you asked a simple question that seems an obvious one to me."

"What's that?"

"Since the fire, have you been able to retake control of the situation?" The young woman stepped aside. Now the light threw her profile into relief: the straight nose, the high cheekbones, eyes bright as a spring sky. Her youth, her beauty, and the energy that Vincent sensed within her were so many odes to life. He did not feel he had the right to tarnish them with problems that the young woman could unfortunately do nothing to solve.

"It's too early to say. What about you? Are you getting used to these surroundings?"

"This place is so unusual that I'm able to forget everything that exists elsewhere."

"How is Pierre?"

"He worries about not seeing you enough and wonders what the future holds."

"We all feel that way. Don't you?"

"I spoke with fortune tellers and card readers. Several of them come each night."

"What did they predict?"

"Always very different and contradicting things, to the point that none of it means anything. They promise me love, chubby-cheeked children, and often fortune, but none of them spoke of the danger of death. Don't you find that surprising?"

After his experience with the twins, Vincent would not venture to comment on oracles, spirits, or prophecies. He was no longer certain of what he thought about them.

"If they promise you only happiness, you should believe them."

They both smiled. Vincent motioned to the camp with his chin. "I heard that to free up a caravan, you and Pierre now share one."

Gabrielle blushed. "Pierre is behaving like a perfect gentleman."

"I have no doubt about that."

"He put Henri to work; a second-hand dealer brought him some textbooks, quills, and a notebook. And even a copy of *The Mysterious Island.*"

Perceiving Gabrielle's reluctance to discuss her relationship with Pierre, he came to her aid by changing the subject. "I was told that Eustasio sent a reassuring message and that he'll be back in a few days."

The young woman nodded. Gabrielle didn't dare look Vincent in the eye, but she had to ask, "Are you going to make it through this?"

"I hope so."

"When you're not here," she admitted, "it's not the same. We all feel a bit lost. Pierre and I talk about you a lot. We're able to keep Henri occupied, but Konrad broods."

"I miss you all very much."

A trail of dust on the horizon caught Vincent's attention. A horseman was galloping toward them. Perhaps he would continue on his way westward, but Vincent's instinct told him otherwise.

The man, who rode at full gallop, gradually came into sight. He wore a long coachman's coat and the signature hat. Vincent straightened and stared at the newcomer. Gabrielle spotted him as well.

"Will you have to leave again so soon?"

"Perhaps."

The coachman entered the camp and made his way between the tables, hardly slowing, just enough to hail Victor in passing, who pointed to where Vincent and Gabrielle were sitting. At the foot of the embankment, the horseman jumped down from his mount and climbed to the top. He wiped his dusty forehead on his arm. "Mr. Adinson sent me to fetch you," he panted.

"What's going on?"

The man glanced at Gabrielle.

"You may speak freely," Vincent reassured him.

"Men are working in the house on Rue de Montmorency, and also near the manhole where you descended the other night."

Vincent jumped to his feet. "Damn it! They're going to try to force the tunnel."

"I'm to take you to Paris straight away."

Vincent turned to the young woman and took her hands gently in his. "I have to go, Gabrielle. But before I do, I need your help."

"If I can..."

"Give my regards to my brother and my friends. Don't alarm them, just tell them I couldn't stay, that they shouldn't worry, and to continue to live their lives. Take care of my family as you did in our home; that, too, is your gift."

"Your strange family..."

"You're now a part of it."

"You can count on me."

"Tell Pierre that I always come back."

Vincent gathered up the notebooks and raced down the embankment with the messenger. The man jumped nimbly into the saddle and helped Vincent up behind him. Vincent waved to Gabrielle, who watched him ride away, until the two men were indistinguishable from the dust they raised.

71

The coachman pulled in the reins and gave an order; the horse slowed from a trot and the fiacre pulled up to the intersection of Rue Beaubourg and Rue des Gravilliers. In the midst of the activity on the heavily traveled street, no one noticed the cab, from which no passenger descended.

Concealed behind the cab door curtain, Charles and Vincent observed the worksite that had been set up around the manhole through which they had previously descended.

"We counted nine men," explained Charles. "They brought only tools: picks, pickaxes, shovels. Their intentions are clear."

"Have they started bringing up dirt?"

"Not yet."

Vincent nodded, quite impressed by the effort that had been made. "They're clever. The worksite looks like any other blocking the street. They could be mistaken for actual sewage workers. They're going to dig undisturbed."

"Could they get past the landslide?"

"You were there with me when the tunnel collapsed. The tremor felt like a real earthquake. The passage is most likely blocked for several dozen yards. I'm not saying it's impossible to reopen, but it's going to take a lot of time and effort."

"I'm going to have them watched day and night."

"The amount of rubble they bring up will be a good indicator of their progress. Tell the men to count the carts. And if they start receiving beams or planks for shoring up, that means they made

it through and have to fortify a passage. Then we'll have to act."
Vincent turned towards Charles: "What's happening on Rue de Montmorency?"

"They sent about fifteen men. Some are sleeping onsite. We saw the same kind of tools arriving over there. They must be giving it everything they've got."

"Their enforcer, Joshua, assured me: they will keep working, with or without me. As they await my return, they've chosen the only method at their disposal: the use of force."

"Do you seriously think they expect to see you again?"

"Why else would they have let me go? Only by returning voluntarily could I prove my devotion. By the way, I haven't ruled out giving them that impression if it might be useful to us. In the meantime…"

"What will happen if you don't join them?"

"They'll start attacking us again, more determined than ever. But I'm not afraid of them. All that matters is that my loved ones are safe. Are they, in the embassies?"

"I give you my word."

Charles suddenly appeared uneasy. "Did you remember what happened after your spiritism séance?" he ventured.

"No. Not the slightest memory, which is very strange. It's as if those two days never existed, or as if they had been erased from my memory."

"Their activity on this site raises another problem."

"What?"

"Are they here because they spied on us, or because you gave them the address?"

Vincent was about to protest, but Charles held up his hand. "I'm not accusing you of anything, and I don't even suspect you. I'm only asking if they might have administered substances that would have made you negligent. After all, we know they master the use of poison, and you witnessed their unusual—to put it mildly— talents."

"You think they may have drugged me?"

"Or hypnotized you. That would explain why you remember nothing, not to mention the state in which we found you."

"Let's hope you're wrong."

Vincent carefully opened the curtain and watched the men busy at work around the manhole. Some of them climbed out, more or less covered in mud, to be replaced by others who crawled down in turn. They drank a little water and exchanged a few words. One of them lit a cigarette. They looked like quite ordinary workmen.

"I hope I didn't reveal anything in spite of myself," grumbled Vincent. He sighed and added, "What do you think they're up to?"

"Do you regret that we didn't undertake this work ourselves?"

"Definitely not. I believe it is more effective to focus on the existence of other entrances, as suggested by Loyola's account. Speaking of which, I've already thought of several lines of inquiry that might be useful to us."

"For their part, my companions have also clarified certain points that have proved surprising, to say the least. Would you like to meet them?"

72

The Paris Observatory was relatively calm on that early afternoon, since a portion of its staff spent their nights studying the stars. The majestic building—the pride of the Royal Academy of Sciences founded by Louis XIV—stood in the center of the gardens that had once been the site of pioneering experiments. This is where the meridian determining "true noon" had been plotted, the standardized notions of the meter and kilogram determined, and the sciences of cartography and geodesy developed.

At the moment, its round dome, home to one of the world's largest astronomic telescopes, was closed.

"The astronomy observatory?" said Vincent in surprise.

"It's one of our meeting places," explained Charles. "One of our most eminent companions works here, and the site can be accessed through several entrances, some of which are underground and connected to old quarries. It is an excellent option for meeting unobserved. Even the revolutionaries failed to discover what was hidden here, although three hundred of them searched the area."

Weaving his way through the alleys while staying close to the hedges, Adinson led Vincent toward a side entrance to the grand building.

The guard recognized Charles and let them in through the service entrance. The two men climbed an inconspicuous staircase and quickly reached the first floor, where they headed toward the rotunda in the western tower.

As they entered, Charles whispered to Vincent, "Don't be offended: no one will tell you their name. It will be a little confusing for you at first, but you'll quickly find your footing. Don't be put off by my companions' bluntness. They don't beat around the bush. Say what you know, ask your questions without fear, and do not be ashamed of what you do not know."

Imposing pedestaled globes and blonde wood wall panels embellished with moldings gave the large octagonal room an air of elegant nobility. Everything in the kind of objects on display and the sobriety of style was an invitation to travel, liberated from borders and gravity. A majestic portrait of Louis XIV hung over the fireplace. To its left hung a portrait of the observatory's first director, the astronomer and engineer Jean-Dominique Cassini. As for his son, grandson, and great-grandson, who went on to direct the institution after him, they were granted far more modest portraits dispatched between a map of the Moon and a territorial survey of France. A fresco on the ceiling depicted a beautiful woman floating in the sky facing a gilded chariot pulled by four white horses and driven by a being surrounded by a halo of light—an allegory of Venus crossing the Sun.

Six people were already seated around the central table standing directly below the mural. They were bent over documents that were quite different from the star charts and terrestrial maps typically studied in that venerable place.

Adinson approached them. "Greetings, my friends. I am pleased to introduce you to the specialist in secret passages, the former student of our late magician brother."

Each of the guests welcomed Vincent with a nod, to which he responded awkwardly. Five men and a woman stared at him. He was by far the youngest in the room. Adinson invited Vincent to sit next to him. "Thank you for responding to my call so quickly. Time is running out. We just verified for ourselves that individuals are already busy at work around the two previously identified tunnel entrances."

An anxious murmur ran through the audience. A man with an impressive mustache and a monocle declared, "Yet another reason to get straight to the point."

He set the engraved key on the table. "My theologian colleague and I have studied this surprising piece in every possible way. We first examined the complex engravings that adorn it, which led us to an initial, unsatisfactory conclusion: besides originating in what are usually considered to be enemy cultures, there is in all likelihood no coded message."

The historian held up the solid ring with the entwined characters for the gathered scholars to see. "We have here together Latin and Arabic writing, while this key likely dates from the Crusades, a time when these two civilizations were engaged in violent conflict. I would like to draw your attention to the way the artist purposefully wove the designs together to create something that went beyond contemporaneous confrontations."

The fair-haired man wearing a three-piece suit and matching waistcoat sitting next to him offered clarification. "Although we were very impressed by the spirit of union that may have motivated the object's creator, we did not discover much else. Only when my historian and theologian colleagues left the key with me so that I could study its physical structure did I make a fortuitous discovery. The key was sitting on my worktable when I noticed that it seemed to react to the presence of metal. It was lying on my notes when it actually pivoted on its own toward the foot of my steel easel. I realized then that it was magnetic. We immediately attributed this to its iron-based composition, which struck us all as being quite ordinary compared to the quality of the craftsmanship."

The physician picked up the key and went on. "You have no doubt noticed the tiny hole in the shaft. We ran a very fine thread of cotton through it and suspended the key, as I am doing now. We were able to confirm that it comes to a balance in this way and indeed reacts to magnetic masses by moving in their direction."

He reproduced the experiment, teasing the suspended key with a small steel bar. The two elements interacted; the key seemed to pull toward the steel.

"From this we believe we may deduct that it is not intended to open a lock. It is more than a key: it is likely some sort of compass."

The physician passed the object to the woman seated across the table from him. She looked at it carefully, then said, "The fact that it was discovered in the coffer with Ignatius of Loyola's account does not guarantee a connection."

Adinson leaned toward Vincent and explained quietly, "Madame is our devil's advocate today. Her job is to question the hypotheses we formulate. We take turns playing this role. She is formidable at it."

"What role does she usually play?"

"Mathematician and geographer."

Vincent was captivated by the natural authority that emanated from the woman. And he was incredibly excited to see eminent specialists from diverse disciplines conversing freely, without prideful resistance to fields beyond their own.

He raised his hand. The devil's advocate let him speak.

"It seems logical to me that this key could be a compass, but beyond that, what interests me most is that its appearance may divert attention from its true function: a real tool concealed by the illusion of another. This, I'm convinced, connects it to the devices I encountered in the tunnel. In fact, in the case of both the air vents that reproduce the sound of ominous howls and the hinged floor of the cellar, simple, clever processes are used in ways other than what they are intended for, as is the case with this key."

"Yet," the woman said, "if we have been correctly informed, you never had to choose between multiple directions on your journey through the tunnel. What would be the use of a compass, then, if one has no need to orient oneself?"

"True, we were presented with no choice but to follow the tunnel," confirmed Vincent. "But we didn't explore everything, because we were prevented from doing so."

The theologian, a small man with a cleft chin wearing a cassock, spoke up. "Are you alluding to the passage that collapsed under the water?"

"Precisely."

"We learned that you had discovered a grate, and that our late companion lost his life trying to force it open. Is that true?"

"I've given it much thought, and I think it's more than that. I don't believe it was an accident caused by a state of dilapidation or a weakening of the structure due to the water's influence. Instead I think the passage was protected by a mechanism, and because inappropriate means were used in an attempt to open it, it auto-destructed to prevent a breach. As spectacular as the disaster was, the passage simply closed itself off to keep us from going any further."

"Which implies that whoever built this tunnel was ready to sacrifice it permanently, for themselves as well, rather than see it desecrated?" said the devil's advocate.

"You bring up a crucial point. That's why I think another entrance exists, one I suggest we look for."

"If, as suggested by the account Loyola recorded, what lies at the end of this tunnel is exceptionally precious, why create multiple access points, thereby increasing the risk of discovery?" she asked.

Vincent met the argument with a smile. "I don't have the answer to your judicious question, but in the same way two renters can each possess a key to the same house, we may be looking for a site shared by several entities. Two entrances would have left each of them free to come and go as they pleased, while keeping them united."

The archivist, who had been silent until this point, spoke up. "Then we must turn our search to the groups that would have been powerful enough, at the time of the Crusades, to decide to create a sanctuary with others like themselves."

"There are not many," the devil's advocate pointed out.

The historian with the monocle looked at each of the participants in turn. "The real question is what could have urged them to undertake such a project. History has taught us that men require much convincing to overcome their differences. This sanctuary was quite obviously built for a reason, and its creators most certainly had something important to protect, a treasure exceptional enough that they did not feel justified in protecting it on their own."

Vincent was immediately taken with this point of view, especially since it resonated with his own conviction: the complexity of design and construction in the tunnel and passages transcended the capacities and expertise of each community taken independently.

"This sheds new light on the case," remarked Adinson. "Let us continue our research and not waste a minute. And let us hope that our combined insights are more efficient than our enemies' picks and shovels."

73

The participants gave themselves time to think before considering their research in relation to other sites that might conceal an entrance. Some of them conversed informally, while others went over their notes. Charles was having a quiet discussion with the archivist. Off to the side, Vincent stretched his legs and thought about what he had just heard.

Crucial information had emerged, brought to light by people who knew what they were talking about. Although he knew nothing about their identities or their backgrounds, just hearing them was enough to make him realize that they all had knowledge, stature, and much more experience than he did—enough for him to be intimidated.

It was the first time that Vincent had attended a meeting of this caliber. Until this point, he had only very rarely come into contact with such erudite minds, and at best, he had been providing a service. This gathering was different. Was he a spectator or a member? Each of the participants was an expert in their field. Was he really one in his? Even if he had managed to uncover the secret of the tunnel entrance—with Henri's help and a good dose of luck—he had not been able to disarm the submerged grate.

One of the giant globes caught his attention and he walked over to it. The areas of land were represented in ocher and the oceans in off-white. The object was truly a work of art, and what it symbolized was dizzying: every continent of this vast planet on which so many civilizations coexisted or succeeded one another, each with its own history, high points, sometimes even its decline, and every one of them with its share of mysteries. Vincent suddenly considered the planet in its entirety. He could set it spinning with a single finger. Although the sphere was quite large, he could wrap his arms around it or, like Atlas, carry it on his shoulders.

The globe's cartography was only a few decades old, and yet it was already out of date. Vincent was troubled when he noticed this. The increasing number of voyages had proved false many of the contours believed to be true at the time of its creation.

The globe on display in the other corner was much older and even more striking. Faced with its faded blue seas and contours of fantastical continents, even someone with an education as basic as Vincent's could now point out the numerous errors that had once been presented as truths by the most eminent scholars and explorers of their time.

He heard the geographer speak behind him. "Does our Earth intrigue you?"

"To say the least. Everything humanity has discovered is blindingly obvious when you look at these two versions."

"The building we're standing in was created precisely for that purpose. Information brought back from the great maritime expeditions over two hundred years ago was verified and indexed here. Coronelli, the Italian geographer monk who created this globe in 1688, was perfectly educated in scientific knowledge."

"For the layman that I am, it's surprising to be able to evaluate with the naked eye everything that our ancestors did not know. It's glaringly apparent, even on the more recent globe. So much progress has been made."

The woman smiled. "They had the same thirst for knowledge that we do, they simply lacked the same resources. Each day science and experience provide us with new ones. I believe that the phenomenon is even intensifying and accelerating. We have a better and better understanding of our world. We can all now make the surprising observation that a child today knows more about our world than a scholar of the distant past."

Vincent ran his finger along the inaccurate coasts of the South American continent. "I never realized that."

"One question has always stayed with me, to the point of obsession. What do we do with everything that we have learned? What is the use of this knowledge and these resources that develop with increasing speed? Do they really make us better, or just spoil us more? Are we not wasting the opportunities that are offered us? Despite the growing body of knowledge, there is one legacy that we are unable to overcome: our animal nature. We still have our animal reflexes, those instinctive fears that prevent us from thinking big and elevating ourselves. The Ancients dreamed of ideals that we now neglect, that we degrade by lowering them to the level of laws or dogma gutted of their deeper meaning. The paths to commerce are multiplying faster than the paths to wisdom. We are losing sight of our true interests and the road traveled. We consume today without a thought for tomorrow. When I see people content to be entertained, I grow fearful; for what has been won can yet be lost. But we must keep the flame and spirit alive if we hope to survive."

She pointed to the older globe with the approximate cartography. "What will our descendants think of our civilizations? How will those who come after us judge our actions? Will they reveal that the contour of our mentality is as primitive as those imaginary shores that have no basis in reality?"

Unaware of the moment he was interrupting, Adinson appeared at their side. "Please forgive me, but our archivist has just informed me of an element that appears to be of the utmost importance."

Charles motioned the archivist to join them. "Please, repeat what you just told me."

"We have already established that, prior to the construction of Nicolas Flamel's house, a tomb that probably concealed the tunnel entrance was located on the same site."

Vincent nodded. The man continued. "Logically we focused our research on buildings from the same period, around the thirteenth century, that would have been likely to be connected to the Crusades, religious orders, or chivalry. My research unearthed so many possible solutions that not a single one stood out, but my theologian colleague directed me to another field of inquiry. In the archives, I discovered the existence of another tomb from the same period as that of Enguerrand de Tardenay, one located close enough to place it within the tunnel's supposed path."

"A Templar sepulture?" asked Vincent.

"Even better: it was located in the very foundations of the Tour du Temple."

"The imposing fortified tower of the Templars' estate?" said Vincent in surprise.

"The very same, the centerpiece of their vast domain."

Adinson and Vincent exchanged looks. The archivist continued. "But this poses a serious problem: the Templars' estate was destroyed and the tower demolished. There's nothing left of it. If this tomb was there, it has been struck from the map! Just as we discover a glimmer of hope, we already see it fading. This is what distresses me."

Vincent froze, then yelped like a madman. "Good Lord!"

Adinson recognized the agitation that had so worried him when Vincent had returned from his absence. "What is wrong, my friend?"

Vincent pulled the notebooks from his pocket and flipped through them feverishly. "I read something about that tower being demolished in Robert-Houdin's notes. I'm certain of it. He mentions a strange affair involving that very same Tour du Temple."

74

The sky darkened quickly on that gray morning, and rain poured down on Paris. When Charles and Vincent reached the north end of Rue du Temple, the square of the same name gradually came into view.

The two men slowed to observe their surroundings. To prepare for this crucial visit, they had each spent a good portion of the night studying on their own. They hoped, together, to figure it out.

Surrounding the vast central esplanade, opulent buildings were being completed in the last remaining open spaces. The Carreau du Temple market drew second-hand clothing dealers and tailors. More and more businesses were setting up shop there.

Adinson turned up his collar. He eyed Vincent's bowler mockingly. The rim had become a gutter from which a thin trickle of water escaped down the side of his face. Despite the seriousness of the situation, Charles could not resist teasing his companion. "Now do you understand the purpose of a hat?"

Vincent smiled thinly and shook his head like a dog drying itself, sending water flying onto his partner. But he never took eyes off the Square du Temple that stretched out before him.

Some of the trees had already grown to respectable heights. The paths were deserted; no one was strolling in the rain, and no children played near the ornamental pond and its decorative waterfall. There was not a single newspaper vendor in sight, only workers and delivery men who had no choice but to carry on in spite of the weather. Sorry-looking horses pulled their dripping carriages along the road that skirted the island of greenery.

The new town hall rose above it all, proclaiming its official status. Completed barely twenty years earlier, the Renaissance Revival construction, flanked by two wings, housed the administrative services of the third arrondissement.

Vincent had recently studied the area's history using maps and now discovered the reality. He began to explain it, as much as to review things for himself as to inform his companion. "The entire perimeter once belonged to the Templars. In the thirteenth century, at a time when the city of Paris still reached nowhere near this far, they had settled in the swamps, which they drained and dried before establishing what would become one of the most thriving estates in existence. By 1210 the area was a third the size of the capital and included farms and vegetable gardens, as well as many outbuildings protected by an outer wall. The Master's house was located on the square, and at the far end, precisely where the town hall now stands, rose the Tour du Temple."

Adinson turned to look where Vincent was pointing.

"One hundred sixty-four feet tall, fortified, flanked on all four corners by turrets with arrow slits, this fortress was the symbol of the Templars' power. It was visible from a great distance, and the king himself could see it from his windows on the Ile de la Cité. The order was all-powerful, and their immense property formed a city within the city. Early in the morning on October 13, 1307, when King Philip the Fair ordered the premeditated arrest of Templars throughout France and had them sentenced under vague pretexts, their numerous assets were confiscated for the Crown. They could have withdrawn behind their fortifications, but they surrendered without resistance, confident in the king's justice. The searches that were immediately carried out on their estates, and particularly in this tower, revealed nothing, and the legend of a hidden treasure began to spread."

Adinson walked beside Vincent, considering the ground that had been witness to another story, and where people now tread without a thought for or even an inkling of what had previously taken place.

"Several centuries later," continued Vincent, "Crusades and Templars were nothing more than a memory, and as Paris expanded, their tower became a building like any other. It was abandoned for a time before being repurposed for other uses, including a granary, a protected armory, and then as barracks. During the Revolution, the tower became a prison for King Louis XVI and his entourage, until he was led to the scaffold."

"Is that what Robert-Houdin mentions in his notes?"

"His curiosity was piqued by a development that occurred much later, more recently. Early this century, in 1808 to be exact, Napoléon Bonaparte ordered the demolition of what was left of the Temple complex and its buildings. The official version of the story is that he feared the site would become a royalist pilgrimage destination in memory of the king's suffering there. But the historian discovered nothing in the prefecture archives that suggests such a phenomenon occurred. The theologian shed light on what are probably the real reasons behind the measure: while the Emperor's decision seems to have been based on fear of a royalist tide, he was ultimately convinced by one Ernest Blanchard, who evidently had other ambitions. The man directed a materials company specialized in salvaging and reselling old stones. He was awarded the contract to tear down the last Templar buildings, including the famous fortified tower. It would have been a mundane story of profit, if events hadn't taken a strange turn. Although it took the businessman less than three months to tear down six massive buildings near Montparnasse, it took him over two years to destroy this tower alone. Quite unexpectedly, he did not dismantle it starting at the top: he emptied the interior first."

"As though he were searching for something?"

"Exactly.

"Perhaps he was hoping to lay his hands on whatever had escaped Philip the Fair."

"That's what your friend Robert-Houdin suspected. Publications from the time also mention the presence of secret societies in the area that practiced black masses and occult ceremonies."

"Nothing about a sepulture?"

"Yes, there is one account, years later, in 1867, during the inauguration of the town hall that stands before us today. One of the guests declared to a journalist—probably to get attention—that his father, who had participated in the demolition as a young laborer, had discovered a tomb there."

"The one we're looking for?"

Vincent nodded. "He made it clear that it had been neither destroyed nor moved, and that it still lay underground, below the new building. The press relayed his story and two days later, he was found dead in his home from unexplained causes, although he had been in perfect health. That's when Robert-Houdin took an interest in the affair and made the connection."

Adinson peered at the town hall in the renovated neighborhood. "So the tomb is still there, intact, somewhere beneath the new construction."

"Why don't we have a look?"

75

With seven children to feed, the night watchman did not cling to his integrity for long. A few pieces of silver had convinced him to look the other way while they made a simple nighttime visit. One of the coachmen had stayed behind in the guard's station to share—or rather to pour—a bottle of spirits that eventually put the man into a deep sleep.

Two coachmen equipped with lanterns escorted Charles to the cellar, who explored the area as he tried to work out where he was on his map. Vincent followed him, studying the walls and floors, looking for the slightest clue that would lead him to the ruins.

The small squad followed a modern corridor that serviced the foundations, methodically investigating every last niche. On either side of the corridor, a series of doors opened onto small rooms, most of them used for archiving purposes. Each one was numbered and assigned to a department. Napoléon Bonaparte's desire to formalize birth, marriage, and death records had considerably increased the volume of documents that required storing.

Using the watchman's pass, one of the men unlocked a new room and entered with his lantern. Charles joined him and began by verifying their position on the map. He turned it around and around, trying to orient it.

"We are nearly at the center of the area where the tower stood."

"'Nearly' doesn't sound very convincing," said Vincent ironically. He glanced at the wooden racks heaped with paperwork and tried to see what lay behind them.

Countless brown envelopes and bound files stood in piles, all of them carefully labelled with rounded penmanship. The unit was assigned to land registers and property surveys.

Vincent grabbed the lantern and crouched down at the back of the room to examine the base of the wall where it was visible in the spaces between the filing cabinets. Charles looked around without a clear idea of what he should be searching for.

"Well?"

"The tilework is recent and perfectly level, as is the stonework."

"But how can the tomb be concealed?"

Vincent bent forward and leaned into the floor to get a better view of the edge where the floor and the wall met.

"Two sets of craftsmen worked one after another onsite: the first tore down the fort, and the second constructed this building in its place. The decision to keep the sepulture here had to have been made by the first set of workers. Logically, they must have protected it using the materials they found in abundance around them."

"Is that why you're paying particular attention to the stones?"

"Older stones would be telling." He stood up, rubbing his hands together. "In the meantime, there's nothing of interest here. Let's head to the next one."

Back in the corridor, Vincent glanced at Charles's map, then turned around to count the nooks they had already inspected.

"You're right, we're approaching the center of the former tower."

The next room they entered had shelves full of organized files like the dozens they had already seen. This unit, assigned to urban planning, also held rolled-up maps.

As he stepped into the room, Vincent immediately noticed something: the room was slightly warmer than the others, and there was a hint of humidity in the air.

"Do you feel that?" he asked Adinson.

"Yes, we're going to have trouble if we don't hurry!"

Charles took his watch from his vest pocket. "We still have much to see," he said, showing it to Vincent, "and yet we must leave soon."

Vincent crouched at the foot of the wall without rushing. He ran his hand along the floor. A new feeling of relative warmth confirmed his initial suspicion. A faint dust, stickier than what they had found in the previous rooms, adhered to his palm and fingers. He smelled them. "Something is different here."

Walking over to the shelves, he tested the texture of the maps, rubbing the paper between thumb and index finger like a piece of fabric. There was no denying it: the room was humid. Adinson repeated the gesture, but his sense of touch was not as refined; he was incapable of perceiving what Vincent had detected.

Vincent removed several documents to reveal the back of file cabinets. He shook the structures to see how they had been fixed in place.

"Do you suspect something?" Adinson asked him.

"Let's just say I'd like to understand."

"Could the humidity be the result of a leak?"

"Possibly, but we would find traces of mold in that case, and there are none."

Vincent slipped his arm behind the cabinet to reach the wall. He extended his hand as far as possible, feeling around with his palm as he had done on the ground, to collect a bit of dust. He removed the spiderwebs that came along with it and tasted the substance on his whitened fingertips.

"It's nothing like the others. We're going to have to move the cabinets."

"Do you realize how long that's going to take us?" exclaimed Charles.

"Another reason not to waste any time."

Vincent grabbed an armful of files and set them near the door. The two coachmen and Charles followed suit.

The four men quickly lightened the cabinet enough to move it an arm's length from the wall. Vincent managed to slip behind it and examined the stonework, which he had done many times before. His experience in Flamel's cellar had taught him to leave nothing to chance. He palpated the wall as a doctor would a patient while the three other men watched him attentively.

"This wall is warmer than the corresponding wall in the neighboring rooms. Perhaps that's because of the nature of the material, but it could also be due to empty space behind. Help me finish moving the cabinet."

"The night is almost over," Charles objected. "We cannot run the risk of being caught searching an official building."

"This difference in the rooms is intriguing. Don't force me to leave with that question hanging. Grant me a reprieve and your help. Don't you want to know?"

With their combined efforts, it was quickly done.

"Notice the uneven shape of the stones and the order in which they were laid. Unlike the stones in the other dividing walls, they aren't uniform, as would be expected of industrially manufactured stones," said Vincent.

"Yet the surface looks the same," remarked one of the men doubtfully.

"They were probably recut to blend into the background, removing the antiquated appearance that would have given them away."

Vincent picked up a lantern and moved it slowly along the wall, angling the light to illuminate it. Charles examined the floor. "Do you think the floor might be lower here as well?"

"If it were made of beaten earth, I might wonder, but see for yourself: it's solid tile."

Vincent reached the corner formed by the back and left walls of the room. He stopped. "Now this is odd," he said. "None of the stones overlap the two walls. That's very surprising."

"What do you mean?"

"Look: the two walls share no stones. Those on the back wall have all been cut to stop cleanly at the corner."

"Which means?"

"Which means that the two sections are not joined together as they should be. The joints interlock everywhere but here."

"What is your hypothesis?"

"This is typical of an opening." Vincent knocked on the wall. He put his ear to it and repeated the operation a little further along.

"I hear a very slight resonance." He tapped in a few more places, then turned to his companions. "This wall isn't built against the bedrock. We must find out what's hidden behind it."

"Break through it? We would need pickaxes and crowbars."

"Not necessarily. Help me move the cabinet a little further away so I can get a bit more momentum. And then, how about putting our shoulders to work?"

76

The men took turns hurtling themselves at the wall, eventually cracking the plaster in one corner. Encouraged by the sight, Vincent, Charles, and their companions redoubled their efforts and, with a great wrenching of stone, finally managed to open a thin crack. A current of air and a pungent stale odor seeped into the room.

The men were galvanized by the possibility of having discovered a passage and forgot about the pain. Even Charles rushed forward with renewed strength, using all his weight to enlarge the opening.

Vincent caught his breath before charging again, keeping a firm eye on the base of the wall. "Keep going! One more and we'll have done it!"

Inch by inch, a portion of the wall gradually pivoted, like an unwilling door. Adinson grimaced and rubbed his shoulder, but his eyes were gleaming. "Whoever built this didn't try to block the access permanently. They probably intended to come back."

The scraping of stone on the foundations grew less difficult with each charge, and soon the opening was large enough for a man to slip partway through. Vincent grabbed a lantern and poked his head in. After a moment's hesitation, he ventured all the way into the darkness.

"Be careful," said Charles in alarm. "We didn't use conventional methods to open this passage. Last time, this kind of maneuver…"

"This wall wasn't built by whoever created the tunnel," Vincent interrupted. "But I assure you, I'll be careful."

Turning his back on his companions, he raised his lamp above his head. He could only see a few yards in front of him, and it took him some time to adjust to the darkness; but it was enough to make out a small square vestibule that gave onto a staircase leading into impenetrable darkness.

Vincent made up his mind to continue cautiously onto the strange landing. The odor of earth and dust, typical of underground spaces, filled his nostrils. He inhaled, torn between the desire to venture further and a strong feeling of caution.

"Is everything all right, Vincent?"

"You should come have a look."

Charles didn't wait to be asked twice and slipped through the opening. He squinted. Vincent took him by the arm to guide him in. Pointing to the staircase, he whispered, as though they might be overheard. "If you allow me, I will go down first."

He placed a foot gingerly on the first step to verify that it was in fact stable and free of any traps. Once he was satisfied, he brought his other foot forward and stood there as though he had conquered an outpost in enemy territory.

"The carving technique appears to be the same used in the tunnel on Rue de Montmorency," he said as he examined the walls.

Charles nodded silently. Step by step, Vincent began his descent, inspecting each inch won from the darkness. Charles carefully placed his feet exactly where Vincent had. The staircase descended rapidly; the lamp did not shine bright enough to be able to guess where it led.

"Where will this passage lead us?" asked Charles quietly.

Vincent didn't have an answer. He ran a hand along the wall, intrigued by a faint white deposit. As they descended, the fine cottony film grew more abundant, mostly likely the sign of a cellar left too long unopened.

Suddenly the halo of his lantern revealed a landing below them. Vincent struggled to contain a desire to rush down the stairs, so curious was he to see it, but he knew what too much haste could cost him. When he reached the last step, he stopped. He leaned slightly forward, as though standing on the edge of a frozen pond, hesitating to walk across it for fear of the ice breaking. At last he carefully ventured a few steps on the ancient stone floor.

What he saw when he looked up was beyond anything he could have imagined and left him stunned. Beside him, Charles bore the same astonished expression.

They had discovered far more than a simple tomb. An entire crypt emerged from the shadows, a large round room with thirteen vertical alcoves bored into the perimeter, each containing an upright stone sarcophagus. Between each alcove, a lancet arch soared to the keystone, marked with the Templar's cross.

In the center of the cobbled space gaped a square-rimmed well carved with gothic arches and surmounted by an ironwork crossbar equipped with a pulley.

The site, frozen in time, had a regal atmosphere about it. Even the silence was grandiose.

Charles and Vincent made their way humbly forward; they were the first to set foot inside since the entrance had been walled up. They were quite literally surrounded by sepultures. Stone coffins were displayed standing, as if the remains they held might step out of them at any moment. A shiver of excitement tinged with super-stitious fear ran down Vincent's spine.

Oddly, the tombs included no recumbent statues and not a single coat of arms or title. The edge of each lid, engraved with Latinate script, framed a different sculpted scene. Each one seemed to lead into the next, forming a kind of fresco that stretched across the tombs.

The two men remained silent. Only their breath marked the passage of time, at first reverberating, then gradually calming after the initial shock, to eventually become one.

They had taken a leap into the past, descending a staircase to climb back through the centuries, traveling from a modern cellar to a buried medieval necropolis.

Torn between prudence and respect, Charles reached out a hand toward the closest sarcophagus, but did not touch it. "Do you think this is the sanctuary?"

"I have no idea. If so, that would mean the Templar fortress provided an entrance that circumvented the labyrinth."

Vincent began to take a closer look at one of the sarcophagi, when he noticed the same snowy film he had seen in the stairwell.

A fine layer covered the entire crypt and everything in it. He drew his lamp closer to examine it, then suddenly jumped back and pulled Charles aside. "Whatever you do, don't touch anything! Don't put your hands anywhere!"

Adinson was startled. "What is it?"

"Saltpeter! The walls and sarcophagi are covered in saltpeter. It's even on the vault."

Charles shrugged. "It's just ordinary cellar mold. The place has been shut up for too long. Why are you so alarmed?"

"It's not just mold, Charles. Its scientific name is potassium nitrate. While it does indeed form naturally in moist cellars, it's also one of the main components in gunpowder. Robert-Houdin used it in his smoke explosions."

"Good heavens!"

"If we had walked in here with a live flame—like anyone in the thirteenth century would have done, when torches were used for light—this room would have burst into flames instantaneously."

Charles examined the downy film cautiously. "There is indeed a lot of it."

"This can't be coincidence," said Vincent. "The humidity level in this room was most likely designed to encourage development of this highly flammable substance. Perhaps it's the trial by fire promised in the labyrinth?"

He inspected the walls, careful to keep his lamp as far from them as possible. "Come see this: tiny holes were pierced at regular intervals at the top and bottom to allow humidity to enter..."

Fascinated by his surroundings, Charles spun around, then walked around the room. As he did so, he glanced quickly into the well. "I understand why the demolition workers didn't dare to destroy this place."

Just as Vincent bent down to look at the bas-relief that unfolded across the sarcophagi, they were surprised by a voice from the landing above. "Gentlemen! The guard is awake. He informed us that the employees won't be long in arriving. Get up here fast! We have to put everything back and get out of here quickly."

Vincent and Adinson exchanged glances; intense was their frustration and bitter the taste of unfinished business. Charles sighed, resigned, but not Vincent. Spying the gleam in his eye, Adinson guessed what he was thinking. As Vincent opened his mouth to speak, Charles declared categorically, "Don't even think about it, my friend! I refuse to leave you here, in the middle of this powder box and who knows what other traps. You're leaving with me. Now!"

77

A fiacre entered the courtyard through the tall doors, which were immediately closed behind it. It pulled up alongside other cabs, where men in shirtsleeves were busy at work, calling out to each other. The coachman jumped down from his seat and gave his waybill to his superior. Grooms quickly unhitched the horses. Further down the line, a wheelwright examined damaged ironworks; a farrier changed the shoes on a docile bay while a stable boy greased the harnesses.

From the windows of Adinson's office, Vincent turned a mechanical gaze on the ordinary activity as he paced the room. His mind was elsewhere.

"Vincent, please, stop pacing about like a caged lion. I can't concentrate. I'm just as frustrated as you are that we had to interrupt our exploration, but we didn't have a choice. Help me prepare our return instead."

Charles was seated at his table, trying to make a list of necessary equipment, which he read out loud. "We should bring the key, and safety lamps. As for tools . . ."

He stopped, uneasy, and addressed his companion. "Do you think we will have to open the sarcophagi? I'm loath to break into sepultures."

Vincent, lost in thought, didn't reply.

"Good heavens!" said Adinson, annoyed. "May I have your attention? If we want to solve the mysteries of this crypt, we had better be ready. Who knows what lies in store for us? While we're forced to wait, we should use the time to get our questions in order. Don't you have any?"

Vincent stopped pacing without taking his gaze from the courtyard. "All I have are questions. My head is so full of them, it's going to explode. The more I think, the further adrift I become. Did we find the sanctuary? Who are the thirteen men buried there? Why are the tombs arranged as they are? What story do they tell? Like you, I have no desire to disturb their eternal slumber, but we must resign ourselves to doing so if we wish to obtain answers."

"Then we should bring the crowbars." Adinson seemed truly sorry as he added them to his list.

"Don't forget ropes," added Vincent, "and a lifting tripod, to move the lids. And bring a good knife."

Adinson wrote. "How many men should we take with us?" he asked.

"Two should be enough. Choose the most trustworthy and morally sound. Our investigations, which are strange to say the least, could prove too trying for the less seasoned."

"Understood."

"Everyone must wear cotton gloves."

"Noted."

Vincent went over to the desk and leaned on it with his arms outstretched, as he did when he was developing a strategy at his own work table.

"Charles, you have much more experience with religious architecture than I do. What does your instinct tell you about this crypt?"

"My instinct...," thought Adinson. "One thing is certain: I'm puzzled. It would have been much more logical to find it... under a church. While the circular shape of the room is not unusual, the rest of it is: the arrangement of the bodies, the sarcophagi used to form a fresco. The presence of the well might also be surprising on first glance, but if we consider the fact that this room was originally located under a fortress, and that sources of water were vital there and always protected, then it makes sense."

"I agree with your analysis."

"Our companions who specialize in history and theology will be much better placed to study the site than I am. Should we ask them to accompany us?"

"That's an excellent idea."

Charles noticed that Vincent looked drawn. "We can't return until tonight. You should use this time to get some rest."

"I can't."

"Why don't you spend some time with your friends at the embassies? Take the day, it will do you a world of good."

"I thought about it. I would really like to, but I'm not sure I have the strength to act as if nothing has happened. I can't get my mind off of this crypt, but I can't tell them about it. I mustn't. I don't even know if I'll ever be able to. It's awful, Charles: they matter most to me, but for their own good, I'm forbidden from confiding in them about the thing that preoccupies me."

He paused for a moment. "Ultimately, you're the only person with whom I can speak freely. We haven't known each other long, but oddly, you're probably the one who knows me best. You, and a killer who spends his time spying on me."

Vincent looked up at Adinson and asked, "Have you ever felt that way? Have you ever felt like you're living a double life that's leading you away from the ones you love?"

Charles shook his head. "Jean-Eugène sometimes confided in me, and I shared some of his secrets, but they weren't mine. My wife and daughter passed away before I had my own to keep. But I can easily understand what you're going through, and it certainly isn't easy to cope with. But, if it might lighten your burden, hear this: as complicated as this may be, I envy that you have people who connect you to this life. Whatever you have to endure, they are the antidote to the feeling of solitude that poisons us all eventually. It had settled within me, year after year, despite my illuminating collaboration with my companions—until we met. I will never be able to thank you enough for that. So, my boy, take my advice: don't enter the same desert I have. You're fortunate; you still have a life outside of the shadows where our struggle is taking place."

Charles was right. Vincent sighed. "Do you ever fear losing yourself in the face of what we're discovering?"

"No, Vincent, for the simple reason that I am already lost. That is not your case. Don't forget that."

Charles sank into his armchair and took a deep breath before adding, "You know, when I promised that I would do everything in my power to protect your loved ones in exchange for your help, I wasn't looking to make a deal. It wasn't necessary. I knew that, sooner or later, you would join us, simply because our activities are consistent with your values. Robert-Houdin predicted so, and he was right. In revealing our existence to you, I only completed what my old friend didn't have the time to accomplish himself. I defend your odd little family with a concern that is not rooted in any desire to buy your loyalty, but rather in a desire to do what I can no longer do for myself. Having failed to help my own family, I am healing my wounds by taking care of yours."

Vincent looked down. "Thank you, Charles. I sometimes wonder if you overestimate me. I'm not sure I'm worthy of the life that you have the courage to lead. I'm drawn to it, but I sense that it could destroy me. I feel myself changing, and it frightens me."

"I am well aware that you're changing. I see you enduring the pressure, the fear—and all of that is warranted. But I also see how you remain true to yourself and that you don't give up. If my extra years give me an advantage over you, it's that I have lived enough to see you not as a drowning man, but as a man who is growing into himself in the face of adversity. Do not be afraid of yourself; we have enough to contend with, with the threats we face."

The words spread through Vincent like an elixir soothing his doubts. He remembered feeling this way in the past, when his father, Étienne Begel, or Jean-Eugène Robert-Houdin spoke to him as the very young man they sought to elevate, each in his own way. That was a long time ago, but Charles's words echoed the reassuring voices that resonated within him, stronger than his own doubts.

"Thank you, Mr. Adinson."

"At your service, Mr. Cavel. Try to relax. We need you at your best tonight."

Vincent stood up. "I'm going out."

"Will you be needing a cab?"

"Thank you, that won't be necessary. I need to be alone. Don't worry about it."

"Don't leave through the front door; your Mages may have thugs watching our building. I'll show you a less conspicuous way out."

78

Vincent made his way through the crowd that meandered along the city's Grands Boulevards. In contrast with the mysterious world he had discovered the previous night, the activity on the street seemed somewhat unreal: day following night, pointless abundance following what was essential, everyday frivolity following ancient secrets. Finding one's place is difficult when navigating between such extremes.

He peered at the many faces he encountered as if they were parading past him in a dream. Men, women, children, and the elderly of all social classes mingled on the street. Their features didn't really come to life unless the individuals were accompanied, and they were never so expressive as when they were conversing. From these connections arise feelings. Vincent noticed them, and drank them in without ever really being satisfied, but it was reassuring. No one noticed him—people rarely observe their surroundings.

As he walked, he caught snatches of conversation. A policeman lectured a delivery man whose pushcart crammed with rolls of cloth was blocking the road. A bell tinkled as a shop door opened; peals of laughter escaped. The barely audible cries of a distant newspaper vendor overlapped with the bellowing voice of a singer. Vincent regularly checked to see that he wasn't being followed. At an intersection, he ran into a peddler selling clever pieces of sculpted horn to help women slip their feet into their shoes. Further on, a young man weighed down by a bag of coal as large as he was cut across his path. The adolescent ducked into a building as a woman threatened a harsh retaliation if he dirtied the floors. The trick was to walk smoothly to keep the black dust from drifting through the thick canvas. Vincent didn't know if he had just watched the scene, or if he was reliving a memory. When he used to make this kind of delivery, the concierges scolded him in the same way.

What had happened to him? While he knew the date, time, and place, the rest escaped him. What had happened to the young man he had once been? He missed the time when mysteries had been just magic acts masterfully performed by his tutors: each mystery eventually gave up the secret to which they held the key. It was probably under their influence that he had created for himself a rational vision of the world, convinced that life followed strict rules and that work and integrity could always triumph. He had recently discovered that some feelings and other kinds of mysteries could challenge the limits of anyone's conscience. Now he knew that if our rare certainties have so much value, it is only because our lives are guided by doubt.

As he left Rue de Châteaudun, Vincent caught a brief glimpse of a peculiar individual reflected in a shop window. He feared he was being followed, before realizing that it was his own reflection. A stranger to his own image, he hadn't recognized himself. The beard, hat, and ordinary clothes belonged to another man. There was a change in his posture as well. His stomach was in knots.

He could already make out the sign depicting Quasimodo at the end of the street. The line was even longer this time; it stretched past two stores where the owners were complaining because the crowd interfered with their business. Vincent joined them.

In returning to this place, Vincent hoped for an encounter with himself, with that which escaped all logic, with whatever woke within him when he was struck with one of those flashes that made his heart beat. Because he feared he was dead, he had come to resuscitate himself. He was there to make a promise.

He had not forgotten the intense personal upheaval triggered by his first visit: a true moment of eternity.

Vincent had experienced these states on many occasions; they were fleeting, but so powerful that he remembered each and every one. He remembered very clearly the rush he had felt when Begel had shown him Robert-Houdin's little automaton building.

The vestige of that wave of enthusiasm mingled with elation was still strong in him. He had been overwhelmed by an infinite energy that had lifted him above a mundane and laborious life. In that moment, he no longer thought of anything but the joy of understanding and discovery. He had experienced other, even more intense, moments after that, when he had been introduced to his first secret passages by Robert-Houdin himself.

The magic had worked once again when the passage in Flamel's cellar had revealed its secret to him and young Henri. When he thought about it, the best of these moments were those he had experienced in the company of someone else—like those rare sentiments that illuminate the faces of passersby when they are shared.

Yet that very same night, discovering the crypt in Charles's company had not had this extraordinary effect on him. It was in thinking of the way Begel or Robert-Houdin might have reacted, had they been in his position, that he became aware of his own numbness. Vincent had not shared what they would have felt. Of course he had been impressed, fascinated even, but above all he had been worried, wondered, and felt responsible for the future of the crypt. This time, he had not been swept away by the intoxication of discovery, even accompanied by Adinson. Could it be that the ordeals he had endured had made of him a cold person who could no longer find warmth, even from the strongest experiences life has to offer?

He had come this morning to throw an anchor into his heart of hearts. If this mooring snapped, he would be condemned to flounder and sink.

He placed his coin on the counter. The man in the booth lingered on his face for a moment, but didn't recognize him—Vincent wasn't the only one who saw a stranger in his face. A weak moan followed by cries of panic caused a murmur to ripple through the line.

His turn finally came. Vincent parted the wall hangings and entered the dark vestibule. He knew the protocol; he took his seat on the stool. The curtain opened; there was the monster. The unhappy creature bore traces of new wounds. Vincent even glimpsed a fire iron being plunged into his ribs to force him to groan convincingly.

Mouthing the words so the poor man could read his lips, Vincent murmured, "Hold on, I'll be back to get you."

He had come for the sole purpose of making this promise. If he didn't keep it, he would prove to be more adrift than the monster. He would have abandoned the only spark within himself that made him feel alive.

Having delivered his message, he let himself fall from his seat in mock terror, got up swearing, and fled.

"Next!" cried the owner, whose business was booming.

Vincent had not won the prize, but he had come away with much more: in the gaze of that deformed creature who had reached the limits of suffering, he had found someone, man to man, who had recognized him without a shadow of a doubt.

79

Each step down took them a little further from what they knew. The secret staircase descended into an eternal silence that augured a meeting with the past.

When they reached the threshold of the crypt, the historian, the theologian, and the two coachmen handpicked by Adinson stopped. Even the scholars had never seen anything like it.

Vincent motioned to the two coachmen. "Please leave the equipment at the foot of the well and place the lamps along the rim. Whatever you do, keep the lamps away from the walls to avoid igniting the saltpeter."

Vincent unloaded his equipment; the historian was already inspecting the sarcophagi. "Fascinating, quite astonishing."

Adinson handed him a pair of white cotton gloves. "Put these on, and don't move anything without consulting our resident trap expert."

The man with the monocle slipped his hands into the cloth gloves. The theologian lingered over the ogives and the cross pattée that united them directly over the well.

"Do you notice any symbolism in this place, Father?" asked Vincent.

"Forty-two steps to walk down, thirteen sarcophagi without any religious symbols, a well, and the Templar's cross looking down on it all. If there's a hidden meaning in this surprising layout, I must admit that for the moment it escapes me."

Vincent opened his collar and freed the key-compass that hung from a thin cord around his neck. He held it like a pendulum and walked around the room with it. He moved extremely slowly, on the lookout for the slightest shiver or the smallest change in orientation. He walked as closely as possible to the walls and sepultures, but the key did not react.

One of the men leaned over the well with a lamp. The bright halo was not strong enough to illuminate the bottom. He picked up a stone and threw it in, under his colleague's curious gaze. It was a few seconds before they heard the sound of a distant echo.

"The water in such an old well is probably stagnant," he said.

Making notes on sheets of paper he pulled from his cassock, the theologian was already hard at work copying the inscriptions engraved on the edges of the lids.

The historian, standing at his side, remarked, "The sepultures are clearly linked by style: a border of text framing a sculpted scene appears on each of them. The same counter-relief technique is used, and the same importance is given to the characters in the image. However I find it surprising that these scenes do not focus on a single individual per tomb, as if whoever was inhumed there wasn't the main subject."

"I also find that surprising," agreed the clergyman. "These tombs plainly form a visual message. They complement each other, like stained glass windows in a church or the panels of a tapestry, to tell some kind of story. But which one?"

"No battle scenes," remarked Adinson, "no glorious feats of arms, just simple encounters. In some of them, it appears that the men depicted are offering objects to one another."

The historian adjusted his monocle and chimed in. "What if what matters isn't in the foreground? Have you noticed? The background elements seem to be inspired by different regions of the world. Perhaps these sarcophagi allude to travels?"

He pointed to a scene. "This one appears to depict the lines typical of Asian architecture, which is very unexpected on a medieval European tomb. And if I were not afraid of the historical aberration, I would venture to say I recognize South American monuments on that one."

"At first glance," pointed out the theologian, "the dates engraved along the edges all fall between 1220 and 1305."

The historian remained thoughtful. "The height of the Knights Templar. The order was all-powerful at the time. But if..."

The man stopped, suddenly paralyzed. Vincent had felt it too: the floor was trembling faintly. He looked at his other companions. They all nodded. No one dared to move.

Vincent crouched down and flattened his hands against the cobblestones. The last time he had encountered a similar phenomenon, the floor had given way rapidly beneath his feet, sending him into one of the biggest panics of his life. He would not be surprised a second time.

"If I give the signal, leave the room as fast as you can and head for the stairs."

"Has a trap been triggered?" asked the theologian, now very pale.

"Considering the people who created this place, I'd be ready for anything."

A second tremor ran through the structures. Vincent stood up and said to the coachmen, "One of you watch the vault: if you see the slightest speck of dust fall, tell me. The other will wait in position on the stairs, ready to evacuate our elders."

Another dull, muffled thud sounded. Suddenly the theologian stiffened, his mouth agape, his eyes bulging in terror. Incapable of anything more than a gasp, he stared at something behind Adinson.

"Father, what's wrong?" he asked with concern.

The clergyman pointed a trembling index finger to one of the sarcophagi.

Another jolt. Charles saw what had terrified his companion and was overcome with fear as well: the lid of the central sarcophagus had just come loose and began to open. The sound seemed to be coming from inside.

Keeping his eyes on the tomb, Adinson called out in a strangled voice. "Vincent! Look!"

They were all looking at the sepulture when another impact flung it further open.

The historian chewed at his lips. "Do you believe in spirits?" he asked the group.

"Just a few days ago I would have said no," replied Vincent.

The man at the foot of the stairs stifled a cry and fled, bounding up the steps four at a time. His colleague cast panic-stricken glances from the sarcophagus to the exit and back again, debating whether to follow him.

The phenomenon repeated, as if the occupant of the upright tomb were opening his own final resting place to extract himself from it.

The historian fell to his knees and clasped his hands in prayer. "Have mercy on our souls! We have profaned this place. We have awoken the anger of the dead! We are damned!"

Vincent motioned to the coachman to pick up the scholar, who had lost his composure and was rocking back and forth and babbling.

Another shudder shifted the stone, further widening the gap. Vincent grabbed the lamp. Keeping a cautious distance, he stepped forward to examine the interior of the sarcophagus. But he was still too far away. He would have to venture closer.

Fear gripped his belly; he raised his lamp... and squinted in disbelief. He was expecting to see a skeleton, most likely covered with its shield and dressed in chain mail. He even imagined discovering the deceased brandishing a vengeful sword. But he saw nothing. Absolutely nothing.

He took another step. Another tremor unveiled more of the stone coffin.

This time there was no doubt about it: it was empty. Vincent frowned. Not only was the tomb empty of any remains, but it had no bottom. Vincent found himself facing the gaping opening of an underground passage.

80

The tremors continued, but they grew less frequent. The theologian was still trembling from head to toe. Adinson and Vincent had finished moving the heavy lid and were inspecting the entrance to the gallery it concealed.

"Are you thinking what I'm thinking, Charles?"

"I believe so. This tunnel is devilishly similar to the one we explored together."

Vincent turned to Adinson with disapproval. "Did you purposely use the word 'devilishly'?"

Realizing his carelessness and the effect it had on the clergyman, who collapsed to the floor, Adinson apologized to the poor man. Vincent held out his lamp. "Are you coming with me? Or would you prefer to stay here?"

Adinson was already on the move. "There's no way you're going alone. Our friend, however, should wait for us here."

The two men entered the tunnel. They quickly lost sight of the opening as the room with the sarcophagi disappeared behind them. Cautiously, they made their way steadily forward.

"We must be walking under the Square du Temple," ventured Adinson.

"Most likely. Don't forget to count your steps."

As they continued on, they felt with increasing clarity each of the rare tremors that still occurred. It now seemed evident that the passage led toward the source of the quaking.

The light from Vincent's lamp suddenly revealed something odd. Several yards ahead, the walls had a different appearance: they were swollen and deformed with strange protrusions, unusual textures and bulges. Wary, Vincent turned to Adinson. "Wait here while I see what this is all about."

Vincent padded softly forward. He cautiously examined each rocky protuberance, fearing what it might conceal. The outcroppings diminished the width of the passage, creating a bottleneck.

"Perhaps they simply didn't take as much care with this portion as they did with the others?" Charles called out.

"Would you be willing to bet your second life on that hypothesis?"

A tremor, even closer this time, vibrated through the floor. More alert than ever, Vincent touched the rock, inspecting it. There was nothing special about it, just those rough, inexplicable protrusions. In several yards, he would be past this suspicious portion of the passage, and he still didn't understand its purpose. It was unsettling.

The walls had smoothed out once again; he signaled to his companion to join him. Charles wove his way down the passage without slowing down in the narrower portion, especially since another, stronger shock indicated that they were approaching the epicenter.

"Does the direction we're traveling seem coherent with our hypothesis?" asked Adinson.

"More than ever, and the distance should soon equate as well."

As the tunnel took an unexpected turn, the floor appeared to be flooded. The further the two explorers went, the higher the water was. After several steps, it was already up to their ankles. Vincent was wading up to his knees when he came out of the turn. He was able to confirm what they had both anticipated: the tunnel abruptly ended where a collapsed section completely blocked it.

"We won't get any farther," concluded Charles, who had joined him.

Vincent pointed to the ceiling, which was split by a long fracture that stretched to where they stood. "It would probably be wise to turn back."

Before retreating, the two men took a moment to study the pile of rubble. Judging from the unsteadily balanced rock fragments and the texture of the earth, the collapse was recent.

"There's no doubt about it," reasoned Charles, "this is where we would have emerged if we had managed to open the submerged grate."

"Which means that on the other side, just behind this heap, our adversaries are digging like mad. They probably encountered a section of collapsed rock that they're trying to get past using a battering ram, which would explain the tremors."

"They're really going at it."

Vincent savored the irony of the situation. "Do you realize what this means? We're just a few steps away from them. They have no idea of the confrontation taking place as we stand right in front of them while they hammer away over there."

"So much the better! We have no idea how far along they are, and if the minions of this damned 'Sacred Dawn' end up here, they would only need a few minutes to reach the crypt."

"You're right."

"We must stop them from continuing at all costs. Let's alert the police! Turn them in!"

Vincent shook his head in disappointment. "While some of them might be arrested, too many would remain at large, and they will find a way to come back and finish the job. I would prefer a more radical solution: we must cut them off for good."

"How?"

Vincent looked up to evaluate the condition of the tunnel's structure. "We could bring down another section. The ceiling is already fractured. Adding a few tons of rubble should force them to give up, especially since they have no reason to suspect that we caused the collapse. We would just need to support the tunnel further back to limit the impact of the quake, and they would be faced with an insurmountable obstacle."

Charles rubbed his chin, satisfied with the idea. "And they'll conclude that their own blows made the collapse worse. I approve!"

The two men wasted no time wading out of the water and heading back the way they had come.

With only a few yards left to go, and both men considering their next step, Vincent suddenly stopped without warning at the beginning of a curve and flattened himself against the wall. He concealed his lamp and motioned to Charles to do the same.

"What's wrong with you?"

"Ahead of us: men lying in ambush!"

Charles frowned. "Perhaps they're our men, looking for us."

Vincent already had his knife out, prepared to do battle.

"How many men did you see?" whispered Charles.

"I didn't really have time to count them."

"Why aren't they moving? They aren't making any noise." He took the initiative and called out, "Who goes there?"

There was no answer.

"None of this makes any sense," said Charles suddenly. He moved away from the wall to see for himself. "Give me a bit of light, so we can clarify matters."

As Vincent uncovered his lamp, Charles saw two silhouettes emerge further along the corridor. He could feel something wasn't right. He took the lamp from his companion and moved it left and right, and up and down. Figures took shape and wavered; he smiled.

"My dear friend, we have let ourselves be fooled once again by the brilliant creators of this labyrinth."

Not without a certain pride, he explained the ruse to Vincent. In the play of light and shadow, the stone reliefs in the bottleneck took on the appearance of human figures.

"The contours you were wary of on the way in were sculpted in the rock to create hostile-looking silhouettes in torchlight."

"Simple shadow play," said Vincent, regaining his composure.

He folded his knife. Charles amused himself with the ruse by waving the lantern about, producing a sensational effect. The swaying of the lamp literally animated the profiles of huge men ready for battle. Vincent smiled at the illusion he had fallen for. "The effect is only visible if one comes from this direction," he remarked. "Which means visitors were intended to reach the crypt through this tunnel."

"Everything suggests that the crypt is the sanctuary," said Charles. "The relics and treasures mentioned in the account are probably locked in the other sarcophagi."

"We will have to be very careful," added Vincent. "Whoever created these passages and their traps would not have left them unprotected."

"You're the expert."

The two men resumed their progress. Adinson brushed his fingers one last time over the ingenious reliefs. Neither he nor Vincent had the faintest idea of what awaited them.

81

When the doorway finally came into view, Vincent caught sight of the theologian still on the ground, leaning against the rim of the well. The poor man still seemed to be in shock; he was a pitiful sight. The historian had come to sit beside him, probably to comfort him.

Something about their posture caught Vincent's attention, but he didn't have the luxury of further speculation. No sooner had he stepped through the sarcophagus than a man jumped out and pointed a weapon at him. There wasn't time to warn Charles, and both men found themselves in the revolver's sights.

"Hands up, both of you. And don't get any ideas."

The man waved the barrel of his gun, motioning them to join the coachmen and the night watchman, who were already tied up. One of his accomplices bound their hands behind their backs. The crypt had fallen into the hands of four intruders. Two of them guarded the captives, while the others were already breaking into a sepulture and rummaging eagerly among the remains.

Without an ounce of respect, they upended the body and the contents in their search for jewelry or other valuable objects. Although Vincent was disgusted by their actions, he couldn't help noticing the odd appearance of the deceased: the corpse had neither wasted away nor decomposed. Several centuries after being inhumed, his features were still fairly recognizable, for he had been mummified much like the pharaohs; although the body bore the attributes of a knight, it was wrapped in strips of cloth. An Egyptian embalming technique applied to a representative of Christian knighthood made for a thoroughly strange combination. But the vandals couldn't have cared less, and continued ransacking the contents.

"Aren't you ashamed of yourselves?" roared Adinson, livid with anger.

In response, one of the jailers elbowed him in the face. Vincent tried to intervene but without the use of his fists, he was brutally put back in his place.

"Is this what your Mages teach?" he protested. "Are you building your ideal world by profaning and pillaging tombs?"

One of the dead men's Crusade medal was torn from him so forcefully that his neck dislocated with a crack.

"Barbarians!" protested Vincent.

One of the goons walked over to Vincent and pressed the barrel of his gun to his heart. "Joshua will be happy to see you again. I think he likes you. I don't." He punched him in the stomach. Vincent took it as best he could. He had to think fast. The situation was going to spiral out of control. These vandals would continue to break open the sarcophagi one after another, and then turn Vincent and his companions over to their criminal organization. Adinson and his two colleagues must not fall into their hands at any cost.

"There's nothing else in this one," said a looter as he threw the knight's mummy roughly back in its coffin.

He was already on to the next as he picked up a crowbar. An idea crossed Vincent's mind. "I wouldn't do that if I were you."

The man stopped short. "Why? Isn't that what you were about to do? You're the one who brought these tools. Try to convince me you weren't after the riches lying around in here."

"Not with that method. You may have noticed that this crypt is full of surprises."

Intrigued, the two men listened. Vincent absolutely had to hold their attention. "Take this tunnel, for example. It was hidden. See for yourself; I'm not making it up. You're lucky that nothing happened to you when you broke into the first sarcophagus, but the next one could cost you dearly."

"Explain."

Vincent took his time, as he did when he was delivering his secret passages to his wealthy clients. At that precise moment, the criminals no longer saw him as just a prisoner, because he knew something that could be useful to them. He calmly strengthened his advantage over them.

"Joshua knows it, and you probably do too. Your gang failed to open the cellar in Flamel's house while I on the other hand... You've been struggling ever since, but it's already cost you dearly, hasn't it? *Aurorae sacrum honorem*..."

The looters looked at each other. "You mean to say these tombs are booby-trapped?"

"I'm not just saying it, I assure you they are."

The four men exchanged hesitant glances. One of the goons asked, "Can you open them safely?"

"Not alone. I'll need help from one of my men."

Vincent pointed with his chin toward the coachman who hadn't fled, betting that he would be the most reliable if it came to fisticuffs. The bandit who had his weapon trained on them consulted with his accomplices. "What do we do? Do we chance it?"

They argued and wavered back and forth. Vincent took advantage of their inattention to murmur to his companions. "Prepare to duck and take cover. Bullets may fly."

Adinson didn't have time to ask him what he had in mind. The looters had reached an agreement and one of them was already making his way over to free Vincent and the coachman he had chosen.

"I won't hesitate to kill you. Don't play smart with me," he growled bad-temperedly.

"That wouldn't be like me, especially considering the stakes."

Vincent pointed confidently to a sarcophagus. "I advise you to start with that one."

The man with the crowbar was already in position, and his accomplice moved to lend him a hand.

Vincent grabbed a lantern from the rim of the well. As the crooks began their filthy deed, he heaved the lantern against the wall as hard as he could. It shattered against the stone with a loud clatter, and its oil burst into flames as it spread over the walls heavy with saltpeter.

82

First there was a blinding light, then infernal heat; Vincent dove to protect the two elderly researchers. The entire crypt burst into flames with astonishing speed, generating a raging wind that swept the space in a devastating vortex.

In a matter of seconds the torrent of fire had spread across the walls. It traveled faster than a galloping horse, transforming the entire room into a red-hot bubble that imprisoned the members of both camps.

In a moment of panic, one of the henchmen fired his gun; cries of pain and surprise rang out. The violence of the event was equaled only by its unexpectedness; the storm abated as quickly as it had appeared.

Caught unawares and disoriented, the criminals dropped their tools. One of them, who had been standing near the wall, suffered burns to his eyes. He roamed around moaning, twisted in pain, with his hands covering his face. A second man remained prostrate on the ground, his hair charred and the skin of his hands and face carbonized. One of the looters lay face-down on the ground, his vest still smoldering. The last man tried to get up, but Vincent was faster; he didn't have to hit the man very hard to render him harmless.

Stunned, the theologian and the historian probably did not understand what had happened, but besides being stupefied, their condition was no cause for alarm. The night watchman was still in shock, but he managed to get up on his own, despite his bonds. The coachmen helped each other free.

Everyone's face was blackened, and a suffocating chemical odor hovered in the air, mingled with the smell of singed hair and flesh. Adinson was the only one who didn't get up. He was still lying on his side. Vincent hurried over. "Charles! Charles! Answer me!"

While Vincent was already imagining the worst, the older man finally coughed, rolled over, and lay on his back. His face lit up with a broad smile.

Charles held out his hand so his friend could help him to his feet. Both men's clothes were completely singed and their faces were streaked with soot.

"Your idea was brilliant, Vincent, but you almost got us all killed."

"They found us. I couldn't have been the one who betrayed our location."

"They probably followed us."

"Let's be sure there aren't any more of them up there."

"There aren't," confirmed the coachman who had kept the watchman company at his station. "None of them wanted to stay outside while the others might discover some loot."

"Perfect. Let's get these monsters out of here."

Dazed, the night watchman looked around him.

"Do you understand what I'm telling you, my friend?" Vincent asked him.

"What happened? I almost died..."

"Nothing happened. If you agree to stick to that version of the story, then I promise you enough money to keep you and your family safe. What do you say? How about a house?"

The man smiled broadly. "Now, that I understand. Nothing at all happened."

"Go home like you usually do. One of us will bring you your fortune and you can quit your job."

The watchman pointed to the looter on the ground. "I really thought those animals were going to kill me."

"If you keep your mouth shut, no one will hurt you."

The man nodded vigorously. "A fortune for my family?"

"A fortune from my pocket, I guarantee it. And now, I will entrust you to one of my companions, who will take you home."

Vincent turned over the motionless body. The skull was cracked. "His number is up."

From the bandit's pocket Vincent pulled the Crusade medal that had been torn from the mummified knight. He walked over to the deceased, bowed before his remains, and placed the medal around his neck. He bowed again and backed away. "Charles, could you help me put the lid back over this poor soul?"

While the coachmen carried away the wounded, Adinson went to lend Vincent a hand. "At least their abuses revealed that there are no relics in this tomb."

The two men tried to lift the heavy stone, but Adinson wasn't even able to get it off the ground. "This slab is far too heavy for me," he apologized breathlessly.

Vincent turned toward the coachmen to ask for their help, then realized he hadn't seen the one he'd chosen since the explosion. What had happened to him? He looked around the room and began walking around the well, fearing he would find his body, when he heard a weak voice call out: "Help! Help me!"

Vincent and Adinson exchanged looks. The voice called out again. "Can you hear me?"

There was no doubt about it: the plea was coming from the bottom of the well.

83

Vincent slowly descended into the well. Standing upright, one foot secure in a loop of rope, he held on tightly with one hand and clutched the lantern in the other. A coachman lowered him steadily. When Vincent looked up, he saw Adinson bending over the rim, his face gradually receding from view.

The vertical tunnel passed through a layer of darker stone. He still couldn't see the bottom below, but he heard the echo of the ill-fated coachman's movement in the water.

"Hold on!" he cried. "I'm coming!"

"I can see your light. Be careful, you've nearly reached the end of the well where it opens up."

"Opens up?" said Vincent in surprise. "Opens onto what?"

"Where I fell. I can't see anything, but judging from the echo, it must be pretty big."

Since beginning the descent, Vincent had been steadying himself now and again by placing a hand on the tunnel wall to avoid spinning like a top. Suddenly he no longer felt the wall. The shaft that surrounded him had disappeared. His lamplight was now engulfed in darkness. He had abruptly gone from a confined space to a vast emptiness with no landmarks. He was destabilized, and felt as though he were floating in a boundless void.

"Stop lowering!" he yelled.

"Is everything all right?" came the far-off voice of one of the coachmen.

"I don't really know."

The jolt he felt upon stopping did nothing to assuage his unease, and Vincent began to sway. He tightened his grip on the rope and tried to get a feel for his surroundings.

The light of his lamp briefly illuminated several details. It took him a moment to realize that he was now suspended beneath the dome of an underground cave. Like a spelunker, he was overlooking a vast chamber containing a natural water reservoir. Several yards below, Vincent spotted the injured man submerged to the waist who, thanks to the light, could now see what he had tumbled into.

"Good heavens, what's this now?" grumbled Vincent. He held his lamp at arm's length to cast a wider circle of light, which gave him a better idea of the cavern's size.

"It's enormous!" he exclaimed.

The echo intensified the surprise in his voice. The cavern, with its rough walls, had to be natural. Its dark flanks and sharp furrows had not been chiseled.

"Lower!" called Vincent to the coachmen.

Above him, the well shaft was no more than a small hole that would have been difficult to find in the chaos of the rocky dome without the rope he was attached to.

Vincent was approaching the surface of the underground lake. "Can you touch the bottom?" Vincent asked the injured man.

"Where I am, yes. I managed to find a shallower area. Luckily the water was deep where I fell. I probably only broke an ankle."

"You're lucky you didn't die after a fall like that. This water table saved your life."

He looked up and yelled toward the well. "You can stop, I've reached our friend!"

His message echoed around the underground cave as a distant voice acknowledged reception.

Vincent let go of the rope and slipped into the cold water. Careful to hold the lamp as high as possible, he joined the man with several awkward strokes. Soon he could touch the bottom as well.

"That was some dive!" remarked Vincent. "What were you thinking?"

"I was frightened by how violently the fire spread. Instinctively, I jumped for cover into the well. Everything happened so fast. Did everyone make it out all right up there?"

"We regained the upper hand. Except for you, none of our men were injured."

The man, relieved, held out his hand. "Thanks for coming to get me. My name is David."

Vincent shook it. "Nice to meet you, David. I'm Vincent. What a memorable meeting, at the bottom of a chasm! We'll never forget this place."

"That's for sure. We're probably the first people to ever venture down here."

"Let's not linger. You're going up first."

As Vincent bent down to wrap his arm around his companion, the key hanging around his neck slipped out of his shirt. It bobbed around on the end of its cord, but quickly came to a stop, pointing intently in one direction. Bothered by the movement, Vincent first felt the key move, then saw it when he looked down. He carefully released David and observed the object attentively.

"Did you see that?"

"Your key? Yes, you could have lost it."

"No, I mean what it's pointing to."

Vincent slipped the cord over his head so that he could use it like a pendulum. He held out his arm and moved the key about, turning it every which way, but it continued to point in the same direction. "I need a moment," said Vincent as he ventured into the water.

He walked carefully forward in the lake in the direction indicated by the key. Several times he felt the bottom slip away for a few seconds, but each time he found his footing again. The key was drawing him toward a cove in the cavern.

As he approached a narrow bank, his foot collided with a submerged obstacle. He bent down and felt around under the water, touching what appeared to be wood framing a curved surface. He soon realized that it was the remains of a sunken rowboat. "We are not the first to set foot here, David."

"What do you mean?"

Still guided by the key, Vincent had nearly reached the cavern wall. Everywhere he looked, all he saw was stone. Could the stubbornness of the compass be an error?

Then, in a fold of rock he spotted a crack—a passage large enough to slip through. The key left no room for doubt: it was the path to follow.

"David?"

"Yes?"

"Do you think you have the strength to wait a few more minutes?"

84

The gallery had not been dug by human hands. It was a natural fracture from which a stream flowed, a breach in the rock that wove its way between two rough, slate-black stone walls that swallowed up the lantern light. The crystalline water murmured as it carved a path over the uneven ground that it had smoothed since the dawn of time.

Vincent waded with difficulty into the stream. He supported David, who had joined him, refusing to remain alone in the dark, even though his ankle pained him. He limped miserably and put as little weight on his injured foot as possible. Each contact with the ground made him wince, but he stifled his moans.

"Are you certain you don't want to wait for me?" suggested Vincent once more. "You could rest here, on one of the stones where it's dry."

"I'm slowing you down too much, aren't I?"

"I'm more concerned about the one ankle you have left. Especially since we have no guarantee that this rat hole leads anywhere."

"Please, don't leave me alone in the dark. I'll lose my mind."

Vincent didn't insist. Luckily they didn't have far to go before they came out into a much wider space. The echo of a waterfall's steady rumble was the first noise to reach them. It sounded far away enough to suggest that this new gallery might be incredibly vast. The thundering water was clearly flowing faster than the stream they had followed into the cavern.

In the limited light, it was impossible to see what lay near at hand. They were venturing into the heart of a chaotic stone universe devoid of life.

They had taken no more than a few steps into the cavern when Vincent spotted what appeared to be a stone stela standing erect in the darkness. A moment later he saw that it was chest-high and carved out of a single block of stone in a simple but masterfully executed shape. The summit was carved out to form a basin that was full of a viscous liquid; a black wick rose from the bottom.

"It looks like a giant oil lamp," he said in surprise.

"Let's light it," suggested David, who was growing increasingly uneasy in the profound darkness.

Warily, Vincent pinched the wick and collected a bit of the thick substance that saturated it. He sniffed it, then, skeptical, tasted it and raised an eyebrow. "Oil, indeed. Thick and terribly rancid, but it's oil."

He opened his lamp and, tilting it carefully, tried to light the wick. Quite unexpectedly, it caught fire. The hesitant flame crackled and grew, adding its light little by little to that of their lamp. In the increasing brightness, David spotted a second stela a little further away. "And there's another one!"

Vincent lit the wick while his companion, thrilled to see the heavy shadow of darkness recede, paused to relieve his ankle. He pointed to the stream running through the cave. "It probably feeds into the lake."

"It must come from over there, in the back of the cavern, where we hear the waterfall."

As the second oil lamp came to life, the increasing light revealed a third. The phenomenon repeated over and over. Only after lighting the fifth lamp did Vincent realize how immense the underground cavern was. Looking up, he said, "This room is even larger than the one with the lake."

David said nothing. He was sitting completely motionless, his eyes wide and his mouth agape.

"Are you in pain?" asked Vincent.

Speechless, David gestured with his chin toward the back of the cave.

Vincent turned around and froze as well. Confronted with the imposing majesty of what appeared before him, he took several steps backward, stunned, and nearly lost his balance.

A veritable castle keep rose before them, a huge, round turret fit to grace the most spectacular of medieval castles. It was built into the cave wall and rose so high that the lamplight did not reach the summit, which disappeared into the vault.

"Good heavens," he murmured. He struggled to gather his wits. "Who could have built such a fortress in a place like this? A keep in the bowels of the earth."

The construction emanated such intensity that it was frightening: a silent, slumbering power, freshly woken from the darkness where it had been waiting for centuries, lurking in the far recesses of its lair. Its unusual appearance made it even more mysterious: it had no arrow slits or windows and, even more astonishing, no door. Its streamlined form was completely smooth and gave it the appearance of a giant shield that a Titan might have rested against the wall of his underground den.

It took Vincent several long minutes before he dared to approach it. With every step he took toward it, he felt increasingly overpowered by the spectacular, totally impenetrable fortification.

Only when he was a few yards away did he begin to understand the seemingly smooth structure. The circular wall was composed of thousands of stones cut to various dimensions, laid to interlock perfectly, and assembled without the use of a single joint: a perfect rampart offering neither toehold, nor protrusion, nor weakness, no gap to accommodate even a spike. An impregnable stronghold. What could it be protecting?

Vincent ventured closer to touch and feel it, but an invisible force stopped him mid-gesture. His hand hung in the air. He was too awestruck to allow himself to touch it. He instinctively knelt down and bowed his head at the foot of the silent stone carapace.

"I'm not here to plunder," he murmured. "I've been led to you by a series of improbable steps. But perhaps you already know that. Will you allow me to try to understand you?"

At that moment, he would have interpreted any sign—from the smallest earthquake to the most unexpected sound—as an order to abandon his quest, and he would have obeyed. But the enduring silence and the colossal entity that tolerated his presence without crushing him seemed like peaceful consent.

Vincent stood up, full of gratitude and moved by a strong desire to protect this exceptional place, no matter what happened.

He walked the tower's perimeter, but it revealed nothing more. It was impenetrable, and the way it was imbedded into the wall was an achievement in itself. The perfect craftsmanship combined with the lack of ornamentation set it apart from any human construction, as if the structure were not a built fortification but a being in its own right.

Deep down, Vincent knew that this keep was the greatest mystery he had ever confronted. Just as he was spinning the most outlandish theories about it, David ventured, "I don't think you can do it alone. We have to go back. We're running out of time. We're far from our world, Vincent, and we have a long way to go to get back there."

85

Vincent was just climbing out of the well behind David when Charles held out a hand and helped him the rest of the way.

"Praise God, here you are at last! I was worried sick." Adinson's concern for Vincent made him more loquacious than usual. "Look what a state you're in. You didn't even answer our calls! I thought I was going to have to go down there myself to find you. What were you doing all this time?"

Vincent steadied himself on the cobblestones. The odor of burned saltpeter still hovered in the air. He contemplated the crypt, which had regained its calm. It appeared more chiseled, now that it was rid of the traces of struggle and the faint white coating that had blanketed every surface.

Charles continued talking uncontrollably, but Vincent only half listened. He waved to David, who was already being helped up the stairs by a coachman. He and Adinson were left alone.

"I found it, Charles."

Adinson cut short his monologue, surprised at the interruption. "What?"

"The sanctuary."

Stunned, Charles fell silent. He quivered from head to toe.

"I didn't manage to get inside," explained Vincent, "but I know it's the one: an enormous underground keep built into the rock, an impenetrable tower with no visible entrance."

Charles's breathing resumed heavily. He squinted and peered at his partner. Besides being stunned by the revelation, he felt that something had changed in Vincent. He heard it in his voice and saw it in his movements. Vincent was no longer quite the same as he had been when he entered the well.

Vincent gestured around at the crypt. He was unusually calm and relaxed. He now understood and saw beyond the mise-en-scène of his surroundings.

Vincent looked at his companion with unusual intensity. "These sarcophagi contain no treasures," he said. "They probably hold the sanctuary guards. Everything is clear to me now: the labyrinth and the buried site described in the account, the traps defined by the four elements that nearly destroyed us."

"An underground keep?"

"It's immense, majestic, a masterpiece in a remarkable setting. It doesn't resemble a temple, but it has the same aura."

"Tell me more about it, please!"

"There's little to say, and certainly much to hope for. It's an impenetrable building hidden at the bottom of a cave in the bowels of the earth, as imposing as if it had been constructed out in the open. You must see it for yourself." Vincent spoke with respectful admiration, almost as if he were speaking about a living, mysterious presence that both fascinated and eluded him.

"But time is of the essence. We have much to do."

Vincent gathered up the sheets of paper and the pencil abandoned by the theologian. "Charles, if you don't mind, I would like to entrust you with some messages to be delivered urgently to my loved ones."

"What do you have in mind?"

"I'm going to need backup from you, my team, your coachmen, and still others."

"Why don't you explain to them yourself?"

"Because I'm going to stay here. I'm going back down."

Charles protested. "Out of the question! We're not leaving you alone!"

"You must. I cannot abandon the sanctuary. You'll meet me there this evening."

Vincent's calm demeanor contrasted with the older man's outburst, as if their roles had been reversed.

"Do you realize what you're saying?" protested Charles. "Alone in this underground labyrinth that you've only just discovered? I refuse to collect your body after you've been massacred by who knows what diabolical machinery!"

Vincent looked deep into Adinson's eyes. "You have to trust me, Charles. Please, don't prevent me from staying. I won't be able to succeed if you're against me."

Vincent turned and walked toward one of the sarcophagi, reaching out to touch it. He closed his eyes and seemed to find inspiration, energy, and answers there.

"Everything I've experienced has finally found its place within me. Each meeting, each challenge, each doubt. I know nothing about this keep, but it was my destiny to find it. When I stand before it, the mysteries we have faced find meaning. My entire life has served only to make me the man I am at this very moment, in this place that we have discovered together." He spoke these words in a deep voice; each one carried a conviction and determination that nothing could oppose.

"I'm no longer afraid, my friend," he said, turning once more to face Charles. "I know what I must accomplish from this moment on. Our meeting was no accident. The Great Watchmaker who guides us ends up taking us where we need to be."

Charles smiled. "Do you remember what you said during one of our first conversations? You said, 'I admire you, Charles. Not only for everything you seem to know. You fascinate me because you believe. I envy your hope, your faith in a better world. I would very much like to share that with you.' Today, I could repeat that back to you, word for word."

"We will share this hope, Charles. It's my turn to quote you. 'I'm counting on your help to reach a complete resolution.'"

Besides his determination, Adinson perceived in Vincent a sagacity that he had not seen in anyone but his dear departed friend.

"Write, Vincent," he sighed. "I will be your messenger."

Vincent sat down on the ground and leaned against the well. He quickly filled several pages explaining what each of his friends must prepare. Then he folded each letter, addressed it with the name of the recipient, and gave the stack to his partner.

Finally the two men climbed the staircase, leaving the crypt to settle back into the silent darkness in which they had found it.

When they reached the pivoting wall, Charles placed a hand on the younger man's shoulder. They didn't say a word, but the look they exchanged spoke volumes. Then Charles reentered his century and Vincent pushed the wall shut behind him to conceal the entrance.

Adinson was in for a busy day; and Vincent, for an infinite night.

86

The act was already nearing its finale. The man hoisted himself deftly onto his partner's shoulders. Surrounded by a seasoned crowd, the supporting man spread his legs to make sure he was stable as the aerial acrobat rose to standing, perfectly balanced. They were ready for the climax of the show. The acrobat focused his attention, then bent his legs and coiled in on himself. Suddenly, with incredible force, he sprang back and executed an impeccable back flip. He landed perfectly, while his partner absorbed the shock without flinching.

The audience applauded wholeheartedly. The duo of Spanish acrobats was the star act that day in the camp, where they had stopped by for the first time. After cheers and a few embraces, they had been admitted into the informal fellowship that welcomed new talents daily.

"I propose a toast to their health!' cried the mime artist.

The troupe roared with enthusiastic approval. Tankards, cups, and glasses were quickly filled with beer and wine in their honor. Everyone toasted according to their customs and conversed in their native languages.

Off to the side, Gabrielle and Pierre were seated face to face, indifferent to the merrymaking around them.

Pierre finished reading the message from his brother and looked up at the worried young woman.

"What does he say?" she asked quickly.

"We're to meet tonight. Charles knows where."

"Is he all right?"

Pierre was thoughtful. "I don't know what's going on, but when I read his words, I'm reminded of when an idea is gnawing away at him and he doesn't want to waste another minute. He mentioned nothing about the situation, but insists that we must prepare ourselves."

"Prepare ourselves?"

"Some equipment... but he also mentions 'in spirit.'"

"Do you know what's going on?"

"I have absolutely no idea. He writes that 'we're going to try to discover a passage leading to a place unlike anything anyone has ever seen.'"

A dog trainer commanded his animal to jump up on the bench near them. Seated side by side, master and beast shared the same bowl with equal appetite. The couple didn't even notice them.

"His letter also mentions you," continued Pierre.

"What does he expect of me?"

"That you stay safe for the moment. A cab will take you to the home of the Countess de Vignole, where you'll remain under Eustasio's protection until I return."

Gabrielle was disappointed.

"He says that your help will be required very soon," added Pierre. "He even uses the word 'indispensable.'"

Pierre hadn't noticed Konrad walk up. The big bearded man was also holding a message from Vincent. He remained standing and said pointedly, "This seems serious. We're being asked to put together a proper battle plan by tonight."

The carpenter pointed to Adinson and Victor, the guardian of the embassies, who were deep in conversation near the caravans on the distant hillside. Charles, usually so dignified and self-restrained, was making many sweeping gestures as he spoke.

"I didn't hear much," said the German, "but apparently there's talk of bringing the whole troupe."

"The acrobats?"

"That's what I said."

Pierre pointed to the paper in his friend's hand. "What does he want from you?"

"It makes no sense. He asked me to gather the equipment necessary to shore up a tunnel. He even made a sketch with measurements that he himself calls 'approximate.' Within the next few hours, I need to procure 'particularly strong' timbers. He specified that my reinforcements must be strong enough to withstand an explosion. Do you have any idea what that means?"

"My word, I have no idea what Vincent is up to. I hope he's not going to drag us into a bombing."

"And if he were? Knowing your brother, there would be a good reason behind it. As strange as his instructions are, we must trust him and do as he asks."

Pierre acquiesced. Konrad waved his message about. "He writes here that we'll have just one chance, and that this will probably be the most important mission of our lives!"

He pointed to the caravans again. Henri could be seen near his, sitting on the ground hugging his knees. "You should go see the Nail. He's not doing so well. I think he might be upset that Vincent didn't write to him. I couldn't comfort him."

Pierre got up. "Actually I need to speak to him anyway."

Konrad watched him walk away, along with Gabrielle, who was still pondering what role might be in store for the rowdy group around them that never stopped drinking and singing.

87

When Henri saw Pierre walking toward him, he hurried to dry his eyes. He tried to gather his composure as the older man climbed the hill.

"Why are you on your own like this?"

The Nail sniffled. "What everyone's preparing for doesn't concern me. I'm just the 'kid'—the one no one wants underfoot."

Pierre sat down next to him, facing the camp where paper lanterns were already being lit.

"This promises to be an important night, Henri. Vincent even wrote that it would be 'historic.' He's never used that word for any of our projects."

"He didn't write to me," the boy interrupted bitterly.

"Is that why you've worked yourself into such a state? I don't think it's worth crying about."

Henri turned to face Pierre. "Have you read *The Mysterious Island*?"

"No, but I've often seen you absorbed in it."

"I reread it again over the last few days. Do you know why I like it so much?"

"Because it's captivating?"

"Because it's the story of a team, united like a real family, that goes on adventures. It reminds me of us. And then there's Captain Nemo, a very intelligent man who used his imagination to invent machines that no one had ever thought of before."

"I suppose this captain reminds you of Vincent."

"Yes, they're similar. But I've been wondering more and more why I like this book so much, because when it comes down to it, it's very depressing."

"Depressing?"

"Ultimately, Captain Nemo is alone, and his tragic destiny saddens me. Do you know what his dying words to his friends are?"

"So he dies?"

"He says, 'I die of having thought it possible to live alone!'"

"What does that have to do with Vincent?"

"Isn't he alone as well? Do you think we matter as much to him as he matters to us?"

Pierre stared at the boy. "Do you for a moment doubt that? Don't you see how much he does for us? For you in particular?"

"Then why doesn't he trust me?" cried the Nail. "Why didn't he write to me?"

Pierre handed the boy the letter he had received from his brother. "Here, go straight to the end. It's about you."

Feverishly, Henri skimmed the last few lines. "'P.S. Don't forget to ask Henri to come this evening. We'll be in great need of his observation skills.'" The boy's face brightened.

"You see," said Pierre, "in our story, the captain doesn't die alone. We'll have the honor of dying with him!"

Henri burst out laughing.

"Another thing," whispered Pierre, "if I may offer a word of advice: you should read *The Three Musketeers*. You won't feel left out, because despite the title, there are four of them."

The two friends hardly had time to enjoy the joke, for Charles's tall figure appeared before them. His grave demeanor immediately brought them back to the serious situation at hand.

"Gentlemen, excuse my interruption, but Victor and I need your help."

Pierre was already on his feet.

"You're used to solving mysteries using unexpected methods. Perhaps you can help us out of our predicament."

Pierre and Henri were all ears.

"Here's the problem: when night falls in a few hours' time, we will meet Vincent at a location that absolutely must remain secret.

But we learned the hard way that the people who tried to kill you have eyes and ears everywhere. We can bet on the fact that their spies will notice our movements. To keep them occupied, Vincent came up with the idea of organizing a vast diversion across the entire city, a great commotion that should allow us to slip away without attracting attention."

"That's why he's counting on the acrobats!"

"Exactly. But to be effective, their action must be coordinated with a precision that can't be assured with a few watches."

Victor chimed in. "We're looking for a way to send a signal that will indicate exactly when to begin the operation. The best we came up with for the moment is to fire a cannon, but we don't even know if one exists that is powerful enough to be heard everywhere in Paris."

Adinson looked disappointed. "Impossible."

"In other words, we have nothing, and time is running out," concluded Victor, disheartened.

Pierre thought for a moment. Just then, Henri's face brightened. "I know what to do! I have the solution!"

88

Charles Adinson stood solemnly on the steps overlooking the interior courtyard of the coachmen's headquarters. That evening, he was dressed like them. At his feet lay a bag—which he was careful to keep away from fire—containing several sticks of dynamite and what little wick he could scrounge up on such short notice.

He checked his pocket watch once again. The hour was drawing near.

Before him, the twenty-five carriages stood lined up and ready to spread across the city in waves, one after another. The steeds snorted and stamped, their horseshoes ringing out on the pavement. The men stood in wait, silently reviewing routes and instructions.

Charles gave his watch a final glance. The time had come. He signaled to the watchmen and the immense doors opened immediately.

In a loud voice he declared to everyone gathered, "Gentlemen, you have twenty minutes to get into position. I wish you a safe journey."

Whips cracked and the first rows of carriages set off. The fiacres left at a steady pace, the street ringing out with the hammering of horseshoes. Some headed to the same neighborhood together before separating to take up their assigned positions. Each knew exactly what task they had to perform. The most experienced were sent to the Square du Temple to block traffic and clear the road for the convoy for which everything had been organized. The plan was carried out with military precision.

In theory, the city was calmer in the evening and traffic lighter. Stores and businesses were closed, and only restaurants and places of entertainment or diversion generated activity on their doorsteps. However this evening many night owls noticed that the streets were unusually busy.

On the deserted market squares, at the intersections of avenues, on the parvises, and even outside the cabaret Le Chat Noir, small groups of artists had gathered and were waiting. Unsettled to find themselves out on the job when there were so few passersby, they felt a growing pressure. They were overcome by a combination of stage fright and anxiety. Tonight they would give it their all. Together, dispatched across the center of Paris, they waited for the signal to appear in the sky.

While Henri's idea was not the easiest to carry out, it was certainly the best. There was only one point visible from the entire city, a single monument that rose above the others, which, since its recent opening, had lit up the night sky with its beacon.

89

For the two coachmen, the most difficult part had been to avoid being locked into the most renowned metal tower in the world. After hiding in a small technical room in the second-floor theater, all they had to do was wait.

As soon as the last employees left the platform in the final elevator of the day, they were free to do as they pleased. Things were about to get serious, and they were forced to take the stairs to the upper floors.

Clouds obscured the stars in the sky above Paris. The Exhibition was closing up for the night after the now famous luminous fountain musical show. The crowd, which could be heard even from such heights, was leaving the Champ de Mars.

The two men didn't have time to admire the extraordinary view before them. The illuminated capital served only as a backdrop to an unusual race, one that they absolutely had to win. They had about 1,300 more steps to climb before reaching their goal, and they had less than ten minutes to do it.

They sprinted up the stairs, not even stopping to catch their breath on the landings. The record for ascending the tower from the ground, held by an American athlete, was just over fifteen minutes. No one would ever know that the two men were going to at least match that pace on the last section, and without the benefit of daylight.

The night wind increased as they climbed higher, forcing them to redouble their efforts. They held on to the guardrails to avoid being thrown off balance by the gusts, while being careful not to miss a step.

Between the second and third floors, the shape of the staircase changed to accommodate the tower's narrower structure. The feeling of vertigo was ever-present, reinforced by the gusts that threatened to throw the men off-balance, and fatigue was setting in. One of the coachmen, his heart beating furiously, suddenly felt dizzy.

"Wait," he said to his companion as he bent over. "I don't feel well."

"We can't slow down. Everyone is counting on us. Keep going! Concentrate on the stairs and follow me. We're almost there."

The man took a gulp of air and stood up. They were off again.

Out of breath, they reached the third-floor terrace, the highest, where the apartment reserved for Mr. Eiffel himself and his distinguished guests was located. Looking in through the bay windows, they saw decorative wallpaper and furniture in precious wood. At the moment, only the caretaker was present, seated on a stool and absorbed in a novel.

The beacon was located higher still, on a tiny platform between two crisscrossed girder arches that crowned the monument. Its light was blinding, and the drone of electrical installations mingled with the whistling of the wind through the structure. The beam it cast over the city and its monuments was so intense, it could be followed with the naked eye.

The coachmen would not need to venture onto the tiny openwork stairs that wrapped around the central column rising to the summit; according to their information, the switches that controlled the beacon's power supply were located in the control room adjoining the engineer's apartment.

Crouching below the bay windows, the two men found the door to the control room. One of them looked at his watch. "It's almost time."

The other pointed to the caretaker in the adjacent room.

"I hope his book will keep him busy enough so that we don't have to knock him out." He pulled a club from his bag all the same.

They slipped into the control room. It was hot and the air was dry. The control panel was there, equipped with four large needle gauges and four toggle switches. Above the one on the left, an engraved plate read "Beacon."

The men exchanged a look, and the bolder of the two lowered the switch. A fine spark cracked when the blades left the pins. His partner went outside to confirm and quickly returned. "It's out!"

In extinguishing the summit of the world's tallest construction, they had given a silent signal to begin.

Suddenly a voice called out hotly. "What are you two doing here?"

90

The sky had just lost its brightest star: the Eiffel Tower went abruptly dark. Positioned on the Rue de Turbigo, the coachman, who had been keeping an eye out for the sign, signaled that it was time to leave with two short raps on the fiacre roof. Inside, Charles and Pierre were seated side by side across from Konrad and Henri.

The carriage quickly picked up speed on the empty road. As the cabin tilted into a bend, Adinson opened the curtain slightly and watched Rue Réaumur come into view. At the far end stood the Square du Temple and the cellar leading to the crypt.

Seeing them approach at top speed, the teams responsible for cordoning off the area made way to let them through. Adinson silently prayed that nothing had happened to Vincent during his day of solitude underground.

Pierre kept an eye on Henri, whose face was hard to read. "Are you worried?"

"What I am is in a hurry to see Vincent again. Will you be sure to tell him the beacon was my idea?"

Pierre nodded. "You can count on us."

The carriage accelerated further. Charles pulled his watch from his pocket. At that hour, David and another team must have dropped off another load of wood and tools in the crypt.

The carriage headed up Rue de Bretagne and began to slow as it neared the service entrance of the town hall.

"Gentlemen, we've arrived," said Charles. "I must be honest with you: I do not know what awaits us. I've seen only the entrance to the underground complex we're about to enter. I know little of what Vincent found, and I must admit that I did not much approve of his confronting it alone. We don't know each other, but he has often spoken of you. Of each of you. I know how much he respects you and how much you mean to him. So I have faith, and I believe there could be no better team than the one we form tonight."

The carriage came to a halt before he could finish his sentence. It was time.

91

Charles was more than relieved to hear Vincent's voice when he finally answered his calls. The anxiety that had weighed on him since their last meeting evaporated.

He was the first to descend into the well. After a frantic day with so much to organize, this aerial experience brought him back to the present.

"Hold on tight," Vincent called up to him from the water below.

Following a straight path, but spinning around on the rope, Adinson dropped down to Vincent, keeping his eyes closed the whole time.

"You're in for a nice bath," teased Vincent in greeting.

Charles found the courage to open his eyes. Astounded by the volume of the cave surrounding him, he ended up in the water without even realizing it.

He recovered from his surprise and stared at Vincent. "You shaved your beard?"

"I had to get cleaned-up; this place deserved it."

"Did you manage to enter the sanctuary?"

"Not yet. In any case, even if I had found a way in, I would have waited for you."

Vincent didn't appear tired. Adinson thought he even looked younger. Was it the clean-shaven face or elation brought about by the quest?

Vincent led him across the lake to the narrow bank.

"Excuse me for asking, but how in the devil did you shave?"

"With my knife! As you're about to see, there's no lack of stones to sharpen it with. Were you able to arrange everything?"

"The diversion worked like a charm. Everyone played their part, without exception. You should have seen it; everyone in the troupe threw themselves into it wholeheartedly. They caused quite a stir, which the press no doubt will be buzzing about! In any case, seeing those artists rally around us warmed my heart."

"We'll thank them; I already have an idea how. Were you able to get the explosives?"

"I have three sticks of dynamite, but only thirteen feet of wick."

"That's more than enough."

They climbed out of the water at the entrance to the fissure. Charles was not bothered about having to wait for the others; it would give him time to catch his breath.

Konrad, Henri, and Pierre soon joined them. The sight of the underground lake had a spectacular effect on each of them. Konrad pronounced every expletive he knew in his native tongue; the Nail didn't even wait to reach the water before jumping in. As for Pierre, he made the most dignified entrance as the only one who avoided spinning around on his rope.

Pierre embraced his older brother. "How on earth did you discover this extraordinary place? Did you decipher secret texts? An encrypted map?"

"Even better: one of our colleagues fell into the well. Luckily he made it out all right."

Pierre assessed the drop with a whistle. "Holy mackerel, that's some fall!"

"Holy, indeed. I'm happy to see you here, brother."

Pierre raised an eyebrow and stared at him. "I'm not 'little' anymore?" Vincent smiled. "Is this where we have to search for your treasure? Is it underwater?"

"No, you'll see. We have a ways to travel yet. This lake is just the entrance hall."

92

Exiting the fracture in single file, the little group reached the end of its journey. Vincent, leading the way, moved aside to let his four companions appreciate the sweeping cave that opened before them. Illuminated by the stelae, it now appeared in all its colossal splendor.

"There's a river!" exclaimed Henri when he heard the waterfall.

Adinson walked forward, and as he mounted a natural rockfall, the keep suddenly came into view. He was stunned; his head spun. The sight of the construction filled him with enthusiasm and left him flustered.

"I told you it was beautiful," murmured Vincent.

"It's much more than that."

"I didn't see the time pass as I sat contemplating it. The more I observe it, the more fascinated I become."

Pierre, Konrad, and Henri were transfixed as well. Vincent read in their faces what he himself had felt upon discovering it: astonishment, a boundless wonder tinged with admiration, and a hint of dread.

"No openings," remarked Pierre. "Is there a secret passage by which to enter?"

"I need you to help me find out."

Ignoring the stones that littered the ground, Adinson walked toward the monument. He stumbled but paid no mind, as though hypnotized by the structure. Suddenly he said, "This tower might not be meant to be opened."

"What do you mean?" asked Vincent in astonishment.

"It could be a mausoleum, a spectacular funerary temple."

"A tomb?" said Konrad in surprise.

Vincent frowned. "It doesn't have any of the features," he remarked. "Of all the monumental tombs discovered anywhere in the world, none looks like this one. If you compare it to the Egyptian pyramids, or even to the sculpted caves..."

Adinson objected sharply. "You must admit that none of the paths that led us here resembled anything in the known world."

"Who would have themselves buried so far underground," asked Pierre, "in such a structure? No one less than a king."

Adinson kept walking toward the monument, as though drawn by an invisible force. Vincent followed him.

"This sepulture may not have been conceived by whoever rests inside," remarked Charles, "but by those who deemed that the remains should be placed here, protected for centuries and centuries."

Vincent hadn't considered the keep from that angle. This hypothesis called into question everything he had imagined.

Charles continued his line of reasoning. "The sanctuary mentioned in the account brought back by Loyola could very well be the altar for the most important relic discovered in the Holy Land. The final resting place of the King of kings."

Instinctively, Vincent did not agree with this idea. Charles's supposition, as tempting as it sounded, could not replace what he had experienced during his hours spent in solitude near the fortification, as if the visceral connection he had felt upon first seeing it enabled him to confirm that Charles's hypothesis did not explain the underlying truth of this place.

Adinson had reached the foot of the fortification. Like Vincent, he didn't dare touch it. He made the sign of the cross. Vincent stopped and stood by his side. "The account mentioned several relics and a spiritual treasure."

Charles didn't respond, lost in thought before the monument. His lips moved silently. He was praying.

"Whatever lies within this keep," declared Vincent when his companion had finished, "we will not profane it. That's not why I asked you to join me. If we use anything other than our minds, we won't be any better than our enemies. All I hope for is a chance to find the entrance that leads to its secret. If there is no such passage, or if we don't find it, then we will leave this place to its eternal slumber."

Adinson nodded in approval.

93

Konrad and Charles had gone off to explore the cave, and Pierre was finishing his walk around the rampart.

"What do you think?" asked his brother.

"The surface is surprisingly smooth and the stonework assembly is perfect. If I had to define this tower, 'hermetic' would be the first word to come to mind. It offers no information, and reveals nothing but an outer wall that resists all attempts at investigation; not the slightest symbol, no marks, not even a stonemason's signature. Yet if we consider the amount of effort it would have taken to build this giant, then there must have been many people involved."

Vincent acquiesced. His younger brother continued. "I suspect that its form is the result of an unconditional search for efficiency, a radical commitment to protection. Everything was done to make it as resistant as possible. This desire surpasses all other considerations, and leaves us without any identifiable architectural style that would allow us to date its construction."

"The sarcophagi in the crypt date from the thirteenth century."

"We should take that into account, but something else intrigues me: the construction technique doesn't seem to be one used in this part of the world. Have you ever heard of such a puzzle? Look at these L-shaped blocks and these stones of different shapes. These are nothing like the rectangular blocks used by the constructors of cathedrals and medieval castles. It seems as if the builders made use of stones of every size and shape they had access to, even if it made their task more complicated."

"Perhaps the combination of techniques indicates an alliance between whoever built this tower?" Vincent thought of the spirit of communion that had motivated the engravings on the compass-key. He turned back toward the cave and made a sweeping gesture. "Look around us. Does nothing surprise you?"

"What am I supposed to see?"

"Nothing, actually. The stones used to build this tower came from this cave; they were extracted from it. Yet nothing remains of the construction site, which was surely enormous, that would have been necessary to erect this colossus. Not a scrap of scaffolding, no structures that might have served the many different trades involved in its construction. I didn't even find any shards of stone! There's nothing but this keep surrounded by these lamps, as if it had grown here alone of its own will, like a tree in a meadow."

"You're right," remarked Pierre with a nod.

The brothers contemplated the building in silence. Then Vincent asked, "What do you think of the fact that it's built into the rock wall?"

"I don't really know," said Pierre. "A wish to further strengthen it? Even though it doesn't really need it. What do you think?"

"To prevent it from being surrounded. That's the only reason I can see."

94

Henri had climbed to the summit of a rocky spur that afforded him a large view over the keep and the cavern. Seated on the overhang, swinging his legs, he mulled things over. The rumbling of the waterfall echoed in the space. Vincent climbed up to join him.

"When I found myself alone here," he confided to the boy, "I chose this very same observation point."

As if the Nail had been waiting for his visit, he started questioning Vincent straight away, continuing the line of reasoning he had been mentally working away at. "The tunnel where we were so scared led to the crypt with the well, right?"

"Indeed."

"You know, I'm not sure that whoever created the traps we ran into would have gone to such lengths for a tomb. Instead, they must have come here as if it were some kind of a safe, whenever they needed to and in complete safety. In that case, the mechanisms and the hidden galleries would make sense. I'm willing to bet that there's a secret entrance into this tower."

"I agree with you, but how do we find it?"

"I'm trying to use the rules you taught me, but it's not easy. 'The best passage is one nobody suspects exists.' That was true of the cellar, and even of the crypt, but this is different. Looking at this blind, sealed château, you have to believe there's an opening."

Vincent let the Nail continue his reasoning uninterrupted. "'A passage must play on the illusions of the person looking at it.' There's nothing to see in this underground cavity but cut stone and sheer rock, from the ground to the vault. No matter where you look, it's tempting to say that it would be absolutely impossible to get through it. And yet, somehow, it must be possible. That's for certain. Which means that the entrance could be anywhere."

Vincent smiled. Henri went on. "The third rule gave me some ideas: 'The passage must always be triggered by unexpected means.' I searched everywhere, next to the oil lamps, behind the rocks. I even looked under a fair number of stones, but I didn't find anything that could serve as a trigger."

The Nail turned to face Vincent. "You never told me the last two rules."

"It's now or never, right? Listen carefully. Rule number four: 'The energy that controls the movement of a passage's mechanism must be timeless.'"

"In other words?"

"Only forces that remain constant over time should be used: a spring, two elements in equilibrium, a counterweight subject to gravity. Elements that can remain suspended indefinitely, ready to be triggered even if the passage stays closed for a very long time."

"For decades?"

"Centuries, if necessary."

Henri wondered what kind of energy could be lying in wait behind the wall.

"And the last rule?"

"You're going to think it seems obvious, but be warned; it's more complex than it seems, and I must admit, I've been mulling over it quite a bit here. Rule number five: 'A passage must be reversible, otherwise it isn't a passage.'"

The Nail looked puzzled; Vincent clarified. "You said it yourself: whoever designed this place had to be able to come here whenever they needed to. Every checkpoint on the path to accessing it can therefore be opened and closed as many times as necessary. In other words, if we manage to enter this tower, it can't remain wide open after our visit. Do you follow me?"

Henri nodded, but without conviction. Vincent explained. "All right. Let's try a counterexample. Let me introduce you to a type of secret entrance that isn't a tunnel: the one used in the ancient tombs of the Valley of the Kings charted by Napoléon in Egypt. The blocks that sealed the entrance were moved into place using a clever flow of sand contained in clay jars, whose tips were broken when the time came. The process could only occur once; the trigger was irreversible. Once the blocks were in place, it was impossible to move them without destroying them."

Henri began to understand, but was about to ask a question when a voice called up to them. They both turned their heads.

Konrad was at the foot of the stone, his hands cupped around his mouth to be heard over the sound of the waterfall. "You should get down here now. We found something strange."

95

Water was gushing vigorously from a natural opening in the rock. It surged forth in a sweeping curve and fell several yards to land in a square basin carved into the rock itself. A set of steps led to the foaming reservoir. As the waterfall broke the surface below, it produced a light mist that humidified the air, which had encouraged the growth of a fine layer of tiny mushrooms that carpeted the dark stones with a beautiful iridescent gray.

Adinson and Pierre stood on either side of the basin discussing their observations. They broke off their conversation when Konrad returned with Vincent and the Nail.

"Did you come this far?" the German asked Vincent. The watery din forced him to raise his voice to be heard.

"I shaved here!" Vincent cried.

"We were wondering why this receptacle is the only constructed object in the cave—except for the keep, of course!"

"This basin calls to mind those used in baptismal ceremonies on the River Jordan, or ritual washing basins at the entrance to mosques and certain Hindu temples," Adinson interjected. "But there's nothing that indicates a relationship to religious worship."

"Oddly enough," added Pierre, "the basin was carefully crafted, while the water was left to flow freely past it." He pointed to the overflow that spilled out at the foot of the basin into the cave's natural field of stone.

Vincent tried to see the bottom, but the water was too turbulent.

"Did you by any chance get in the water when you shaved?" Konrad asked him.

"What an idea! Of course not, I crouched on the steps."

"I had a swim, because I wanted to see how deep it is." To demonstrate, the German once again walked down the steps into the water, which rose halfway up his chest. Vincent watched him uncomprehendingly.

Konrad didn't appear to be cold, and moved around in the reservoir, explaining as loudly as he could. "The walls are covered with a thin layer of silt." He wiped a bit off and held it up. Henri pinched his nose in disgust. "But as I walked around, I discovered something surprising."

He motioned Vincent to come over. Without a moment's hesitation, Vincent joined him in the water. Following Konrad's lead, he ran his hands along the wall, under the water's surface.

His hands soon encountered a thick protruding border. Running his fingers along it, he made out a rectangular shape—a frame. He found the corners by feeling around, then tried to identify the material through the viscous silt.

"It's not made of stone."

"It's metal," revealed Pierre.

"Did you manage to see under the water?"

"It's too agitated, but if you scrape it with your nail, you'll come away with bits of rust," said Pierre.

"It's probably a hatch," noted Konrad.

"A hatch?"

"And that's not all." Konrad took Vincent's hand and guided it under the water's surface to what appeared to be a handle.

The two men looked at each other. Adinson crouched on the ledge just above them. "Now that you know as much as we do," he said, "two questions beg consideration: if we open this hatch, where does it lead? Or, then again, what might come out?"

Vincent looked at Pierre before replying. "There's only one way to find out. Henri, come help us!"

96

The sliding panel was literally welded to the supporting frame with rust. Konrad, Pierre, and Vincent took turns holding their breath and diving under to hammer around it using fragments of rock that Henri brought them.

It was slow-going work, but little by little, methodically and meticulously, they managed to restore the gap between the moving component and its stationary support. The element began to work loose.

"Let's try to open it," Vincent called out.

Together, Adinson and Henri leaned deep down from the edge to pull on the handle while the other three struggled to lift the plate. After several tries, the five men finally succeeded in lifting it slightly. Water poured into the gap that they continued to enlarge. They had barely managed to move the metal barrier halfway when the water began to flow faster, quickly emptying the basin down to the level of the opening.

The friends took a moment to catch their breath. Henri suddenly called out to Vincent, "Rule number four! 'The energy that controls the movement of a passage's mechanism must be timeless.'"

The boy smiled broadly. He got up and hurried toward the keep. He leapt over obstacles as he ran as fast as he could across the cavern, almost as fast as the water, which he was convinced was flowing through an underwater canal in the same direction as he was running.

He was extremely excited by the time he reached the foot of the tower. Despite the waterfall's ever-present rumbling, he thought he heard something else. He placed his hands on the rampart and pressed his ear to it. This time there was no doubt about it: he heard a muffled but steady sound.

Vincent arrived shortly, soaked. The Nail motioned for him to listen. For the first time, Vincent dared to make physical contact with the monument. He heard a muffled thud, then a second; some kind of hammering was working up to a rhythm. An image came to him, that of a heart beating, as if the keep were coming back to life after centuries of slumber.

"Does that remind you of anything?" Vincent asked the boy.

"Yes, it's the same kind of sound the floor made when it began to lower beneath our feet."

The Nail glanced around in panic, down at the ground and up at the ceiling, worried about what the ancient mechanism they had just activated might set off. But the keep didn't move.

Suddenly Vincent pointed to the wall of the cave beside the tower. A rectangle of rock was sliding back. Slowly, steadily, a perfectly outlined slab the size of a door withdrew into the mass of rock to reveal an entrance.

Their three companions arrived just in time to witness the sight. The block of stone, which blended into the cave's natural escarpment, disappeared into the wall as if a giant hand were spiriting it away, like an opening leading to another world.

97

For the first time in centuries, the passage was open. When the dull striking of the rack and pinion ceased, the rock came to rest deep in its hollow. In moving back, it had freed a space; beside it appeared the first few steps of a rising stairway.

Like curious but wary animals, the five explorers peered at the entrance that had appeared in the dark rock and the few steps they could make out.

"I'm going to get the lamps," said Vincent. "But before we go in, we should decide who's going to stay outside."

"Why don't we all go in together?" grumbled Henri, who already feared being left out.

"Because if anything happens, and if for some reason this door closes, no one will ever find us."

Konrad raised a hand. "I'll stay."

"So will I," chimed in Pierre. "You'll tell us about it."

Henri looked woeful. "I really wanted to go."

Vincent handed him a lamp. "Promise me you won't touch anything."

"I swear I won't!"

Vincent, Adinson, and the Nail entered the opening; the outline's extreme precision contrasted with the raw material from which it had been cut. It was just tall enough for Vincent to pass through. On the floor, he noticed metal spans aligned like rails that had served a wagon that carried the slab to its resting place.

Adinson looked up toward the stairs. "So that's why the keep was built into the cavern wall. That's where the entrance is."

"After you, Charles," encouraged Vincent.

"Aren't you the most qualified to face whatever might catch us by surprise?"

"I don't think we are at risk of anything in this keep. We've reached the heart. But keep your eyes open all the same."

Adinson climbed the steps sculpted in the rock, counting them under his breath as he went along.

Vincent let Henri go next and prepared to bring up the rear. He waved to his friends who had remained on the threshold.

When he was out of sight of the entrance, and Henri and Adinson had walked some distance, he paused. He needed this moment alone, even if his team was not far off. He had difficulty realizing that he was now in the antechamber of the keep. Visions of everything he had imagined about the sanctuary surfaced in his mind, but none came close to the actual experience. He thought of his colleagues, of the men who had set him on this path, and with great feeling dedicated his visit to them. He placed a hand on one of the steps. This time he was not afraid to enter into contact with this place that continued to astonish him, as though he were one with the keep. Silently, he sent his heartfelt emotion to the tower that welcomed him. The attachment he felt for this unique place was now coupled with true devotion.

He tried to imagine the men who had built it. Whatever had motivated them, their talent and the perseverance they had demonstrated spoke volumes about their courage and the worthiness of their ideals.

Charles's voice rang out above him; his cry of astonishment filled the space and was soon bolstered by Henri's. Vincent rushed to catch up with them. He literally bounded up the steps, which led to a small landing. The men found themselves standing before a simple arch without grate or door, which opened onto a round room sheltered inside the rampart and covered from top to bottom with racks of shelves that held a multitude of chests of all shapes and sizes. There were hundreds of them, all perfectly arranged. In the center of the room stood a simple, round wood table, etched with twelve equal parts.

Henri wandered from one end of the room to the other, intrigued by the mysterious chests, many of which were within his reach.

Some were reinforced with metal hinges, sheathed in tanned leather, or finely worked, while others were of much simpler construction. Next to an engraved metal box, Vincent spotted a strongbox with mosaic inlay. Next to that stood an urn carved from marble. The variety of styles attested to different eras and origins. There were small casks and finely decorated triangles; they ranged from simple poplar, to artistically carved ebony, or oak partly covered with canvas or decorated with embossed leather, to studded wood or boxes inlaid with bone, ivory, or mother of pearl. The accumulation of disparate genres called to mind the merging of symbols that adorned the key that still hung from Vincent's neck.

Several shelves contained nothing more than simple wooden boxes covered in irregularly woven fabric that hid their contents. Charles carefully lifted one of these cloths. A flash of gold made him throw caution to the wind. "Vincent, look!"

Henri rushed over as well, and they all discovered a treasure chest of gold coins. Hundreds of ancient coins were heaped together in the box. Charles quickly looked in the next compartment and discovered another fortune, this one silver. His eyes widened and he gingerly picked up an oxidized coin. He examined both sides by the light of his lamp, but did not recognize the worn profile stamped on it.

Vincent shone his light around him. He was beginning to understand the importance of what surrounded them.

Charles was already taking stock of the other containers, each of which revealed new riches. Age-old currency of every origin, phenomenal quantities of precious gemstones, countless reserves of gold in every possible form, and all kinds of valuable objects dazzled him. Henri's fingers itched; despite his promise not to touch anything, he had also peeked under the cloth in another compartment. "Vincent, gold nuggets!"

Vincent joined him, but he had noticed something: each niche was labeled with a Roman numeral etched in the wood. "The contents of these compartments are not arranged randomly. Each one must correspond to a precise use, or perhaps to an owner."

Charles had just picked up a thick bundle of bills of exchange. The parchment was dry, the ink had darkened, and the writing had the fine, sweeping first letters of another century. He looked over several of them, captivated by the dates and wax seals that served as authentication.

"What are they?" Henri asked him.

"During the Crusades, these documents allowed pilgrims to complete their journey without having to carry real money with them. Before their departure, they deposited money at a commandery in exchange for this kind of certificate. At their destination, they could present it to a Templar establishment, where the equivalent sum would be returned to them. That way, they no longer risked being robbed on their journey. The Templars invented this process and established the network."

Vincent listened with one ear as he continued to inspect the various chests, moving from one to another with increasing speed. He didn't find what he was looking for.

"What is it?" asked Adinson, sensing his restlessness. "You look disappointed."

"More like disillusioned."

"Do you realize that we have probably discovered the Templars' treasure, the very same one that kings have lusted after but never managed to find?"

"The account spoke of a spiritual treasure, and these chests contain only gold or gemstones. I don't see any relics, or anything that might resemble one."

He returned to the entrance and looked down at the stairs they had climbed. "The staircase leads directly to this room and nowhere else. There is no alternative but to climb all the way up here."

"So?"

"Sixty-two steps led us about sixty-five feet high."

He rubbed his chin and wondered out loud, "Why would whoever worked so hard to build this keep use only a portion of it?"

"Vincent, what are you thinking?"

"What is the purpose of taking us so high?"

Vincent suddenly looked down. He struck the floor with his heel. "What lies below this gallery of riches?"

He began to examine the floor, inspecting it feverishly, venturing into the smallest nooks and crannies. "Help me look! There has to be an opening somewhere."

Henri joined the hunt. He moved chests out of the way so he could slip into the lowest storage compartments. Some of them were so heavy that he couldn't shift them, and he was forced to twist his body to get a look behind.

"There! Under the table!" cried Charles. "Look!"

Vincent hurried over. There was no doubt about it: a fine circular groove had been cut into the floor. The two men moved the piece of furniture that was standing over it.

Using the blade of his knife as a lever, Vincent tried to lift what looked like a large round lid. To his great surprise, it came away easily.

The three companions leaned over the gaping hole that plunged into darkness.

98

To get down, they had to take a straight, heavy ladder with thick oak steps that barely creaked, despite their age.

As he climbed down it, Vincent felt as though he were plunging into an extraordinary world. This room had an entirely different atmosphere; nothing echoed in the muffled silence. A fragrance both strange and pleasant hovered in the air. Vincent stopped a moment and breathed it in. Among the different notes, he picked out a combination of old leather, parchment, and precious wood.

At the bottom of the ladder, Vincent stepped onto a stone floor similar to the one in the crypt where the sarcophagi stood.

He turned around, unsure of where to look. On the walls hung shields, some bearing coats-of-arms whose colors had faded over the centuries along with the traces of blows from ancient combats. Pennons and garments hung scattered about; a yellowed shirt stained with dried blood, a brown coat so old that it might disintegrate into dust. Vincent noticed a green cape in a pitiful state that appeared to have been sliced in two.

The walls were in large part taken up by a bookshelf full of tall stacks of grimoires, as well as parchment scrolls and an impressive quantity of documents—simple pamphlets of all shapes and sizes, roughly bound notes, sketches, codices, ancient maps. The accumulation of documents also spilled from two long, low chests made of dark wood that had mostly disappeared under the heap. Thousands of works were piled before him. Here too, East met West, but there was more to it than that; the ages and languages of humanity also overlapped here.

The rest of the room was crammed with a variety of objects stored on pyramids of crates and trunks: military helmets from different eras, statues, fragments of stelae engraved with different languages. A funeral mask covered in fragments of polished jade seemed to stare at him with its white eyes.

Vincent walked toward the compendium of civilizations. Some of the crates were imposing and covered with cloth or sealed with enormous wax seals, still intact. Three small amphorae stood in a row at the foot of one.

When he reached the room, Adinson observed the chaotic abundance around him. Henri was the last to climb down the ladder. "It's a proper museum!" he exclaimed in astonishment.

"Probably the most precious one of all," murmured Charles, who lingered over a volume of anatomical drawings bound with strips of wood.

He closed it delicately and moved on to other archives. Some of the works were held closed by leather cords; many were equipped with metal corners so they could be set down without damaging their covers. Each bundle and binding represented a sum total of knowledge—everything that formed civilizations: mathematical treatises in Greek and Arabic, medicinal plant herbariums in Latin, ancient collections of laws, and dozens of other manuscripts with subjects that escaped him. He caressed the pages with a blissful expression on his face. Further on, another section seemed to hold a collection of registries, inventories, and accounts of voyages.

"All of this knowledge united, all of these languages."

"As if this shell protected the essence of the knowledge the Ancients collected. So many sources. Probably the fruit of expeditions to far-off places, intended to gather in a single place the collective experience of all mankind."

Adinson pointed to a drawing in a portfolio; it depicted a church in the form of a cross with equal arms that literally seemed to be buried in a land planted with exotic trees.

Vincent gestured to a volume with a metal clasp adorned with mysterious symbols. "So many studies, and all from a time when only the essential was written down. These messages from the past have much to teach us."

Henri took his time examining the objects. He lingered over the various antiques. "Have you noticed?" he called out.

"What?"

"Despite the many objects connected to knighthood that are stored here, there's not a single weapon. No swords, lances, flails, or maces, as if all violent tools had been banned." Adinson agreed, impressed by the young man's analytical mind.

Drawn by what appeared to be an annotated map, Vincent moved a pile of books and carefully unfurled it, blowing away a veil of dust. It didn't have the polished layout of an academic document; it looked more like a survey. The lines were repeatedly interrupted, suggesting that they had not been drawn at the same time, but perhaps over the course of a voyage. The coasts were scattered with comments; Vincent couldn't tell where they were located. These small notes, dense and finely written, seemed to be made by the same traveler exploring new lands. It was probably one of those pioneers that the geographer defined as being bold enough to blaze a trail. Vincent thought he could make out a date: Anno Domini MCCCVI.

Vincent looked up, thoughtful. "1306. It looks like an expedition report. Whoever brought these treasures together probably went looking for them farther away than we suspected."

Charles acquiesced. "Their odysseys were not only geographic, but spiritual and scientific as well."

Vincent knelt down to examine a clay tablet. "The sarcophagi in the crypt probably hold the explorers who collected all of this."

"That would explain the different regions suggested on the lids and the scenes of exchange they depict."

Charles looked around the room. "It will take us years to study and try to understand all of this."

"Probably a lifetime," replied Vincent.

He turned to the pile of closed trunks. "What might these contain? It must not have been easy to carry them back from the limits of the known world. As spectacular as this place is, it was created first and foremost for them. Those men must have been truly impressed by their contents for them to unite despite their differences."

"The limits of the known world," repeated Adinson. "You have probably put your finger on the common denominator between everything that surrounds us. We must meet it without preconceptions. Some of this knowledge, this magic, has perhaps been lost for a long time."

Vincent picked up a sphere of oxidized copper that seemed to symbolize a skull; several areas bore inscriptions in an unknown script. "The relative disorder suggests that whoever stored these priceless treasures here didn't have the time to dedicate themselves completely to it."

He spread his arms before the countless objects. "The real treasure is here," declared Vincent. "The keep, the labyrinth, and everything that was designed and built exists only to protect it. Whoever created this sanctuary initiated the mission that you and your companions carry on: to unite knowledge and protect it from oblivion and the convulsions of History."

"To protect it from the madness of men," murmured Charles, as he paused over a manuscript. "We'll need all our companions' scholarship if we hope to have a chance at grasping the full significance."

Vincent agreed. All three men remained silent, considering their discovery and everything that it implied.

After a moment, Vincent looked up. "Charles, you told me that your fellowship of researchers has no name."

"Indeed. We have always remained anonymous."

"Don't you think that this sanctuary alone could justify having one? After all, it is the most dazzling symbol of your quest."

"Of *our* quest, Vincent. It is yours as well."

"The Fellowship of the Keep. That has a nice ring to it."

Adinson repeated it to himself, pronouncing the words silently. His face lit up with a smile. "Why not?"

99

When it was time to leave, Henri asked permission to borrow a gold denarius to show Konrad and Pierre, who had agreed to wait outside.

The Nail was the first to take the staircase carved in the stone and come out into the cave, his gleaming coin in hand, eager to show it to his friends and already delighted at the idea of describing to them the marvels they had found in the keep.

Despite his enthusiasm, he froze. Vincent, following close behind him, immediately understood why: Konrad and Pierre were sitting on the floor, their hands bound, held at gunpoint by Joshua.

Vincent stiffened at the awful sight. Following on his heels, Charles turned pale and let out a muffled curse.

"Good evening, Vincent," jeered the gunman. "So we meet again." He savored the impact he had made and added, "Some of us hoped to see you join us. I admit that I was among them, but as the days go by..."

He shook his head. "I was very disappointed by your defection. And after the Sacred Dawn had opened its arms to you."

Vincent didn't respond. The miserable expressions on his companions' faces seemed all the more tragic in contrast to their attacker's triumphant smile.

The man gestured toward the keep. "Very impressive! So this is what we've all been chasing after?"

Joshua suddenly stopped and looked at Henri. With the barrel of his gun, he pointed to the coin in the Nail's hands. "What have we here? My word, it's the gleam of wealth! Bring it to me."

Henri tightened his fist around it and held it close, refusing to obey. Without hesitation, Joshua aimed the weapon at his head. "You were very lucky to survive Flamel's cellar, kid. Don't push it. Give that to me. I won't ask again."

Vincent motioned him to comply. The Nail, his face twisted with anger and hate, stepped forward and gave up his precious denarius.

"Calm down, kid," muttered Joshua. "You're old enough to know that sometimes it's best to submit."

Vincent tried to divert his attention. "So you managed to get past the collapsed tunnel."

A flash of surprise in the man's eyes suggested that he had come another way. But Vincent had to know for sure. The response would determine the scale of the disaster to manage. "How did you find us?" he insisted.

Joshua smiled broadly. "What an absurd idea to offer such a fortune to a simple night watchman. Did you really think he would keep his mouth shut? You're so naïve. At his first drunken evening in a foul tavern, he couldn't help but brag. He told us about a fabulous crypt filled with tombs and treasures. In the seedy parts of Paris, that kind of secret spreads like wildfire."

Vincent shook his head in disappointment.

"You know, Vincent, this misfortune ought to teach you that not even profit appeases men. They are insatiable. The only way to ensure their silence is to kill them."

Vincent looked up at him defiantly. "Is that what you're going to do to us?"

The brute didn't respond. He played with the gold coin, which had replaced the leather cord between his supple fingers. "I imagine this came from that strange tower and that it was not alone. A promising sample, very promising. I can't wait to see for myself. Tell me about this place."

"You wouldn't understand. Neither you nor your Mages will ever grasp the true value."

"Who said anything about the Mages? I'm the one who took all the risks; I'm the one who found you. I've done enough for them. Doesn't a treasure belong to whoever finds it first?"

"Not this one."

"So it's that big? You're making my mouth water. How about you show me around?"

Vincent stiffened. Seeing his reluctance, Joshua grabbed Pierre by the collar and jabbed the barrel of his gun under his jaw, dragging him to his feet. "Do I have to prove my determination to you? You've already been told: beginners often need proof, but it always comes at a price."

Vincent's mind began to race. He couldn't stand seeing his brother threatened like that. He was overcome with a visceral anger, and his blood began to boil. Without thinking, he threw himself at the killer.

Joshua reacted with terrifying calm. He turned his weapon away from Pierre and fired coldly at Vincent's legs; Vincent collapsed with a moan, stopped brutally in his tracks.

Vincent twisted in pain on the ground, clutching at his thigh as blood seeped through his fingers. Konrad and Pierre were about to intervene, but Joshua turned his gun on them. "Sit down!" he yelled, "or he won't be the only one dead."

Then he bent over Vincent and growled, "I'm not going to kill you right away because I want you to see what's going to happen."

He stood up and grabbed Pierre again. "So, are we going to take that tour? For the moment, I only have one gold coin, and that's not enough for me!"

"Leave him alone," said Adinson, "and take me hostage. He's never been in the tower. I have."

Joshua hesitated a moment, then released Pierre. "You're right. You'll be a much better guide."

He didn't mind the switch; not only would the old man who volunteered probably know more than the other, but an older prisoner would spare him any more rebelliousness.

At least that's what Joshua thought. Charles Adinson was right: people don't often look beyond first impressions.

100

As Joshua grabbed Charles firmly by the arm, ready to force him into the keep, the situation changed abruptly. Adinson pivoted suddenly and stabbed his attacker in the chest with the knife that he had discreetly unfolded.

The criminal was thrown off balance by the attack; the gold coin slipped from his fingers and sailed through the air, spinning around as the man collapsed, firing two shots as he did so.

The detonations resonated in the cavern, eventually merging into one in the echo of suspended time, followed by the ringing of the gold denarius as it hit the stone.

On the ground, Joshua was still breathing, the knife blade sunk deep into his chest near his heart. He groaned and grimaced, feeling about for the weapon that had slipped from his hands. Henri hurried to kick the revolver away while Konrad, his hands still bound, threw himself on the killer.

Adinson also fell. Everything happened so fast that no one could say if he had thrown himself to the ground out of self-preservation or if the unspeakable had happened. Vincent gritted his teeth, overcame his pain and, putting pressure on his leg, dragged himself as best he could toward his friend. "Charles, Charles!"

Adinson remained lying on his side.

"Your idea was brilliant, Adinson, but you nearly got us all killed. You're as crazy as I am!"

Charles smiled, but bloody foam filled his mouth. A red stain seeped from his stomach through his vest. He had taken a stray bullet.

"Charles! For the love of God!" cried Vincent in panic. "Whatever you do, don't move. We're going to take care of you. You'll make it out!"

Henri and Pierre rushed over. Vincent opened the vest to reveal the wound. The bullet had been shot at close range, wreaking havoc. Vincent tried clumsily to stop the hemorrhage by applying pressure to the wound, but the blood continued to flow.

"What got into you?" asked Vincent, feigning reproach.

"You specifically said that we should all have a knife. I figured out what to do with mine." Charles's gaze faded, and his eyes rolled back. Pierre held his head to try to help clear his airway, but his breathing grew congested. Silent tears streamed down Henri's face.

"Hold on, Charles," Vincent begged. "Hang in there. We're going to get you out."

He took Charles's hands and kissed them. His face was covered in blood.

He had witnessed this once before, one night kneeling on the cold cobblestones outside an inn, while his father lay dying before his very eyes. The child he had been could not save him. But tonight, he was a man. Would that change things?

It all had to be a nightmare. Yet Vincent recognized the very real pain fed by absolute rage. He did not want to feel it again. He pushed it away, but he had no choice. The faces of Charles and his father merged; the feeling of hot sticky blood on his hands came back to him, along with the feeling of powerlessness. The roar of the waterfall became the commotion of the crowd that had formed in the street.

"Charles, please. You can't leave me when there's so much for us to discover. We've only just begun. I need you."

Adinson tightened his fingers around Vincent's. With difficulty he said, "You'll know what to do. You are the first Fellow of the Keep."

Vincent was crying; he pulled Charles's wrists toward him, as though that could keep him in the world of the living. Feeling his strength ebb, Adinson gently freed himself to place a paternal hand on his young friend's cheek. "Thank you, Vincent. You made my second life as wonderful as the first. May my death help you to live in freedom."

For the second time in his life, Vincent took in the final gaze of someone he loved—this last unspoken and definitive message that made him realize that life would have to continue onward without the one he held so dear.

101

It was a beautiful day. The chickadees perched on the ruins of the boardinghouse were singing loudly. It was now their home.

David had posted coachmen around the block of houses to ensure that no one would disrupt the peculiar ceremony underway.

Pierre, Henri, Konrad, and Eustasio, as well as Gabrielle and Hortense, stood side by side in the garden behind the rubble. They wouldn't go any further; they would remain at the edge of the kingdom of life.

Victor was there too. But Vincent alone carried Adinson's body to the cellar that had once been a workshop. He hadn't wanted to share that terrible honor.

Broken with sorrow, he had not understood Charles's last words right away. Yet their meaning had been obvious. "May my death help you to live in freedom."

Bent under the weight and limping, Vincent had set his friend at the map table, in Vincent's usual seat. There where he and his friends had spent so much time thinking and seeking solutions. He settled him in the chair exactly as if he were working. Without really knowing why, he slipped a pencil into his hand. Seeing him like that, for a moment he had the impression that Charles was going to turn around and discuss the best way to protect the keep. Tears filled his eyes, but Vincent resisted the emotion. He kissed the icy cold forehead of his companion and covered him with a sheet.

Then, dragging his bandaged leg, he went over to the armored cabinets and flung them wide open. He furiously emptied them of their archives. He pulled out all the files related to their projects and threw them haphazardly on the ground around the body.

Covers opened, notes and sheets of paper scattered and jumbled together. This information, these addresses and sketches, all of it was a burden; it would be obliterated into ashen secrets.

Vincent felt no regret as he threw the fruit of years of labor to the ground. The past was of no importance. Two final gazes had taught him that all that matters is what you decide to do in the present.

His movements expressed neither anger nor bitterness, only a fierce determination. He set up pyres around the cellar, piling up scale models, equipment, and even the wood scraps he had found Gabrielle hiding under. He gathered anything that could burn, scattering, collecting, and tossing as he went. Despite his seemingly careless behavior, he meticulously orchestrated the destruction that he himself had planned.

Vincent grabbed cans of lamp oil and emptied them assiduously. He doused furniture, papers, Konrad's workbench, and Eustasio's easels and painted works. He emptied bottles of turpentine and every jar of flammable product he could find. Nothing must survive. Turn the page and erase all trace—this was his only chance to return to life clean and unfettered.

After all that, Vincent returned to the foot of the stairs. A pain stabbed at his leg, but he was composed. Despite the circumstances, he was filled with a sense of peace and calm.

He felt no regret as he contemplated his workshop. He was not weighed down by memories; he knew who he was doing this for. They were waiting for him outside, miraculously safe and sound.

He addressed a final goodbye to Charles and flung his lantern at the drawing table. As it fell, it shattered on the first saturated documents, which burst into flames. Images of the blazing crypt came back to him.

The fire spread quickly in the cellar, traveling from pyre to pyre, following the trails of flammable liquids. The basement took on a blinding orange glow, the temperature rose quickly. The crackling became a low, continuous hum that betrayed the blaze's growing appetite. Fire is always hungry.

Dragons, goddesses, and angels seemed to dance the same saraband in the flames that were already licking the ceiling. Blueprints burned, drifting and twirling in the burning coils of smoke from the blaze that had taken possession of the cellar. Vincent was no longer at home here. The smoke began to blur his vision. Tears came to his eyes, but they were not tears of sadness.

His gaze fell on the cabinet that held the automaton. The violent inferno had just torn one of the doors off. The velvet cover disintegrated into incandescent shreds. This time, the woman, the man, and the cat could not be rescued by the firefighters. The heat of the blaze was no longer an illusion.

In the space of a few minutes, the workshop had become an inferno, and Charles had disappeared behind the curtain of fire. The workshops had become purgatory. A forgotten can of gasoline exploded, while all around furniture collapsed in clouds of swirling embers.

Vincent couldn't resist the devastating force much longer. He was going to go back upstairs, close the door forever, and let the fiery blaze finish its work. He tried to catch one final glimpse of Charles, without success. The hell he had conjured forced him to retreat. He covered his nose with the only thing he had wanted to save: the cap his father had given him.

102

Vincent Cavel died this morning in a tragic fire that completely destroyed his cellar. Inspector Clément Bertelot himself visited the site of the tragedy. He recognized the remains of a folding knife like the one his friend always carried, and signed the death certificate, despite the condition of the body.

The funeral was simple and held in the ruins of the small Saint-Pierre de Montmartre church, according to the deceased's last wishes. It was attended by a handful of close friends who remained very dignified, and the neighborhood's regular mourners, who never missed a chance to attend one of these sad celebrations.

His body lies in the Saint-Vincent Cemetery, not far from the grave of a long-forgotten watchmaker.

The gravediggers wouldn't soon forget the elegant stranger, slightly limping and in an overcoat and top hat, who, with a generous tip, asked them to take care of the grave.

Six days later, the chamber where Quasimodo was exhibited was inexplicably overrun by a dozen extremely determined men claiming to belong to an anarchist movement. Without causing any damage or leaving any victims, they kidnapped the unfortunate creature, who has not been seen since.

In the month that followed, the coachmen's company paid cash for the brand new building overlooking the Square du Temple, across from the third arrondissement's town hall. Although the building was equipped with the latest facilities, heavy construction was carried out, particularly in the basement. The neighbors were surprised, and complained of "nocturnal underground vibrations." Some went so far as to claim they had heard an explosion. The police eventually carried out an investigation, but they found nothing in the foundations, other than new and perfectly intact walls.

Konrad became the happy owner of a magnificent apartment on Rue Lafayette. He was rarely there, and no one knew where he spent his days. He provided lodging to the parents of an Italian friend, whose French mother had returned to her native country. The carpenter continued to buy large quantities of wood, but his supplier had no idea what he did with them. The last time the building concierge had run into him, concerned about his abnormally pale skin, she had advised him to get a little sun. Konrad couldn't care less; he had what he desired most in the world.

Eustasio had taken up residence in the countess's home, and began making a living from his art, painting portraits for high society. For amusement, he returned to Montmartre every Sunday, where he painted the crowds at the dance halls and balls. He was tempted to take up photography.

In October, as the Fair came to a close—with more than sixty thousand exhibitors, half of them French, and more than thirty-two million visitors—Henri began studying medicine. He lived with Pierre and Gabrielle, who had moved into a small house next to the Château des Brouillards, where their growing family would soon be cramped.

Many years later, Montmartre had not changed that much after all. Paris had not devoured its soul. The construction of the Sacré-Cœur dragged on for so long that the church struggled to shed its scaffolding. The World's Fair was remembered as a success. The Galerie des Machines was dismantled, but the Iron Lady still towers over the capital, thanks to the army, who saw its potential as a remarkable radio antenna.

Our story has come to an end, but its legend is just beginning.

The guardian at the Saint-Vincent Cemetery was shocked to regularly find glasses and a bottle left on two graves. The first few years, he chalked it up to the eccentricities of artists; they were appearing in growing numbers in the neighborhood, which had become a haven for bohemians. But eventually he realized that the mysterious event happened every year on May 5th. He was beyond relief when a man showed up to relocate the two graves. He never learned where they were transferred.

Henri Royer would soon become a doctor. He had already opened one of the first secular clinics for mendicants. He also worked in the bourgeois neighborhoods. On his desk, among the contemporary objects, which included a telephone, a certain rusty nail was never absent. Each time a patient arrived, he began by observing their hands, to understand how they lived.

The rest remains secret, buried in the heart of Paris, where a tower and two graves have found their guardian who, each day with his companions, tries to learn and disseminate the best of those who came before him. Together, they discovered the sixth rule: "The secret of a good passage must never sink into oblivion."

The henchman had been wrong. It is not necessary to kill to ensure the silence of men.

On certain summer nights, it is whispered that a nameless elegant stranger and a monster sit side by side on the steps of Sacré-Cœur to contemplate the night sky, sharing a glimpse of eternity.

THE END

JUST BETWEEN US

Now that you know Vincent's secret, I would like to share several other—entirely true—secrets with you. They might inspire you to go for a stroll, to seek out and visit certain monuments, and to look beyond the surface.

*

Existing in various forms over the years, Saint-Pierre de Montmartre church is, in fact, the oldest place of worship in Paris. There, on August 15, 1534, Ignatius of Loyola, Peter Faber, and Francis Xavier, accompanied by Diego Laínez, Simão Rodrigues, Alfonso Salmerón, and Nicolás Bobadilla, spoke their first vows and established what would become the Society of Jesus. Pope Jules III would later recognize the order on July 21, 1550. Ignatius of Loyola was canonized on March 12, 1622.

Today the Jesuit order has more than 16,000 active members on all five continents, and Pope Francis—the 266th supreme pontiff of the Catholic Church, appointed in 2013—is the first pope from the order.

The history of the building, where the initial vows were spoken, is as turbulent as it is fascinating. A crypt, carved into the gypsum, was actually discovered there during construction work on July 16, 1661. Today it is inaccessible. After falling into ruin, the church narrowly escaped demolition thanks to the support of Georges Clemenceau, then mayor of Montmartre, who put the church's rescue to a vote in 1897. If you decide to visit, be sure to find the gravestone of Adelaide of Maurienne, queen of France and founder of the abbey; the stone was moved from the center of the choir, where her tomb is believed to be. Carefully observe the column capitals, and the marble ones in particular, which were taken from a very ancient temple built by Romans in Lutetia. You might also consider the unusual floor tiles, a very uncommon choice for this type of building.

The cemetery adjoining the church is the smallest but—more importantly—the oldest in the capital. The ancient tombs make for a truly unique atmosphere.

*

In 1852 the sewer system sprawling beneath Paris included fewer than 99 miles (160 kilometers) of tunnels. In 1870, less than twenty years later and following intense construction, over 310 miles (500 kilometers) of pipes of various sizes ran under the city. At the end of the nineteenth century, the Paris sewer system was one of the most dense and sophisticated in the world, boasting more than 715 miles (1,150 kilometers) of tunnels—95 percent of which had been dug in just fifty years.

Only a handful of reports related to the opening of these public health facilities mention intersections with other underground tunnels connected to former quarries; Paris contains a dense network of these quarries, located mostly on the south bank of the Seine River. The gypsum quarries in Montmartre—among the oldest that were exploited to provide the capital with building materials—were filled in again, little by little, although some significant sections, now closed to the public, remain. They provided the raw material for a good deal of plaster—obtained by heating gypsum—used in city construction and embellishment, which led older residents to say that Paris will always contain more of Montmartre than the other way around.

*

In addition to natural underground galleries carved out by water flowing through the earth's subterranean layers, some connected to the water table, nearly twenty "exceptional" cavities—often gypsum dissolution zones—have been identified beneath the capital. One of the most impressive, located beneath the Gare du Nord train station, was injected with several thousand cubic yards of concrete in the 1980s to stabilize the area.

Over the last twenty years, more than a hundred such injections of various quantities have been carried out under the capital to eliminate the risk of collapse.

*

Today, Paris includes over two hundred places of worship, most of them chapels, churches, and consecrated buildings. In the nineteenth century, and particularly during the period of vast construction initiated by Baron Haussmann, over eighty other buildings, most of them centuries old, were destroyed or, in fewer instances, reconfigured. Specialists estimate that about a quarter of these buildings contained identified or secret crypts. Today, the most extensive crypt in Paris is located under the Saint-Sulpice church, where traces of the primitive church can be found.

*

In November 1881, Rodolphe Salis—a wine merchant, aesthete, and poetry enthusiast—opened a cabaret on Boulevard de Rochechouart that he called Le Chat Noir, because he found and kept a black cat that was in the building. The establishment was eccentric and libertarian, and soon attracted artists and fringe elements who contributed to the scandal-soaked and festive spirit of the Butte Montmartre. Le Chat Noir became fashionable, attracting the capital's talented writers, actors, musicians, satirical singers, painters, and illustrators, including Alphonse Allais, Charles Cros, Toulouse-Lautrec, and Aristide Bruant.

The cabaret became one of the first truly seedy establishments in the capital to overcome the social divide; it was also frequented by thugs and other petty criminals on the hunt for victims, which earned it frequent visits from the police.

Salis decided to leave the establishment to Bruant and set up shop in a larger building on nearby Rue Victor-Massé, where he developed his extraordinary sets and his true vision for a cabaret: singers on the second floor and shadow theater—in color!—on the third. Théophile-Alexandre Steinlen created the famous Tournée du Chat Noir poster in 1895, after the establishment's golden age had already come and gone, nevertheless giving it prominence in the imagery associated with bohemian Paris.

During the same period, Paris was in the grip of a feverish excitement over spiritism and paranormal activity. For several decades, "miracles" had no longer been the preserve of the clergy, and countless spiritualists, soothsayers, and magicians possessed extraordinary powers in which they traded at public or private seances for a wealthy clientele. There is evidence that several of these dubious characters gathered at Le Chat Noir starting in 1885. Many would be thwarted and their mystique stripped away, but some—more skillful or truly gifted with powers—fascinated the public and earned themselves a genuine reputation. One of them, Le Grand Orion, performed alone; but it was suspected that he had a twin, enabling him to appear in two places at once. He was accused of fraud and eventually fled to Switzerland in 1890. At the time, he was thought to possess genuine psychic powers that he supposedly used to establish his authority over a cult.

*

To this day, at the corner of Rue Mouffetard and Rue du Pot-de-Fer in Paris, there stands a fountain that provided the setting for a strange discovery. Built in 1624, it acquired its current form in 1671: a curved building with a faucet on the "Mouffetard" side and an entrance on the other.

In 1899, while the interior equalizing tanks, inaccessible to the public, were being replaced, workers made a surprising discovery. In the false bottom of the rear metal tank, they found about sixty gold napoleon coins, in three cylinders, each containing twenty pieces. The coins represented a fortune large enough to frighten the workers, who did not keep it for themselves. No one was ever able to explain where they came from, and the mystery remains unsolved to this day.

*

In January 2015, during foundation reinforcement work in the basement of a building at the corner of Rue Réaumur and Boulevard de

Sébastopol—formerly the headquarters of the Félix Potin retail business and today the site of a Monoprix department store—eight mass graves were discovered containing a total of 200 skeletons.

*

In 1892, a certain Victor Fink, after receiving a spectacular inheritance from a distant relative, created a "charitable residence" near Montrouge, just south of Paris, for acrobats and other impoverished artists. The initiative was so surprising and the source of the funds so mysterious that the story made all the headlines.

The man acquired land with several farmhouses that he renovated to make lodgings, where he took in those he referred to as "entertainment's needy." One of the farms was reserved for abandoned or mistreated sideshow curiosities.

*

Between 1989 and 1992, the Parisian subsoil was subjected to five sounding operations using impressive truck-mounted seismic vibrators: the machines sent tremors into the ground and the seismic echo was recorded using an array of measurement and analysis tools to produce an ultrasound image of the earth's deep subterranean layers. At the time, the media talked about a search for hydrocarbons or gas pockets in the bowels of the capital.

*

Between 1397 and 1407, Nicolas Flamel—who is remembered as an alchemist—had a mansion built for himself in Paris that he never lived in. Currently located at 51 Rue de Montmorency, the house has retained much of its original appearance despite several partial reconstruction efforts, notably in 1900 when its gable and high windows were modified. It is the oldest house in the capital that can be dated with any certainty, and the facade has been classified as a historical monument since 1911. Today it is a restaurant.

Flamel offered lodgings to workers and the needy, on one condition—that they say a prayer every day. No one could explain Flamel's extraordinary fortune, which he often used to philanthropic ends, earning himself the ardent admiration of alchemy enthusiasts to this day. The original wording, inscribed across the pediment, is still visible: *Nous homes et femes laboureurs demourans ou porche de ceste maison qui fu fte en lan de grace Mil quatre cens et sept, somes tenus chascun en droit soy dire tous les jours une patenostre et I ave maria en priant dieu que sa grace face pardon aus povres pescheurs trespassez, amen.*

(We, men and women laborers, living in the entryway of this house that was built in the year of our Lord 1407 are all required to recite an Our Father and a Hail Mary daily, praying to God that his grace brings forgiveness to the poor deceased sinners, amen.)

*

An exceptional magician responsible for developing most of the great principles of his art and an inspiration to his successors, Jean-Eugène Robert-Houdin is an extraordinary figure: an inventor, researcher, creator, and founder of a theater dedicated entirely to magic. It's impossible to summarize the magnitude of his contribution and his personality in a few lines, but I encourage you to learn more about this man, who was unfairly forgotten in the shadow of Harry Houdini—the Austro-Hungarian Ehrich Weisz—who appropriated his name and many of his methods, largely relying on the media to build a sensational career in the United States.

Our remarkable role model Jean-Eugène Robert was born in 1805. He developed a fascination for mechanics as a child observing his father at work in a horology workshop. He became a watchmaker at the age of twenty-three. An encounter with a magician specialized in sleight of hand would change his life.

In 1830, he married Cécile Houdin, the daughter of a Parisian watchmaker, and added her name to his own. In the following decade, Jean-Eugène Robert-Houdin focused his efforts primarily on watchmaking and registered several patents for inventions, including a lighter-alarm, which ignited at a scheduled time. He reinvested the money he made building automatons and entertainment gadgets, including a mysterious pendulum with no visible mechanism, into his research. Despite his financial difficulties, he was eventually recognized for his talent. A patron lent him the funds to create his writing-and-drawing automaton that met with great success at the World's Fair in 1844. Following Cécile's death, he devoted himself entirely to illusionism.

The first of his "Soirées Fantastiques" ("Magical Evenings") was held on June 25, 1845. His illusions Foulard aux Surprises (Surprising Handkerchief), Pâtissier du Palais-Royal (Palais-Royal Pastry Cook), and L'Oranger Merveilleux (The Marvelous Orange Tree) caused a sensation. His fame grew when he presented La Seconde Vue (Second Sight), a divination exercise, and when he put his young son Émile in ethereal suspension. In November 1846, his shows were so successful that spectators had to reserve seats months in advance. King Louis Philippe I invited him to the palace for a special performance, and he also performed in London for Queen Victoria.

His own theater proved to be an exceptional laboratory for his illusions, where he developed trap doors on the stage floor and rope systems for sleight-of-hand tricks. Later, Georges Méliès would hold film projections there and drew inspiration from Robert-Houdin's special effects for many of his films.

In 1855, Napoleon III called on him for help in fighting against the Arabic marabouts who were encouraging the people in Algeria to rebel. In June 1856, Robert-Houdin pretended to be an all-powerful sorcerer with supernatural powers by performing tricks like Le Fusillé Vivant (Surviving the Killing Shot) and Le Coffre Lourd-Léger (The Light and Heavy Chest). The marabouts' influence diminished, though it did not disappear entirely.

Robert-Houdin installed many inventions on his estate: all of the electric clocks on the property were connected to an electric regulator and perfectly synchronized. The estate's entrance gate was equipped with a bell and an electric strike so that it could be opened remotely. He also kept many of his automatons there.

Robert-Houdin also registered patents in a number of other fields, and some of his inventions, like the fencer's electric plastron and the odometer, are still used to this day. He died on June 13, 1871, leaving behind no less than a hundred tricks that still fascinate and inspire generations of illusionists.

An event in 1904 set the small world of European scholars abuzz. Nearly sixty manuscripts, some of them very old—many dated prior to 1400—were inexplicably and anonymously given to institutes and libraries, but mostly to museums. The operation occurred mainly in Paris, but reports also came in from London and Rome. The documents came from a variety of places—some far from Europe—and were all determined to be authentic and priceless. No connection was immediately made between the different bequests, and no one managed to determine who had donated them, or more importantly, why. The official theory gives credit to a mysterious collector who had no doubt gathered the exceptional pieces illegally and, realizing his days were coming to an end, could not bring himself to destroy them.

A thorough investigation was never carried out; at the time, the public was far more captivated by a case of fraud: a major trafficking operation of diplodocus bones had just been uncovered. For months, hundreds of unsuspecting buyers had paid a fortune for these "prehistoric bones" that in reality were nothing more than horse or cattle femurs aged in chemical baths. At the time, it was said to be the fraud of the century—but there were many others.

Acknowledgments

The author would like to thank the teams
and staff of the following institutions:

The Inspection Générale des Carrières
The Observatoire de Paris
Numdam.org

and especially:

The Bibliothèque Nationale de France
and Gallica, its exceptional digital archives

Research and documentation:
Chloé Legardinier

Key points of interest (see endpapers):

1 Saint-Pierre de Montmartre church (west)
and the Sacré-Coeur construction site (east)
2 Saint-Vincent Cemetery (west)
and Lapin Agile cabaret (east)
3 Vincent Cavel's house
4 Alfred Minguier's house
5 Galerie des Machines at the World's Fair
6 Le Chat Noir cabaret
7 Tour du Temple